'If you're wanting a crime novel to sink your
teeth into, then this is the perfect fit.'
Chat magazine

'An addictive revenge story set on a remote island,
it's another hit for this must-read author.'
Woman

'Detective Elin Warner is back in another atmospheric thriller. Pearse
cleverly develops intrigue and ramps up the tension relentlessly as
the stakes become deadly. Fans of *The Sanatorium* will love it.'
**Gilly Macmillan, *Sunday Times* bestselling
author of *The Long Weekend***

'Be careful who you get attached to . . . no character
is safe in this tense thriller!'
Yours

'I absolutely loved it. So many threads, more red herrings
than a North Sea fishing trawler. It's a riveting, twisty
turny read, a classic whodunnit with a killer final twist.'
John Marrs, bestselling author of *The One*

'A delightfully creepy thriller set in a fantastic
gothic location. I loved it!'
G. R. Halliday, author of *From the Shadows*

'*The Retreat* is designed to keep you guessing to
the very end. A great one to read on holiday.'
The Herald

'Long may Sarah Pearse continue to ruin the
idea of luxury-resort travel for us all.'
**Catherine Ryan Howard, No.1 Irish bestselling
author of *The Nothing Man***

7.23

...sychological thriller...
...reworks Christie's
...the relationships
...ds.'

...of *The Couple at...*

'An eerie, atmospheric thriller that will have yo...
your shoulder as you read. A wonderfully chilling st...
grief, revenge, and family secrets. An absorbing escape!'
Ashley Audrain, *Sunday Times* **bestselling author of** *The Push*

'Pearse skilfully builds a sense of foreboding throughout
this creepy thriller packed with satisfying twists.'
Sunday Express

'Full of foreboding and high-stakes tension, Sarah Pearse's latest is a
page-turner. The past doesn't stay buried for long, at sea or on land,
and what comes to the surface is both shocking and chilling.'
Nita Prose, *Sunday Times* **bestselling author of** *The Maid*

THE
RETREAT

SARAH PEARSE

PENGUIN BOOKS

TRANSWORLD PUBLISHERS
Penguin Random House, One Embassy Gardens,
8 Viaduct Gardens, London SW11 7BW
www.penguin.co.uk

Transworld is part of the Penguin Random House group of companies
whose addresses can be found at global.penguinrandomhouse.com

Penguin
Random House
UK

First published in Great Britain in 2022 by Bantam Press
an imprint of Transworld Publishers
Penguin paperback edition published 2023

A CIP catalogue record for this book
is available from the British Library.

ISBN
9780552177320

Typeset in 11.25/14.5pt Minion Pro by Jouve (UK), Milton Keynes.
Printed and bound in Great Britain by Clays Ltd, Elcograf S.p.A.

The authorized representative in the EEA is Penguin Random House Ireland,
Morrison Chambers, 32 Nassau Street, Dublin D02 YH68.

Penguin Random House is committed to a sustainable future
for our business, our readers and our planet. This book is made
from Forest Stewardship Council® certified paper.

For my mum

'You can be a king or a street sweeper, but everyone dances with the Grim Reaper.'

Convicted murderer Robert Alton Harris's last words

Prologue

Summer 2003

Thea's scream rips through the clearing, startling the birds from the trees in a flurry of flapping wings.

The sound isn't human; it's high-pitched and desperate, the kind of scream that turns your stomach inside out, makes your ears burn.

She should have waited until they got back to camp. He told her to wait.

But Thea had insisted. Half an hour and three beers since they'd snuck away from camp for some time alone, and she couldn't hold it any longer: 'Don't look at me like that, it's your fault for bringing so many cans. Shout if you see someone coming . . .'

Laughing, she'd walked a few paces away, carefully positioned herself so Ollie could see only the sandy tips of her white pumps, the thin trail of wet already winding through the dusty floor.

The scream intensifies.

Ollie freezes for a moment, but instinct kicks in: he lurches into action, pivoting towards her. But almost instantly, he comes to a halt, a cloud of dried soil and leaves kicking into the air.

A movement: someone stepping out from the tangle of branches.

The rock on the cliff above, the island's namesake, is casting them in shadow, but Ollie can see right away that this person isn't from camp. They aren't in shorts and a T-shirt like the kids, or the cheery green of the camp leaders; they're wearing something dark and shapeless.

Ollie's eyes dart to Thea. He can now see her frantically thrashing in the dense undergrowth.

He wants to move, to do something, but his body is locked. All he can do is stare, his heart lunging in his chest – hard, knocking thuds against his ribs.

A violent flurry of movement, and then a sound: the sharp liquid crack of something bursting and breaking.

It's a sound he's never heard before.

Ollie closes his eyes. He knows it's Thea, but in his head, he's turned her into something else. A puppet. A mannequin.

Anything but her.

His eyes flicker open and it's then he sees it: the watery trail has become something darker, thicker.

Blood.

It splinters into a fork – the liquid tip of a snake's tongue.

Another strike: this time harder, faster, but it barely registers, and neither does Thea's second scream – blistered, cut off, like it's clotted in her throat – because Ollie's already running.

He darts into the woods, making for the cove he and Thea found yesterday while the others were building the fire. While they'd both pretended they had stopped there just to talk, to drink, it was obvious it was going to become something more.

His hand on the soft band of skin above her shorts, her mouth pressed against his . . .

The thought is too much; he speeds up. It's as though he's running blind – the setting sun flicker-flashing through the trees overhead, his eyes seeing nothing but a blur of shadowy green and the grey-brown carpet of leaves. His trainers are slipping out from under him, the dry ground as slippery as mud.

Barbed branches pull at his shirt. One catches his arm, snags the soft skin on the inside of his wrist. Blood flares – a ragged line of tiny red beads bursting through his skin.

It feels like he's done this before – a weird déjà vu, as if in a dream, one of those panicky ones where you wake up sweating and panting, the type that sticks with you for a while afterwards.

A few metres on and the trees start to thin, the woodland floor giving way to sand, the rock beneath, flattened elephant-folds of dusty limestone. He's reached the steps Thea found yesterday, nothing more than wooden treads knocked into the soil. Momentum tugs his body forwards with each step and he's forced to lean back to stop himself from falling.

When he reaches the bottom, he jumps on to the sand and runs towards the small overhang he and Thea had lain in last night, contraband bottles in their hands.

Ollie drops to all fours, hollowing his back to crawl under. Once he's inside, he sits with his knees drawn up to his chin and concentrates on breathing. In and out. In and out. Being still. Staying quiet.

But his body won't cooperate; he's shaking with jerky spasms that he can't control.

Ollie clamps his hands over his head as if the pressure will force away the scream still ringing in his ears. But now it's not just the sound, it's the sight: Thea's body folding, collapsing – like a puppet master had violently jerked at her strings.

He bashes his hand against the rock above him. Bashes again and again until there's ripped-back skin and blood.

Red smears across his knuckles, a sharp thread of pain

pulling through him that he tries to hold on to, to distract him, but it doesn't work.

The truth is still shouting.

He left her. He left her. He ran.

Ollie puts his head between his legs and takes a long, shuddery breath.

Minutes pass, but no one comes. It's getting late, he can tell. The last of the sun is almost gone, the sand in front of him now in shadow.

He'll wait a little longer, he decides, then he'll try going back to camp. As time ticks by, Ollie half convinces himself that it was a joke, a prank Thea got roped into by the boys. He clutches at the thought: he'll get back to camp and she'll be there, laughing at him for running away like a kid.

A few minutes later, he drags himself from under the overhang. Straightening up, he glances carefully around him, but the beach is deserted; there's nobody there.

As he runs back through the forest, he's still clinging to the thought: *It's a joke. Thea is fine.* But as soon as he enters the clearing, he knows. The dark trail from before is now a stream of blood forming a winding downhill path.

Ollie tries to look at her, but he can't bring himself to see past her white pumps, now perfectly still and streaked with red.

It isn't real. Not Thea. She can't be . . .

He turns away, bile rising in the back of his throat.

It's then that he notices something on the ground, sitting on top of the dusty leaf litter.

A large stone, about thirty centimetres long. The surface is mostly weathered, with tiny scuffs and dimples where it's been battered by the waves and sand, but it's also smooth in places, the outline softly contoured.

Crouching low, Ollie picks it up. It feels warm, gritty against his palm. Something about it is familiar, he thinks, slowly turning it between his fingers.

It hits him, and he holds the stone still.

Tipping his head, he glances up at the rock on the cliff face behind, then looks back at his hand.

Ollie looks from one to another until his eyes blur.

He realizes that what he's holding isn't just a stone.

The subtle curves and contours resemble the rock above him.

Reaper's Rock.

'So here's the update as promised . . . we're at the beach waiting for a boat to take us to the retreat, but what I didn't realize is quite how remote Cary Island actually is . . . I reckon it's a twenty-minute boat ride from the mainland at least.' Jo flips the phone's view from her face to show the sea, a glimpse of the island visible in the distance.

'I've had loads of people asking about LUMEN, so I'll explain the vibe. LUMEN's a luxury retreat on the gorgeous island you've just seen, off the South Devon coast. The architect was inspired by Mexican legend Luis Barragán, so we're talking luxe, candy-coloured villas nestled in woodland with views out to sea. There's some pretty special stuff: an outdoor yoga pavilion, a glass-bottomed pool, and this crazy rope swing stretching out over the water . . . you can drop straight off into the sea. One of the most spectacular features is an amazing villa on a private islet – that's for all you honeymooners. I couldn't get my mitts on that one as it's already booked, but it looks stunning.

'I'll be taking you out on the kayaks with me later today, but to give you an idea of the wellness activities on offer, they've got paddleboarding, meditation, kayaking, hydrofoil surfing, and loads more.' She pauses. 'Now for the creepy bit: I love the backstory to this place. The rocky outcrop on the side of the island, you can just about see it from here, it gives the island its nickname: Reaper's Rock. Spooky, right? And according to a lot of the locals, the island is cursed. Apparently' – she lowers her voice to a hushed whisper – 'the rock is said to be a manifestation of the Grim Reaper. During the plague, people were quarantined here and then left to die. So the story goes, their souls are still wandering and will only be at peace when the Reaper takes a new victim. Stay too long and you'll be next . . .'

Jo flips the camera again to show her mock-terrified face. 'Eerie, isn't it? But that's not the only thing. There was an old school on the island that burnt down back in the day. Abandoned until it was used by the local council as an Outward Bound centre in the late nineties. All fine and dandy until a group of teenagers were murdered at the hand of the island caretaker, Larson Creacher, in 2003.' She lowers her voice again. 'Is it wrong to say all the spooky stuff kind of adds to the appeal?'

1

As Elin Warner runs, the air feels sticky like gum, catching in her eyes, hair.

Only six a.m., but the heat is already bouncing off the pavement, solid walls of it, with no breeze to sweep it away.

The route she's taking is part of the South West Coast Path – houses on either side, lavish Victorian and Italianate villas that stud the wooded hillside. Gleaming pinpoints of sunlight are bouncing off the windows as her reflection shifts alongside her in the glass – cropped blonde hair mushrooming up and out with each step before settling back around her face.

The exteriors of the houses seem flimsy in the heat, their edges blurred. The verges outside are parched yellow – grass not just suspended in growth, but withering and dying, bare patches opening up like sores.

Summers have been hot before, but none like this: weeks of sunshine; spiking, record-breaking temperatures. Newspapers printing endless images of cracking motorways, fried eggs cliché-cooking on the bonnets of cars. Forecasters had predicted a reprieve several weeks ago, but it never came. Just more sun. Nerves are fraying, people ready to snap.

Elin's just about holding on, but her internal landscape is at odds with the external. With each day of blistering heat that passes comes the exact opposite inside her: the cold grip of fear creeping back.

It keeps her up at night, the same thoughts on repeat. With it, the control strategies: the running, relentless exercise. The past few weeks, an escalation – earlier runs, longer runs, secret runs. *Self-flagellation.*

All because her brother, Isaac, had mentioned her father had been in touch.

A few metres on, the houses on the left give way to a green. The coast path runs behind it, hugging the lip of the cliff.

Leaving the pavement, she darts into the opening for the path. Her stomach lurches.

No fence, only a metre of land between her and a forty-metre plunge to the rocks below, but she loves it: it's coast path proper – no houses between her and the sea. The view opens out: Brixham on her right, Exmouth to her left. All she can see is blue – the sea a darker, inkier shade than the chalky pastel of the morning sky.

With each step, she feels the heat from the ground rising up through the soles of her trainers. She wonders for a moment what would happen if she kept moving: whether she'd eventually implode – an engine overheating – or whether she'd simply carry on.

It's tempting to keep going until the thoughts stop, and she doesn't have to try to hold on any more – because that's what it feels like sometimes: as though she's having to grip too hard to normality. One small slip, and she'll fall.

At the top of the hill Elin slows, her thighs screaming, thick with lactic acid. Hitting pause on her Fitbit, she notices a grey car cresting the hill. It's moving fast, engine throaty, scattering the seagulls picking at a flattened carcass on the road.

Something registers as she takes in the shape, the colour. It's

Steed's car, she's sure of it, the DC drafted in to help her on secondment. It speeds past, a blur of dust-dulled alloy and flying gravel. Elin catches Steed's profile: slightly crooked nose, strong chin, fair spikes of hair gelled into submission. Something about his expression pulls the last bit of breath from her. Elin immediately recognizes it: the quiet intensity of someone flooded with adrenaline.

He's working. On a job.

The car stops at the bottom of the hill. Steed flings open the door, jogs in the direction of the beach.

Pulling her phone from her shorts, Elin glances at the screen. The Control Room haven't rung. *A job, just down the road, and they called Steed instead.*

Familiar worries resurface, the same ones that have consumed her ever since HR and Anna, her boss, decided that she wasn't ready for full duties after her career break.

Steed's a speck in the distance, moving towards the beach. Elin shifts from foot to foot. She knows the right thing to do is to stick to her plan – to run home to breakfast, to Will – but pride gets the better of her.

Running hard down the hill, she passes Steed's car and crosses the road. No other cars; only a cat slinking across the tarmac, fire-striped undercarriage nearly touching the ground. She crosses the scrubby patch of grass to the empty beach beyond. No Steed.

Walking left, along the shore, she passes the restaurant jutting out on metal pillars above the beach. A rustic-looking shack, name emblazoned in driftwood above the door. *The Lobster Pot.* It's shuttered. Last night, the terrace would have been heaving, strings of fairy lights illuminating wine bottles in coolers, baskets of shiny mussels and fries.

A little further on, she finds him; there, beneath the overhang of the restaurant. He's kneeling on the sand, muscles straining through the fabric of his shirt. The raw physicality is always the first thing Elin notices about Steed, but he's a dichotomy: the hard, honed body belied by the softness of his features – heavy-lidded, sensual eyes; a wide, full mouth. He's that rare kind of man: the type women simultaneously feel protected by and protective of.

They've slipped into an easy working relationship. He's younger than her, late twenties, but there's none of the thrusting bravado you sometimes get in men of that age. He's astute, has a knack of asking the right questions, an emotional intelligence that's all too rare.

A woman is standing beside him. She looks to be in her late forties, tall and muscular. Her blue swimming hat is still on, the same hue as her costume, the thin layer of rubber emphasizing the shape of her skull. Despite the heat, she's shivering, jiggling from foot to foot in a nervous rhythm.

Steed turns, and as he moves Elin sees it: a leg, splayed against the sand – a pale calf, lettuce-like fragments of seaweed suckered to the skin.

She finds herself stepping forwards to get a better angle.

A teenager. Ugly wounds – slashes to the face, chest, and legs. Their clothes are almost completely shredded, the polo shirt split down the seam, across the torso.

Closer again, and her vision blurs, the syrupy haze of the air giving the scene a sloppy focus. As she takes another step, reaction tips over into realization.

She sucks in her breath.

Steed swivels round to face her at the sound, eyes widening in surprise. 'Elin?' He hesitates. 'Are you—'

But the rest of his words bleed into the air. Elin starts to run.

She knows now why they'd called Steed instead.

Of course.

2

Hana Leger and her sister, Jo, are waiting on the jetty for the boat to take them to the island, suitcases and bags piled around their ankles. Hana rubs the back of her neck. It feels as if the sun were homing in on the soft skin there, direct as a laser beam.

The water is thick with people: paddlers, swimmers, dinghies bobbing, lone figures tracing the horizon on paddleboards. Children splash in the shallows, kicking up spray. Chubby toddler arms punch at froth.

Hana's stomach tightens, but she forces her gaze back to the squatting toddler.

Don't look away. She can't be blind forever.

'You okay?' Jo looks at her through her aviators, blows out over her upper lip. The motion lifts up the thin strands of white-blonde hair that have fallen loose from her ponytail.

'Just hot. I didn't expect it to be so bad down here. Sea breeze and all.' Hana's dark hair, cut in a bedraggled bob, is damp, sticking to the nape of her neck. She ruffles it.

Jo rummages in her backpack. It's one of those technical, lightweight ones, covered in zips and pockets. Pulling out a bottle of water, Jo swigs and then offers it to her. Hana drinks: it's warm, plasticky tasting.

Her sister cuts a striking figure. Tall, tanned, she manages to elevate the white cotton beach dress and leopard-print Birken-stocks, slightly fuzzy from wear, into something hip and effortless. Every part of Jo is lightly muscled from a regime of yoga and running and skiing.

Hana follows her to the end of the jetty, squinting. The island itself is a blur – the bright circle of sun behind casting it into shadow. Only one thing is clear: the infamous rock pro-truding from the top left of the island – the side profile that gestures to a hooded figure, a protuberance jutting out like a scythe.

Hana's stomach tightens, the sight a hit to her solar plexus. 'I didn't expect it to actually look like—'

'A reaper?' Jo turns, ponytail swishing against her face.

'Yes.' Despite her sunglasses, a murky shadow of the rock appears every time she blinks. It's a stark contrast to the brochure – all white sandy beaches, lush foliage.

'But you're looking forward to it? The break, I mean.' Jo raises her voice above the whine of a jet ski.

'Of course.' Hana squeezes out a smile, though she's secretly been dreading this trip.

She'd actually said no when Jo first called. The idea of a holiday with Bea, their older sister, and Maya, their cousin, boyfriends included, seemed odd. They hadn't seen each other in months, after steadily drifting apart over the past few years. While Jo said it was all about *getting them together again*, Hana struggled to understand it. Why now? After all this time?

She offered up what she thought was a solid excuse: without Liam, it didn't feel right. But Jo was persistent: phone calls, texts, she'd even turned up at her flat – a rare occurrence – with a hard copy of the retreat's brochure.

Jo wore her down, making Hana feel simultaneously old and prissy for declining. This was Jo's modus operandi: she's a leader, not in a bossy way, but by the sheer force of her personality. Somehow, you got caught in her slipstream, unaware you were even being led.

It never bothered Hana as much as it irked Bea. Bookish, and fiercely introverted, Bea found Jo's energy and extroversion overwhelming. Perhaps it washed over Hana more because she was in between: academic, but not Bea's level. Sporty, but not an athlete like Jo.

'I'm going to post a view of the island from here . . .' Jo takes a photograph.

Hana turns away. It pisses her off – this constant documenting of every move they make – but she can't complain. This trip is a result of Jo's frenetic social media activity: as a travel influencer she gets paid in kind with free holidays. She has nearly four hundred thousand followers who like that she's natural, regularly commenting on her 'relatability' – her slightly too-wide mouth, the Streisandesque kink to her nose.

'That can't be ours.' Jo slips her phone back into her pocket. 'Not already.' A boat is making its way across the water, leaving a foamy spume of white in its wake. Hana glances at the blocky lettering on the side. LUMEN. Jo checks her Fitbit. 'Actually, it's already five to. Where's everyone else?' She turns to the beach. 'Saying that, I think that's Seth over there . . .'

Hana follows her gaze. 'Is it?'

'Is it?' Jo mimics. 'Conjure up some vague enthusiasm, Han.' She shakes her head. 'I know you're not a fan. He's too "risky" ' – she makes quote marks with her fingers – 'for you, isn't he?' Jo's face tightens. 'I wish I'd never told you now. It wasn't exactly serious.'

A bead of sweat trickles between Hana's shoulder blades. Jo's the master of this: the sudden turn. 'A criminal record *is* serious. We were only looking out for you.'

'He got in with the wrong crowd. End of.' Jo's eyes flash. 'Not everyone's perfect, you know, not everyone can do happy-clappy songs all day, teach kids how to add up.'

Hana looks at her. *There it is. The sting in the tail.* This is why this holiday is a bad idea. Because Jo, as usual, is able to chop her down with a few choice words. The worst thing is, it's not just a jibe, it *is* what the rest of the family think of her – a reductive cliché, knee-deep in Play-Doh, sing-song saying the register.

They'd never imagine the reality: the kids' sticky, pinchy fingers in hers, the nitty-gritty machinations of their brains that slip straight from their mouths, no filter, and how, after a term with them, Hana knew exactly what kind of humans they'd become.

Jo puts up her hand, waving, all smiles again as Seth approaches. *Switch flicked.*

'Yay,' she shouts. 'You're here!'

Hana does a double-take. A well-built man in shorts and a T-shirt is walking towards them. The height, gait, the baseball cap pulled low over his eyes – it's gut-wrenchingly familiar. With the sun in her eyes, his face is hard to make out, the similarities uncanny. Despite what her logical mind is telling her, her heart leaps before reality hits.

Of course it's not him. Liam is gone. Dead, dead, dead.

Swallowing hard, she collects herself. It's then she notices another, slighter figure behind Seth. It's Caleb, Bea's boyfriend. But no Bea. She asks Jo, 'Where's Bea?'

'She cancelled.' Jo's voice pitches higher. 'I told you, didn't I?'

'No,' Hana says tightly. 'When did this happen?'

'Last week. Something came up with work, I think. A trip to the US.' *Bea cancelled.* It shouldn't be a surprise. She's always been a workaholic, but the past few years have taken it to another level.

'So she sent Caleb instead. A placeholder.'

Jo shrugs. 'It'll be good to get to know him.'

'You didn't want to rearrange it for when Bea could come?'

'No. Too late, and besides, we need this, Han.' There's a look of quiet determination on her face. 'To reconnect.' Before Hana can reply, Jo starts walking up the jetty, long, loping strides. 'I'll go and meet them.' But as she walks past Hana, Jo knocks over her own backpack, balanced on her case. Unzipped, the contents immediately scatter: hairbrush, diary, a purse. A half-empty bottle of water careers across the jetty. 'Shit . . .' Jo grabs it, clumsily shoving everything back in before resuming her jog to Seth.

Hana's about to follow when she realizes that Jo's missed something: a crumpled piece of paper. Bending down, she picks it up. Her eyes skitter across the page.

It says *Hana*, then three small sentences all the same, but the first two crossed out, and started again.

~~I'm sorry.~~ ~~I'm sorry.~~ *I'm sorry.*

3

When Elin reaches the flat, sweat is pouring off her, a damp ring marking the neck of her vest a deeper shade of blue. Her skin is burning, not from the exercise but the conversation she'd had with Anna walking back up the hill. They'd exchanged small talk, but Elin knew the real reason for her call. *Steed had been in touch. Told Anna he'd seen Elin.*

She replays their exchange in her head: 'Steed messaged you, didn't he?'

'Yes, he was concerned—'

'It's Hayler, isn't it? He's back.'

It's like a pulse in her head: *Hayler. Hayler.* The first case to work its way inside her like a parasite, scrape her clean. Hayler had murdered two young girls, tied their bodies to a boat, let the propeller do its work. She'd let him slip away. It broke her: the Hayler case triggered her career break, the rapid, brutal excision from the MCIT, the Major Crime Investigation Team, the job she loved. Marked the start of her panic attacks, her anxiety.

It was only when she found her brother's fiancée's murderer in Switzerland that the darkness haunting her loosened its grip. Though devastating, the experience reaffirmed the question she'd grappled with for months – that she *did* still want to be a detective. She made the decision to come back, but so had Hayler. The worst possible timing: her slow return to the MCIT will become a crawl. They won't want her anywhere near . . .

Her mouth was thick, her words clumsy. 'I can cope with it, Anna. If I come back on the team, I don't have to be involved, I can sit it out.'

A weighty silence. *Anna's embarrassed.* 'No, it's not Hayler. That kid you saw on the beach went missing a few days ago. Suicide. Already dead when the boat went over him.'

It wasn't Hayler.

She'd leapt in, jumped to the wrong conclusion. She'd panicked, like she always did. The thought snags in her mind, but Elin forces it away as she opens the door.

She walks down the hall of the flat. She can't yet refer to it as home, still feels as though she has to treat it carefully, a precious object that belongs to someone else, and she knows it isn't right. Two months in and it *should* feel like hers.

It isn't the flat's fault. It's spacious, beautiful – part of a Regency-style crescent overlooking the sea. They'd made the big decisions together: a simple design, neutral palette, carefully chosen soft furnishings: an L-shaped sofa, jute rug, a love seat in egg-yolk yellow.

All of it, Elin had raved over – wanted to make a fuss of her flexibility, prove to Will that she'd turned a corner, and that this time, there was no looking back. But she *is* looking back, can't help it. She misses her place: her squashy two-seater, watching the rain fall on next door's flat, book time while eating, uninterrupted.

Will's on the sofa, his laptop propped open. Elin catches bits of sentences: *'award prep now the priority . . .'* The phone is pressed to his ear; he's talking in a low, urgent voice.

Will's an architect, his job both a career and a passion. His love for his role is one of the things she loves most about him: how he perceives the world in a different way, privy to a level of beauty that for her will always be just out of reach. Walking to the kitchen, she pours a glass of water.

A few moments later, Will turns. 'You're back early.'

'Cut the run short in the end.' She sips her water. 'Who was that?'

'Jack. The project in Stoke Gabriel has passed planning.' Tilting his head, he scrutinizes her. 'Something up?'

He knows her too well. 'Could say that.' Her voice wavers. 'Made a bit of a fool of myself.' She explains what happened: following Steed, the awkward call with Anna.

Will's face softens. 'I wouldn't stress – Hayler was your last case. It'd be odd if you *didn't* think about it.'

'But it wasn't just that, I panicked . . . it made me think about Sam.'

'Elin, you got the answers you needed. You can move on.' Will's right, but while she got answers about her brother's death, they were ones she'd never, in her darkest imaginings, considered – her older brother, Isaac, wasn't there when Sam died as a child, as she'd believed. *It was her.* When he fell in the water, hit his head on a rock, she froze. Did nothing to help. 'No one blames you. You were a kid.'

'But . . . I think my dad did—' Her voice catches. 'Isaac said he's planning a visit. It made me think about something I never thought was significant at the time, but now . . .'

'What?' he says gently.

'The day Dad left, he'd planned a scramble up to these rocks where you could jump into the sea. I couldn't do it, burst into tears at the top, ruined the whole thing. After, Dad said: *You're a coward, Elin. A coward.* Turned out to be the last words he ever said to me. Later, my parents had an argument. Dad left in the night.'

'But what he said wasn't about Sam—'

'No, it *was*. That's the real reason Dad left, and he was right. I am a coward. I ran today.'

'You're not. You're making progress. Steady steps.'

Elin nods, but the old her didn't need steady steps. She was sharp, ambitious. Going places. The old Elin wouldn't have been on secondment in Torhun. The work is repetitive, grinding; coordinating door-to-door enquiries, CCTV, witness statements. No real meat on the bone.

'I know it's not the same,' he says softly.

She shrugs. 'Nothing is.' It would be hard to match the high stakes of the MCIT, the furious pace in the Incident Room, the intellectual rigour in teasing apart the subtleties of a case, identifying strategies, the plan of attack. Nothing else comes close, but what if it's too much for her now?

Will scans his phone. 'My last meeting's at four. Fancy dinner out? Talk properly?'

'Sounds good. By the way, I heard you mention an award. Good news . . .'

A flush creeps up his cheeks. 'Oh, a project's been shortlisted for an award.'

'That's great.' Elin's surprised to find herself having to force a smile, a small, mean part of her envious. In her head, her career should be soaring like his, but it isn't. Will's the one surging onwards, motor at his back, while she's treading water.

He stretches out, the hem of his T-shirt pulling upwards, trying to be nonchalant, and it all becomes devastatingly clear. *He's trying to minimize it.* Worse than him being oblivious.

'Which project?'

'The retreat. LUMEN.' He smiles, his pride obvious. 'Really unexpected.'

LUMEN. Will's baby: a luxury retreat that he designed on an

island a few kilometres off the coast. The retreat has given the island a new face, Will's firm bulldozing the past away in a bold mix of blocky, modernist-inspired architecture and Mexican colour. A passion project, one of the first things he mentioned when they met: *'We're reinventing, but we've worked with the landscape too, using stone from the old school, quarried on the island . . .'*

'National award, it'll put the firm on the map.'

Not only that, Elin thinks. It's the creative recognition – a verification of his vision to turn around people's perception of the island. 'Congrats, and you don't have to play it down for my benefit. My stuff, it shouldn't put a dampener on you. I've got to learn to deal with it.'

'Easier said than done, I know.' He smiles. 'Fancy a quick coffee? I've got time in between calls.'

'Yes, let me write down my times – only got the first half, but . . .' Elin reaches for her notebook on the side table. Her watch records her stats, but she still likes putting it down on paper. The one area of her life where she's making tangible progress.

Elin looks up, feeling Will's gaze on her. She finds pity in his eyes.

He looks to the floor – found out, embarrassed.

4

Hana watches the RIB slow as it approaches the dock, a ragged line of white foam kicked out in its wake. The words she's just read are on repeat in her head.

~~I'm sorry. I'm sorry.~~ *I'm sorry.*

She was right: this trip wasn't just a way of bringing the family back together. Jo's organized it for a reason and Hana's pretty sure it's linked to the note that fell from her bag.

'Jo Leger?' The driver scrambles out of the boat, sending it rocking against the jetty.

As he ties it up, he greets them from behind polarized lenses, with a practised, enthusiastic smile. He's young, late twenties maybe, clad in a starchy white polo shirt, shorts.

'That's me.' Jo steps forwards, smiling. She's relieved, Hana can tell, that the forced, awkward greetings are done – Jo's overenthusiastic bear hugs with Caleb a sharp contrast to Hana's muted half-embrace.

'I'm Edd.' The driver walks towards them.

Seth steps forwards, smiling, vigorous shake of the hand and broad chest stuck out. This is typical Seth. A jock, but a beautiful one, she thinks, taking in the thick line of muscle in his arm.

Hana remembers the first time they met, at a coffee shop near their house. Seth had introduced himself – all faux humbleness – and then proceeded to semi-flirt with her mother and sisters in turn, holding their gaze a bit too long, throwing out compliments. He'd clearly expected people to find him attractive, and while he is – tall, bearded, muscular – and she did, the expectation was off-putting. The *entitlement*.

She catches Caleb's eye as the handshake finally comes to an end and they share a smile.

It's the first time she's looked at him properly. His safari-style shorts paired with a faded Pac-Man T-shirt display the deliberate, don't-give-a-shit nonchalance of a Silicon Valley tech nerd. It fits somehow; Caleb's an academic, older than them all but still clinging to the student vibe.

Physically, he's the polar opposite of Seth – lean, sharp-featured, with the kind of nondescript mousy hair that makes him blend into a crowd. Hana still remembers her mother's surprise when Bea introduced them last year. Her prior boy-friends had been, to use her mother's cringy expression, 'hale and hearty'.

Her mother's analysis a few days later was undecided: *there's something self-righteous about him*. Over dinner that night, they had glimpses of it: comments about politics and education that slipped under the radar because of the booze. It didn't bother Hana. She admired his confidence in saying the things she also felt but had never voiced. She'd always cared too much about what people thought of her.

When they met again – just the sisters and Caleb this time – she liked him even more. He has a keen intelligence, a dry humour, and the kind of quiet confidence that's often overlooked beside the chest-beating of someone like Seth. Caleb was able to match Bea intellectually and wasn't afraid to challenge her. Most people were. Bea's ferocious brain intimidated almost everyone – rendered them either mute or defensive.

'So how many are we waiting on?' the driver asks.

'Only one.' Jo laughs. 'In fact, there she is now.'

Maya's coming towards them, a half run, half walk down the jetty, one battered canvas trainer trailing a lace behind it. She's in typical Maya attire: a thin grey dress hanging loose over her tanned, sinewy frame. A hot-pink scarf dotted with a white pineapple print is loosely knotted around her head, only just taming her mass of curly black hair.

'Nearly went without you.' Jo's face splits into a grin. 'I—'

She isn't able to finish her sentence before Maya barrels into them, pulling Jo in and then Hana for a three-way hug, but they clash, elbows bumping. There's an awkwardness to the embrace; the action rusty somehow, underused. As Maya steps back, her bag drops from her shoulder – a battered black hold-all that looks suspiciously light and small.

Jo narrows her eyes. 'Sure you've got everything?'

Hana suppresses a smile. Jo had sent them an exhaustive list of supplies for the trip. *Rash vest. Cap. Water shoes. Sun cream.* It went on.

'Of course. I followed *the list* to the last letter.' Maya winks, catching Hana's eye.

'All right, let's go.' The driver is already striding towards the boat.

As Hana climbs aboard, there's a loud noise. She jumps. A couple of metres away, teenage boys are plunging into the sea from the wall by the restaurant, shorts billowing up as they plummet. The sharp crack as they smash into the water goes right through her.

'You okay?' Jo takes a seat next to her, tipping her head so it's close to Hana's. There's sympathy in her tone, but it's touched with something. Annoyance? Frustration?

'Of course. Those kids startled me, that's all.'

'Are you sure you're not still—'

'Still what?' Hana asks sharply.

Jo shrugs, but Hana knows what she's thinking. *You're not still anxious?*

Her behaviour this past year, her inability to dust herself off and go back to normal, has, in Jo's eyes, rendered her flawed, broken. And Jo believes that this is in some way *her* decision, as if by now Hana should have snapped out of it.

It's what she remembers most about last year, after Liam's accident. Jo looking at her, not empathizing, but examining, as if she were trying to find a chink in Hana's grief, some kind of signal that this would only be temporary.

Even now Jo struggles to refer to it, deals in euphemisms instead: after Liam's 'accident' she wanted Hana to quickly be 'better'. You could pin a million different woolly words on it, but they all amounted to the same thing: 'Get over it.'

The boat pulls away from the jetty with a sudden jerk as it accelerates, and Jo laughs as she's jolted into Hana, all smiles.

The switch flicked again.

Hana stares at her sister with an intense loathing.

She shouldn't have come. This was a bad idea.

5

'Not far now.' Edd raises his voice above the sound of the engine. 'Few minutes, max.'

Hana glances at her watch, the face lightly speckled with sea spray. They've been going for more than twenty minutes. She looks back at the beach; the wooden spine of the jetty is barely visible. Already, the hustle and bustle of the mainland seems far away.

Pulling out her phone, Jo gestures with her hand for Hana and Maya to bunch together. 'You two, turn to face out to sea.' They oblige, heads gently knocking together as the RIB bounces across the water.

'We're going to hit the back of the island first,' the driver calls. 'Never been anything built on this side. The forest's too thick.'

Caleb lets out a low whistle. Hana narrows her eyes, feeling a little jolt of anxiety as she takes in the dense wall of foliage. She can tell how dark it would be in there – sunlight watered down to almost nothing where the tree branches curve over one another like laced fingers, obscuring the sky.

'It's been too long.' Maya turns to Hana. 'We've been shit at keeping in touch, haven't we?'

'I know.' Hana observes her cousin. Her face, close up, suddenly unfamiliar. She hadn't remembered how beautiful Maya

27

is – the wild, curly hair and tanned skin, inherited from her Italian mother. Maya looks young still, but perhaps it's just Hana's perception – she'll probably always struggle to see Maya as grown up. Six years younger, for ages Maya *was* a child, someone Hana looked after. It wasn't just her personality; there was something uncertain about Maya, as if she weren't yet sure about her place in the world. Maya seemed to drift, travelling light, place to place, person to person.

'I shouldn't say *we*,' Maya continues. 'I've been crap at replying.'

'It's fine,' Hana says, but the words sound flinty, and she makes an effort to soften her tone. 'I didn't expect everyone to keep up the hand-holding.'

Because that's what Maya did, for months after Liam's death. The accident had drawn them back together, albeit temporarily. Maya was her rock – quiet, unwaveringly reliable when everyone else returned to their own lives. Even now, Hana's not sure if the rest of the family got bored or simply forgot, the minutiae of life taking over. It's been one of the hardest things after his death itself – that feeling of being alone at the time she needed people the most.

'How are you feeling about it all now?' Maya meets her gaze. 'Liam . . .'

'I just miss him. I didn't know it would feel like this, so . . . physical.' She can't put the bodily sensations into words; the horrible catch in her throat when she sees his side of the bed, the hollow in her chest when she thinks about the future they'll never have.

Everything they'd lost. Because that's what grief is: loss.

Hana's lost it all: Liam's perpetual five o'clock shadow, the way he made things come alive, talking about the world so viscerally it was like he was spreading out a map in her head. For

28

Liam, life was one big adventure. Rivers to be kayaked, hills to be biked down. He made the world full of colour, and without him it is now dark. *She* is dark and she doesn't know how to get back from that.

The driver interrupts her train of thought. 'On your left, you'll see the villas.'

He's right: nestled in the trees are glimpses of buildings – a right angle of powder pink against the blue of the sky, a large square of window, sunlight bouncing off the surface.

The retreat is perched high above the beach, a winding set of steps snaking their way up the cliff from the cove beneath. Several large, low-slung buildings are painted in other vivid tones – blues, peach. Just below on the right, slightly offset, is a glass-bottomed pool jutting out over the rocks.

'So what do you reckon?' Seth nudges Caleb. 'Bea's missing out, isn't she?'

'She is.' Caleb shrugs. 'We'll have to come another time.'

Hana notices Seth's response to the muted reply: how he's subtly examining Caleb. He's clearly discomforted by Caleb's body language, or rather the lack of it – the fact that he isn't trying to be matey.

Maya leans in, lowering her voice. 'So what do you make of that? When Bea cancelled, I thought he would too.'

'You knew she wasn't coming?' Hana picks up on her use of the past tense.

'Yes. Jo messaged a few weeks ago.'

Hana nods and it dawns on her that it wasn't an oversight – Jo not telling her – she withheld the information deliberately so that Hana wouldn't cancel too. She's not sure she would have come if she'd known Bea wasn't – they'd always needed all three of the sisters to balance one another.

Bea and Jo were two extremes – quiet versus loud. Introvert

versus extrovert. Academic versus sporty. Hana, in the middle, found that if she was with one without the other it felt wrong, like she was pulled too much to either extreme.

'I'm glad you made it,' Maya says quietly. 'I keep thinking, we let the whole promise thing slide, didn't we?'

The promise: *Stick together. Never forget.* Hana flinches at the naivety in the phrase. They'd made 'the promise' as kids, after the fire at Maya's house during a family sleepover, a fire that devastated not only their house, but their family too. They'd all managed to escape, bar Sofia, Maya's younger sister. Her room was empty when they searched, so her parents assumed she'd already gone out ahead of them. When they realized she hadn't, they tried to head back in, but the fire crew stopped them. They were the ones to eventually find her, hidden, frightened, under her bed, but by the time they did her burns were so severe, they led to a devastating stroke. The resulting brain damage and care requirements had proved too much for Maya's parents, and Sofia now lived in a residential care facility outside of Bristol.

The promise was to stick together, the three sisters and Maya, but their once unshakeable bond didn't survive late adolescence.

'We're here!' Jo's already gathering up her bags as the boat approaches the jetty. A member of staff is standing by, holding a tray of juice in tall glasses, the liquid inside a dramatic sunset orange. 'Those look incredible – just what we need before kayaking.'

Maya looks at her quizzically. 'Kayaking? We've only just arrived.'

'I've booked us a slot in' – Jo glances at her Fitbit – 'half an hour.'

'What about unpacking?'

'I thought everyone would be desperate to get in the water.'

Maya nods, face impassive.

When the boat comes to a stop a few minutes later, Jo's the first to get out.

Turning, she thrusts out a hand to Hana. 'Sorry for what I said before, asking if you were okay,' she murmurs, helping her up on to the jetty. 'I just want this to go well . . .'

There's a vulnerability in her expression as she searches Hana's face for a reaction. Jo doesn't usually do this – show her feelings, let alone apologize – and it makes Hana start to doubt her earlier assumption about the letter she'd found. Maybe this is all it was – an apology for not being around. Nothing more.

But as Jo loops an arm through hers, Hana can't help but stiffen.

She should know better than to let down her guard.

6

Elin picks half-heartedly at the remaining piece of grilled chicken on her plate before pushing it aside. Although the doors to the restaurant terrace are open, there's no breeze and the space is packed, only intensifying the heat. Three or four large groups are clustered by the bar, overspill leaking into the seating area.

Will squeezes her hand and Elin smiles. With the sweet-sour tang of wine on her tongue, it feels like their early dates – the ritual and festivity of eating out; the choosing of drinks and food, people watching.

'Hey, budgie alert.' Will points to the doors at the back of the restaurant.

Elin follows his gaze. A man in his sixties is striding up the beach in a green pair of budgie smugglers. It's her and Will's in-joke during summer. They've become connoisseurs; grading them according to cut on the butt, waist height, colour, transparency.

'What do you reckon? A nine?'

'Nah ... seven,' she replies, deadpan. 'There's coverage in key areas.'

Will laughs, but as it winds down she senses a tension in his expression. 'On a more serious note, there's something I wanted to ask you.'

She picks up her wine glass. 'Sounds ominous.'

'Not really. I wanted to show you this.' Reaching for his phone, he tilts the screen to face her. 'Message from Farrah. Says she can't meet this weekend. Busy at work.'

Farrah, Will's older sister, works at LUMEN as a manager. Fingers always in each other's pies – it always seemed slightly odd to Elin, too close for comfort, but then that was Will's family. Constant phone calls and texts.

'And? You've said before it's been hectic this season.'

'I know, but she's been acting odd recently. Not herself. Mum and Dad said she seemed distracted when she went round there last week. I've asked her about it, but you know what she's like. Never show a weakness.'

What you're all like, Elin mentally corrects. As a family, while they make a show of their openness – family meetings, heart-to-hearts over lunch – over time she's learnt that the openness is selective. They struggle to reveal anything that puts them at a disadvantage.

'Maybe boyfriend stuff?'

'I don't think so.' His fingers worry his battered silver ring. 'There hasn't been anyone since Tobias.' He pauses. 'I sometimes wonder if she'd confide in someone outside of the family.' He hesitates again and she knows what he's about to say. 'You never did go for that drink, did you?'

She pulls her plate back towards herself slowly, a delay tactic. 'Drink?'

'Didn't Farrah mention it the last time we saw her? You and her?'

Elin nods. She knows she should make an effort but has never quite got around to it. It hasn't been an easy relationship, awkward from the off, their first meeting a lunch together, several weeks before she met Will's parents.

You'll like her, Will had said, while they waited in the café, teeing her up – *she's sporty and fun like you* – but all Elin remembers is Farrah's assessing gaze, that immediate sense that she'd found something wanting. Elin knew what it was: a message. *You're not right for my brother.*

Ever since then, she and Farrah have circled each other warily. They talk a good game: lots of empty promises about meeting up, but it never materializes because she suspects neither of them actually want it to.

'I'll message her,' she says finally. 'To arrange it.'

Leaning over, he kisses her lightly on the lips. 'You can stop pretending.' He smiles. 'I know you're not keen, but she's probably more intimidated by you than the other way around. You've got to give people a chance. It's the same with the secondment. Roll with it. See how it goes.'

Elin nods, looking at him, absorbing everything: the freckles, the dirty-blond hair, the black-framed glasses that ever so slightly magnify his eyes, and she feels a surge of love.

He's right. There'll be hurdles as she gets back to work, but she needs to do as he says. *Roll with it. See how it goes.*

7

'So, do you like it?' Jo gestures at the main lodge a few metres away and smiles.

Juice still in hand, Hana stops beside her, breathes in the holiday smells: pine and flowers, sunbaked earth. 'It's beautiful.' She turns, taking in the candy-pink walls, the flat roofs and glass. Everything about it is striking, but her gaze keeps being pulled to the sea.

The view is breathtaking: sparkling bands of unreal colour, luminous blues and greens, framed by the cypress trees around her. The horizon beyond looks like it's simmering in the heat: a giant pot ready to boil.

'Restaurant on your right, yoga pavilion and exercise studios on your left.'

Hana nods. It's as she thought on the boat: the communal parts of the retreat are built across this plateau, all benefiting from the same view. It's clever – it gives the illusion of total isolation. No land, just water: an endless stretch of blue.

'Love it.' Seth puts an arm around Jo's shoulders. 'You picked well.'

Caleb's face is impassive. It's impossible to tell what he makes of it – either he's ambivalent or simply isn't one of life's enthusiasts.

'I think we'll be spending most of our time here.' Seth walks right, in the direction of the restaurant, flip-flops slapping loudly on the stone. 'Or more accurately, the bar.'

Hana follows, taking it all in. The indoor restaurant is flanked by a large outdoor space – a terrace and bar jutting out over the cliff, with sweeping views of the sea.

Although it's close to lunchtime, staff in white uniforms are still serving breakfast. A wooden pergola is wound with trailing plants and flowers, a large sail-shaped awning above, protecting it from the sun. Small festoon lights are strung from pillar to pillar. Acid-bright planters housing large cacti circle the terrace.

From this angle Hana can see the rope swing: the most Instagram-worthy spot at the retreat. A guest is swinging from one of the ropes, feet ruffling the surface of the water.

As they turn, walk the other way, starting to skirt the perimeter of the yoga pavilion, Hana's eyes pick out the villas dotted below, blending into lush foliage.

'It's a bit of a walk to ours,' Jo says, following her gaze.

'How far? I—' But she stops, suddenly hit by the sight of the rock above her.

Hana was expecting the shape to be less dramatic close up, but if anything, it's more pronounced – a side profile of the Reaper. She takes in what could be interpreted as the dipped curve of the hood, an arm extended, and the scythe.

It's this that her eyes fixate on – the slight hook to the stone blade.

She looks away, catching Seth's eye. He glances up at the rock and then at her, a smile playing on his lips.

Despite the sun warming her bare shoulders, Hana shivers.

8

'The guide said the caves are about ten minutes from here.' Jo's voice bounces off the water, magnified, as she turns from the front seat of the double kayak. 'Apparently you can paddle right through, come out a hundred metres or so down.' As she digs the paddle into the water, every muscle in her upper back and arms is perfectly defined by a slick layer of sun cream.

Maya, in a single kayak about a metre away, pulls an expression of mock horror. 'Having fun?' she mouths.

Hana smiles, but it's forced. Although it's not hard work – the kayak steadily powering through the calm water – she feels queasy and can still taste the acidity of the fruit juice they had on arrival. She shouldn't have drunk it, not before exercising. The heat doesn't help, she thinks, feeling sweat prick the back of her rash vest.

In truth, Hana would prefer to be back in the villa, feet suspended in the turquoise square of their plunge pool, a glass of ice water beside her. It was every bit as beautiful as the photographs – white walls; honeyed limestone floor; leafy, tropical plants in the corners. A holiday, hacienda vibe – rattan furniture, large terracotta vases, woven patterned rugs. Artworks in fierce rust red, pinks, and blues.

Why did they have to rush out? Why can't Jo just enjoy the moment?

Bea wouldn't have done that, she thinks, irritated. She, like Hana, would have lingered, analysed the little touches together – the tiny abstract artwork composed of pieces of bleached driftwood attached to the walls, the surreal clusters of cacti.

Hana had tried to hang back, make her excuses, but her pleas had been ignored. It's where Bea would have been useful. She's one of the few people who put Jo in her place.

'Hey, you three. Enough chat. We need to up the pace if you want to make it back for lunch,' Seth calls.

He and Caleb are up ahead, also in a double kayak. The two make an unlikely pairing – Seth's broad, tanned back a sharp contrast to Caleb's narrow build, clad in a shiny blue rash vest. It looks like Seth's doing most of the work – Caleb's strokes are messy, his paddle skimming the surface of the water rather than slicing through.

The island curves around towards the villas, and with it, the water turns a darker, inkier blue, huge ropes of seaweed standing upright from the bottom. Hana shudders, feeling the resistance as they wrap around her blade.

As they paddle past the last of the villas, the gentle landscape gives way to something wilder: the enormous walls of trees that she'd glimpsed when they arrived. Pines meld with conifers, oaks, brambly shrubs. A few metres on, the cliffs slope sharply inwards, forming a small cove. It's deserted – no people or paddleboards.

Jo steers them closer. Raising her blade, she points. 'Pretty sure this is it. I recognize it from the photos of the entrance. It loops around once you're inside.'

Hana looks uneasily at the small archway of limestone, barely wide enough to allow the kayak through.

'It's pretty narrow.' Caleb rests his paddle horizontally across his lap. 'You're sure this is the right spot?'

'It'll be wider inside. Other people have done it . . . we'll go first, won't we, Han? Show you guys the way.'

Hana can hear the challenge in Jo's voice. Still tasting the acid in the back of her throat, she swallows it away and nods. 'Of course.'

They paddle slowly towards the archway of rock. Caleb's right: when they reach the opening it's so narrow that they can't paddle, have to stop to let momentum carry them through and into the cave. Hana tenses as the sides of the kayak scrape the wall, a rough, rasping sound, but a few moments later, they're inside.

Instantly, the cave dims to a murky gloom. The limestone ceiling is low, blotchy with moisture. Barnacles and limpets lace the stone. It's a little wider now, with room to paddle on both sides.

'Everything all right?' Jo turns.

'Fine.' Hana's voice echoes off the low ceiling and walls. Paddling further in, it gets even darker, the water nearly black. A musty smell pervades the air, fishy and stale.

Up ahead, the passage narrows again. 'Are you sure it follows around?'

'Sure.' Hana can hear the hint of impatience in her sister's voice. 'Hold on.' Jo reaches for the slim tube of the torch hanging on a bungee cord around her neck, flicks it on. The beam picks out a curve in the wall about twenty metres ahead. 'See?'

Hana's fear gives way to a sudden euphoria, something she hasn't felt in a long time. Adventures like this have been off the cards since Liam died. He was the active one. Her default, without him, has been sofa surfer.

The channel of water finally widens enough for them to paddle side by side. Jo directs the torch straight ahead, a thin shaft of light spilling across the water. It turns the surface smoky – an eerie blue-green – and casts long shadows against the cave wall. Unfathomable shapes appear within the stone, a frenzy of colour and texture.

Hana paddles ahead, absorbing it all. 'This is amazing,' she says, turning. Jo grins. Hana realizes that this is what they were missing these past few years – a shared experience like this. Coffees, quick meals, actual adventures together. Making new memories.

She's about to voice as much when she hears the low murmur of Jo's voice. Hana watches, dismayed, as Jo directs the camera around her and Hana realizes that the smile she thought was at her is in fact directed at Jo's phone. So much for family time. Was Instagram and TikTok what this trip was all about? An exercise in self-promotion?

'Can't we just have a few minutes without that bloody phone? You documenting every single thing . . . Don't you ever want to be in the moment rather than recording it?'

Jo turns, her face tight. 'Han, for God's sake, lighten up, it's partly why we're here. I've got to produce content about the retreat to justify the gifted stay.' She shakes her head. 'It's always the same with you. So bloody judgemental.'

Absorbing the hurt in her sister's expression, Hana hesitates, regretting saying anything. Perhaps she *is* too quick to judge.

But before she can speak, Jo's face softens. 'But you're right, I'll put it away.' The edge has left her tone. 'I forget how all-consuming it feels to other people; Seth says the same. I get it, but sometimes all this . . .' She nods at her phone. 'It's easier than the real world.'

Hana looks at her curiously. 'What do you mean?'

'This edited version of life I'm putting out there. I prefer it sometimes. None of the messy stuff in real life, the weird dynamics between people.'

Hana smiles. 'You're trying to say *we're* messy . . .'

'A little.' Jo grins. 'It's just still a bit odd, between us all, isn't it? I keep wondering if it *is* a good idea, trying to force something that isn't there any more. You, me, Maya.' She hesitates. 'How's Maya been with you?'

'Fine, I mean, we're still catching up, but apart from that . . .'

'You're sure? She hasn't said anything?'

'About what?'

A flicker of something in Jo's eyes before she smiles. 'Nothing in particular.' But as they paddle away, the smile stays fixed in place. A beat too long to be genuine.

9

Hana closes the toilet door and crosses the restaurant, threading her way between tables packed with diners. She inhales the delicious smells, the air heady with the smoky char of meat, the resin note of the pines above. The strings of lights criss-crossing above illuminate half-empty wine bottles, glistening puddles of olive oil, and pillows of focaccia.

The view from here is otherworldly, the harsh blues of daytime sea and sky peeled away to reveal something softer and subtler. The distraction costs her: as she steps forwards, she stumbles, ankle giving way as her sandal catches on the uneven stone.

Too much to drink, Hana thinks, feeling the fizz and spin of the alcohol. She's in the lovely phase of inebriation: her senses heightened so the air feels warm, liquid against her skin. *It* is *liquid*, she thinks, doing a double-take, then realizes the heat of the grill pulling upwards is making the air in front of her shimmer and wobble.

Despite that, the person standing to the left of the grill is clear: Seth. He's talking to one of the female members of staff, head thrown back in laughter. *Typical Seth*: his need to charm and flirt extended to waiting staff, anyone around him.

Whether it ever leads to anything more, Hana's not sure, but it shouldn't, she thinks, looking ahead at Jo, in conversation with Caleb, phone in hand.

She's dazzling tonight. A few drinks in and her face is relaxed, open, the black broderie anglaise dress emphasizing her sun-streaked hair and her tan. Their mother is half Swedish, and Jo had snagged most of the clichéd Nordic genes – blue eyes, blonde hair, and also her mother's eclectic dress sense. The brightly coloured wrap slung over her shoulders – with splotches of green and pink – would look over the top on Hana, but on Jo it somehow works. Doesn't overwhelm her.

'You were gone a while.' Maya smiles. 'I was about to send out a search party.'

'I—' But Hana doesn't get to finish her sentence. Jo's holding up her phone, playing something back. It's *her*, Hana realizes, as she'd tripped. Jo's managed to slow it down, Hana's expression of panic – wide eyes, mouth ajar – played back frame by ugly frame.

A broad grin spreads across Jo's face. Seth, back at the table, is also smiling.

'Sorry,' Jo laughs, the green crescents of her wooden earrings lightly knocking her cheeks. 'I was panning around to get some footage of the restaurant and . . .' She bursts into laughter again.

Hana looks at her, senses suddenly and painfully heightened. 'You're not planning on putting that up, are you?' A flush crawls up her cheeks.

'No, of course not.' Jo reaches a hand across the table. 'God, you're not actually *bothered*, are you? I was only teasing.'

Hana can't help but recoil from her touch. 'Teasing . . .' But she stops as Maya catches her gaze: a warning shot. *Don't react.* She nods in assent. Maya's right. It'll be her who comes off worse if she snaps back.

It's at moments like this she wishes Liam were here. He'd have squeezed her hand under the table, changed the subject.

It was what he was good at: empathizing, boosting people. It was one of the first things Hana picked up on when they met, at a birthday party.

Tall, dark, lightly muscled, she'd spotted him immediately, but when they spoke, she was surprised at how shy he was, an endearing lack of self-awareness of his good looks.

Later in the evening, they'd ended up around the fire pit in the back garden together. She watched in admiration as Liam stepped in to defend a colleague being grilled about why she didn't have kids. It touched Hana how he'd reacted, and they'd ended up chatting – one of those uninhibited drunken talks you can only have with strangers because you think you'll never see them again.

She came away from the night certain of two things: that she wanted to see him again, and that if she did, she'd end up on a mountain bike. Liam's biking obsession consumed at least half the conversation. Hana finds herself smiling at the memory, but then remembers. She has to nudge the thought away, an unwelcome visitor.

'I get it,' Caleb says, looking at Hana. 'Sometimes I wish we could roll back twenty years, have a meal the old-fashioned way.'

'What did you say?' Jo nudges her chair closer.

'Just that all the video stuff, it's too much sometimes.' Caleb shrugs.

Jo wearily shakes her head. 'I've seen that look before. You think it's beneath you, don't you? Bea's said as much.'

He frowns. 'What do you mean?'

'I've seen Bea's posts on social media. All that naff pseudo-intellectual bullshit about TV shows and books. Bea never used to be like that. She always said that if you're truly intellectual, you don't feel the need to ram it down people's throats,

44

what you read or watch worn like some bloody badge to prove how intelligent you are.'

Caleb stiffens, mouth pressed together in a thin line. *Jo's hit a nerve.* He changes the subject. 'You know, I read about this place before we came, thought it was probably a fuss about nothing, but when you're here, see the rock close up . . .' He cranes his neck so he can see past her. 'It's got a presence, hasn't it?'

Seth nods. 'It makes me think there's something to it, what people say.'

'And what do people say?' Caleb mocks Seth's dramatic tone.

'That it's cursed, among other things. Not surprising given what's happened here over the years.'

'Like?'

'The plague stuff, the old school burning down . . . Creacher . . . don't think I need to say any more—'

'No, you don't,' Maya interrupts. 'While it makes for a good story, it's not exactly conducive to holiday vibes.'

'Speaking of holiday vibes, I fancy another cocktail.' Picking up the drinks menu, Jo reads aloud: '*Sunset Sailor. Bacardi Oro, Diplomático, Angostura, pineapple, orange.*'

'Bea would love that,' Caleb says, gesturing one of the waiting staff over. 'She's in a cocktail phase at the moment. Even bought one of those shakers for home . . .'

'Wish Bea could have come,' Hana murmurs when their drinks arrive a few minutes later. She takes a sip of hers. It's strong, heavy on the rum. 'Not the same without her.'

'Well, we'll toast her.' Jo holds up her cocktail, the vibrant liquid catching the light. 'To Bea.'

Maya's the only one who doesn't raise her glass.

Hana glances at her, shocked to find Maya blinking back tears. 'What's wrong?'

'It's not just Bea we're missing,' Maya blurts out. 'Sofia should be at things like this.'

'Oh, God, of course.' Hana squeezes Maya's hand, kicking herself.

'It just hits me, sometimes, what she's missing out on.' Maya wipes her eyes.

Jo raises her glass again. 'To absent friends . . .' Despite the sympathy on her face there's something dismissive in her tone. They drink in silence before she speaks again. 'Shall we go to the beach in a bit?' She throws out a comment about whether they're too old for skinny-dipping.

The conversation quickly moves back to the jokey, light-hearted tone from earlier, but Maya's outburst has bothered Jo, Hana can tell.

It's as if Maya has caused a ripple in the evening Jo had planned, thrown a rock into the otherwise perfectly flat lake.

10

Day 2

Michael Zimmerman walks through the restaurant, cloth and polish in hand.

His gaze picks over the scene: the empty chairs, the soft grey of the stone floor, the festoon bulbs, each reflecting a tiny, glowing sun. He likes this time, before the guests are awake. This early, the sun feels heavy-lidded, like it's barely opened its eye over the horizon, reluctant to meet your gaze.

Plus, this shift is easy work. The retreat has already been swept clean the night before. All he has to do is hunt out the final bits the night staff have missed – a bottle jammed into a corner, open mouth still dribbling beer; greasy finger smudges on the balustrades.

He's not good for much more, he thinks, feeling a sharp twinge in his lower back. His days of heavy exertion are over, his body worn out from years of teaching PE and playing weekend rugby. It was time to take his foot off the pedal, but he didn't want to retire completely, which made this job the perfect in-between.

Enough company to keep him out of trouble, that's what his wife would have said, and it was true. It didn't do you any good to be on your own. Too much time to think.

Michael wipes his cloth along the railing one last time, fingertip pressed into the fabric to catch the worst of the grease, then makes his way across to the yoga pavilion.

He hasn't yet reached the entrance when he notices a piece of clothing on the grass outside the glass balustrade surrounding the front of the pavilion.

The brightly patterned material bothers him; something like this shouldn't have been missed by the night cleaners.

Slowly walking over, Michael leans over the balustrade to retrieve it, but as soon as his hand closes around the slippery fabric, something on the rocks below draws his gaze.

He startles. *You're seeing things.*

But as he looks closer, it's clear that he isn't.

Michael starts to tremble. His hand falls open, wrap slithering back to the ground.

Wrenching his gaze from the rocks, he turns, retches. With each spasm, regurgitated lumps of the muesli laid out for the staff every morning splatter the pale stone of the floor.

11

Elin sits down at her desk, thighs still tingling from her run. She loves early mornings in the office – the silence and citrus-fresh bite of cleaning fluid, the loamy light picking up dusty computer screens. Tiny details she sees only at this time, when her brain has space to roam, not yet weighed down by the detritus of the day.

She needs any help she can get on this case; a vital spark that's been missing so far. There'd been another burglary yesterday, the latest in a spate of similar crimes, the thieves making off with thousands of pounds' worth of jewellery and electrical goods, petty cash. In the past few weeks, she'd widened the net. They'd gone to the press to appeal for witnesses and dashcam footage, but they'd drawn a blank. Forensics had turned up nothing.

The pressure is weighing on her: *if she can't make headway on this, why would they think she's ready to go back to the MCIT?*

Elin sifts through the witness statements. The gang, and she's certain it *is* a gang given the volume of crimes, are professional: identifying targets without any kind of security or CCTV either on the house or in the vicinity.

'Morning.'

She looks up. *Steed.* He gives her an easy grin and slips off his rucksack, dropping it to the floor. Heat is radiating off him, sweat patches blooming under his arms.

'Christ, it's hot already. I was going to cycle in, but changed my mind.' Pulling a protein shake from the side pocket of his bag, he pops the cap.

'It's going to be in the thirties by the afternoon.' Elin appreciates the small talk, certain he won't mention seeing her on the beach. He's too discreet. It's something she's picked up on since they've worked together; he knows when to leave things.

'What's on for today?' Steed swigs from his shake.

'There was another burglary last night. We need to double-check all CCTV within half a kilometre of the property. I know we've got a few restaurants nearby, the yacht club on the other side, see if we can pick anything up that way. Hold on—' She stops, noticing Anna's name flashing on her phone.

A flicker of nerves as she recalls their last conversation. But there's no reference to the day before. Anna's voice is oiled with urgency. 'We've received a report of a body on the rocks out on Cary Island, at the retreat.'

'LUMEN?' A catch in her throat at the synchronicity: Will's award.

'Yes. You okay to attend the scene and assess the situation? You're closest. Ambulance and CSI will meet you on the jetty at Babbacombe. The police boat will pick you up from there.'

You're closest. It makes sense, but she knows that Anna suggesting she go isn't just because she's in the vicinity. It's a vote of confidence in her, her abilities, after their discussion yesterday.

But the doubts of the last few weeks jostle for position, crowding her head. What if she can't handle it? But Elin quickly squashes the thought; she's capable. Ready. 'Absolutely. I'll get my things together and go.'

As she says goodbye, she notices Steed is listening. 'Something on?'

'A body's been found on Cary Island. Fancy coming?'

'Of course.' He straightens – excitement that he quickly tries to temper by making a fuss of checking his phone.

But as she starts methodically packing her grab bag, everything from evidence bags to forensic clothing, a wave of trepidation sweeps over her.

Despite Will's involvement in LUMEN, she's never visited the island. Never wanted to – no local did. The island's past had always weighed far too heavily.

12

The police boat slows, engine dampening to a throaty purr as they approach the jetty.

The CSIs, Leon and Rachel, and the two paramedics gaze up at the retreat with admiration, but as the boat steadies to a stop, all Elin feels is a bottomless dread.

She's seen the island in photographs, but this is different. There's a wildness about it, something raw and uncompromising. Although she tries to focus on what Will's created, it's nature that dominates, drawing her gaze: the tangle of woodland, looming cliff faces, birds perched high in the shadows, and the rock.

Reaper's Rock.

Memories flicker.

A ticker-tape stream of images from the press: police boats, people searching through the forest, the bloated face of Larson Creacher's mug shot all over the news, straggly rat's-tail hair curling around his shoulders.

'Ready?' One of the medics turns, breaking Elin's reverie as she begins to clamber from the boat, bag in hand.

Elin nods, distracted. Someone is walking towards them, waving. *Farrah.*

'You know her?' Leon looks at her curiously.

'Will's sister. She's a manager at the retreat.'

'It's not going to be awkward?' Rachel brushes her dark, wispy fringe out of her eyes.

'No.' Elin's not offended by her bluntness. It's one of the things that makes Rachel so good at her job. That, and an inexhaustible ability to go the extra mile.

Farrah stops to direct the medics to the body. When she reaches the dock she greets Elin: 'I didn't realize it would be you.'

Elin nods, skimming over a reply by making introductions. 'This is DC Steed, and these are the crime scene investigators.'

Farrah gestures at the medics, scrambling over the rocks to the left. 'I told them where she is, but I don't know if there's much chance . . .' She tails off. 'Our first-aider said as soon as he got there he knew.'

'The paramedics still need to check.'

'Of course.' A fleeting frown crosses Farrah's brow as if she's questioning Elin. She's done this before. It makes her feel that Farrah doesn't take her seriously. 'I'll walk you over.'

'Do you know who she is?' Elin says as the group fall into step beside Farrah.

'No, she's not a member of staff, and as yet, none of the guests have been reported missing, but it's still early. People might not be awake yet.'

'Where exactly did she fall from?'

'Yoga pavilion.' Farrah points up at the wooden structure perched atop a sheer cliff face that looms dizzyingly high above them. Elin can make out a glass balustrade circling the front of the pavilion: the only barrier to the rocks below.

'She fell *over* the balustrade?'

'Yes.'

'How high is it?' Steed asks.

'Maybe waist height on me.' Farrah shakes her head. 'I'm still not quite sure how it could have happened.'

But Elin knows it's possible to fall over a balustrade of almost any height. She's seen a couple of catastrophic balcony falls – one residential, one in a hotel. On both occasions, alcohol was involved, but she can't make that assumption here. Not yet.

Farrah seems ill at ease as she glances towards the rocks. 'Michael, the cleaner who found her, said he saw a wrap on the other side of the barrier. Maybe she leant over to get it and lost her balance.'

'Perhaps, but until we know more we have to look at every possible explanation.' The golden rule in an unexplained death: treat as suspicious until proven otherwise.

'Where's Michael now?'

'At the yoga pavilion. The officer on the phone said he should stay there, stop anyone getting too close. We've put a rough cordon up with some rope, put a member of staff outside to guard it as he instructed.'

'Good.' Elin thinks on her feet: she's going to have to divide and conquer, split Rachel and Leon up so they can examine both scenes simultaneously. 'Leon, can you head up to the pavilion with Farrah, start there? Steed and I will go with Rachel.'

'Of course. Lead the way.'

13

Elin and Steed follow Rachel, clambering over the rocks at the base of the cliffs. Small, flatter stones are interspersed with huge boulders piled on top of one another; a cliff fall of old.

Elin, already sweating, wipes her forehead with the back of her hand. Rounding the cliff, she can see the paramedics leaning over the body, talking quietly.

She absorbs the scene: a slim, fair-haired woman in her early thirties, sprawled across the rocks. She's in a black dress, her arm bent backwards at an unnatural angle. The side of her head closest to the rock is caved in, the massive trauma shattering a large section of her skull. Brain matter and white bone fragments are visible against the pale grey of the rock and the dark pool of blood under her head.

Disturbed, Elin swallows hard. Some scenes, like this one, are so graphic that you can never be prepared. She knows it will stay with her long after the case has been closed.

'Wouldn't have stood a chance from that height,' Steed says thickly.

The older medic, Jon, a tall, stocky man, says, 'She's dead.' He turns his wrist. 'Life extinct at 7.33 a.m.' Turning to Elin, he peels off his glove. 'She's already in rigor. Obviously massive head injury, multiple injuries to spine and pelvis. Surface wounds consistent with a fall from that height.'

Elin tips her head up, struck by an awful, vertiginous sensation as she looks at the jagged ridges of the cliff. She can't help but see the fall in her mind's eye: the woman's body twisting and turning in mid-air, skull loudly cracking on the rock below.

Looking back to the woman, Elin's eyes track up to her face. Her eyes are closed, the right one obscured by a bloody abrasion. Her full mouth is slack, drawn downwards.

Her gaze moves lower, alights on the woman's black dress and her shoes. One strappy sandal is half off, the woman's perfect inky-blue pedicure visible. Elin wants to preserve this fragment of the woman in her mind – the one part of her untouched.

'Any ID?'

'No, and I don't see a bag or phone. Either she didn't have them on her, or they've got lost somewhere in the fall.' Jon clears his throat. 'I think we'll take the boat back, leave you to it, if you're good to take it from here.'

His words propel her into action. Reaching into her bag, Elin pulls out her kit, forensic suits, overshoes, and gloves, then passes a set to Steed.

'Okay for me to go in?' Rachel pulls up the hood of her own suit.

Elin nods. They scramble into their suits, the rustling of the paper amplified in the quiet. They wait while Rachel photographs the body, the pool of blood around her head.

A few minutes later, Rachel puts the camera aside, starts patting down the body, examining the small pockets at the sides of the woman's dress. She confirms they're empty.

'The rigor?'

She considers. 'I'd say it still isn't complete. She's been here longer than a few hours but not more than twelve.'

That gives Elin something to work with – the woman probably fell in the early hours of the morning.

'Can we turn her over? Look for any other wounds?' In particular, Elin's looking for signs of an attack: a gunshot, puncture wounds.

Steed steps carefully around the body until he's directly opposite Rachel. On the count of three, they turn the woman. Rachel examines her back and legs. 'Nothing. Can't see any other abrasions apart from collateral damage from the fall, scratches to her hands and arms. No obvious defensive wounds either, no bruising or signs of restraint around her wrists. Fingernails look clean.'

Elin nods. From what Rachel's said, this may have been just a fall, but she can't discount the possibility that she was pushed. A well-aimed, careful shove from behind would result in the same outcome without any obvious defensive wounds.

As Rachel picks up her camera, Elin turns to Steed. 'Let's cordon off the area with tape. Establish a common approach path and start a scene log. I can't imagine there's going to be anyone wandering about, but just in case. If you're okay to preserve the scene, I'm going to update Anna, then check in with Leon.'

'Sounds good.' Steed steps forwards, face flushed.

Elin hesitates. 'You okay?'

'Fine.' He clears his throat. 'It's just – we had something similar happen with a family member . . . It brings it back.'

As Elin says a few reassuring words, it's clear from his rapid blinks that he's still riding the feeling. She wants to offer comfort, but knows if she gives in to any kind of emotion she'll lose the focus she's desperately clinging to.

'Right,' Elin says finally, giving a nod. 'I'll see you in a bit.' Taking off her suit, she starts back over the rocks, but a few metres from the scene, she stops, blinded by a sudden, sharp glint from the cliff above. When she turns her head, it's gone, but the glint reappears as she walks: a hazy semicircular glow flickering in the centre of her vision each time she blinks.

It takes a while to leave her, but even when it does, Elin still feels unsettled.

She's picking up on something scorched about the island, a strange stillness that seems unnatural somehow, malevolent.

14

Hana wakes up sweaty, sheets twisted around her in a knot. Her head is pounding, the room is shifting on its axis as she sits up, the rattan chair in the corner and the cheese plant beside it stretching and elongating before her eyes.

The sensation makes her feel disorientated, anxious, and for a moment, she's back there – the panic-filled days after Liam's death. Not just one grief but two: the loss of Liam and also the loss of their dream of starting a family, snuffed out before they'd got off the starting blocks. A few months before his accident, they'd taken tentative steps towards IVF.

Hana was consumed by regrets.

Why hadn't they started the process sooner? Taken action rather than just talked about it? At least she'd have had something of Liam. Something to hold on to while everything else fell away.

Another surge of nausea.

Swinging her legs out of bed, Hana walks to the sink in the bathroom and refills her glass. She reaches for her transparent zip-up toiletry bag filled with medical supplies. She's turning into her mother, she thinks, popping two tablets from the foil packet of paracetamol. *Always be prepared.*

Slipping them into her mouth, she takes a large swig of

water, followed by the greedy gulps you only take when you've been drinking.

Her phone is on the bedside table. She picks it up, takes it over to the window.

A perfect square of summer: blue sky, trees, canary yellow curve of the hammock stretching across the terrace.

Hana takes a photo, flicks through the ones from last night. The first makes her smile: a grinning group shot on the beach, their backs to the water. The image is out of focus, the photographer – Caleb – obviously moving as he'd snapped it.

After the meal they'd gone to the beach as Jo had suggested. No one swam in the end, but they'd paddled their feet in the water, set the world to rights. She'd had some cringingly intense conversation with Caleb, perched on the rocks at the edge of the beach – something about his work, environmental policy. At one point, Jo and Seth had a drunken row that sputtered out as quickly as it began.

The beach interlude ended with a call to Bea that went to voice mail, after which they'd sent her the group shot. Hana smiles, imagining Bea's grin when she saw it, their sunburnt, moon-faced smiles. What did the message below their photo say? Something sloppy, sentimental. *Wish you were here. Caleb's doing kisses down the phone . . .*

A text in reply: *Guys . . . love you but I'm at a work event. Speak soon.*

Hana can picture Bea at this event – busy and solicitous, saying all the right things in just the right tone. This is what she thinks of as Bea 2.0: smart, expensive clothes, discreet jewellery, fair hair swept away from her face. Nothing like the unsure, bookish sister she grew up with, who loathed dressing up.

She keeps swiping: Caleb's taken a few of the same group shot, but when she reaches the last image, a ripple of disquiet moves through her. He'd obviously snapped the photo as the group had started to disperse, the effort of holding a fixed smile too much. *I can't do it*, she remembered Seth laughing.

Hana's still half smiling, but Jo has turned away. She's looking at Hana, clearly unaware the photograph is being taken. The expression on her face pulls Hana up short, Jo's features frozen into a strange mask of something dark.

Hana can't quite make out what it is. *Fear? Hate?*

Her thoughts slide to the note that had dropped from Jo's bag. Maybe there was more to it than she thought.

Walking over to her holdall, she rummages in the side pocket where she'd shoved the letter on the jetty. Carefully smoothing it out between her fingers, she looks again at the words.

Hana,
~~*I'm sorry. I'm sorry.*~~ *I'm sorry.*

Her stomach twists. Part of her feels compelled to knock on Jo's door right now and ask her what it means, but another part of her recoils at the idea, knowing the drama that will inevitably ensue.

Keep calm and carry on.

It's all she needs to do. One week together and then they can go back to minimal contact. Now she's an adult, she can decide how often she sees her sister, the kind of relationship they have.

It's one of the few good things that came out of what happened. Hana had realized these past few months, after everyone had drifted away, left her alone in her grief, that if she can survive Liam's death, then she can survive anything.

She's stronger than she thought.

15

When Elin reaches the top of the steps from the beach it's a few minutes to eight.

The retreat is stirring to life; white-shirted staff busy in the restaurant, a group of early swimmers walking towards the beach. It's clear that some of the guests have clocked something is up. They're milling around the yoga pavilion with that studied, false nonchalance – not wanting to appear as if they're staring but doing so anyway.

About to pull on a suit and overshoes, she hesitates, noticing Farrah approaching.

'I take it she's definitely—'

Elin nods. 'A little while, I think.'

Farrah's mouth tightens before she composes herself, gesturing to the restaurant. 'Michael, the man who found her, is waiting in there. You wanted to speak to him . . .'

'That's right. Give me two minutes. I need to . . .' She gestures at Leon.

'Of course. Come over when you're ready.'

Slipping the suit and overshoes on, Elin ducks under the tape. Leon's crouched beside the balustrade, dusting the glass. 'All going okay?'

'Fine.' He nods at some vomit near by. 'Apart from the occupational hazard.'

'The guy who spotted her?'

'Yep.'

Peering over the balustrade, Elin quickly draws back. However daunting it is looking up, looking down is worse – the sudden visual dive and plunge to the hooky spikes of rock below. The splayed, broken form of the woman's body hits her anew from this angle.

'What do you think about the height of the balustrade?'

Leon continues dusting the glass. 'Definitely low enough to go over accidentally. I'd have had something higher in place given the location of the pavilion.'

'Anything on it?'

'Yes. Unusual pattern of prints all over the other side – fingers and palm. I'm pretty sure from what the guy said that they're hers. Apparently the glass is cleaned every night and he'll mop up anything left in the morning. Everything points to her falling frontways, and then twisting – like she tried to hold on but lost her grip.'

Elin leans closer to the balustrade. Silvery fingerprint powder highlights the various marks covering the glass – a blotchy segment of a handprint, smeared fingerprints – but she knows it doesn't prove anything. Those marks could result from an accidental fall as well as a push. 'Did she drop anything here?'

He shakes his head. 'I've done a quick search, but apart from the wrap' – a nod at a bagged-up piece of clothing on the floor – 'nothing.'

'Where was it exactly?'

'On the grass on the outside of the balustrade, but I don't think it necessarily lends weight to the falling idea. It might have dropped *as* she fell.'

Elin examines the wrap through the bag. It's brightly

patterned – a modern abstract print with bold splashes of pink and green. 'You haven't found anything else?'

'Only this . . .' He points through the balustrade. 'There's an indentation in the grass here, before the cliff drops away. Looks consistent with something fairly heavy being placed on it.'

'Heavier than the wrap?'

'Yes, and it's in a different location anyway, a bit further forwards than where I found the wrap. Given the lack of wind or rain, it's held. Can't say for sure it's from last night, but if it was over a few days ago, I think the grass would have recovered.'

'Any conclusions?'

'Not really. It's small and square. Maybe something else she dropped on the way down. Could have got dislodged in the fall.'

'I'll get Rachel to have a look down there.' She hesitates. 'Right, I'll leave you to it. I'm going to speak to the guy who found her.' Tugging off her suit and overshoes, Elin notices that the small crowd of guests has swollen, big enough to prompt a member of staff to shepherd them away towards the restaurant. She tags behind, then splinters off, walking towards Farrah, who is sitting beside an older man, talking quietly.

Farrah glances up. 'Elin, this is Michael Zimmerman. I've told him you'd like to speak with him.'

Michael gives a tentative smile. Elin immediately notices his eyes. They're striking – heavy-lidded, a pale blue that conjures images of a sky yet to deepen. She guesses he's mid- or late sixties, and judging from the deep lines on his face and wild castaway beard, most definitely what Will would call a 'sea dog' – the older soul surfers born and bred on the coast.

Taking a seat opposite, she pulls out her rough book. 'Michael, I understand this isn't easy, but I was hoping you could take us through what happened this morning. Starting with where you were before you saw her.'

He nods, picking up the cap laid beside him on the table as if to put it on to his head, then setting it back down. The peak is bleached by the sun, salt stained. 'I was up around five, like I usually am, early shift. I do all the final checks, cleaning-wise, of the public spaces. Can't guarantee that the night crew haven't missed something, or the guests haven't been out overnight, made a mess—' He looks up, tries to catch Farrah's eye in shared solidarity about the unpredictable nature of guests, but she's looking at her phone.

'What time was this?'

'Just after six. I'd finished up in the restaurant area and was walking over to the yoga pavilion. I was going up the steps when I saw a piece of clothing, the wrong side of the balustrade. Bright, you couldn't miss it.' Michael picks up his cap again, turns it between his fingers. The gesture is oddly familiar, and Elin has a swooping sense of recognition, as if she's seen him or perhaps someone else do it before.

'Go on,' she says softly.

'I walked over to pick it up and that's when . . .' He licks his lips. 'That's when I saw her, down on the rocks. I could tell she was . . .' A pause. 'I was sick, you probably saw, but when I got myself together, I called 999, then Farrah.'

'And you didn't notice anything during your shift? Nothing suspicious, out of the ordinary? No one walking around who shouldn't be there?'

'During the shift, no, but . . .'

Farrah looks up: a sharp glance in his direction.

He changes position in his chair. 'Look, it's probably nothing to do with this, but last week, something odd happened, during the night. I woke up as you do, nature's call when you get to my age. Getting back into bed, I saw someone walking about, near the rock. It struck me as strange, someone out that late.'

'You saw this from the staff accommodation?'

He nods.

'And exactly what time was this?'

'Four, maybe a bit later. Whoever it was, they had a torch, was shining it up at the rock, like they were looking for something.'

'Probably a guest.' Farrah's tone is dismissive as she turns to Elin. 'Some of them take photographs of the rock at night. No idea why, you can barely see anything.'

Michael gives a mirthless laugh. 'This place, nothing would surprise me.'

Elin's skin prickles. 'What do you mean?'

'This island, it's hardly had a glowing report card, has it? Don't get me wrong, they've transformed it, but you can still feel it sometimes, early in the morning, when no one's around.'

'Feel what?' Elin leans forwards, uneasy.

'Something . . . bad.' He visibly swallows. 'A guest, a few weeks ago, said the same.'

'Really?' It's an effort to keep her voice steady.

'Yes. The artist that did the piece in reception told me he went to the old school here, the one that burnt down. Said he'd come to see his piece, check out the retreat,' Michael continues. 'Loved it, but he said . . .' He pauses, his features frozen for a moment in thought. 'He said he could still feel it,' he says finally. 'The evil here.'

Farrah shakes her head at his words, the melodramatic delivery, but as Elin thanks him, closing her notebook, she can't dismiss what he's said quite so easily. She, too, can feel it the longer she's here – a presence and an energy that goes beyond all the stories.

Something intrinsic to the island itself.

'We'll need a formal statement later, but that's all for now.

Thank you again.' As Elin picks up her bag she notices a man walking towards them. On reaching Farrah, he murmurs something inaudible in her ear.

Farrah turns. 'This is Justin Matthews, the security director. He's found the CCTV for the pavilion. I wasn't sure if there was a camera close by, but there is apparently.'

A flicker of relief. 'Can we look now?'

'Of course.'

But she's only taken a few steps when she hears a noise: a skitter of gravel.

There's a tug on her arm. Elin pivots to find Michael behind her, uncomfortably close.

His hold tightens to a squeeze. 'What I said before,' he murmurs. 'I mean it. What that man told me, he's right. There's something rotten here. You need to be careful.'

16

Hana, now washed and dressed, scrapes her hair back into a ponytail, a ponytail that never really works since her hair is too short. *Stubby*, Liam used to call it, ruffling the ends. *An attempt, Han, but a misguided one.*

Retying it, she slips on her sandals and makes her way out into the corridor. The scent of coffee, bitter and fragrant, is filtering in from the living space.

Jo. She's the early bird. It will be her in there, making coffee. *Act normally*, she tells herself, pasting a smile on her face. *Don't react.*

But she finds that it's not Jo, but Maya, sitting on a wicker chair in the sunshine, a green scarf knotted around her curls.

She glances up, smiling. 'You just missed coffee . . .'

'It's fine, I'll make one.' Hana looks down at the book lying open on her lap. 'What are you up to?'

'Drawing.' Maya gestures at what Hana can now see is a sketchbook. 'I couldn't sleep. It's always the same when I've been drinking. Wake up in the night, can't get off again.'

'I know what you mean, I didn't sleep well either. I think the whole beach thing was a bridge too far.' She pauses. 'Did you hear Jo and Seth's row?'

'Bits of it. He took a call, didn't he? A friend.' Maya shakes her head. 'Not sure why Jo's surprised – he's always been like that. Loads of women "friends".' She makes quote marks with her fingers.

Hana pauses, picking up on the significance of Maya's words. 'What you said, about always being like that – do you know Seth, I mean, outside of Jo?'

Maya hesitates, flushing. She lowers her voice. 'Well, I wouldn't say *know*. I've climbed with him a few times. A mate of a mate. It's how Jo met him, through me. A night out.'

'You never said.' Not just about how Jo met Seth, but the night out, she thinks, stung.

'Didn't seem important. And for Jo, probably not quite the romantic story she wants out there for her followers – some drunken hook-up in the pub.'

'What did you make of him? Before Jo, I mean?'

'Thought he was a bit of an idiot. All smiles, charm to your face, but behind your back . . . shallow's the word.' Shrugging, Maya glances towards the corridor, dropping her voice a notch lower again. 'There were rumours about him being aggressive too, before bouldering competitions. Trying to psych out his rivals.' Her fingers worry the stud at the very top of her ear.

'What is it?' Hana's voice is barely more than a whisper as she, too, looks to the corridor, part of her convinced Jo will burst in at any moment.

'The aggression, I reckon it's spilled over with Jo. He was going on about her drinking last night, that she shouldn't go so hard.'

'Maybe he's just worried. She was pretty wasted . . .'

Maya's face clouds. Hana changes the subject, nodding at the sketchbook as she waits for the coffee machine to start gurgling into life. 'I didn't realize you still drew.' Art had always been Maya's thing. It started after the fire: intricate, dreamlike pictures.

'Bits and bobs here and there. Fame and fortune has most definitely eluded me.' She looks up. 'It's funny, isn't it? When you're young, you're convinced you'll make it, that you've got all the time in the world. I really thought that after college I'd get there. Success, recognition, that it would all somehow magically slot into place.'

'It still can. You're only twenty-eight.'

Maya laughs. 'Dreams. You need time, Han. The concentration. Enough cash. The reality is I'm good, but I'll never be brilliant.'

Hana, taken aback, makes a fuss of putting her cup under the nozzle of the coffee machine. When she glances at Maya, for the first time she sees how thin she is, the harsh morning light picking out the hollows of her cheeks. Her burn is visible: puckered, melted skin creeping in a line up her calf. Jo has one too – her scar ragged, bubble shaped, on her arm. Bea's is barely noticeable, a blotchy pattern on the side of her right foot.

Permanent reminders of the fire that changed Sofia's life forever.

Hana was the only one who came out unscathed. It made her feel guilty when they were younger, but looking at Maya now, she wonders if everyone focused too much on the external scarring to the detriment of what was going on inside. At the time, they all assumed that Maya had coped okay. *Children are adaptable*, her mother said, but perhaps she'd suppressed it – only now was it catching up with her.

'Enough about me. We didn't finish our conversation yesterday. How are you doing?'

Hana's touched. No one has asked her how she is – and meant it – for a long time. She shrugs. 'Bad days and not-so-bad days. I think . . .' Hana pauses, working out how to word it. 'I think *how* it happened doesn't help, not having all the facts.

70

If I knew, it might be easier to process.' As it is, all she has are the lurid, graphic projections of her own mind. The bare facts: that one sunny April morning, Liam went on his own to Haldon Forest bike park.

He was on the hardest trail, attempted an obstacle called Free Fall, a wooden plank structure with a pivot point high above the ground. At the inquest, they worked out that he'd never made it over the pivot point, tumbled, landing directly on his head. He broke his neck, fracturing his C6 vertebra.

Instant death.

'Morning.'

Hana turns, reverie broken. Seth's standing in the doorway in a pair of boxers emblazoned with tiny palm trees, his dark hair wild, electrified. 'Jo not back yet?'

'What do you mean?' Hana says.

'Gone for a run, but she didn't message to let me know. She usually does.'

'A run, in this heat?'

'Her thing after a night out. We normally get images of "broken Jo" at every mile in her stories, complaining about running with a hangover.' He looks down at his phone. 'Saying that, none so far today. Perhaps she's feeling the booze—'

'She must have gone pretty early,' Maya murmurs. 'I've been up since six.'

'Probably,' he shrugs. 'But I thought she'd be back by now. Breakfast's calling.'

Maya stands. 'I need a shower, but I can be ready in fifteen if you all want to go?'

Seth nods. 'I'll knock for Caleb and then message Jo, let her know we've gone up.'

As everyone drifts from the room, Hana's left alone with her coffee. She's about to take it outside when she notices Maya's sketchbook on the chair. Curiosity getting the better of her, Hana wanders over. Putting her coffee down on the table, she nudges open the book, flicking through, one eye on the corridor. Sketches of the rock face, each one slightly smaller than the last. A Russian doll of an image.

She keeps flicking, but the rest of the pages are blank. About to close it, she hesitates, catching a glimpse of a sketch towards the back. *A drawing of Jo.*

Hana's skin prickles. Although Maya has drawn Jo accurately – slightly crooked nose, full mouth, the slight dimple to her chin – she realizes that it's *how* Maya's drawn it that's odd. Each line is leaden, as if she's pressed the pencil so hard that it's nearly gone through the page.

The effect is curious: it's as if she's captured Jo but at the same time is trying to overpower her with her pencil, battling her image into submission with each mark and line.

17

'Sorry, I didn't know Michael was going to be so full-on,' Farrah says as they follow Justin along the main path.

'It happens. People often need to vent after something like this, a way of coping with what they've seen.' Elin keeps her tone light, but she's still chilled as she picks over his words. 'What did you make of what he said, about someone wandering around?'

Farrah shakes her head. 'Made no sense. You can't get up there, not any more . . .' She tails off as Justin stops at the entrance to the main lodge and the glass doors slide open automatically.

Inside, it's another world. The reception space is beautiful – wide and open, with pale wooden floors. There's a glass ceiling and, on the left, a glass wall, flooding the room with light.

Whitewashed walls on the right are pulled into sharp relief by floor-to-ceiling panels in the same chalky pink as the exterior. The panels roughly divide the space into two zones: a seating area with a view of the rock through the glass wall and ceiling, and the reception on the opposite side. A row of tall cacti stud the back wall.

Elin's eyes lock on the huge textile artwork hung on the wall behind the reception desk. It's abstract, swirls of line and colour interspersed with smaller, almost primitive markings.

It's only when she gets closer that she realizes what the markings are.

Her pulse picks up. Not abstract shapes at all, but Reapers.

Small versions of the rock, dotted throughout the textile.

Elin looks on, discomforted, as she sees more and more – some woven into the fabric in the same colour as the background, camouflaged.

Farrah follows her gaze. 'Beautiful, isn't it? A contemporary British textile artist who went to the school here back in the day. It's something else, seeing it here.' She glances over at the glass wall. 'Under the rock itself.'

It's only then that Elin properly absorbs the mass of stone above, looming through the glass ceiling and the transparent wall. She baulks. The sheer scale of it from this angle is overwhelming; one more metre and it would be invading the building.

'Elin? You okay? Justin's ready if you are.'

'I'm fine.' She has to force a smile as they walk down the corridor leading off the lobby.

Justin guides them into the room at the end. 'I've got it ready.'

Elin briefly glances around. Multiple screens cover the back wall, all showing different images of the retreat. The room is thrumming with a familiar office odour: coffee mixed with a plasticky tech smell.

Expertly minimizing one screen, Justin brings up another. 'The camera is positioned in front of the lodge looking out to the pavilion. Sweeps from left to right.' His fingers move rapidly over the keyboard. 'This is the live scene.'

Elin immediately makes out the pavilion where Leon is kneeling, examining something.

Justin's fingers hover over the keyboard. 'What time shall I go back to?'

'Let's try from about eleven p.m. last night.'

He starts scrolling. The picture is fairly clear because of the exterior lighting but still holds the shadowy grain of night-time. 'Stop me if you see anything.' Images rapid-fire across the screen. All similar; the same grey static.

11:00, 12:00, 12:30, 1:00 . . .

'Wait – I saw someone. There . . .' Elin points.

Justin rewinds, slows the footage to real time. At the bottom left of the screen a woman weaves unsteadily past the camera, something dangling from her hand. Despite the dim light, Elin's certain that it's the dead woman, the same length hair, clothing.

The woman stops at the centre of the yoga pavilion and walks towards the barrier. She lays her wrap over the balustrade. It slips, falling to the other side.

A few seconds later the camera glides away to the right so she's no longer visible. Elin leans forwards, frustrated, as the camera image jitters slightly then slowly glides back again. When the woman reappears, she's leaning over the balustrade, as if bending to retrieve the wrap.

All at once, her foot jerkily slides backwards, so she's further bent over the railing. It's enough for her to begin to tip, and the forwards movement once started is unstoppable. The weight of her body, its momentum, propels her over the barrier head-first, her legs upright, face and body pressed against the outside of the glass panel.

Her hands are still clamped to the rail. There's a brief moment when Elin thinks the woman might be able to right herself, but it doesn't happen. In an instant, her right hand loses its grip, and her left becomes an awkward pivot point, twisting in its socket as her body swings around below it, pulling her legs below her in a complete reversal of position.

Elin watches, her breath high in her chest; it's clear that the woman won't be able to hold on for long.

Staring at the screen, time seems to slow. This woman is a stranger to her, but it's as if Elin knows her intimately in this moment. She's inside her head, imagining her panic, the mounting sense of desperation as her hand becomes slick with sweat and she can feel herself slipping.

The weight is too much. She falls.

No one says anything: they're still staring at the blank space where the woman had been. A void has opened up and no words will be able to fill it.

18

The morning air is still, full of the musky scent of flowers. The group slowly weave their way up the winding stone path towards the main lodge, crossing fine streaks of light scattered among the long branches of the pines.

The drunken bonhomie of last night has dissolved – the awkwardness emphasized by low blood sugar and the lack of social lubricant that is Jo. It's only when she isn't there that Hana realizes how much Jo fills in the gaps between them all.

Seth's holding forth as they round the corner, bouncing from one subject to another: *digital epicentres. A trip to San Francisco. Bioweapons*. He's speaking quickly, as if it will somehow kick the group chemistry to life, but it doesn't. They fall into silence again, distilled into individual sounds: birdsong. Voices escaping from one of the villas. The slap of Maya's sandals against the ground.

Maya loops her arm through Hana's, her skin surprisingly cold. 'Seth doesn't like it without Jo, does he?' she whispers. 'You never really see that side of him.'

Hana nods. It intrigues her. She'd always assumed Seth was the one who bolstered Jo, but perhaps it was the other way around. Without her, he seems adrift.

Maya turns to look at Seth. 'Still no word from Jo?'

'Let me ...' Seth pats his shorts – left pocket, then right. 'Shit, I've left my phone in the villa.'

Everyone stops in their tracks.

'We'll wait.' Caleb shrugs as Seth starts walking back. 'No hurry.'

Maya says, 'I need to send a few emails anyway.' She starts tapping out a message on her phone, but as Hana watches, she senses a frustration in her movements – a slight shake of her head as she types.

'What's up?' Hana stops beside her.

She shrugs. 'Just the usual. Job stuff. If I don't find something soon, I'm going to have to move out into an even smaller flat.'

'What happened to the job that Jo recommended you for?'

Maya's face tightens. 'Only temporary. Got the boot a few months ago. Haven't found anything since.'

Hana couldn't understand Maya's roadblock with work. So strong in every other part of her life – scaling rock faces, punchy in her politics – she lacked drive with her career. Her Fine Arts degree had never really amounted to anything, and although she'd taken jobs, her heart didn't seem to be in them: work experience in a gallery, library assistant, virtual PA.

Maya looks at her. 'Han, you go, get us a table. I'll wait here with Caleb so Seth doesn't think we've abandoned him.'

'Okay, I'll leave you to it,' she replies, getting the message. 'Meet you up there.'

Hana slowly follows the path upwards. Although it's hard work in the heat, her chest loosens; a weight removed. Horrible to say about her own family, but on her own she finds she can breathe more easily.

At the top, she sees a group of guests milling around the yoga pavilion. More people are joining, and she cranes her head to see what they're looking at.

Her eyes take in everything at once: the twisted snarl of blue-and-white tape strung up around the pavilion, the solemn member of LUMEN staff in front of it, but what strikes her the most is the flash of colour.

The only colour against the muted neutral of the pavilion floor.

There's a strange moment when her eyes focus in and then out on the crinkled plastic bag, the bright, bold fabric folded up inside it. She feels herself growing hotter, not only from the sun on her face, but from the realization dawning on her.

It's the wrap Jo wore last night, the one their mother brought them back from holiday in Liguria. Splashy, bold colours like paint splotches.

But why would it be here?

She notices a man beside it, dressed in one of those crinkly white suits.

It's then that it all comes together in her head. The man and the blue-and-white tape and the fabric all squished in the bag. She feels seasick, heady, as if the island had suddenly become a boat and the ground beneath her were moving.

Hana takes a breath, and then another, feels herself sway, and she actually puts her arms out to steady herself. She registers that the man's mouth is now opening, saying something, but she can't hear it. Only the gulls as they criss-cross overhead, and the roaring of the blood in her ears.

Hana jerks forwards, towards the pavilion.

Two steps in and she slips. Her shoes, her strappy sandals that she chose because they had a flash of something cool and young about them, have completely flat soles. The fine layer of sand on the path acts like oil. A strange, comic split, her left leg splayed.

Straightening, she starts moving again, pushing through the

crowd of people gathered outside. The member of staff guarding the pavilion puts out an arm to stop her, but Hana throws the full weight of her body forwards and his arm gives way. She bursts into the pavilion, half running, half walking towards the white-suited man by the balustrade on the far side. He turns, eyes widening in surprise.

He puts up his hand, mouth moving in slow motion. 'No,' he says, and it reverberates in her head, big and boomy and exaggerated, like she's hearing it underwater.

It's only when her eyes find the little Sharpied arrows on the glass balustrade that it all comes together.

Stepping towards the balustrade, she leans, waist pressed against the glass, looking down to the rocks below. Her eyes skim past a man and a white-suited woman to the body slumped on the ground.

A black dress, fair hair splayed across the rock.

Hana's breath catches in her throat.

In her head, she's kicking and screaming like a child, lung-bursting screams that make her throat raw.

When her breath finally comes it's as a gasp.

She's dead. Her sister is dead.

19

Elin breaks the silence: 'I'll need a copy of the footage.' Not just for the case file, she thinks, but to examine the moment of the fall more closely. Something about what she saw is niggling at her, but she can't quite pick it apart. Perhaps . . .

She doesn't get to finish her thought process. A loud click.

The door opens and a member of staff walks into the room, visibly stricken. 'Farrah, sorry to disturb,' he says falteringly, 'but there's a woman, outside, at the yoga pavilion. She's screaming.'

The dark-haired woman on the floor beside Leon has her arms wrapped around herself, knees brought up to her chin. Her hair, a messy bob, is falling over her face, hiding her features.

Elin feels a horrible sense of disquiet as she puts on her overshoes and ducks under the tape. This close, she can see that the woman's knees are grazed and bloody, specks of grit and sand dimpling the broken skin. She's hugging the evidence bag, fingers clutching so tightly she's puckering the plastic, the bright fabric beneath. She reminds Elin of a child, refusing to let go of her favourite blanket.

Leon, crouched beside her, is speaking quietly, probably trying to somehow persuade her to give it up, but the woman isn't responding. As she glances up, hair falling back from her face, her eyes are glazed with a vacancy that pulls at Elin.

The look Leon gives Elin is desperate. 'Sorry, I couldn't stop her. She ran right past one of the LUMEN staff standing outside on the path, ducked under the tape.'

'It's fine. I'll take it from here.' Elin squats down next to the woman. 'Hello,' she says softly. 'I'm Detective Sergeant Warner. Do you know what's in this bag or who it belongs to?'

The woman drags her gaze up. 'It's a wrap. My sister's.' Her voice is so quiet Elin has to strain to hear her. 'My mother brought it back for her, from Italy.' Her voice splinters. 'I've just looked down there. It's my sister.'

Elin nods, feels the prickle of sweat on her hairline. 'Look, let's get you up so we can talk about it, but before we do that, will you give me the bag? It's important that what's inside stays safe, so we can try to understand what happened.'

The woman nods wordlessly, passing it to her. After depositing it with Leon, Elin helps the woman to her feet, starts leading her across the pavilion. They're about to slip under the tape and on to the path below when a voice rings out.

'Hana? What's going on?'

Elin glances up. A statuesque, fair-haired woman is striding towards them, phone in hand. She's in exercise gear – a pair of electric-blue running shorts, a black vest. The navy BUFF pulling her hair away from her face is blotchy with sweat.

'Han?' the woman repeats. 'What's wrong?' She steps up, as if to enter the pavilion, then stops, noticing the tape.

'I'm afraid there's been an accident,' Elin replies. 'Someone's fallen from the pavilion. Hana thinks it's her sister.'

'It is her, I know it is.' Hana glances back towards the balustrade. 'Jo, it's Bea.'

'Bea?' Jo's trainer is tapping the floor in a nervous rhythm. 'That's impossible.'

Hana's voice wobbles as it raises a notch. 'It's Bea.'

Jo's hand skims Hana's arm. 'But Bea's in America. You know that.' Turning to Elin, she lowers her voice. 'I'm sorry, my sister's had a rough time recently. She's probably in shock, confused after seeing whoever—'

'I *know* it's her.' Hana's voice is tremulous as she points at the evidence bag beside Leon. 'That's her wrap, the same as yours – the one Mum bought you both. I saw her on the rocks. It's Bea. She's dead.' The wavering voice gives way to a soft crying.

Elin waits for Jo's reaction, but it's as though Hana's last few words haven't hit home. 'Look, let's ask Caleb.' She addresses Elin. 'That's Bea's boyfriend. He's probably spoken to Bea this morning. Hey, Caleb?' she shouts.

Elin analyses the group walking around the outside of the pavilion. A mixed bunch; a small, slight, brunette bookended by two men. The taller one is dark with a thick beard, the other shorter, with a cap. All look uneasy as they absorb the tape, Leon, and his equipment.

'What's going on?' The woman stops beside them, petite with a wiry, lightly muscled body. *A climber*, Elin guesses, clocking the callused hands and baggy Patagonia shorts.

'Someone's fallen. A horrible accident.' Jo pauses, trying to deliver the words with a slow seriousness that somehow imparts the opposite – a condescension that says, *Humour us while I explain something ridiculous.* 'Hana thinks it's Bea.' She turns to Elin, gesturing at Caleb. 'This is Caleb, Bea's boyfriend. You've heard from Bea today, haven't you?'

Caleb opens his mouth to speak and then closes it again. 'Well, actually, no, I haven't,' he says slowly. 'But she messaged me last night, when we got back from the beach.' Tugging his phone from his pocket, he taps the screen. 'Said she'd finished dinner, was going back to the hotel.' His voice softens. 'So she's

83

fine, Han. Whoever fell, it's not Bea.' After a beat, he says, 'Look, I'll call her. That'll clear it up.' Tapping at the screen, he puts it to his ear, hears a faint dial tone. The tension is palpable as the ringing continues, but a few seconds later, there's a loud buzz. 'It's gone to voice mail.'

'Caleb, the time difference, mate,' the taller man says awkwardly. 'She won't be up.'

'Well, if she isn't, Della, her assistant, will be. She's in the UK.' Caleb steps away, agitated, tapping the phone again. As he paces backwards and forwards, Elin hears him quietly talking. His speech is very slow, deliberate. She's not sure if he's trying to delay the moment or it's just his natural pattern of speech.

When he walks back a few moments later, phone still in hand, Elin notices his eyes slide towards the balustrade. 'She—' He stops, collecting himself. 'Bea never went to the US. She cancelled her trip yesterday.'

His words act like something seismic.

The group's expression lurches from disbelief to horror.

Jo shakes her head. 'I'm going to check for myself.' She makes a dive for the pavilion, ducking under the tape.

'No,' Elin says, but she's too quick. Three, four strides, and Jo's at the glass balustrade.

When she walks back to them a few moments later, her face is drained of blood. 'You were right, Han. It's . . .' She stops, tears welling in her eyes. 'It's Bea.'

20

Elin's chosen to speak to the Leger group at a corner table on the restaurant terrace, overlooking an almost deserted pool. Peering through the still of the water to the glass bottom, the jagged rocks below, her stomach flips: *she'd never trust that glass*.

Waiting for everyone to settle, she pulls her notebook from her bag. A member of staff places a jug of water and some glasses beside her.

Jo leaps on it. 'Han, have this.' She pushes one of the empty tumblers across the table, but Hana doesn't respond – she's mechanically shredding a tissue in her hand, tiny white pieces fluttering to the table.

Elin clears her throat. 'Thank you for taking the time to speak with me. I know it's hard, at a moment like this, but it's important for me to understand a little more about Bea, specifically why you didn't think she'd be here.'

'Of course.' Caleb meets her gaze, his eyes now puffy from crying. 'Bea was meant to be working this week, in the US. She's a corporate lawyer in London, but her firm has an office in New York.'

Elin nods, slightly thrown by his precise diction, somehow at odds with the emotion in his face. 'Was she originally planning to come?'

'Yes.' Jo swivels her phone on the table. 'This holiday was meant to be a family thing, with partners. We hadn't seen each other in a while.'

'And whose idea was the trip?'

'Mine,' Jo says. 'Well, I arranged it after someone else initially suggested it, and I thought it sounded good. I'm an influencer, so I got in touch with LUMEN's marketing team and they asked if I'd like to come to the retreat. I invited the others.'

'When did Bea cancel?'

Jo considers. 'A few weeks ago, said she had a business trip she couldn't get out of, but that Caleb would still come, so we could spend some time getting to know him better.'

Elin nods. 'And there was no indication Bea had changed her mind? No messages you might have missed?'

'No. She even told me the flight landed in the US on time,' Caleb says. 'We've been in touch via message ever since she's been out there.' He corrects himself. 'Since I *thought* she was out there. Like I said, she even messaged me last night. We'd been to the beach, sent her a group photo. She didn't pick up, but she sent a few lines back.' Tapping at his phone, he thrusts it towards her. 'Look. This was . . .' He checks the screen. 'Eleven oh three . . . we'd just got back to the villa.' He tips the phone towards her again.

Elin glances down at it, nods. 'No one left the villa again?'

'No.' The others shake their heads.

She turns to Caleb. 'And when did you last speak to Bea?'

A pause. 'Not since she left on Thursday,' he says slowly. 'That's usual when she's away on business. We don't feel the need to keep checking in, especially on a short trip.'

Elin nods, her sense of disquiet growing ever stronger. Bea's fall was an accident, the CCTV makes that clear, but the fact that she wasn't *meant* to be on the island in the first place is bothering her.

Why come here unannounced? For what purpose?

There's only one thing she can think of, but that feels spurious – surely she'd have had to tell the retreat, at the very least? She decides to voice it anyway, gauge their reaction. 'Is it possible that it might have been some kind of surprise?'

'No,' Hana says immediately, the first thing she's said since they've sat down. 'That's not Bea's style. She's a planner.'

'She's right.' Caleb nods. 'And why go to all that trouble?'

A heavy silence falls, and as she looks at them, Elin notices a flush creeping up Jo's neck. 'Actually, I do think it's possible she might have done it as a surprise,' Jo says quietly. 'A gesture, maybe.'

'Gesture? I don't get it . . .' Caleb swivels to face her.

There's another pregnant pause that Elin knows better than to try to fill.

'When she first told me that she wasn't coming . . .' Jo's voice is tight, strained. 'We had a rough conversation. I'd spent ages planning this. Arranging everything – it isn't easy – and then she backs out, just like that. I was upset, it felt like she didn't give a shit about the effort I'd gone to—'

Seth puts a hand on her arm. 'Jo, not now—'

'No, it's how I felt. When we spoke, I ended up giving her a few home truths.'

'Like what?' Hana's voice sounds high, untethered.

'Just that she needed to get her priorities straight. Put the family first.' She hesitates. 'Don't look at me like that, Han. It's true. She doesn't prioritize us, Mum and Dad especially. How many family things has she cancelled on? Dad's birthday, last year . . .'

Sensing emotions running high, Elin interrupts. 'So you think that her coming, it could have been to make amends?'

Jo gives a tight nod.

Elin's about to ask another question, but she stops: Farrah's walking towards them.

When she reaches her, Farrah leans down, murmurs in her ear. 'Hate to interrupt,' she says. 'But I think we might have an answer as to how Bea Leger got to the island.'

21

Giving her apologies, Elin follows Farrah to a table about a metre away, where a member of staff is waiting.

'This is Tom, one of the water sports instructors.' Farrah smiles at him encouragingly and he nods an awkward hello, ruffling a hand through his dark hair.

'Sorry, I'd have come forward earlier, but I'm not on early shift today. Sleeping in.' It's obvious that he's dressed hurriedly. His blue shirt is buttoned in the wrong order, the khaki shorts beltless, hanging low on his waist.

'No problem. Can you take me through what you know?'

Flipping his sunglasses to the top of his head, Tom nods. Elin mentally revises his age upwards: mid-thirties maybe, looking at the fine lines around his eyes. 'Bea and I met at uni. Same halls. She told me a few months ago that she was coming. It was a nice coincidence. I was looking forward to catching up.'

'And you were aware she'd cancelled?'

'Yes. She contacted me a few weeks ago, explained that she'd had to drop the trip because of work, but said the rest of her family were still coming. I didn't think any more of it until she messaged me early yesterday, saying she'd changed her mind. She asked if I could help, told me she wanted to turn up unannounced, surprise her family.'

Messaged him yesterday. Did it imply a last-minute decision, or did she simply not tell Tom until just before she was leaving for the island? 'What exactly did she ask you to do?'

'Pick her up, sneak her in.' He glances across at Farrah, sheepish. 'Crappy move, I know, but she was going to check in first thing, and as she'd booked in originally, I knew there was space . . .'

'What time did you collect her? Morning? Later?'

He wrinkles up his brow. 'Evening, around eightish. I moored at one of the smaller coves, so no one would see us arrive, then we went to a meeting room in the main lodge.'

'Did she say why she didn't want to go straight to see her family?'

'Said she'd had a long journey and wanted a drink to unwind, catch up.'

'How many did she have?'

'Not a lot. Maybe two or three? I don't think she realized how late it had got.' Tom glances out to sea, his gaze automatically ticking over a group of paddleboarders with a well-practised eye. 'But she wasn't drunk, if that's what you mean.'

'And nothing seemed odd about her behaviour?'

A shrug. 'Pretty hard for me to judge. We don't know each other well, not any more. Uni was a long time ago. We only kept in touch occasionally, through social media.'

Elin nods. 'Roughly what time did you finish having drinks?'

'About half eleven. She said she was going to head to the villa, surprise them. I pointed her in the right direction and left her to it.'

Half eleven. They had her on the CCTV at the barrier at one a.m. What did she do during the time between leaving Tom and when she fell? From what the family said, she never made it to the villa.

'Did she take her luggage with her?'

'I assumed she had.' He frowns. 'You haven't found it?'

'No.'

'It might still be in the meeting room.' He inclines his head towards the main lodge. 'I can show you where it is.'

'Please.' Elin starts pushing back her chair.

'Wait,' Tom says. 'Before we go, there *is* something: when you asked if anything seemed odd . . . it's only just come to me. Just before she left, she got a message on her phone. She said she needed to call someone. I left her to it, but it sounded like she was pretty upset.'

Elin mulls over what he's said with a nagging sense of disquiet.

She can't shake the feeling that she's missing something about what's happened here, a vital part of the narrative.

22

Hana watches Jo walk over to Seth and Caleb, who are standing by the breakfast buffet, plates piled high with sticky pastries, sourcing food no one wanted but Seth insisted they get. *Keep their energy up.* It's not that at all; it's a distraction. A way to avoid processing what's happened.

Hana can't blame him. She can't process it either: *Bea's dead. Bea was here, on the island, and now she's dead.* Nothing about it seems real.

'I keep going over it, Han.' Maya swivels the silver ring on her finger. 'What it must have felt like, to go over that drop. When I'm climbing, sometimes I get this sensation, as if I'm about to fall. All part of the rush, but going over this, she must have been so bloody *scared.*' Her voice cracks.

Hana takes her hand in hers. 'I know, doesn't bear thinking about.' Yet she is: horribly graphic images – the moment Bea fell, realized she was tumbling into nothingness. A sob rises up in her chest.

'It's not just the fall.' Maya's eyes are tearing up too. 'I don't get it, the fact that she was here, and we didn't know. It's not like her to pull something like this.'

It's true. Bea doesn't do spontaneous, never has. Ever since she was a kid, she's been ordered, almost to the point of obsession: pens lined up, schoolbag packed and by the door the night before.

Pulling a fresh tissue from her bag, Hana takes a breath. 'But you heard what Jo said, about calling her out. Perhaps she did feel guilty, wanted to surprise us.'

'Maybe.' Maya looks unconvinced. 'I . . .' She stops mid-sentence, as if she's struggling to formulate what she wants to say.

'What is it?'

'It's just,' she says finally, wiping her eyes, 'I think someone lied, about what happened last night.'

'Lied about what?' Hana says weakly.

'About not leaving the villa.' The words come out quickly now, as if Maya's glad to be rid of them. 'Someone did leave. I heard them.'

'But everyone said—' Hana replays the moment in her mind, the negative responses to the detective's question.

'I know. But someone left, I'm sure of it.'

'When was this?'

'About an hour or so after we got back . . . a quarter past twelve. I was still on my phone when I heard the door go. I looked through the window, saw someone going along the path beside the villa. I couldn't make out their face, it was too dark.' Maya's voice pitches higher. 'But it was definitely our door that went. Someone left the villa, Han, I'm sure of it.'

23

Bea's silver suitcase is sleek and expensive-looking, compact enough to be carried on board, pushed into an overhead locker.

Neatly placed under the long wooden table in the meeting room, it's the only clutter in the space. The meeting room, despite the official connotations, has the same laid-back vibe as the rest of the lodge. It's hard to place Bea here after what Elin's seen of her; imagine her wheeling this case in, anticipating surprising her family, full of life.

Slipping on a pair of latex gloves, Elin hauls the case on to the table. As she sifts through the contents, she finds typical holiday attire. Several cover-ups – silky, flimsy bits of material low in the neckline, slit up the sides. Elin recognizes the chevron pattern immediately from magazines – Missoni. Expensive. The rest of the clothing clearly is too – a bohemian mix of fine knit tops, textured cotton skirts and shorts.

It gives her another insight into who Bea was as a person. Someone not only successful, but ordered. In control.

Yet, something's bothering her. Elin rummages through the case again. This time, it strikes her: no swimwear. Why come to a retreat like this and not bring something to swim in? It might be an oversight, but it also might imply that Bea had packed in a hurry, was in some way distracted.

She thinks about the fact that Bea let Tom know she was coming only yesterday, and about the phone call he'd overheard. She picks it over, once again gripped by the sense that another narrative is running alongside what she already knows.

No way to tell at this point if it's important to the case, but it's niggling at her.

Piece by piece, she puts the clothing back in place.

She's nearly done when there's a ping from her phone: a message from Rachel.

All done here. Can you come down when you're ready?

Elin taps out a reply. She's about to zip the suitcase back up when she notices a Filofax in the woven netting in the top half of the case. It's clear from the battered cover that it's well used. Bea, like her, still prefers paper over digital when it comes to making notes.

Flicking through, her eyes immediately alight on the calendar section. It's meticulously filled out in neat, precise handwriting up until the last few days, which are blank. Moving on, she finds notes from various meetings. It's only when she hits the end page that she finds something that piques her interest: a couple of website addresses.

It's not the sites themselves that draw her attention, but *how* they've been written. The messy script is nothing like the ordered handwriting style in the rest of the organizer, and the addresses are scrawled diagonally across the page, underlined several times.

Definitely Bea's handwriting, she thinks, comparing the shapes of the letters.

www.fcf1.com, www.localhistory.org

Taking a photograph with her phone, Elin places the organizer back into the case.

The addresses, like the packing oversight, might be nothing, but still, she can feel something stirring to life – that sense of momentum that comes with questions starting to pile up, loose threads pulling free.

24

'Right.' Rachel shoves her camera into her bag. 'I think I've gone as far as I can on the forensic front.' Her voice is flat with the kind of weariness that comes with extreme concentration.

Elin's eyes once again travel over Bea's body. Maybe she's imagining it, but she can smell the blood in the air, starting to turn – a musky, metallic tang. Her stomach flips.

'Any sign of a phone?' she says to Steed, thinking of the call Bea made when Tom left her in the meeting room.

Rachel pulls down her hood to reveal wet hair, a ring of indentation marking her forehead where the hood has gripped her flesh. 'Doesn't look like she had anything on her when she went over, unless it went into the sea. Unlikely, given where the body was found. Nothing with Leon?'

'No. I did find her suitcase, but no phone inside.'

'She'd have had it on her, wouldn't she?' Steed steps forwards. He, too, is now red – the telltale mark of sunburn forming on his cheeks. He stretches, his shirt patchy with sweat, individual continents starting to overlap across his muscles like tectonic plates.

'I'd have thought so. No sign of anything else? Leon found a mark in the grass on top of the cliff. We thought she may have dropped something, knocked it over with her.'

'Not that I can see, sorry.' Rachel's climbing out of her suit. 'Is Leon finished?'

'Yes. He's packing up.'

'You're happy with everything?' Steed murmurs.

'More or less. CCTV's pretty conclusive, an accident rather than anything more sinister, but a few things are bothering me about why she was here. I need a bit more time to think it through.'

'Makes sense. What are you going to do about the scene?'

'Release it, get her to the mortuary. I'm going to run everything past the DCI now. If she agrees, I'll call for the police boat.' It's a big decision to release the scene, but they have the evidence they need, regardless of the backstory to Bea being here. Steed nods.

Elin picks her way back over the rocks, but this time as she navigates the uneven surface, she's slower – it feels like she's wading through mud. Her stomach growls. She glances at her watch: past lunchtime. Food and drink are calling.

Jumping off the rocks and on to the beach, she walks towards the shade beneath a rocky overhang of cliff.

About to pull her phone from her pocket, she pauses. A woman is striding towards her, her gait erratic, struggling with the soft sand. *Hana.*

She stops in front of Elin, nervously plucking at her dress. 'I wanted to speak to you alone.' Her dark bob has separated into thick clumps clinging to her cheeks, the oval of her face pronounced. 'I know what happened to Bea was an accident, that probably this isn't relevant, but I'd never forgive myself if I didn't say anything. It's important, isn't it, in a situation like this, to say everything, even if it sounds stupid?'

'Of course. Shall we sit down first?' Elin points to the large boulders squatting at the edge of the beach. 'Get some shade.'

But Elin hasn't even pulled out her notebook when Hana starts speaking. 'My cousin, Maya, thinks that someone did leave the villa last night. When you asked us about it, some-one . . .' She stops, struggling to get out the words.

'Someone lied,' Elin finishes for her.

Hana nods. There's a pause before she looks up at her, her expression tumultuous. 'You know, I thought this trip was a bad idea from the off. Everything I've heard about the island, those murders, the rumours about that school . . .'

Elin's pulse picks up. 'What do you mean?'

'Maya's father's friend worked at the old school for a while. Didn't last long. He told her this place was bad news.' Her expression darkens as she looks around her. 'Now we're here, I know exactly what he meant.'

25

'CTV is clear?' The ugly shriek of a gull overhead almost drowns out Anna's words.

'Yes. She leant over to pick up her wrap. Overbalanced.' Elin stares out at the white gold of the sand, the glimmering band of water beyond. 'Doesn't appear anyone else was involved. Leon thinks forensics on the glass corroborates, but we'll only be able to confirm once we establish the prints are hers.'

'Alcohol?'

'Possible, but we'll need to wait for the toxicology results once the PM's been done. Anything else you can think of before I release the scene?'

'No, sounds like you've got it covered.' A pause. 'Elin, is something up?'

She always forgets how well Anna knows her. 'Something's jarring, not the fall itself, but why she was out here. If it's all right, I might stay on over the weekend.'

'You want to keep Steed?'

'Moral support?'

'If you want to put it like that. I know I've thrown you in at the deep end . . .' Elin smiles. Yet again, Anna's pre-empted her. She hadn't thought about it until she mentioned it, but it makes sense. Not being on her own. 'And it's all gone okay so far?' Anna says softly.

Elin knows that this is her way of asking if she's coping, if Anna made the right call in asking her to go. She has a brief urge to blurt it all out: the doubts, her uneasiness about the island, but she doesn't miss a beat. 'Really, it's been fine.'

The dull drone of an engine prompts her to look up. She can make out the rough outline of the police boat in the distance, speeding towards the island.

'Anna, I'd better go. The boat's here.' The RIB is slowing as it approaches the rocks, the individual figures on board pulling clear from the blur.

Game face on, Elin starts walking back the way she came.

Bea Leger's brief stay on the island is coming to an end.

The zip of the body bag makes an excruciating sound in the still air, a creaking wrench as teeth meet teeth. Halfway up, the zip jams. Rachel's hand is shaking as she yanks, tries again, rocking the pull forwards and back. A fresh band of sweat breaks out on her forehead.

Steed shifts uncomfortably. She can tell he's itching to step in, get it done.

Elin turns away, her mouth dry. She hates this bit: the impersonal closing of the body bag, the efficient transfer of the body to the mortuary.

They watch, silent, as the two officers carry Bea off the rocks and on to the RIB. The ordeal over, Rachel follows the police driver on to the boat. 'Right,' she calls. 'We're out of here. I'll accompany the body to the mortuary for continuity of ID. Call me if you need anything.'

Elin's sure she can hear relief in Rachel's voice. She's proven right: as the boat speeds away a few minutes later, Rachel doesn't even give them a backwards glance.

'You don't have to hide it, you know,' Steed says as they pick their way back to the beach. 'Not around me, anyway.'

'Hide what?' Elin glances out to sea at a group of paddle-boarders who are fanned out in a triangle formation. The person on the lone board in front moves effortlessly into a downward dog. Amazing how Bea's death has barely made a dent on the world. *It isn't their person*; the juggernaut of life rolls on.

'How you feel. People bang on about getting used to it, but I think they just get better at covering it up.'

Elin's momentarily thrown by his openness – they've never spoken like this before. Chitchat, surface stuff, but nothing beyond that. 'You think most people hide it?'

'Course they do, we all have a game face, a defence mechanism to pull us through the shitty bits.' He gestures down at himself. 'This is mine. I was a skinny kid, used to run a lot with my mum. Psychologist would have a field day, say it's armour, defence mechanism . . .'

Elin struggles to picture a skinny him beneath the bulk. 'Against what?'

'Verbal bullying, physical. All the rugby boys didn't exactly approve of the running and I was pretty nerdy. Into history, archaeology. People took the piss.'

Elin gives him a sideways glance. 'Brave of you to say. Not many people admit stuff like that, especially in this job.' They scramble down the rocks on to the sand. 'I've never felt I could share, not properly.'

'This to do with the career break?' Steed asks.

'Partly. Keep thinking I'll choke on the job. Something happened before, and I froze. Part of me's convinced I'll do it again.'

He grins. 'Ah, so that's why I'm out here: backup.'

'How'd you guess?' Smiling, Elin feels something shift between them, a tentative bond becoming firmer.

They reach the bottom of the steps. 'Right, I need to call Will. You go up.' She wants Will to hear from her what's happened before he finds out another way. 'Then I need Farrah to tell me where my villa is.'

'Villa?' Steed pulls a face. 'Not slumming it in staff accommodation with me, then?'

'Pulling rank.' Elin laughs as they begin walking up the steps. 'It was actually all they had left. A cancellation.' She hesitates. 'But one thing I didn't think of – clothes. I've always got stuff in my bag, but . . .'

Steed smiles. 'Don't worry. I brought some. The Scout in me. Always be prepared.' Climbing the last few steps, he asks: 'Anything you want me to do now? I was going to get something to eat.'

'Maybe speak to some of the staff. Be discreet, but ask if they saw or heard anything out of the ordinary.'

Nodding, Steed lowers his voice. 'Don't look, but you've got a fan. On the right.'

She gives it a few seconds and then glances up. Michael Zimmerman is standing near the restaurant, broom in hand, openly staring at Elin. Realizing that they've noticed him, he rapidly starts sweeping again.

Elin scrutinizes his bent frame, and once again she feels a sense of familiarity. It's confusing: she's now certain that it isn't only that he reminds her of someone; she recognizes him, has seen him somewhere before. 'That's the guy who found the body.'

'Ah, I never asked. Helpful?'

'Not sure. He was . . . rattled. Kept banging on about the

island. The curse. Reckons he saw someone at night, walking around the rock.'

'Guests?'

'Assume so.' Elin clears her throat, eyes still fixed on Zimmerman. 'Right, I'd better call Will. Can't put it off any more.'

'Good luck.'

'Thanks.' Elin strides towards the side of the main lodge, hoping for some privacy.

Although she's sure that Michael Zimmerman can't see her from this angle, she's certain she can feel his eyes on her, watching her every move.

26

'You're at the retreat?' On the final word the FaceTime screen judders and pixelates, Will's next sentence unintelligible, staccato.

Elin moves her phone around to get a better signal, but the only thing pulling clear is her own sweaty reflection lurking at the top right of the screen. It's a few seconds before Will resolves, and with it, his office, the framed architectural drawings on the wall behind.

'Yes. A woman died. Fell from the yoga pavilion on to the rocks.'

Will takes a sharp intake of breath. 'An accident, presumably.' The tension in his voice clips his words. Concern, obviously, but something he'd probably never admit to considering. *The award.*

Elin feels a tug on her heart. 'Yes. I've seen the CCTV. I know you don't want to ask, but as far as I'm aware, the guests took it in stride after Farrah shared the news. Life goes on. They're more focused on their holiday.'

His features soften, relief writ large across his face. 'It feels shitty even caring when something like this has happened—'

She nods. 'I know. Her family are here, in total shock.'

'I bet.' He rubs a hand over his forehead. 'What about Farrah? Have you talked?'

'It's actually her I've been dealing with. The general manager is off for a couple of days. Farrah's holding the fort.'

'How is she?'

'All right, given the circumstances.' She tips the screen again, away from the sun, and as she does, her eyes hook on a flash of colour in the distance. A figure in a blue T-shirt and cap moving quickly past the rock.

'Good.' Will nudges his glasses up his nose with his finger. 'So when are you back?'

'That's the thing, I'm going to stay out here with Steed, tonight at least. A few loose ends I want to tie up.'

His expression is unreadable. 'You're comfortable doing that? After we talked about you taking it slow. Was this Anna's request?'

'No, but she wouldn't have sent me in the first place if she didn't think I was ready.' Elin looks past the screen to where she'd seen the figure. The person is still moving, heading in the direction of the woodland beyond. As if they've sensed Elin watching, they briefly glance in her direction. The figure turns back before she can make out any facial features, but she feels a catch at the very edge of her mind.

'I get it, but I'm worried . . .' He looks away from the screen. A heavy sigh. 'Something's come up, on Twitter. You know I follow Torhun Police?'

She nods.

'Well . . .' His gaze pulls back to meet hers. 'Someone's put out a tweet with a photo, and they've tagged Torhun Police. I'm pretty sure the photo is of you.'

'What kind of photo?' Her voice wavers.

He can't quite meet her gaze. 'It's probably best you take a look yourself. I'll ping it over. I reckon they've scraped it offline.'

She opens the message, pulse quickening.

It's her at a training exercise in Exeter a few years ago. She was standing next to a senior officer, although here he's been cut out of the shot. That in itself already makes the image disconcerting, but it's nothing compared to what has been done to her face.

Someone's gone to the trouble of digitally scratching away her eyes.

Two precisely etched-out hollows.

Her flesh crawls. The effect . . . it's horrifying. It makes her look soulless . . . a blank.

Her hands are clammy around the phone, the blood pounding in her ears.

Jabbing at the screen, she closes the image.

'So . . .' Will tails off. 'Pretty odd, isn't it?'

'Weird, but I've had something like it before, do you remember?' She desperately tries to project a nonchalance that she doesn't feel. 'During the Hayler case?' She'd had several messages then, threatening in tone, from different accounts.

In the throes of the investigation, she hadn't given it more than a passing thought – she'd guessed it might be Hayler's acquaintances or family, maybe even someone random. An oddball using the fact her name was in the press.

'But none of those had a photograph in the tweet, did they?' Will persists.

'Well, no . . .' She hesitates, aware this could escalate. 'I'll tell Anna, and look—' The words are out before she can stop them. This is her default: to try to stop an emotionally difficult conversation in its tracks. 'If you're worried, why don't you come out for the weekend? Farrah has a spare villa. A cancellation.'

The tension in his face dissolves. Will breaks into the smile she loves most – an instant, face-cracking smile, as if the sun has suddenly pulled out from behind a cloud.

'I'd love to.' This is his kind of thing, a random weekend away. 'Do you want me to bring anything?'

'Just some summer stuff. Not much, it's only a few days max.'

He nods. 'Right, it's nearly three now. I can get a water taxi over at, say, sixish?'

'Sounds good.' Stepping out from beneath the overhang, Elin looks to the rock. She can only see the back of the figure as it's swallowed up in the dark mass of woodland.

As she walks away, two images take turns in her head: the figure walking past the rock and the strange, scored-out hollows in place of her eyes.

27

The glass of water slip-slides across the wooden counter like an ice-hockey puck, caught on its own condensation. Grabbing it, the barman steadies the glass before placing it in her hand.

'Thanks.' Hana forces a smile, but it wobbles, her lip trembling as she catches a glimpse of herself in the mirror above the bar.

The harsh daytime light is brutal. Her hair is a mess, her skin sallow.

Heat floods her cheeks as she imagines how she must have looked to the detective, rattling on about someone leaving the villa, about the island . . .

Awkward under the scrutiny of her own reflection, she gulps her drink, returns the empty glass to the bar. She can't put it off any more; time to head back to the villa.

Walking towards the yoga pavilion, she sees a rustic rope has replaced the police tape, along with a discreet sign pronouncing: NO ACCESS AT THIS TIME.

Her eyes lurch past it to the part of the balustrade where she'd leant over, glimpsed Bea's body. The silvery fingerprint powder and Sharpied arrows on the glass are still visible. It's hard to look away.

Half turning, Hana realizes that she's not the only one.

Jo's standing about a metre away. She's changed, only the silhouette of long legs visible beneath a loose maxi dress.

Her neck is bent, as if she's looking down at something.

A surge of anger. *Not her phone, surely? She's not snuck away to record something. Some stupid selfie for her followers?*

'What are you doing?'

Jo turns, the movement uncharacteristically sluggish. Her eyes are laced with red. There's no phone in her hand after all.

Hana feels a pang of guilt. She's done it again; made an automatic judgement.

'Just looking, trying to make sense of it.' Jo gestures at the pavilion. 'But it's not really working . . .' She tails off. 'Where did you go?'

'To speak to the detective about what Maya told me.' Hana pauses. 'I was going to tell you anyway; she thought she saw someone leave the villa last night, after we got back.'

'Someone left? When?' Jo frowns.

'About a quarter past twelve, which, as we now know, was when Bea was already on the island. Seems a pretty strange coincidence.'

Shaking her head, Jo's features relax. *She's dismissed her. Thinks she's clutching at straws.* 'Han, sometimes there aren't answers for things, someone to blame. She fell, a horrible thing to happen, but that's it. No conspiracy theories. One of life's shitty curveballs.'

Hana takes a deep breath. No use pushing the point; she'll end up saying something she'll regret. She changes the subject. 'Where's everyone else?'

'Back at the villa. I think Seth was going for a swim maybe.'

'A *swim*?'

'Yes.' A hint of defensiveness in Jo's tone. 'Not exactly the nicest of vibes in there. Caleb's in a state and Maya . . . well, she's hardly Seth's biggest fan, as you've probably noticed.'

'Hard to miss.' Hana pauses. 'By the way, I never realized that they knew each other, before you, I mean. You never said.'

'Didn't seem a big thing.' Jo shrugs. 'They climbed together back in the day. She's never said as much, but I think Maya's convinced Seth tried it on with her at some point.'

'And did he?'

'He was honest when I asked him. He doesn't remember. Probably some night out. Obviously more significant for Maya than it was for him.'

Jo can be cruel, Hana thinks, watching her smile morph into a smirk. She thinks about Maya's sketch of Jo; the lines drawn so hard they'd made grooves in the paper.

'Even so, Seth's answer is to leave you to it while he goes off for a swim ...' A dig, but she can't help herself. She wants to puncture Jo's air of superiority.

'No,' Jo says quietly, the smile slipping from her face. 'He's not escaping. It's his way of dealing with things. Not everyone can emote, Han, like you. Seth does, but only when he lets down his guard.' She hesitates. 'Same as me. Probably why we make a good match.'

An awkward silence opens up between them. They haven't shared confidences like this in a long time, and it feels strange, the intimacy between them unfamiliar.

'Right, I'm heading back.'

Jo nods. 'See you later.'

As she heads down the steps, Hana glances back at her sister. Something about Jo's posture makes her stop in her tracks. She's in the same position, but her eyes are locked on something just in front of the pavilion.

The rope? The planter?

Something stirs in Hana's memory, but it's gone before she can make sense of it.

28

'This is it.' Farrah stops outside one of the smaller villas, just off the main path. On tiptoe, she peers through a window. 'Once the cleaning staff finish, you can get in.'

It's the first time Elin's seen one of the villas up close. A small-scale version of the main lodge, it's so deeply nestled in the lush greenery that the building itself seems a part of it; a blocky structure bursting from the earth, all angles and glass, painted the same blossom pink as the flowers spilling from the pots outside. She feels a pang of pride for Will.

'Stunning, isn't it?' Farrah says, watching her.

'Gorgeous. Will's so clever.' Elin smiles. 'Wish I could be more eloquent.' But she's getting better, she thinks. While she's still no expert, because of Will she sees a poetry and a personality in buildings that she never did before. 'I need Will here, to describe it. He makes this kind of thing sound better than I do. It's his enthusiasm, I think, his positivity.'

Farrah opens her mouth as if to say something, but then hesitates, as if she's internally debating if she wants to confide. Finally, after a beat, her expression softens. 'But that positivity is one of the Riley family curses. We like things bright. No sheen. There's a weird kind of pressure in that. We're allowed our allotted sad time, and then that's it, move on. Seeing that things don't always have to be that way, it's good for him.'

'But I think he struggles with it, sometimes.'

'That's because Will's never had to be the strong one. He's always leant on me.' Farrah laughs. 'But it works in your favour. He leans on me, so he doesn't have to lean on you.'

Elin smiles. 'He's lucky, having you.' She realizes that perhaps she's misjudged Farrah, misinterpreted her protectiveness as something personal. 'I haven't had any family to confide in, not since Mum died.' A pause. 'Will's probably told you about Isaac.'

Farrah nods. 'He has . . . How's it going?'

'I thought we'd turned a corner, but it hasn't really worked out. He was meant to come to the UK, but keeps putting me off.' Elin falters. 'Sorry, I'm not good at this opening up.'

'It's fine. I don't like being vulnerable either.' Farrah looks down at the ground. 'I always think it's like you're giving up part of yourself. Especially when there's a difference between what people see and what you're feeling inside.'

Elin's eyes smart. Apart from Will, no one's really *seen* her like that or cared, not since her mother died. A flush creeps up Farrah's cheeks and Elin realizes that Farrah has revealed something about herself too. 'And is everything okay with you? Will said you'd been a bit stressed recently.'

Farrah hesitates. 'I don't want to put anything else on your plate, not now . . .'

'Is it work?'

'No, my ex. Not exactly an amicable break-up, and he's still hassling me. Actually came out here a few weeks ago with a friend. Pretended he wanted nothing to do with me, but I could tell he was watching. Since then, I've had a few odd messages.' She gestures to her phone. 'Not his number, but I'm sure it's him.'

Tipping the screen, Farrah shows Elin: *I'm watching. Waiting.* Farrah swipes the screen. Another: *I won't give up.*

'Nasty stuff. If it carries on, we can look into it for you. Slap him with a warning.'

Relief floods Farrah's face. 'I wish I'd said something before, but I was hoping it would go away.' She takes a breath. 'And there's something else, I—' She stops as Elin's phone beeps. A brief shake of her head. 'Don't worry, you need to get on. I'll tell you later.'

'But—'

'It's fine, really. It'll wait.' Farrah presses the key fob into Elin's hand. 'Let me know when Will's arrived.'

Once she's gone, Elin looks at her phone.

A message from Steed. *Know you didn't ask, but did some digging on Zimmerman. Started working here a few months ago. Squeaky clean.*

Thanks, she taps back. *You ok to take a look at the family too?*

Already on it.

Good work.

Elin smiles. There's an eagerness to please in Steed that she recognizes in herself. An insecurity – it's as if your own word isn't enough, you have to hear it from someone else's mouth.

Still waiting for the cleaners to finish, she decides to do some digging of her own. Finding the photo of the web addresses in Bea's planner, she types the first into her phone: www.fcf1.com. The site quickly loads: Financial Crime Fighters. Detailed exposés of financial scams and crimes. The article at the top references a scheme that had robbed investors of their savings.

Elin closes the tab, disappointed. Most likely something Bea's law firm was involved in. The next address brings up a local history site about Cary Island. She skims over the text: the grim history of the island, the curse, the fire at the school, the Creacher murders. The wording has a macabre tone, the author obviously relishing the grim detail.

'We've finished now, if you want to go in,' one of the cleaning staff says, smiling as she opens the door.

Elin thanks her, but makes no move to stand up, focusing on one paragraph of the text.

> Rumour has it there were mass cremations on the island, plague victims burnt to stop the spread of the disease. It's said that even to this day, ash from these cremations makes up more than 40 per cent of the island's soil.

As the cleaner bumps her trolley out the door of the villa, Elin closes the tab. Maybe she's right to think that the darkness in this place doesn't solely come from the rock: perhaps it's in the very soil they're walking on.

29

'This is delicious.' Will extends an arm around Farrah's shoulders, squeezes.

The table Farrah reserved is at the edge of the terrace, overlooking the sea. Food has been laid out feast-style – platters of wafer-thin beetroot drizzled with herb sauce, strips of sticky beef, sprouting broccoli. Another plate is piled high with battered vegetables, pickled chillies, flatbreads dimpled with char.

'Perks.' Farrah smiles openly, easily, but Elin notices a worry line creasing her brow. She recalls their earlier chat about Farrah's ex.

'So, did I choose okay?' Forking some salad on to his plate, Will gestures at Elin's dress.

'Ooh,' Farrah says and smiles. 'You let Will pack for you. Risky move.'

As Will pulls a mock-wounded face, they both burst into laughter. Elin's smile, when it comes, is hesitant – she's pulled up short, as she always is when the siblings are together. The physical similarities are an arresting sight.

Will takes Elin's hand in his. 'Anyway, it's good being here, with both of you, even if it is under these circumstances.' He hesitates. 'What about Steed? Didn't fancy joining us?'

'I asked, but he's already eaten. Said he's following up on a few things.' Elin actually thinks work was an excuse for some

116

time alone. Despite Steed's bonhomie, she senses from his remarks about lengthy solo runs that he's a bit of an introvert at heart.

Farrah nods. 'Have you got much left to do tomorrow? Might be nice to get some fun in as well as work.'

'Not much, only statements.' Reluctant to go into any more detail, Elin ends the conversation by forking a vegetable into her mouth. The batter collapses, impossibly thin. There's ricotta inside, flecked with some kind of herb. It's delicious, but she feels her stomach clench as she swallows. The heat, she thinks. Even now, it's unbearable.

Farrah's phone beeps and as she taps out a message in reply, Will puts his hand over Elin's. 'I feel better, now I'm here. That Twitter thing, it got to me. Hated the thought of you being out here with that hanging over you . . .'

Elin doesn't get a chance to reply. Farrah's phone rings loudly, drowning out the end of his sentence. Shaking her head, Farrah glances at the screen.

'Take it,' Will says and Elin nods in agreement. Farrah meets her gaze, smiling.

'So it looks like things are going well between you two, then?' Will says lightly as Farrah pushes back her chair, leaves the table.

'Yeah, we had a good chat earlier. What you said, about her ex, you were right, I—' She stops. Farrah's already walking back towards them.

'Got rid of them.' Farrah slips her phone in her pocket. 'A supplier. Never allowed to switch off.'

'Maybe another glass will help.' As Elin reaches for the bottle of wine, starts to pour, she notices Hana Leger, Bea's sister, weaving her way through the restaurant. Her hair is limp, the white dress grubby, a shade darker, as if it's absorbed the detritus of the day.

Elin's immediately struck by Hana's awkwardness, by her not quite being at ease inside her own body. Craning her neck, she looks past her, to see if the rest of the group are there.

'Who's that?' Will takes the wine from her, pours himself another glass.

'The sister of the woman who fell. She saw her, on the rocks.'

He frowns. 'She doesn't look in a good way.'

'No.' Elin pauses, wary about how honest she should be. 'We spoke earlier. She was obviously upset – about her sister, but she mentioned the island too, the curse, the old school . . .'

Will shakes his head. 'Christ, I don't get it, all this banging on about the past.'

'I know.' Farrah nods. 'Time to move on.'

Elin stiffens, not only at the instant dismissal, but at how instinctively Will and Farrah have formed a unit. 'But I think it's natural for people to make associations with the island's history. Surely for some people it's part of the reason why they come. Curiosity. It's creepy, the Creacher murders, the curse. You can't pretend it doesn't exist.'

'The whole point of this place was to create something new,' Will says stiffly. 'To reimagine.' He gestures around at the other diners. 'Seems to be working for most people.'

'Even so, you can't just wallpaper over it.'

The smile slips from his face. He and Farrah sit there, silent. Two blank, impassive faces. Elin flushes. She's done this before with Will's family – ruined the convivial mood, splintered the tempo of the night mid-bar by saying something controversial. She kicks herself. She and Farrah had made progress earlier. Now she's ruined it.

Farrah changes the topic. The conversation carries on for a while, but the dynamic is off, stilted and awkward. It's a relief when Elin's phone sounds a few minutes later. She tips the screen towards her. Another text from Steed.

Might be of interest: Seth Delaney has a criminal record. Dealing. Class As.

She texts back: *Thx. Will ask about it tomorrow.*

No action needed now, but it's the perfect excuse. Draining her wine, she pushes back her chair, stands up. 'Steed's sent something through I'd better check on. I'll leave you to it.'

Will nods. 'See you back in the villa.'

Elin turns and quickly walks away, but not quickly enough to miss the pointed glance exchanged between him and Farrah.

30

Nursing a lukewarm tea in her hand, Hana heads out to the terrace. The sun is almost grazing the horizon, but it's as stifling as it was a few hours before.

'Hey,' Caleb says. He's on the edge of the pool, feet dangling in the water. Thick smears of sun cream on his legs have seeped into the water: a thin, oily film settling on the surface. Beer bottles are scattered around him, another in his hand. He glances up at her, and his eyes are bloodshot, rimmed with red. 'Sorry, I don't know what else to do.'

'Understandable.' She puts her cup of tea on the small table a few paces away, sits down. 'You're in shock. We all are.'

'There just seem to be so many questions still . . . why she came but didn't tell me. I can't wrap my head around it.' He takes a swig of beer. 'This big surprise, I get it, but it wouldn't have been for my benefit. I keep going through all the lies she must have told me to keep up the whole charade.'

Hana nods. 'It's normal to have questions when something like this happens. I did, with Liam, couldn't stop. It gets better eventually.'

'Really?' Caleb meets her gaze. 'It's been more than a year since my dad died, and some days it's as bad as it ever was.' As he leans back, his hand jolts the bottle. Amber liquid chugs on to the tiles, pocked with tiny bubbles.

'I'm sorry, I didn't know.'

Shrugging, he picks up the beer, puts it to his lips. 'It was pretty shit, the whole thing. Unexpected. He was just starting to get his life together after a crappy few years, then gets the rug pulled from under him . . .' Caleb tails off and they both look up, hearing footsteps.

Seth's in the doorway.

Post-swim, he's changed. Preppier Seth: all white linen shirt and pressed blue shorts, his hair slicked back. 'I'm going up to the restaurant. Want anything?'

'Not for me,' Caleb replies. 'Hana?'

'I'm fine, thanks.'

Seth hesitates, as if about to say something, before nodding, heading back inside.

When he's out of earshot, Caleb shakes his head. 'He can't even fake it, can he? All dressed up like nothing's happened, still on his jolly.'

'I don't know . . . people deal with things differently. Jo mentioned earlier that he finds it hard to open up.'

Caleb barks a short laugh. 'When people say that I always think it's just a convenient excuse to do what the hell you want. His type isn't bothered by anything.'

'His type?' Hana probes, although she can predict what he's about to say from the snippets he's let slip since they've been here. His politics are clear.

'Spoilt, entitled, used to riding roughshod over everybody. Bea said as much, and she's right.'

Bea said as much. 'What do you mean?'

He shrugs. 'Bea wasn't exactly a fan, put it that way, but I don't think she was surprised they'd found each other. She thought they were well suited, Seth and Jo.'

Hana hesitates, taken aback. 'I'm not sure about that, I know

Bea was worried when they first got together. The whole drugs thing.'

'That was before the argument. I think that's when she finally saw Jo's true colours.' Caleb paddles his feet in the water. The movement makes little circles ripple outwards.

'The argument about Bea cancelling?'

'No, before that.' Caleb raises an eyebrow. 'You don't know?'

'No. When was this?'

'Only a few weeks ago. Jo came to ours and they got into a fight. A pretty nasty one, from the sound of it. Bea ended up walking out.' He shrugs. 'I was convinced that's why Bea cancelled. Didn't fancy round two. Part of me thought the US trip was a neat way of getting out of it.'

'Bea never told you what the argument was about?'

'No, but I always got the sense that Jo was picking away at her, grinding her down argument by argument, for no particular reason other than that she was jealous.'

'Of *Bea*?'

'Yes. Bea never voiced it, but I think that's partly why she didn't make more of an effort to keep in touch. She was busy, yes, but I think it was an excuse for her to not have to do it.'

'Do what?' Hana's voice falters. She wonders if they'd also thought the same about her – that she was jealous – because she was. She, too, found herself jealous of Bea at times.

'Play herself down to make everyone else feel better. Protect their fragile egos. Other women in particular. She never felt like she could be herself in case it threatened people.'

He's right, she thinks, flushing, reflecting on her own workplace, the whispered, snide takedowns of their female headmistress. Hana had often wondered if some women are hardwired to begrudge another's success: an evolutionary mechanism to try to temper it or put it down, and failing that, ignore it. She's been guilty of it too.

Caleb takes another pull of beer. 'I think Bea was happier when she wasn't with the family. I know it's a shitty thing to say, but it's true.'

31

Elin slips across the path towards the main lodge, bypassing a group of diners in flimsy dresses, laughing loudly. She keeps walking, quicker and quicker, as if each step will push her embarrassment away, but it doesn't; her cheeks are burning as she relives the conversation.

Why do it? But she knows the answer: deep down, part of her is threatened by Will and Farrah's intimacy. Horrible to admit, but there it is.

Rounding the back of the lodge, she stops a metre or so from the back doors, settling on the low wall at the edge of the terrace. The cool of the stone is a delicious relief as it seeps through her dress to her thighs.

Her eyes are pulled past the grassy area below the wall to the dark mass of the woodland beyond. With the sky fading to a soft pastel, the sun is no longer strong enough to penetrate the sweeping arms of the trees, meeting in places to form a dense canopy. Her skin is prickling, senses on high alert.

Total silence.

She can't even hear the sounds of the restaurant. No cutlery clanking, laughter, conversation. It feels wilder here, like stepping into another world. As she looks around, she can't help but feel as though a clear line has been drawn between the front of the retreat and the back.

Before now, Elin hadn't really appreciated how little of the island the retreat actually covers. As her eyes sweep over the mass of trees below, she has the unnerving feeling that despite the retreat, nature is the dominant force here, firmly in control.

Suddenly uneasy, she starts walking back around the side of the building to the front of the lodge.

A few moments later, she stops in her tracks.

A sudden flicker of light between the trees below.

The beam momentarily catches their trunks, bouncing them into colour, the dull brown of the bark alive with lurid fingers of moss.

A crisp snap of twigs.

Elin's pulse quickens.

Silly, she reprimands herself. Probably a member of staff, a guest, but the fear is instinctive. Despite her bravado only moments before, her mind flickers to what Michael Zimmerman had told her about the person he saw near the rock, the figure she'd glimpsed earlier.

The light flashes on again.

This time the beam is moving more erratically, jerkily twitching from tree to tree, intermittently swallowed by the undergrowth as the person moves. Elin wills herself to stay calm: *there'll be an explanation.*

But what? Why would someone, even staff, be in what looks like pretty impenetrable woodland at this time of night?

Disconcerted, she walks quickly around the side of the building, then stops, her back against the wall. Waiting a few moments, she peers around the corner of the lodge and into the gloom.

A silhouette pulls clear from the tree line.

The person is wearing a hooded top, the hood pulled low

over their face so it's impossible to see any distinguishing features.

Stopping, the figure glances about as if looking for something, and the torch comes back on, the beam bouncing across the ground to the back of the lodge.

As if they're searching for someone. *For her?*

Elin stays back, against the wall, heart pounding, but the torch is extinguished. She waits for a few moments, but it doesn't come on again.

Whoever was following her has melted away into the darkness.

Nearly at the villa, Elin's about to take the hard left on to the path when someone steps out from the shadows.

There's a soft shuffle of footsteps. Her thoughts lurch to the silhouette she'd glimpsed in the woods.

'Elin?'

Farrah. 'I thought you were back in the villa.'

'I took a walk instead.' Exhaling heavily, Elin puts a hand up to her hair, immediately aware of how she must look – hair bedraggled and coming loose from her ponytail, her red, clammy skin. She pastes on a smile. 'What about you? Seeing Will back?'

'No, I was going to, but . . .' She pauses and Elin notices something that she hadn't picked up on in the midst of her own embarrassment – Farrah is flushed, her eyes moist.

She's struck by the thought that Farrah's been crying, then dismisses it.

'Sorry about earlier.' Farrah breaks the silence. 'Will's stressed about the award, and like I said, I go into protective sister mode, defending him.'

'It's fine.' Farrah's words had immediately neutralized the

awkward atmosphere, and Elin reflects on how *she* must have come across, leaving the table. '*I'm* sorry, I probably shouldn't have put a downer on things, midway through the meal—'

'Forget it. It's been a tough day for everyone.' Farrah smiles. They talk for a moment before she looks down at her watch. 'Anyway, it's late, I'd better let you get back. My brother will be in full-on search-party mode if we talk much longer.'

Saying goodbye, Elin starts back down the path. She's only gone a few metres when she spots a figure at the top of the steps leading down from the yoga pavilion. She turns, confused. *There's no way Farrah's got up there that quickly . . .*

Looking up, she finds she's right: Farrah is still making her way up the path.

Elin lingers, watching, and something curious happens: rather than move on, the first figure is stationary, waiting.

For Farrah?

Her assumption is right. When Farrah reaches the bottom of the steps a few minutes later, she and whoever it is stand there for a minute talking, before they move in unison up the steps.

It takes a few seconds for the realization to hit. She remembers Farrah's hesitation when Elin asked if she'd walked Will back.

Was the apology just now actually a deflection? Had Elin almost caught her with someone she didn't want to be seen with?

She feels a bitter sting of disappointment. It's always the same with Farrah. Two steps forwards, one step back.

Raising her fob to the door of the villa, Elin can't help but feel naive, as if Farrah's pulled the wool firmly over her eyes.

32

Day 3

Elin jerks awake the next morning after a broken, fitful sleep. Despite the bright glare of the sunshine flooding the room, fragments of a dream are lingering: flashes of her running through woodland in darkness, brambles snagging on her face, clothes . . .

'Hey,' Will says, and lays an arm across her stomach. 'You're okay. Just a dream.'

'Horrible. One of those hyperreal ones.' She waits for her breathing to settle. 'I'm probably just on edge, first proper case back, the Twitter thing, all the talk of the island.' Tipping her head to meet his gaze, she says: 'Sorry for going on about it last night.'

Reaching up a hand, he brushes a hair away from her face. 'It's fine. I shouldn't have been so touchy. The island's past . . . it's a bit of a sore point.'

'Why?'

He shrugs. 'Press, mainly. At the launch, even though we had reassurances from journos that coverage would only be about the retreat, some of them snuck in references to the Creacher murders, the old school.'

'But I shouldn't have pushed the point. I think sometimes . . .'

Elin stops, finding it hard to say the words. 'Sometimes I struggle with your relationship with Farrah. Makes me see what I'm missing.'

'Isaac?'

'Yeah. It hurts, that we're still not close, and then finding out that Dad's been in touch with him and not me.' Her throat thickens. 'The whole coward thing, for him, has clearly stuck.'

Will pulls her closer. 'Don't let it inside your head. His bad parenting. What kind of father would blame their kid because she froze when she saw something traumatic?'

'I know, but part of me still thinks that what he said will trip me up, that something will happen here, and I'll freeze.'

'Elin, if you're having those thoughts, then maybe you're not ready—' He stops. A knock at the door. Neither of them makes a move to get up. Elin snuggles in closer.

Will groans. 'I get the hint. I'll go.' Gently dislodging her, he hauls himself out of bed and pulls on a T-shirt, making his way to the door.

A low murmur of voices.

When he comes back into the room a few minutes later, his expression is sombre. 'It's Farrah. A guest is missing, from the villa on the islet. Someone called Rob Tooley.'

'The cleaner found his room disturbed?' Elin probes, trying to cut through the hurried jumble of what Farrah's saying.

'Yes. Rob's friend asked her to go in early, he's been trying to get hold of him since last night. No sign of Rob anywhere on the islet and the cleaner says the room's in chaos. Looks like the bed hasn't been slept in either. Friend was worried because of the circumstances of the holiday.' Farrah pushes closed the front door with her foot. 'He was meant to be here on honeymoon on the private islet, but the wedding was

129

called off a few weeks before. He decided to do the honey-moon alone.'

'So the friend was concerned about his state of mind?'

'Seems that way.'

Elin nods. Someone going missing after an emotional trauma of that magnitude doesn't bode well, only magnified by the fact that it's happened so quickly after Bea Leger . . .

She doesn't like it. 'I'll come now.' Pulling out her phone, she texts Steed. *Just had report that a guest is missing. Will keep you posted.* She turns to Will. 'I'll call you.'

Although Will nods in reply, his face impassive, she senses the underlying tension. She knows what he's thinking about – guilty as he does so: his baby, the retreat. The award.

33

Access to the islet is over a wooden bridge that sways as they cross it: narrow wooden planks shifting beneath Elin's feet.

She tenses. Every movement emphasizes the gaps between the planks, the glimpses of glimmering sea and rocks lurking below the surface.

'Okay?' Farrah says, about a metre ahead. 'Not the easiest access, but it adds to the seclusion.'

'Secluded is right. I can't even see the villa.' Elin clamps her hand around the rope-style handrail to steady herself as Farrah steps off the bridge on to the islet. All she can make out is a narrow track meandering between a dense thicket of towering pines and conifers, mature oaks.

'That's how Will designed it. Total privacy from the main island.'

Stepping off the bridge, Elin follows Farrah on to the track. A hundred metres or so on, the wall of foliage breaks open to reveal a larger version of their villa. The pastel blue of the exterior walls is only a shade lighter than the sky, so it seems to disappear into the sea and sky, boundaryless.

'Probably best if we put on overshoes, just in case.' Elin pulls two new pairs from her bag and hands one to Farrah. After putting them on, Farrah raises a pass to the door. It opens noiselessly into a large open-plan space that is roughly zoned out – a large, low-slung bed on the right-hand side, sofas on the left.

Elin's eyes are drawn to the glass doors at the back that open out on to wooden decking, the sea beyond. Looped rings of handholds mark the edge – a ladder to take you straight into the sea. It's an idyllic private oasis, the perfect honeymoon spot, but a huge space for one, she thinks with a pang, imagining Rob walking in alone.

As she moves further in, it is immediately clear why the cleaner was concerned. The bed is still made, but it's the eye of the storm – the only thing not in disarray. The wardrobe door on the right is flung open, meagre contents lying messy on the shelves.

A duffel bag has been upended on the floor beside the bed, books scattered around it.

Elin notices a small photo album splayed open. After carefully stepping around the books, she pulls on a pair of gloves and starts flicking through the pages.

Polaroids.

Images, mainly selfies, of two people who she assumes are Rob and the woman who was his fiancée, in the first hit of love, eyes sparkling, arms wrapped around each other.

Elin carefully scours the space – bathroom, kitchen area – and then heads out of the back door to the decking. The daybed and table and chairs in the centre are undisturbed, the sea revealing nothing but blues.

'So what do you think?' Farrah says as Elin comes back inside, foot tapping the floor.

'Hard to say. No way of telling if the mess was made by him or someone else.'

But glancing around again, her gaze settles on the cables snaking out of a cube-shaped multi-adapter attached to the wall. Cables, but none of the tech you'd expect to see attached to them – a phone, a laptop, maybe a camera.

A robbery gone wrong? Had Rob come back to the lodge and disturbed someone?

'Any issues with burglaries here?'

Farrah shakes her head. 'Not as far as I'm aware. Do you think that's what this is?'

'It's possible. Someone could access the islet unnoticed. Particularly given the seclusion. Especially at night.' Elin looks beyond Farrah to the water, unable to shake off her growing sense of unease. This isolation *is* beautiful, but the privacy comes at a cost. If anything happened here, no one would see or hear it.

'Is there CCTV?'

'No, but I'm starting to think that it's probably something we should consider, given—' Farrah stops. 'Hold on, someone's calling.'

Nodding, Elin scopes the vast expanse of water beyond. Someone could go anywhere from here by boat – straight out to sea, unnoticed from the main island.

Farrah turns back, a worry line niggling her brow. 'That was someone from the water sports team. Some dive equipment's missing.'

Elin's pulse picks up. 'Since when?'

'Apparently it was there when they locked up last night.' Farrah hesitates. 'They've also spotted a bag floating on the water.'

'I'm going to need to take a look.' As she picks up her phone to call Steed, alarm bells are ringing.

Michael Zimmerman's words are echoing in her ears: *There's something rotten here.*

The longer she stays, the more she can't help feeling that he's right.

34

A hive of activity surrounds the water sports shack as Elin approaches; staff and guests milling around a half-empty rack of paddleboards.

Steed stands next to Farrah, off to the side, sweat already glistening on his forehead.

Farrah gestures in front of her. 'Tom, whom you met before, is probably the best person to speak to about a boat. He's just finishing up with some guests.'

Tom is striding up the beach, bookended by two guests, a paddleboard under each arm. Thick stripes of zinc stick mark his face, warrior-style. His blue rash vest is speckled with salt stains, the material stretched thin against the hard musculature of his body.

'So you've spoken to the Control Room?' Steed says quietly.

'Yep. They've created another incident log.'

'Thoughts?' His feet sink in the soft sand, spilling over his shoes.

'Interesting timing, but not much more to go on. Sounds like he was upset after the wedding got canned.'

Steed looks at her uneasily. They watch in silence as Tom reaches them, hauls the boards up on to the rack. After murmuring something to the guests, he turns. 'Farrah said you wanted to go and take a look at the bag we spotted?'

Elin nods. 'How far is it from here?'

Tom screws up his face. Fine creases appear in the zinc across his nose. 'Minutes by boat, but obviously longer to swim. Fifteen minutes or so.' He pauses. 'You want to go now?'

'If we can. We probably need dive equipment, just in case.'

The implication of her request is clearly not lost on him. As he starts issuing instructions to one of his colleagues, he visibly swallows, Adam's apple bobbing jerkily in his throat.

The RIB slices cleanly through the water. The surface is as still as glass, a perfect mirror of the cliffs above.

It's a few metres before the seabed starts to drop sharply away beneath them. Elin can't take her eyes off it, the shell-studded sand on the bottom visible even at this depth.

The underwater landscape evolves as they pass the cliffs. Huge boulders lie just below the surface, hulking masses bookended by pendulous ropes of seaweed pushing up through the cracks, swaying in the current.

Elin notices Tom's furrowed brow as he turns the RIB slightly, so they're a little further out to sea. 'Are we far?'

'No, nearly there.' Only a few minutes later, he kills the engine, loudly exhaling. 'Here we go.' He points. 'The guys gave good directions.'

Moving to the edge of the boat, Elin peers down. A bag, only the top end visible, bobbing out of the water. It's waterproof, similar to the one she uses for kayaking.

'It's caught on something.' Steed cranes his neck. 'A rock from the looks of it.'

Elin's about to move closer when she notices something a few metres away, on the left-hand side of the boat.

A dark shape protruding above the surface of a rock. Pulse picking up, she absorbs the curves, the material. *Part of a flipper?*

'What is that?' she says, but Tom's already leaning over the side of the boat, staring into the water.

'Christ,' he gabbles. 'I—' But no other words emerge.

With a horrible sense of trepidation, Elin gazes down.

The flipper she'd glimpsed is attached to a body in full diving gear.

'Look at the angle,' Steed murmurs. 'Doesn't look right.'

It's true: the body *is* at a strange angle – on its side – somehow wedged between the rocks, lower arm and leg pushed into the gap, rig balanced on top of the rock.

'Does it look like LUMEN gear?' Elin asks.

'Yes.' Tom's voice pitches higher.

Silently, she grapples with her thoughts. Though there's little chance the diver is still alive, there's no time to wait for medics.

'Tom, can you go in, check on them?'

He gives his head a little shake, as if trying to rid himself of the excess emotion. 'Of course.' With trembling hands, he reaches for his rig, straps it on. Diving backwards off the boat with a practised ease, he hits the water with minimal splash.

As they watch him descend, Elin holds her breath, clinging to a small piece of hope that somehow, through some miracle, the diver – perhaps trapped – has had enough oxygen to wait it out.

Tom resurfaces a few minutes later and clambers back into the boat. She waits anxiously as he rips off his mask and removes his respirator.

'He's dead,' he says, his expression grim. 'I managed to get my fingers into the hood to get a pulse, but honestly, you can tell it's been a little while. I think—' He's almost choking on his words, breath pulling in and out in short, sucky gasps.

'What is it?' Steed urges.

Tom's hands are trembling as he takes off his rig. 'The guy down there, I'm not sure it's who you're looking for. I took a photo.' His hand is still shaking around the phone and as he passes it to Elin their hands collide. The phone jumps from his hand, hitting the bottom of the boat with a loud clash. Crouching, he picks it up, passes it to her.

The screen is blurry with moisture, and Elin wipes it with the bottom of her shirt. As the image resolves, her heart quickens.

Tom's right.

35

When Hana gets out of the steaming cocoon of the shower, she immediately feels like crying again, but the tears won't come. The initial flare of emotion of yesterday has solidified into something harder. Not shock – it's more than that, a deadened feeling, all nerves removed.

She quickly gets dressed, then makes her way down the corridor. Already she can hear murmured voices; her name threading through a jumble of words. *Hana said . . .*

Jo and Maya.

They're not in the living space as she'd assumed, but outside, on the terrace, coffees in hand. Maya's green jumpsuit and Jo's T-shirt dress are all holiday, but the puffy eyes and greasy hair make the whole effect look off.

'Hey,' Hana says, stepping outside. The stone floor is warm beneath her bare feet. 'What are you guys talking about?'

'Not much.' Maya replaces her coffee cup on the table with a clatter.

She tenses. 'But I heard my name . . .'

'We were just wondering how you were,' Jo says quickly. 'After seeing Bea like that, the shock, we're worried, that's all. You went to bed early last night.'

Hana absorbs her look of concern – furrowed brow, blue

eyes crinkling at the corners – and immediately lays it against what Caleb told her about the argument between Bea and Jo.

An unfamiliar anger ignites inside her. 'Worried? I think you should be feeling guilty more than anything.'

The words are out before she can stop them. Hana's surprised at herself, but part of her is glad. Glad she's not doing what she usually does – tempering herself, biting her tongue. Being *nice*.

Jo stiffens. 'What do you mean?'

'I was thinking about it. What you did, Jo, making Bea feel so bad about not coming that she felt she had to arrive here unannounced, go on to have this bloody accident . . . I'd be feeling guilty if I were you.'

Jo sits forwards. 'You don't know for sure that's why Bea came, none of us do.'

'You said so to the detective.'

'Fine, maybe it was the trigger, but you know what?' Jo's eyes flash. 'I'd do the same again. However you want to spin it now, put a halo on her, Bea *had* been selfish recently. Cancelling was a crappy thing to do.'

Maya places a hand on Hana's arm. The stack of silver rings on her index finger catch the light. 'Come on, everyone's upset. Jo's just spoken to your mum . . . she's in pieces. It's a shock, no one's thinking straight. It's natural to want to lash out.'

'No.' The last of Hana's composure crumbles. Her voice is brittle. 'I'm not lashing out. I'm saying it as it is for once in my life. Jo made Bea feel shit. It's what she does, because deep down, she's jealous. It's a pattern—'

Jo blinks, like she's been slapped. 'Jealous?'

'Yes, and I understand it, because at times I've felt it too, but with you, it's worse, always has been. The attention Bea gets from Mum and Dad, what she's achieved . . . you don't think she picked up on it? Caleb implied as much, last night.'

'What do you mean?' Jo says slowly.

'He said Bea knew how you felt about her.'

'Rubbish. I organized this. Why do that if I were jealous?'

Hana cuts her off. 'Because you wanted her to finally see you in your element, to take what you do seriously. You two had a fight a few weeks ago, because for the first time, she'd stood up to you, and you didn't like it.' A guess based on what Caleb had told her, but it sounds plausible.

'A fight?' Jo falters. Her hand, still cradling the coffee cup, starts to tremble.

'Yes. Caleb told me. Some big bust-up, Bea ended up storming out.' Hana meets her gaze. 'Am I right? Had she finally seen through you? Was that what it was about?'

Jo opens her mouth as if to reply, but nothing comes out. 'No,' she says finally. 'Bea hadn't returned some of my calls, that's all. It escalated.'

'That was it?'

'Yes. Sorry to disappoint.' Jo's trembling intensifies, liquid sloshing over the side of the cup and on to the floor.

Hana meets Jo's gaze, then looks away, chilled.

It's not what she sees in it that bothers her, it's what she *doesn't* see.

She realizes that over the past few years, she's lost the ability to read her sister, to know precisely what Jo's capable of.

36

Only an oval of face is visible, putty coloured, greyish in patches, a respirator lolling half in, half out of the mouth.

Elin's heart is hammering as she zooms in to the blurred lens of the mask, the man's eyes open in a glassy death stare.

A wetsuit hood, slightly askew, is compressing his features, but any doubts Elin might have about the man's identity are countered by the glimpse of a dark beard.

Seth.

Her stomach lurches as her mind trawls up the few words they'd exchanged. They hadn't spoken much – he'd seemed awkward dealing with the emotions swirling around Bea's death, but her overall impression was of vitality, of strength. Someone in the prime of life. It's almost impossible to reconcile that image with this one.

Two members of the same group dead in as many days. *What are the chances?*

'You recognize him too?' Tom mutters.

'Yes. He's one of the group . . . Bea, the woman who fell. Seth's her sister's boyfriend.' Elin belatedly picks up on the 'too'. 'You remember him from yesterday?'

'Not exactly. I'll be honest, when you and I spoke, I knew you'd been chatting to Seth, but that wasn't the first time I'd seen him. We'd already met. He's actually been to the retreat a fair bit.'

'A regular guest?'

'Not sure if I'd describe it like that. I don't know if you're aware, but Seth's father owns the island.' A pause. 'Ronan Delaney. Not something many people know. The retreat is leased to a hotel chain, so he's not really involved in the day-to-day.'

'I didn't know.' *Why had none of the Leger family mentioned it? Surely it would have come up when they'd spoken?* 'When Seth comes to the island, does he usually dive?'

'Yes, and that's what I find so odd, that he'd be out there on his own, get himself into this situation,' Tom replies, a bead of water running from his hair down his cheek. 'Experienced divers have the protocol drilled into them – you never dive alone. Seth knows that, usually takes either an instructor or a friend with him.' He swallows hard. 'I also don't like how he's positioned down there, on his side. After an accident a body usually settles cylinder first, following the heaviest part of the body.'

He hesitates, as if finding it hard to get his words out or debating whether to say something.

'Is there something else?' Elin gently prompts.

Tom nods. 'The valve on his air cylinder has been switched off.'

'That would cut the air supply?'

'Yes.' He flinches. 'He'd have suffocated.'

'Is it possible to do that yourself, accidentally?' Steed asks, still looking at the image.

'No, I don't think so, and even if it had, he could have corrected it.'

Elin picks apart his words, his tone, a cold bead of realization settling in her chest. He's not saying it explicitly, but she's getting the gist.

142

'And his hood . . .' Tom reaches for the phone, scrolls, then hands it back to her. 'It's like it's been pulled back.'

Elin looks down at the image; there's nothing natural about the pinches and creases in the fabric. Someone or something has had a hold of it.

37

'I need to make a few calls to get the right team in place, but in the meantime, can we get a boat out here? Make sure no one comes in the vicinity?' Elin says quickly. Even underwater, securing a scene is vital. If this *isn't* accidental and any evidence is disturbed, it could compromise the investigation.

'Of course.' Tom nods, face still pale. 'Anything we can do to help.'

Steed glances back to the shore. 'Is there anywhere off this beach that we can work from?'

Tom considers, then nods again. 'There's a shack, just below the cliff. Not sure how clean it is, but it's private.'

'Thank you.' Elin passes Tom's phone back, reaching for her own, but as she does, it rings.

Farrah's number.

No greeting: 'I've got news,' Farrah starts. 'The missing man turned out to be not so missing. He was snorkelling, apparently, on the other side of the resort. Had his phone with him but it was turned off. Switched it on about twenty minutes ago to find a ton of messages. Bit insulted, I think, that his friend had thought the worst. Said something along the lines of "I loved her, but not that much . . ."'

'And the mess in his room?'

'Looking for his waterproof phone case.'

'Good news.' Elin hesitates, reluctant to burst Farrah's bubble. 'But I'm afraid I've got to follow it with some bad. That bag that was spotted . . . We've found a body nearby.'

'I know it's not exactly up to par with the rest of the retreat, but will this do? I don't know when it was last opened.' Tom turns, feet kicking up a cloud of dust.

Steed starts coughing, pressing a hand to his mouth. 'Years would be my guess,' he manages to choke out.

Elin glances around; the contrast with the water sports shack on the main beach is striking. A musty, saline damp pervades the air, the stale smell of an unused building on the beach, amplified by detritus – battered life buoys, jackets, an old radio on top of a stained icebox. Each scratched square of window is thick with grime, leaving only a small circle of glass in the centre for watery strips of sunlight to filter through.

'It's secluded, which is the main thing.' Tucked in below the cliff above the tideline, it provides the perfect spot to work, away from the prying eyes of the retreat. 'What's it used for now?'

'Pretty sure once upon a time it was used for storing stuff for the old school, then the Outward Bound courses—' Tom stops, radio crackling. 'Sorry, better take this.'

'Go ahead.'

As Tom leaves the room, her phone pings. A message from Will.

How's it going?

She taps out a reply. *Complicated. Can't say too much, but be careful.*

The three-dot jiggle of the reply, then: *Ok. I'm at the main lodge. Will stay put until I hear from you.*

The three dots appear again before disappearing, as if he's started writing something and then thought better of it.

'So what's your gut saying on this one?' Steed murmurs as she puts her phone away.

'Can't say until we get the body up, but from what Tom said, I don't like it. Plus the fact that he was alone . . .'

'And the bag?' Steed stands on tiptoe, peering up at a particularly crowded top shelf. 'So close to where we found him, might explain why he was out there.' He breaks off, craning his neck. 'Jesus, it looks like someone was camping out here once upon a time. There's a Primus, rug, load of old papers . . .' Steed reaches a hand up, and a piece of paper flutters to the ground. He picks it up, scans it. 'A document . . . talk about turning the island into a nature reserve.'

Elin peers over his shoulder. 'I heard about that. Pre-LUMEN, the environmentalists were campaigning for it to be left unspoilt.' Her instinct tells her that it would have been the right call. It seems that the island sends a clear message to each generation that inhabits this place: *We don't want you here.*

Steed holds up something else. 'A photo too. The old school, from the looks of it.'

Elin recoils. The photograph shows a group of boys lined up outside the school, teachers stood behind them in long robes. There's something odd in the children's expressions: an absence of emotion that's somehow poignant. She thinks about the rumours she'd heard, Zimmerman's comments on the artist who'd been a pupil at the school. 'Looking at those boys, probably the best thing that ever happened, it burning down.'

'Those kinds of schools got away with a lot, back in the day.' Steed's still filching around. 'Bloody hell, there's even an old mug . . . pretty weird place to hole up.' He smiles. 'Even for a tree hugger.'

Elin nods. She finds the idea unnerving; someone secretly tucked away in here, out of sight. She changes the subject. 'Any update on timings for D Section?' FSG D Section is the Marine Support Unit, divers specialized in retrieving bodies underwater, key to ensuring they are carefully moved to avoid compromising evidence.

'Actually, yes, the Control Room called back a few minutes ago.' Steed pauses. Elin can tell from the way he opens his mouth then closes it again that what he's going to say next isn't good. 'Don't like piling bad news on bad, but they're not going to be able to get anyone out to us for a while. Sounds like they're committed on a job with Border Force further up the coast.'

Elin nods, her mind already churning through what this will mean for them. There's a fine balance in a situation like this between making sure the body isn't disturbed and ensuring that no evidence is lost by it being underwater too long. If D Section can't get there quickly, there's a risk that any evidence might be compromised. 'I'll run it past Anna first, but I think we're going to need to bring up the body and the bag now.'

Leaving the shack, Elin braces herself. With an inexperienced and, frankly, probably frightened, team this isn't going to be easy, but as her mind churns into a higher gear than she's needed in months, she feels a strange mixture of emotion: the obvious – fear and anxiety at the situation – but something unexpected too.

Exhilaration. A heady, soaring sensation fizzing away inside her.

She's back in control of an investigation. What happens next is up to her.

38

Sucking in a deep breath, Elin slips the snorkel tube out of her mouth and ducks under the water. It's cooler than she'd anticipated, a stark contrast to the humid air. She swims forwards until she's directly above the bag. Pedalling her feet, she tips her body and positions herself near the base of the bag. They were right: it's hooked around a sharp protrusion of rock.

Thrusting out her hand, she grabs the bag's corner, tugs. It barely gives; she's only just got purchase when her fingers slip from the slick surface, the rock it's caught on still refusing to give it up.

Trying to ignore the mounting pressure in her lungs, Elin shifts position, lurches for it again; but this time she feels a resistance.

Not from the bag itself, but her foot.

Something wrapping itself around her ankle.

Only seaweed, she tells herself. Seth's body, still submerged, is a couple of metres away, but for a moment it feels like a desperate hand coming up from the bottom, pulling at her ankle.

As she squirms beneath the water, she feels it again, wrapping tighter.

Panic swells inside her, her chest tight. She's suddenly acutely aware of the water spooling over her lips, nostrils, the sound of her blood beating in her ears.

Her lungs are on fire; burning.

She needs to come up.

Jerking her head, she starts to panic, gestures to Steed, still balanced on the edge of the boat, but his outline is hazy through her mask, the surface of the water.

Starry pinpoints appear behind her eyes.

Move. Do something.

Finally, her body lurches into action. She kicks upwards, the leathery rope of seaweed unfurling from around her ankle. Surging through the water, she noisily breaks the surface.

Elin rips off her mask, the water that's collected inside streaming down her face. Legs frantically moving below her, she pulls in deep lungfuls of oxygen.

'Hey, what happened?' Steed's already reaching down to help her back on board.

'Got a bit panicked. Couldn't get hold of the bag,' she says between gasps, stumbling back on to the boat. It's a lie. She'd been spooked; the same malevolence she'd felt on the island itself, out here, on the water too. *What's this place doing to her?* She's never been superstitious, but somehow this island is blurring the boundaries between her conscious and subconscious mind, hunting out fears she never even knew she had.

She's struck by the same feeling she had in the shack earlier, as if the island, at every turn, is sending a message: *We don't want you here.*

Taking a breath, she composes herself. 'It's stuck fast. Definitely caught on a rock. Think we need some brute force. Probably better if you and Tom go down. With the diving gear, one of you can go a bit deeper, push it from the bottom. I've got enough photos for evidence purposes, so you're good to go.'

Steed nods, still watching her, not quite convinced by her reply. Pulling his mask down over his face, he slips off the edge of the boat with Tom. Seamlessly submerging themselves beneath the water, they make it look easy. No nerves like she has at the bulky equipment, the thought of being totally immersed.

Steed and Tom slowly sink until they're beneath the bag. Their movements are disturbing the water; all she can make out are blurred shapes and shadows.

Pulse still racing, she waits for them to resurface. When they finally do, Steed has the bag in his hand.

'Took a bit of force, as you suspected,' he says, hauling himself back on board. 'But we got it.'

Once Tom is back up too, Elin pulls on a pair of gloves and tugs the dripping bag towards her. Despite the tough, rip-stop fabric, there are deep scratches to the material, where it had snagged on the rock.

Removing his rig, Steed nods at the bag. 'Doesn't look like it's been down there long.'

'I agree,' she replies, taking some photographs, then puts her phone aside. 'Let's see what we've got.'

Carefully unrolling the top, she peers inside.

Elin sucks in her breath.

She's imagined a lot of things, but not this.

Lying at the bottom of the bag is a row of plastic packages – five, no, six, packed with precision one against another, contents mummified by a thick, industrial layer of plastic wrap.

She doesn't need to open them to hazard a guess as to the contents.

Drugs.

39

The little stash, despite its diminutive size, is probably worth a small fortune.

'Quite the coincidence that the body turned up near the bag.' Steed looks shaken. 'Given his record, you think there's a chance he might still be dealing?'

'I'd say so,' Elin says uneasily. She doesn't like this, especially after Tom's suspicions about the body. 'I think it's time we got the body up.'

The tarpaulin they've laid across the floor of the boat is already collecting water from Seth's wetsuit and equipment, swelling pools peppered with speckles of sand.

The bulky rig on his back meant they'd had to place him on his side and at first glance you'd think he was sleeping if it wasn't for the pale colour of his face, the stiffening limbs.

Elin crouches down beside him, the boat rocking slightly with the movement.

Tom reaches out, points. 'Here,' he says quickly. 'This is the valve I mentioned, it's definitely been switched off. Like I said, he could have switched it back on, unless . . .' He gestures to the hood, his hand now trembling slightly.

Elin looks at where he's pointing. This close, the puckering on the hood she'd glimpsed in the photo Tom had taken earlier underwater is clear, slight indentations visible in the fabric.

Her eyes shift between the valve and the hood.

She swallows. They tell a story, an awful one, and she blinks, unable to stop herself picturing it: Seth struggling underwater, air no longer free flowing, a hand weighing him down . . .

'There's something else,' Steed murmurs, moving closer. 'Look, here, at the corner of his mouth. To the left of the respirator.'

A fine, powdery residue.

It's been smeared by submersion in the water but is still visible. Some kind of chalk? It's impossible to tell until it's analysed, but it bothers her.

Steed's looking up and down the body. 'Can't see it anywhere else.'

Elin nods. She can taste bile, bitter in her mouth.

Everything's telling her that this was no accident.

Seth has been murdered. His life brutally snuffed out beneath the water.

40

Elin closes the door of the shack behind her, slipping her phone back in her pocket. 'The DCI thinks we should get forensic PMs carried out now we've got two bodies.'

Steed nods. 'Pretty clear that Delaney wasn't out there on a jolly.' He tugs at the tarpaulin so it sits flat against the floor of the shack. 'Possible pickup spot?'

Water from Seth's body and the tarpaulin is tracking across the dusty floor in a messy line. 'Given what we know about his record, it's plausible. Tom said he's been out here fairly regularly.' Opening the door of the shack, she lets Steed out in front of her before pulling it closed.

'On his father's island, though . . . risky move.' He runs a hand through his hair, still damp from the water.

'Maybe rewards too big to refuse. Perhaps he got in over his head.' Elin hesitates. 'What are your thoughts on timing?'

'So soon after Bea Leger's death?'

'Yes, and someone in the same party. Together with the whole surprise thing, the questions over someone leaving the villa . . .' She shakes her head. 'I think we need to speak to the girlfriend now.'

Steed's eyes flick back to the shack. 'What about the body?'

'Ideally someone should stay, but I'm comfortable with

locking the shack up, leaving be. I think it's best if you come with. Another pair of eyes will be helpful.'

'You want me to let Delaney's family know on the way?'

'Please.' But as she imagines his father's reaction, her mind rubs up against her doubt of a moment ago.

Would Seth really traffic drugs on his father's island?

The question inevitably leads to another: if Seth was willing to do that, exactly what kind of person is his father?

Ronan Delaney, a highly successful property entrepreneur, is one of the most respected figures in the international development and construction industry. Throughout his career, he's constructed award-winning buildings across the UK and in Europe. Delaney is a patron of the Rainbow Foundation, which seeks to engage people from disadvantaged and minority communities in politics and civil society.

As they walk across the beach, Elin keeps scrolling through the feature on Ronan Delaney. Below the first few paragraphs of text is a glossy, corporate shot: Ronan in a white shirt, open at the neck.

'Looks like Seth, doesn't he?' Steed says, looking over her shoulder.

'He does.' While Ronan's hair is speckled with grey, the resemblance to Seth is clear: the same strong features and broad frame. Yet one thing *is* different. Although Ronan's expression is neutral, just a hint of a smile, his eyes give off something she hadn't expected after meeting Seth – vulnerability.

She needs to know more.

Reaching the steps leading up to the main lodge, Elin lingers. 'One sec,' she says. 'I want to check something.' She adds the name of the retreat to Ronan's in the search bar.

A slew of articles about his purchase of the island appear in the results. The contents reaffirm what Tom told her: the retreat was leased by a hotel group known for their upmarket developments in beachfront locations.

Elin clicks in and out of the next article – a generic press release – and is about to give up when one of the results catches her eye.

'What have you got?' Steed asks.

She tilts the screen so he can read it too.

NEW DELANEY DEVELOPMENT DOGGED WITH
COMPLAINTS
TORHUN EXPRESS

Controversy continues to swirl around the proposed development on Cary Island.

Ronan Delaney, new owner of the infamous Reaper's Rock, is planning to build a hotel on the site of the former school on the south side of the island. The application has received over two hundred comments in objection.

Speaking to reporters, local resident Mr Jackson commented: 'The proposed contemporary building doesn't fit with the raw beauty of this island.'

Another protester, Christopher Walden, said: 'I believe our previous plans for the island as a nature reserve, an SSSI (Special Site of Scientific Interest), are more in keeping with the legacy of this beautiful place. If this goes ahead, it will be a travesty.'

The application is scheduled to be decided by Torhun Council later this month.

The comments below are scathing.

Travesty, but not a surprise given the new owner of the island. I've heard rumours about dodgy companies he's been involved in. A shark.
    Worth checking out his other developments.

A shark. Elin rolls the phrase over in her mind. Interesting.

Steed points at the screen. 'Same thing mentioned, about the nature reserve.'

She nods. 'But after reading this, I'm guessing the environmentalists didn't stand a chance. Doesn't seem like Ronan Delaney takes any prisoners.'

'Perhaps not with his own son either,' Steed says quietly. 'Maybe the drug trafficking was some weird kind of rebellion. Pissing on his father's turf.'

41

The group's villa is tucked into a natural plateau at the end of the path. Needles from one of the pines above are scattered across the ground, criss-crossed over one another like pickup sticks.

As she raps on the door, Elin looks at pairs of shoes lined up outside – flip-flops, Birkenstocks, some trainers. A pair of Reefs are noticeably larger than the rest, the rubber insoles still holding the imprint of feet.

Seth's. It touches her. *All the things we leave behind.*

The door clicks.

Elin looks up to find Jo framed in the doorway, phone in hand. Her blue short-sleeved dress pops against her tan but doesn't lift the tiredness from her face; her skin is sallow, the whites of her eyes laced with red. The ends of her hair, still wet, are dribbling on to the fabric, have left half-moons of damp on her shoulders.

'Ah, statements.' Jo moves back to let Elin and Steed inside. The corridor behind is strewn with bags and clothing, as if they've already half-heartedly begun packing.

Elin steps forwards. 'Actually, no. We're not here to take statements.' She clears her throat: this never gets any easier. 'I'm afraid we have some bad news. About Seth.'

'He hasn't done something stupid, has he?' Jo looks between

them, shaking her head. 'I knew it was wearing thin, playing the supportive boyfriend. Since we found out about Bea, he's pretty much checked out. Wakeboarding yesterday, and today I woke up to a message saying he'd gone kayaking.' She pulls a face. 'He's already in the bar, isn't he? Causing a scene—'

'Actually...' Steed starts, but doesn't get to finish his sentence.

Jo's talking again, rambling about Seth's questionable alcohol habits. Elin quickly realizes that it's a defence: she's sensed something's up, is delaying the inevitable. Her voice is too bright, the smile on her face too strained.

Elin gently touches her arm. 'I'm afraid there's been an accident. I'm so sorry to have to tell you that Seth has died.' As she speaks, the air conditioning rattles, and for a moment she wonders if Jo has caught the end of her sentence – her expression is frozen between the forced smile of a moment ago and a curious kind of blankness.

But then she covers her mouth with her palm. 'No ... he can't ... no ...' A dry, hoarse sob emerges muffled from beneath it.

'I'm sorry,' Elin repeats. 'I know it's a shock.'

It takes a little while for Jo to compose herself. 'What ... happened?' she says finally, chest still heaving.

'We don't know yet. We found him in the water in diving gear.'

Jo is hollow-eyed. 'Diving? But he was kayaking.'

'He was in diving gear. Whether he kayaked or not beforehand, I'm not certain.'

'Where was he?' A jerky exhalation.

'A little way out from one of the coves,' Steed replies.

Jo's blinking rapidly. 'But how do you know it's definitely him? You might be mistaken.'

'We'll need someone to formally identify him, but we both recognized him. I'm sorry,' Elin adds.

Jo crumples from her core. She's in a strange kind of crouch – hand clutching the doorframe for support. Elin glances around her, acutely aware of their position in the corridor. 'Shall we go inside, get some privacy?'

Helping Jo upright, Elin leads her through the door on the left and into the living space. The room, like the corridor, is in a state: clothes strewn across the back of the chair, several half-empty coffee cups discarded on the side table. Through the glass doors on the opposite wall she can see swimwear drying on the chairs on the terrace.

Steed gestures to the double doors on the right, leading out into the corridor at the back of the room. 'I'll close those so we won't get disturbed.'

'Who was he diving with?' Jo blurts out.

Elin sits down beside her on the sofa and takes out her rough book. 'As far as we know, he was alone,' she replies as Steed settles opposite.

'But that doesn't make sense.' Jo's foot is violently jiggling against the floor. 'Seth's an experienced diver. He wouldn't go on his own.'

'It appears he did. We need a specialist team to examine everything before we come to a conclusion, but it looks like he got into trouble underwater.' Elin stops, reluctant to dwell on theories when she doesn't have all the facts. 'Look, I know this is hard, but I'd like to ask you a few questions about when you saw Seth last, to help us piece together what happened.'

'Of course. It was when we went to bed. This morning, I woke up late, about eightish.' She sniffs, tears welling in her eyes. 'Seth was already gone. He'd messaged me, saying he was kayaking. Like I said, it didn't surprise me, he hasn't exactly been enjoying the whole grieving family thing.'

'And just so I'm clear on your whereabouts, you haven't left the villa today?'

'No. I've been in my room.'

'You don't know if anyone else has?' Steed pulls a tissue from the box on the side, passes it to Jo.

'Thanks.' She gives him a half smile. 'Not sure, you'll have to ask them.'

Elin nods. 'One last thing: Tom, one of the water sports instructors, told me that Seth's father owns the retreat. Ronan Delaney.'

'That's right.' Jo picks at a piece of peeling sunburn on her hand. 'But he's not really involved. A hotel company leases the retreat and runs it.'

'I suppose you know that Seth's been here before?'

Bringing the tissue to her eyes, Jo wipes. 'Yes. He likes getting away from London. A few years ago, he started his own digital agency. It's pretty hard work so he comes here to decompress.'

'Do you know if he dives when he comes out here?'

A nod. 'He loves diving. Anything adventurous.'

'And have you come with him before?' Steed asks. Despite the fact that he's asking a question, his tone is caring, not intrusive. A fine art, and one that's rare in an inexperienced officer.

'No, this was my first time. I wish I'd come before now. He'd asked me, but I was always busy.' Another sob sounds out.

Elin finishes writing her notes. Waiting until Jo composes herself, she asks, 'Was it Seth's suggestion to come?'

'Actually, no, like I said before, someone mentioned the retreat in passing, and I told Seth. The coincidence seemed funny, so we got talking about the fact that I'd never been. I reached out to the retreat and they offered a gifted stay. Nothing to do with Seth. That's how he likes it. Prefers flying under the radar.'

'Does anyone else in your group know about his connection to the island?'

Jo shakes her head. 'We wanted to keep it that way. People don't always have a very good impression of Seth, my family in particular. If they knew his father owned the island, they probably wouldn't have come.'

'Why is that?' Steed asks.

'I think they'd have assumed this trip was some kind of boast . . .' Jo shrugs. 'He's got form on that front, plus his attitude, it's a bit laissez-faire.' She hesitates. 'He acts like the clown, and it gets people's backs up. It's actually a front. Deep down, he's insecure. His childhood was pretty shit, despite the money. His father wasn't around much and he's always found it a huge pressure, being Ronan's son, all the expectation that comes with it.'

'In what sense?' Elin says carefully, aware that this lends weight to their theory that the drugs thing could be some kind of rebellion.

'People assume he's ruthless, ambitious like Ronan, or some kind of wealthy dropout living off his dad's money. Seth is' – she blinks, corrects herself – '*was*, better than either of those things. I think sometimes he tried too hard to make people like him, but it actually put people off.'

Steed nods. 'Have you noticed any unusual behaviour from Seth recently? Before you got here? During?'

'No. Nothing.'

But Elin picks up on something; a fleeting shadow of an emotion slips across her features. 'You're sure?'

'Yes.' Jo meets Elin's gaze, then Steed's, but it's too direct, as if she's overcompensating.

Elin looks at Steed, disconcerted.

She's hiding something.

It feels wrong, that in the midst of grief someone could be calculating in any kind of way, but Elin knows that people's survival instincts can trump anything. Jo's concealing something, but she can't probe now. *Too soon.*

Elin closes her notebook. 'Would you mind if we take a quick look around your room? It might give us a better idea of why he was out in the water.'

'Of course,' Jo replies, standing up, and Elin catches it again: a faint shadow of an emotion, impossible to decipher.

42

'This is ours.' Jo hovers in the doorway of the room, as if reluctant to go inside.

Elin can see why. Seth's stuff is everywhere – shoes, sportswear, a pair of swim shorts slung over one of the chairs. She glances down at the large case on the bed, a smaller bag on the floor beside it.

'My bag.' Jo follows her gaze. 'I started packing. We were planning to leave once you'd taken our statements.' She glances around. 'Seth hadn't got any of his things together. Always waits until the last minute.' Another strangled cry emerges and this time she can't control it.

'We'll be as quick as we can.' Awkwardly, Elin walks over to the desk, acutely aware of Jo quietly crying behind her, the sound muffled against her tissue. It's the only part of the room that's neat, with a water bottle, a glass, and a notepad on top of a white folder containing information about the hotel. To the left of the folder there's an open laptop, the screen dark.

'The laptop's mine.' Jo steps into the room. 'Seth doesn't use it.'

'Did he bring one?'

She shakes her head. 'He was trying to have a week off work.'

'And his phone? Did he have it with him this morning?'

'I think so. Goes everywhere with him. We're as bad as each

163

other.' She gestures at the cable dangling from the wall. 'It'd be here if it were anywhere.'

Wandering towards the bathroom, Elin puts her head around the door. The tangy citrus scent of the LUMEN toiletries lingers in the air, bubbles of foam still sticking to the floor of the shower. On the unit around the sink there's a washbag, and Elin quickly rummages through. Nothing controversial – aftershave, razor, spare blades.

Back in the room, Steed's rummaging in the wardrobe. Elin joins him, finding the hanging section half stripped of clothes. The ones left are clearly Seth's – smarter shirts for evening, a few T-shirts.

Steed gestures to the top shelf. Two black holdalls, an expensive Finnish brand – a good, solid stainless-steel zip, rip-proof fabric.

'Those are Seth's,' Jo affirms, watching Steed pull them down. She's still talking about him in the present tense and it rubs, a strange friction against how they saw him last: lying lifeless on the tarpaulin in the shack.

Placing the bags on the bed, Steed unzips the smaller one. 'Only a few receipts.'

Elin picks up the larger one, immediately noticing something strange – the bag feels unbalanced, the right-hand side sagging slightly.

Searching through the interior and side pockets, Elin finds nothing until her eyes alight on the front two pockets; a larger, zipped one and a smaller Velcro one on top. With a growing sense of unease, she checks them – empty as expected; an optical illusion, designed to draw the gaze away from the additional width on this side of the bag.

'Oldest trick in the book reinvented,' Steed murmurs.

She nods, pulse picking up. Not a concealed base, but a side.

Jo's watching her anxiously. 'Have you found something?'

'Possibly.' Elin runs her hand along the bottom side seam, feeling the panel beneath give ever so slightly. Hooking her finger up, she lifts the panel to find a zip hidden underneath. She tugs it backwards and slides her hand into the side pocket.

Her fingertips touch plastic – a thin bag, the contents solid inside.

Tugging it down, she slides the bag out through the narrow opening. It's transparent, so she can see what's inside: three large rolls of cash, held together with an elastic band.

A picture is building. Slowly but surely.

'Do you know why Seth would have this much cash on him?' Elin holds up the bag.

'No.' Jo fiddles with one of the friendship bands looping her wrist. 'He carries cash, but not like that.' On the last word, her voice trembles.

Elin turns to Steed. 'Can you bag it and then take another look to make sure we haven't missed anything?'

Nodding, he moves closer to the bag, pushes his hand inside the pocket, right up into the corner seam. A frown. 'There's something here, flush with the seam.'

He withdraws his hand. A glimmer of metal beneath the spotlights overhead.

Elin knows what it is even before he fully pulls it out.

A carabiner.

Why would Seth go out of his way to hide a carabiner?

Steed passes it to her. As she traces the loop of metal with her fingers, the hazy outline of a thought rises up and out of her subconscious.

'Was Seth planning on climbing while he was here?'

Jo shakes her head. 'Not as far as I know.'

The back of Elin's neck prickles as the thought fleshes out.

Briefly closing her eyes, she's suddenly back there, on the rocks, sun scorching her face as she'd stepped sideways . . .

That's it, she thinks.

But the idea renders her mute.

Impossible. A leap of her imagination, surely?

Yet her mind starts putting other, disparate strands together – what Hana told her about someone leaving the lodge, her niggles about the CCTV . . .

She replays the image in her mind; what she'd seen and the assumption she'd made from that. Possibly the wrong assumption.

'Thanks for this,' she says to Jo, slipping the carabiner into an evidence bag. 'I know it's hard, us asking questions when you haven't even had time to process the news.'

Jo nods, her eyes on the carabiner. 'You're finished?'

'Yes, but in light of what's happened, I'm afraid I'm going to need you all to stay a little longer.'

'Of course. I—' Jo stops.

'What is it?' Elin's thrown by the stricken expression on her face. Not only grief, but confusion.

'There *is* something, about Seth. What you asked before, if he'd behaved differently. Well, he had, but only because of what's been happening. The past six months or so, he's been getting emails. Nasty stuff.'

Steed glances at her, raising an eyebrow. 'What about?' he asks.

'He wouldn't show me, but I got the gist. *Spoilt rich kid. Walking over people.* Things about his father too. How he was a bully, had ruined people's lives, stopped them moving on . . . random stuff. Seth didn't make much of it, he's had his fair share of people having a go, but even so, I could tell it had got to him.'

'Any idea who might have been sending them?'

A hesitation, as Elin knew there would be: there had to be a reason that Jo didn't tell her this from the beginning.

'Please,' Elin says gently. 'You need to be honest. It's the only way we're going to be able to find out what's happened to Seth.'

Jo nods. 'Part of me wondered . . .' she begins. 'Part of me wondered if it might be Maya.' A flush has appeared on her neck and begun creeping up her cheeks.

'Maya?'

'Yes. Seth turned her down for a job a few months ago. It's been messy. To be honest, it was a bad idea to suggest it, I shouldn't have got involved.'

'But why would Maya feel so strongly about it?'

'Because of what happened. Maya got offered the job by one of the junior managers. We're friends, so I went to him directly rather than to Seth. I knew what he'd say. Seth found out, pulled the whole thing, said it wasn't a good idea to mix work and family. Maya . . . well, she lost her flat a few months later. Couldn't make the rent.'

'So you think Maya may have done this out of spite?' Steed asks, dropping his voice a notch.

'I don't know.' Jo shrugs. 'I feel stupid now, saying it. Maya's probably got nothing to do with it. I mean, there was stuff about his dad too, and Maya doesn't even know him. Please don't say anything.'

Elin looks at Steed, her first thought: *So why mention it? Why even contemplate the possibility if you didn't think there was a chance it might be true?*

'I won't, but we'll need to speak to both Maya and Hana before we go.'

'Okay,' Jo replies, but Elin's not sure if she's even heard her,

her eyes fixed on Steed as he picks up the money and the carabiner, slips them into his bag.

Once they've left the villa, Steed shakes his head. 'What do you make of that?'

'Interesting. The cash we found starts to make the drugs angle look pretty spot on.'

'And the carabiner?' He gives her a sideways glance. 'You've got a theory, haven't you?'

Elin nods, wary about voicing it yet, bursting the bubble before she's had a chance to ascertain whether it's even a possibility. 'It's to do with where we found Bea Leger's body. If it's all right, I'm going to check it out while you speak to Hana, Maya, and Caleb.'

Steed nods, but Elin senses his unease, the unanswered questions in his eyes.

43

Stopping a few paces from where Bea Leger's body had lain, Elin drags her gaze from the residual bloodstains to the cliff wall itself. It soars upwards, as dizzying as before, ragged lines scored in the limestone, dips and hollows carved out by the elements.

Where had she been standing when she'd seen it?

But it's almost impossible to pinpoint; all she's certain of is that she'd glimpsed it after Rachel had started photographing Bea's body.

Perhaps she'd been slightly higher, she muses, to Rachel's left – she'd been able to see the cliff face as it curved around to the cove.

Climbing left, Elin tries different positions and angles, but all she can see are signs of natural life: pockets of vegetation, grasses, tiny ferns protruding through crevices in the rock. A cormorant, wings outstretched, is perched on one of the crags.

Stepping back, she's frustrated, starting to doubt herself. But as she shifts her head to the side, Elin blinks, suddenly blinded.

Another dazzling flash, identical to the one she'd seen before.

This time she knows what she's looking for, so doesn't make any dramatic steps back and risk losing sight of what might be causing the reflection. Instead, she tips her head slightly, enough to lose the glare.

There. Her pulse picks up. *There it is*, protruding from the rock.

A loop of metal, sunlight bouncing off the smooth silver ring.

A climbing bolt.

Elin's hand wavers as she pulls out her phone and takes a photograph.

Interrogating the site, she puts the pieces together one by one in her mind: *the carabiner in Seth's bag, Maya's belief that someone left the lodge, and now this: a bolt, directly below where Bea fell.*

Is it possible that Bea's fall wasn't an accident?

She'd had the sense that something was niggling her about the CCTV footage of the fall.

Closing her eyes, she replays it in her mind. As the images spool, she realizes that what she saw – the wrap falling, Bea leaning over to retrieve it – might not necessarily be the right narrative. She'd put the two together because it made sense. Cause and effect.

But it didn't *have* to be the case. The wrap may have fallen, but Bea might have leant over for a *different* reason. A human reason.

Elin analyses the bolt, its location. A chill works up her spine. The idea is wild, but plausible; Seth might have been on that cliff face, somehow caught Bea's attention. She thinks about the indentation in the grass that Leon observed.

Perhaps it wasn't Bea who'd dropped something, but Seth, using it as an excuse for a fake fall. He could have called for help, Bea would have seen whatever it was he'd dropped, trusted him, and then as she reached down . . .

Her mind doesn't want to make the next leap, but it does: *he could have pulled her over*. The CCTV, already grainy, didn't show anything below the top half of the glass balustrade, and Bea's body was obscuring most of the glass – so his hand, reaching up, wouldn't have been seen.

But as she churns it over, she stumbles on the logistics; in order to trick Bea, he'd have had to disguise the climbing equipment. Easy enough, she thinks, with some kind of baggy jumper, especially at night, but he can't simply have been hanging there. He'd have had to position himself in a plausible position for a fall.

Stepping to the side to get more of a profile view of the cliff, she spots a small ledge a metre or so below the bolt.

The chill settles deeper in her chest.

Definitely wide enough for Seth to have stood there, asked Bea for help, and when she did, reaching down a hand, pulled her to her death.

The more Elin turns it over in her mind, the more plausible it becomes. Bea, perhaps tipsy, judgement impaired, would have gone to his aid, not picked up on anything awry.

She shakes her head. If it *is* the case, then it's clever. Not an accident at all, but murder. Ingenious as an idea – the perfect murder being one that doesn't appear to be a murder.

But for what motive?

Given the timing, it has to be linked to Seth's death, but what did Bea have to do with Seth?

No way of knowing, not at this point, but whatever it was, it still leaves questions. Something like this needs planning. If Seth was involved, how did he transport the climbing equipment, and where is it now? A carabiner, yes, but the rest – harness, ropes – are bulky, would have drawn attention at that time of night.

It's unlikely that he'd have dumped anything in the water, risked it washing up at the retreat. More plausible is that he's stashed it somewhere close by. Not *so* close as to be noticed when the crime scene was examined, but equally not too far away; he'd have been under pressure to get back to the villa before he was missed.

She doubts he'd have hidden anything on the side closest to the retreat, so that leaves the left-hand side, where the cliff curves around to the next cove.

Picking her way along the cliff, she scours the rocky face for suitable hiding places.

Nothing obvious, until she notices a large hollow in the rock, about a metre wide, stretching from foot level to just below head height. Ducking her head, she squeezes inside. The space is shallow, extending back only a few metres; barely wide enough to turn.

Tamping down a growing feeling of claustrophobia, Elin looks for any natural hiding places, but the walls reveal nothing but barnacles, lumpy protrusions of rock.

After giving it another once-over, she squeezes out of the hollow to start again.

She follows the cliff face around until she comes to another opening, similar in size to the last, but narrower. Once inside, she glimpses it right away: a small opening about fifteen centimetres above the bottom.

Crouching on her haunches, Elin slips on a pair of gloves, pushes her hand inside.

Her fingertips touch something. A crinkling sound.

Burrowing her hands in further, adrenaline rushes through her chest as her fingers grasp a plastic bag, something solid inside.

44

One sharp tug and thin coils of brown and green rope spill from the bag and on to the ground. Sitting half exposed beneath is a metal harness.

Elin stares, not surprised but aghast at what this means: not only the cementing of her theory but how carefully planned it was.

Bea's death was no accident.

That makes it even more likely that her death and Seth's are linked. Most depressingly, the motive is probably drugs.

Senseless deaths over a senseless poison.

After taking several photographs, she roughly pushes the rope and bag back into the hollow.

Too heavy to carry alone across the rocks; she'll have to come back for it.

Outside, Elin peels off her gloves. Wiping her clammy fingers on her trousers, she starts walking across the rocks towards the beach.

She's only gone a few metres when she hears something. A faint noise, from above her.

Tipping up her head, she glances around, but the rocks, the cliff above, are deserted. Despite that, Elin has the strange sensation that she's not alone.

With every step she takes, her unease grows.

She's about to pick up her pace, when there's a flash of movement above her.

It seems to be coming from the rock itself, or rather, a part of it: a small boulder, careering in her direction.

Elin's almost surprised at first – she feels a cool detachment, as if she's watching it fall towards someone else, observing with an almost scientific interest as the boulder bounces against the rock face, tiny fragments of stone splintering with a skittering sound.

She stands, motionless, still expecting it to ping off at an angle, veer away from her.

But it doesn't.

The boulder keeps falling.

Time seems to stand still, each pivot and jerk, as the rock ricochets off the limestone and tumbles, taking place in an agonizing kind of slow motion.

The hairs on the back of her neck lift, but her legs won't move, won't do as her brain is instructing.

Move. Move.

45

'We can't stay here.' Jo stands up from the sofa. 'First Bea, now Seth.' The muscles in her arms are taut with tension as she paces the room.

On the second lap, she brushes past the cheese plant in the corner with such force that the leaves shudder violently, the pot rocking from side to side on its stand.

Catching Hana's eye, Maya smooths a dark curl away from her face with a panicky gesture, as if willing her to say something, but Hana doesn't know what. Jo's right.

This *is* surreal. No other way to describe it.

'It's an awful thing to happen,' Maya says quietly, 'but it's a horrible coincidence, that's all. Accidents.'

'You really think so?' Jo swivels, face brimming with emotion. 'I thought you were being paranoid, Han, with what you were saying about Bea's fall, but now I think you're right, there *is* more to it.'

'But we know Bea fell, and Seth, the detective said his scuba equipment—' Caleb says from the corner of the room. He rubs at his eyes, exhausted from it all, Hana can tell.

Jo's eyes are bright, glittering. 'No,' she interjects. 'She didn't say that explicitly. It was obvious from her questions that she doesn't think it *was* accidental. Something's not right . . . not just the money, but the fact that he went diving on his own, without telling anyone.'

'I know what you mean,' Hana says slowly. 'That *is* strange, especially when you don't know a place well. A massive risk.'

An odd expression flickers across Jo's face. Embarrassment? 'What is it?' Hana asks.

Jo drags her eyes up to meet Hana's. 'I was going to tell you anyway. Seth does know the island. It wasn't his first time here. His father . . . he owns it.'

'We know. The detective told us,' Caleb mutters.

'Oh.' Jo nods, a strange expression on her face. As she leans back against the wall, the movement reveals her scar from the fire. The one vulnerability of her strong body.

'So why didn't you tell us before? Some big reveal for Instagram?'

'No, actually,' she says quietly. 'Like I said—'

Hana cuts her off. 'Stop lying.' She shakes her head, incredulous. 'Even now, with Seth dead, you're lying, Jo, and if I'm being honest, I'm struggling to believe anything that comes out of your mouth.' As she says the words she experiences a liberating sense of release – in not caring any more what people think of her, not having to conceal how she really feels. Maybe she should have done it before, she thinks, slightly drunk on the sensation.

Jo's eyes widen, taken aback, but she quickly rallies. 'If I'm a liar, then I'm not the only one.'

Her voice gives Hana a chill, the cold precision in her diction. 'I don't get it,' she says, faltering. 'Who else is lying?'

'That's what I want to know. Seth's been getting anonymous emails the past few months. Nasty stuff. Threats. Accusations about him, his father. Seems pretty strange that he gets those, and now this happens.' Jo's gaze shifts to Maya, and it's then

Hana realizes what the last few minutes have been building up to – something Jo has been trying to say ever since she started pacing around the room.

'And?' Maya's voice is hard. 'What's that got to do with us?' Her hand comes up to the necklace nestled in the hollow at the base of her neck.

'Well, I'd say it's got more to do with you, Maya.'

'Me?' Shrinking backwards, her dark eyes are liquid, unreadable.

'Yes.' Jo nods, a sudden sharpness to her features; an animal, going in for the kill: 'How pissed off you were with Seth, after the whole job thing.'

Maya hesitates. 'I was,' she says slowly, 'but that doesn't make me a liar. You more or less promised me the job and then Seth reneged on it. Of course I was pissed off.'

'But it's not just that, is it? I know what you did.'

'Know what?' Maya's voice wavers.

Jo tips her head slightly. 'I know it was you, Maya, the rumours about his business doing the rounds on social media.'

Maya stiffens beside Hana. Silence. All she can hear is the faint whir of the air conditioner.

A visible swallow. 'But . . .' She stutters. 'How did you find out?'

'Your ex. Sol bumped into Seth one night, spilled his guts.'

'*Sol* told him?'

'Yes. All the grubby little details.' Jo gives a small, bitter laugh. 'I have to say, I'd never have thought it: you, a keyboard warrior. I didn't tell the detective, but it's making me wonder. If you'd do something like that, then exactly what else are you capable of?'

Maya seems to get smaller as Jo speaks, her shoulders drawing together as if her body is contracting in on itself at the core.

Hana realizes that this is the perfect example of what Jo does – makes people feel small in order to make herself feel big.

Even cornered, she's capable, and Hana knows why she's doing it now; Jo's deflecting. It's her who's lied – about Bea, Seth's link to the island, and so much more besides – yet she's picking up on something Maya's done to shift the focus from her.

Hana stands, turns to face Jo. 'Before you start accusing Maya, I think you've got some explaining to do. Talk about deceiving people – the day we arrived, a note fell out of your bag on the jetty. You'd started writing to me, apologizing for something – I still haven't heard what that is.'

A beat of silence. 'Oh, that . . .' Jo says quickly. 'I wrote it a few months ago. Like I said, I was feeling bad about not being there for you after Liam died. I thought about writing to you, but then we arranged this holiday. I was going to talk to you about it here, a proper conversation, face to face.'

Hana listens as Jo continues, her expression contrite. While she's saying all the right words, laced with all the right emotion – she is somehow not quite hitting the right note.

She's lying again. She's just found out her boyfriend's dead and she's lying.

46

It's only when the boulder is a metre or so above her that her body finally jerks into action, a clumsy flailing of limbs as she propels herself sideways. Elin twists and lands half on her palm, half on her breastbone, the jolt pushing the breath from her lungs in one gasping exhalation.

Elin clamps her hands around her head, bracing for impact, but nothing comes. She doesn't see the rock land, only hears the dull crack of the impact followed by skittish sounds of smaller pieces scattering.

She tips her head, her eyes darting upwards, but no other rocks follow. All that's visible is the looming expanse of cliff, a stripe of blazing blue sky above it.

The thud of her heart in her chest seems out of time with her gasps.

If she hadn't been able to move when she had . . .

Once her breathing settles, she slowly pulls herself to standing.

Her eyes come to rest on the boulder lying about a metre away. It's larger than she thought, roughly split in two by the fall, fresh cleave marks revealing the darker, smoother stone of the interior. Her first instinct is to step back, to try to see where the boulder has come from, but there are no obvious signs of fresh rockfall.

A cliff fall, she tells herself. A piece of rock that's come loose after expanding and contracting in the heat. But as she walks away, Elin glances up at Reaper's Rock. Despite her earlier dismissal, for a moment she can't help imagining that the rock was responsible; as if it had thrown a piece of itself down in anger.

Once again, the island is letting her know, loud and clear.

We don't want you here.

47

Back on the beach, Elin's phone is loudly trilling.

She's half expecting it to be Will, wondering why she hasn't got back to him, but it's a number she hasn't seen since before her career break.

Mieke, one of the forensic pathologists. 'I'm finishing up Bea Leger's PM. Wounds are consistent with a fall from that height and cause of death is from the head injury, as you'd probably guessed, but there are a few things that might be of interest. I've found something a little odd: a trace residue of a powdery substance in her mouth; it's collected around her gumline, very small amounts on some of her teeth.'

A powder.

Elin tenses. There's no way of knowing if it's the same substance she saw near Seth's mouth, but if it is, then it definitively links his death with Bea's. 'Any idea what it is?'

'Can't say until we get the analysis back from the lab, but it looks to me like limestone powder. I've seen it before, a quarry worker. His machinery tipped over and took him with it. We found something similar on him.'

'Could she have picked it up in the fall?'

There's a pause. 'I'd say no. The powder is specific to the quarrying process, working directly with the limestone itself.

It implies it hasn't been processed, so it can't be from a post-production environment, such as a factory.'

'Right,' Elin says, and as Mieke speaks, something occurs to her, something she hadn't given a thought to until now.

The quarry on the island.

Will had referenced it a few times, described how the old school had been constructed from limestone quarried on the island. He'd repurposed some for the build – in the interiors, the reception and communal areas.

Mieke continues: 'I suspect she picked the powder up from somewhere or someone. Some kind of transfer.'

Elin mulls it over, Seth's potential involvement in Bea's death.

It's possible that he could have transferred the powder somehow. But if that's the case, why would he have been in the quarry? Somewhere to stash the drugs?

'Anything else?'

'Yes. Hard to see probably, initially, given the lividity, but I'm pretty sure we've got some bruising on her arms. The pattern is faint, but it looks to me like fingermarks. I need to take a proper look, but . . .'

Elin pulls in her breath: fingermarks that might have resulted from pulling Bea Leger over that balustrade.

'I'm taking from the pause that this makes things more complicated,' Mieke says softly.

'A little. Let me know if you find anything else.'

Saying goodbye, Elin thinks it through, a chill working up her spine. The evidence is overwhelmingly pulling her in one direction: Bea Leger didn't simply fall. She, too, was murdered.

If that's the case, then Mieke's observations might be one of the few leads Elin has to understand what and who is behind these deaths. Once she's spoken to Will, they need to go to the quarry.

Despite what had happened with the rock a few moments ago, her unease with the island, the thought gives her a sharp frisson of excitement, the same she'd had on the beach.

Every fibre in her body is jangling with energy. She feels alive. Vibrantly alive.

48

'The wanderer returns . . . I'd given up on you.' Will pulls out a chair for her.

Elin glances around. The restaurant is quiet – empty tables, only a few staff milling about near the bar. 'Sorry. I was going to call again, but things have become a little more complex.'

His forehead is beaded with perspiration and he roughly wipes it with the back of his hand. 'The missing guest?'

'Actually, no. False alarm. He'd gone snorkelling.'

'Good news.'

'Not exactly.' Elin's voice sounds strained. She doesn't want to tell him. Knows that the minute she does, any hope he had of it not affecting the award, LUMEN itself, is gone. 'But we've found a body in the water. A different guest.'

Will blanches, leaning forwards in his chair. 'Another accident?'

'Can't say, not yet.' Her words are vague, but she can tell he isn't fooled.

'Well, not sure the *keep it quiet* approach is working. Farrah's told me that we're bleeding guests. People have got wind that something's going on.' He makes an incoherent sound.

'People are leaving?'

'Who'd have thought it, eh? They don't like a few random deaths pissing on their holiday.' Will gestures around; one big swooping arm movement. 'Can't you tell? Not exactly buzzing, is it?'

Elin turns. He's right, the retreat has emptied out: the holiday acoustics distilled down from a vibrant hum to a single shout, a sudden, solitary burst of laughter. The beach is empty, and though there are a few people in the pool, the daybeds surrounding it are deserted.

'The boat hasn't stopped going backwards and forwards. Some people have taken their own water taxis.' He bites down on his lip. 'It's been picked up on social media too.'

Elin shakes her head, dismayed. *The last thing they need.*

A sigh. 'I think I'm going to cut the weekend short. I've got loads of work anyway. Should have known it wouldn't be straightforward. Our trips together never are.' Will's eyes meet hers, a shared awareness passing between them. For a moment, there's a closeness between them, but as quickly as it appeared, it's gone. He looks away. 'If I'm being honest, I'm too involved. A shitty thing to say after what's happened, but . . .'

'I understand. It's personal for you.'

'Yeah. It's like watching something precious blow up in your face in slow motion.' His voice splinters. 'Everything I've worked so hard to do with this place, changing people's perceptions – it'll all be for nothing. Once the press gets hold of it, they'll trawl it all up. The Creacher murders, the school. LUMEN will be a footnote.'

A horrible sense of impotence grips her as she feels the situation slipping from her control. She wants to do something, anything, to make it right for him, but she can't. 'Look, we don't know what's happened, not yet. There's still a chance—'

Will looks at her, an odd, stiff expression on his face. 'You don't have to do that, you know. I'm not a kid.'

'Do what?'

'Plaster over it. I know by your face that this isn't good.' He forces a smile. 'I think I've finally heard your bad news voice. All this time together, but only now I hear it.'

As Will speaks, Elin senses something that she hadn't picked up on before, something passive-aggressive in his body language, his tone – almost *resentful*. And while she might be reading into it, she can't help but wonder if he's blaming *her* for what's happening, by fault of simply being involved.

'I'm just trying to be positive.'

He gives a tight nod. 'And you're happy staying?'

'What do you mean?'

'Well, now that the situation's escalated . . .'

'Yes . . .' Elin scrutinizes his face, expression, not sure where he's going with this.

'But this morning in bed you said you were worried about whether you could cope, if you might trip up if things got tough.'

'A doubt, yes,' she says carefully, 'but it doesn't mean I don't want to carry on.'

'But what if you *do* feel like that at some point? Would you be honest with Anna?'

'Yes.'

He meets her gaze. 'Did you tell her about the thing on Twitter?'

Elin hesitates, knowing what this question is: a test. 'I did. She said they'd look into it if it happens again.' She reaches for his hand. 'Really, you don't have to worry.'

A heavy sigh. 'But you here, alone, I don't like it.'

'I'm not alone. I've got Steed.' As soon as she says the words, she knows they're not right, but she doesn't know what to do. From the off this conversation has felt like a minefield, as if anything she says will be the wrong thing.

'Steed,' Will echoes, shrugging her hand loose. 'Well, that's okay then. You're close enough to be able to tell him, if it gets too much?'

Another mine.

Elin fumbles for her words. 'Well, yes, I think I can. We've got to know each other a bit more since we've been here.'

Wrong answer. Will's face closes. She's not sure how they've got to this point – this strange sense that they're dancing to different tunes.

Spotting a white smudge of sun cream by his ear, she reaches up to rub it away, but he flinches, an obvious recoil. Elin flushes, stung, and it's only then that she has a moment of self-reflection, horribly aware of why he's behaving like this.

It's *her*, isn't it? She's made him react like this because of her mercurial behaviour.

At home, these past few weeks, she's been spiky and distant, but out here, she's someone different. Energized. Dynamic.

He gets the worst of her and how must he interpret that?

Elin feels a wave of sadness at the sudden chasm that's opened up in their relationship.

'Well, I have to go,' she says, doing what she always does. Delay tactics. Pushing things under the carpet. 'I'll leave you to it.'

'Call me later.'

'Will do.' Leaning in, Elin lightly kisses him. There's no recoil this time, but maybe something worse: a reticence on his part, a sense he's simply going through the motions.

49

'Maya, you awake?' Hana's body casts a shadow over Maya's prostrate form on the daybed. She's in denim shorts paired with a tan bikini top almost the same shade as her skin, the wide brim of her panama hat pulled low over her eyes.

No response.

'Maya?' she repeats, louder this time, a little note of fear creeping in. After everything that's happened . . . Reaching over, she shakes Maya's arm. 'Maya, wake up!'

Finally, she stirs, roused from her slumber. Sitting up, she grips the side of the daybed, the veins in her hand standing out.

'Sorry.' Her words are slightly slurred. 'Didn't even know I'd fallen asleep.'

Hana perches sideways on the other daybed, but it's uncomfortable, the frame digging into her thighs, so she swings her legs up to lie against it properly. 'Why didn't you tell me the truth?' she says softly. 'About the job?'

Maya sits up straighter on the lounger, rubs her eyes. A line of sun cream is caught in the crease of her stomach, a flash of white amid the brown. 'I was embarrassed. The whole thing – it was humiliating. Jo meant well, but you know what she's like. I'd assumed she'd cleared it with Seth but turns out she hadn't even mentioned it.' She circles one of the rings on her finger.

'Seth pulled it, all apologies, of course, gave me all the *I'll keep an eye out, pass your CV to a mate*, but that was it. Game over.'

'You hadn't signed a contract?'

'It was supposed to be finalized that week. All I had was Jo's word.' Maya shakes her head. 'I was gutted, relying on it to make the rent, and because I thought it was a dead cert, I wasted weeks I could have spent looking for another job.'

'Did Seth say why he wasn't keen on you working there?'

'Apparently he didn't want people assuming it was nepotism, that they needed to go through the proper recruitment process, blah blah, which is all true, but I'd have been willing to do that. I was well qualified for the job. But he was worried about what people would think if he gave a job to someone he had a connection with.'

'And the trolling?'

Maya flinches. 'I spread the rumours online, but the other stuff she was going on about, the emails . . . that wasn't me.' She hesitates. 'Look, it was wrong, putting it on social media, I know, but I had the rage, Han, at how bloody unfair it all was. The same week I'd been to see Sofia with Mum and Dad. Mum was so upset . . . I saw red. It was just the way he did it, like it was nothing. A click of the fingers, no clue what it might mean for me, for my life.' She shakes her head. 'I'd been looking up all this stuff about him, the charity work he's involved in. The poster boy for all these good things, but in the real world, something that isn't some PR stunt, none of it matches up.'

'But there must be some legal thing still with a verbal contract.'

Maya's face is pained. 'I tried that.'

'What do you mean?'

'I went to Bea, Han. Given her training I thought she might be able to help.'

'And she didn't?' Hana falters. *How could she not know any of this?*

'No. Didn't want to get involved. Plus she was busy, and apparently' – she makes quote marks in the air with her fingers – ' "not her area of expertise", that was the phrase she used. Gave me the name of some ridiculously expensive lawyer.' Maya shrugs. 'Getting the job back, it didn't matter that much, it was more the point I wanted to make. All I wanted was for her to help draft some vaguely legal type of letter, make him think twice, but clearly . . . she couldn't. Too busy, or maybe she just didn't want to.'

Hana's struck again with the same destabilizing feeling as it sinks in how little she knew her family. *What else had she missed while grieving?*

'Sorry, I feel pretty shit, talking about Bea like that.' Taking off her panama, Maya shakes out her curls. 'You know what they say, never speak ill of the dead.' A silence opens up between them before Maya speaks again. 'Saying that, it's a rubbish statement, isn't it? Just because someone's dead doesn't mean they're suddenly perfect.'

Opening her mouth to speak, Hana takes in Maya's expression and closes it again. For a moment, she doesn't look like her cousin at all. There's something blank, unreadable about her.

'I'm going inside to get some water,' Hana says finally.

Maya nods, leaning back against the daybed.

As Hana walks up the path, an insect flits past her – two hoverflies attached to one another, jerkily careering towards the pool.

At first glance, it seems like they're in the throes of love, but when she looks again, she can see that the one on top is battling the other one. Pinning it into submission.

50

Elin hoists her rucksack higher up her shoulder.

Fifteen minutes off the main track and it feels like they're going nowhere, the hodgepodge of trees and shrubs eerily similar from one metre to the next, only slivers of sky visible through the thick tree canopy.

The meandering path is narrowing, undergrowth encroaching, wild snarls of brambles edging on to the track. The woodland is growing denser – each tree jostling for space; tall sleeping giants of pine and oak, twitching with insects and animals.

'Everything seems darker down here, doesn't it?' Steed falls into step beside her. Already sweating, he pulls at his shirt, flapping it outwards to try to fan himself.

'I know. It's like we're on a different island.' This far in, it's richer in life – tree trunks choked with ivy, the boulders lining the track rippled with lichen and moss. Hardly any square inch of ground is free from vegetation, a thick blanket of oak leaves. Birds shift among the branches, but Elin can't see them – all she can hear is the twitch and rustle as they flit from tree to tree.

Reaching into his bag, Steed withdraws a protein bar.

'You ever stop eating?' Elin smiles. He's always munching on something, an ever-ready supply of food on his desk or in his bag.

Steed grins. 'Only when I'm asleep.' He thrusts his wrist in her direction. 'Anyway, look, it's justified, nearly lunchtime.' Tearing open the packet, he starts to shovel the bar into his mouth. No pleasure in the process; this is an athlete's fuel-focused efficiency. He mimes getting another one out.

She shakes her head. 'Thanks, but I'll wait until we get back. I meant to get something, but I got caught up with the CCTV guy.'

'Any luck?'

'Some kind of glitch in the system. Meant to wipe itself every twenty-four hours, but it's defaulted to every hour. It's going to take a few days to get someone out.'

Steed nods. 'I've been thinking,' he says, mouth full. 'Delaney staging the fall ... surely to do that, he must have known, somehow, that Bea was here, near the pavilion, for it to work?'

'The water sports guy said she took a call when she was with him. It's possible they were in touch. We need to put in a phone data application request for the Legers ...'

'Already done.' Steed hesitates. 'I'm wondering what else it'll pull up. The dynamics between them ... It was odd, when I spoke to them after you left. Doesn't seem to be much love lost between them.'

'Not exactly crying into their pillows?'

'It's not that, they were actually fairly shaken up when I told them Seth was dead. Tears, the full works; it was more the reaction to Seth's father owning the retreat. Maya and Caleb seemed pretty disparaging.'

'Because they weren't told?' Elin tramps forwards, having to take a large step over a snarl of brambles.

'That and I got the sense they're not particularly keen on the place. Mutterings of style over substance. Said something along the lines of it made sense Seth hadn't shouted about his father owning it, that it didn't exactly live up to all the hype online. All the charity and eco stuff.'

'Pretty strange thing to say given what you'd told them about Seth.'

'That's what I thought.' Steed pushes at a branch in their path, only just catching it before it snaps back in Elin's face.

'They mention any conflict between Bea and Seth?'

'No.'

'A fling gone wrong?'

'Possible.' He pushes the last of the protein bar into his mouth. 'I still can't get over the balls on him, doing something like this at his father's resort.'

'But Jo said he'd been trying to step out of Ronan Delaney's shadow. I reckon the daddy complex is definitely an option.'

Steed's expression is suddenly serious. 'I understand it, in a way, if it is that. Parents . . . they can get to you like no one else. My father wasn't exactly winning any dad-of-the-year awards.'

'The same.' Elin kicks at the leaves on the ground with her foot.

'Shit, isn't it?' he says abruptly, wiping his mouth with the back of his hand. 'When the people that are meant to always have your back over anyone, don't.'

She nods. 'It is.'

Steed meets her gaze and Elin smiles. It's comforting, in a weird way, to think that someone else understands a fact that's usually taboo: not all parents are good parents.

They walk on. A few minutes later, the tree cover thins – blocky chunks of blue sky now visible. 'Think we're near some kind of clearing.' Elin looks along the track as it meanders to the right.

She strides ahead to try to get a sense of where it leads, but a few metres on, her stomach drops as her right foot gives, finds nothing but air.

51

The sickening lurch in her gut is rapidly followed by a sudden pressure on her waist: Steed's arm jerking out to stop her fall.

The movement topples her backwards, to the ground. She cries out, the impact reverberating up her spine.

Stones dislodged by her slip are falling away, pinging off the rock with a tinny echo.

'Shit,' Elin gasps, her heart hammering in her chest.

Steed lets out a low whistle as he helps her to her feet. 'Christ, that was close.'

Craning their necks, they peer down at what's opened up in front of them: the rock face tumbling away, a greyish rubble scree, into a huge, hollowed-out bowl.

They're at the very edge of the quarry and hadn't realized.

What would have been a clear delineation between woodland and the area around the quarry is wildly overgrown, part of the forest itself. Any natural markers that might signal the quarry is near have been smothered by vegetation.

Elin's eyes graze the perimeter, the steep drop to the ground below, littered with boulders and smaller rocks.

Nothing to break her fall on the way down, nothing she could have clung to or grabbed at.

She could have been down there. A bigger step, not such a quick reaction . . .

'Wouldn't have liked your chances if I hadn't been here.' Steed tries to make light of it, but she glimpses the flicker of fear in his eyes.

She nods, still gazing at the drop. 'Pretty dangerous, having this here, no warning sign. It's a good distance from the retreat itself, but guests might still come this far. Why no markers?'

Steed wanders to the right. 'Here!' he says a few moments later, beckoning to her with a flourish. 'There's a sign.'

Walking towards him, Elin sees it, upended in the undergrowth. An official sign, several metres wide, made of a rigid, ribbed plastic. Big red letters: DANGER. QUARRY. A blocky image of a drop.

'Looks like it's been disturbed,' Steed says uneasily, pointing to the bottom of the wooden post that the sign is attached to.

Elin's eyes drop down to the fresh soil staining the timber. She stares, discomforted. 'Fairly recently too.' Her theory that the powder transferred to Bea and Seth came from here isn't beyond the realm of possibility. She's now even more compelled to explore the quarry.

'So how do we get down?' Steed's looking around, eager to get moving.

They kick their way through the scrubby ground, scanning for a route as they skirt the lip of the quarry. They're about a quarter of the way around when Steed calls out, 'Looks like we've got a path here.'

She spots it too: a winding path snaking down to the quarry floor. It might have been made up of well-defined steps once, but they, too, have succumbed to nature, sprouting bleached-out wisps of grass and weed.

When they reach the bottom, Elin walks into the centre of the quarry. Her skin prickles. She's immediately struck with an eerie sensation of recent abandonment, as though it's just been left, mid dig, the floor littered with the cast-offs of the quarrying process – vast chunks of stone interspersed with smaller ones.

'You try that side.' Elin points left. 'I think it's a case of don't know what we're looking for until we find it.'

Taking their time, they walk around, looking for something that might hint at what Seth or anyone else might have been doing here. 'Anything?' she says a few minutes later. 'Looking like a wasted trip from where I'm standing.'

'Same,' Steed replies, then stops. A sudden pull of breath. 'Actually . . . look at this. Here,' he says as she makes her way across, and points to a break in the undergrowth that's smothering the far wall of the quarry. The curtain of low-hanging ivy has been disturbed – strands clearly pulled out from the roots.

Steed tentatively grasps several ropes of the ivy and rips them aside, shuddering as they fall back against his hand and shoulder.

An opening.

'Wasn't expecting that . . .'

Elin doesn't reply, taken aback – the ivy is concealing a hollow in the rocky face, about a metre from the quarry floor.

It's dark, impossible to see what's inside, so Steed pulls out his torch and flicks it on, moving it slowly around in front of them.

The opening is deep, the beam immediately swallowed up in the darkness.

'A cave?' Steed murmurs.

'Looks like it.'

Scrambling up and into the hollow, Steed keeps the torch

out in front of him. While the cave narrows, it doesn't stop as he'd first assumed, but instead bends to the right. 'Definitely a cave, going back a fair way too. Looks like it leads somewhere.' He turns back. 'Want to go in?'

Elin hesitates. A flicker of trepidation: what if someone's in here? Waiting?

Going into a space like this blind is risky, but at the same time, she hears the voice in her head, a voice that's been sounding out ever since she got to the island.

This is what you love. Why you do the job you do. For this: the feeling of pushing yourself to your very limits.

She'd tried once to explain to Will what it felt like, a moment like this. But words can't even begin to conjure it, that highwire fizz, when it feels like you're nothing but your senses, nothing but nerve and muscle and blood pulsing through your veins. *Outside of yourself.* Perhaps that's the appeal: escaping the space inside your head.

Finally, she nods. 'You lead.'

Once she's clambered up into the cave, she pulls out her own torch and they start moving forwards, but within a few metres, Elin is coughing violently. The air is laced with something chalky, as if she's breathing in pure dust. She can taste it, feel it, coating her lips, tongue.

All at once, a gripping claustrophobia – her lungs tightening, as if they're holding on with a vice-like grip to each inhalation. It's been a few months since she's needed anything other than her preventative inhaler, but it's warranted now.

Quickly pulling her reliever inhaler from her pocket, she puffs. *One, two, three.*

'You okay?' Steed asks. 'Pretty dusty in here . . .'

'Fine. Asthma, that's all. I'm usually all right, but this is extreme.' As the medicine hits her lungs, her shoulders relax.

Once her breathing settles, she lightly touches the wall, tips the torch down to her hand. Her fingers are coated in a fine powder.

Steed examines it. 'Reckon it could explain the transfer?'

'It's possible. Perfect place for stashing gear. Can't imagine it sees much traffic.'

Curiosity piqued, she keeps moving, reaching the curve in the wall. As they follow the final section, the column of light thrown from her torch is teeming with powder – tiny, glimmering particles suspended in the air.

The cave opens up again.

Elin sucks in her breath.

Eyes, staring out from the darkness.

Eyes locked on hers.

52

Blurred, dusty faces stare out at her – five photographs, roughly tacked to the cave wall.

Elin feels gooseflesh rising. Panic surges through her and she slowly breathes out, extending the exhalation as long as she can before sucking in another breath.

Bringing up the torch to face height, she hesitantly casts the beam across the images.

It's clear that they've been here a while; each one covered with a thick film of dust, the heavy-duty tape sticking them to the wall peeling away at the edges.

'What the—' Steed starts, but Elin doesn't reply, her gaze fixed on the photographs.

Pulling on a pair of gloves, she reaches up a hand, starts gently wiping away the layer of powder on the image on the far left.

Features appear, but they're pixelated, grainy, as if the photograph has been taken from a distance and then zoomed in. Elin doggedly wipes until the face is revealed – a ponytail, then a wide smile giving a glimpse of crooked teeth.

Her stomach lurches: a photo of a teenage girl, no more than thirteen or fourteen.

Elin moves to the next with a mounting sense of trepidation, because already she knows what these photographs are.

These faces are burnt into her brain, into the collective consciousness of every person in the area all those years ago.

She's seen them countless times, countless places, and in countless ways – plastered across newspapers, TV screens, blogs.

'It's the teenagers that Creacher murdered back in 2003,' she whispers.

A macabre line-up fixed to the cave wall.

These aren't the images that the newspapers used, though. They're candid profile shots; one of the teenagers is frowning slightly, obviously unaware it's being taken.

Another zoomed-in photograph shows one of the boys from the shoulder up, a building Elin recognizes blurred in the background.

Rock House. The school.

'The pictures must have been taken when these kids were on the island. That's the old school behind them.'

Steed peers in, silent, processing like Elin is.

What does this mean? Why would these images be here?

Face by face, Elin carefully dislodges the powdery residue from the photographs, but on the last one she hasn't even wiped half of it away before she stops, hand mid-air.

Her fingers waver.

'What is it?'

'I'm not sure.' She falters. 'This girl . . . I don't recognize her as one of Creacher's victims. I thought there were only four.' She remembers how the newspapers displayed the victims' photographs. Two girls on top, the boys below. There were four; she's certain of it. 'Maybe I'm mistaken, it was a long time ago.'

Elin's about to take a photograph when the light from her torch picks out something else, on the floor, directly below one of the images.

A stone.

As she moves closer, another one pulls clear of the gloom. Hand shaking, she moves from image to image.

One stone below each photograph.

Elin steps forwards, then back, unsure if she's imagined the precision in how the stones are placed, but as she looks again, it's clear: the positioning is deliberate.

'That's weird.' Steed's voice is shaky.

'I know.' She crouches down, fixing the torch beam on the stone beneath the first photograph. 'I—' But she stops, words dying in her mouth.

The stone has some kind of form, has clearly been shaped to create fluid dips and curves.

She keeps the beam fixed on it, not wanting to voice it aloud until she's certain.

Is she imagining it? Seeing something that isn't there?

Steadying the beam, she moves it carefully over the surface of the stone.

No, not her imagination.

The form is a gesture more than something definite, but there's no getting away from it: it's been shaped to resemble Reaper's Rock. Loosely hewn to give the outline, the nod to the scythe.

Elin finds herself recoiling, terror clutching at her gut, a primal reaction.

These stones are a link to the rock. To everything it represents. *The Reaper.*

Death made manifest, here in this cave.

She attempts a photograph, but her hand is sweaty and her phone crashes to the ground.

It skitters across the cave floor. As she searches for it, the beam of her torch dimly illuminates the surrounding space. More wall, stretching back into the gloom of the cave.

'Look,' she bends down to pick the phone up. 'It goes even further back . . .'

Gingerly, they step forwards, moving their lights slowly around them. A few metres on, her eyes pick out something else on the wall.

More photographs.

There's not as much dust as on the first five, the profiles clear without needing to wipe any away.

Bea. Seth.

53

Back outside, Hana finds Caleb on one of the benches near the pool. He's unevenly burnt, only the sides of his legs red, like they've been slapped.

She presses a glass of water into his hand. 'Thought you might need a drink.' She glances at the phone on his lap. 'What are you up to?'

'Morbid stuff. Looking at photos of Bea.' His voice cracks.

Hana nods. She'd done the same last night. As if looking at images of her sister would somehow bring her back, make her real again.

'How are you bearing up?'

Caleb shrugs, taking a sip of his drink, but his fingers are trembling around the glass as he brings it to his mouth. 'It's like torture, isn't it? Someone's idea of a sick joke. All this loveliness while . . .' He gestures around him and Hana takes it in: the turquoise water glimmering in the sunshine, the pine branches above, shifting slightly in the breeze. *It's true.* It's as if this natural beauty is mocking them.

'Apparently not for much longer. There's a storm on the way.' She gestures up. 'Clouds are coming in.' Dark bubbles of cumulus cloud are dotting the sky. Hana's glad. It's what the summer, this island, and all of them need: a release.

He follows her gaze before looking back to the villa. 'Where are Jo and Maya?'

'In their rooms. Don't think anyone feels like socializing.' Hana takes a seat at the table by the pool, tips the parasol back so she's fully in the shade.

Moving to sit beside her, Caleb puts his phone down. He hooks his feet around the legs of the table, but seems unsure of what to do with his arms, awkwardly folding and unfolding them. 'And you? How are you feeling?'

'Probably the same as you. It takes me back to that moment with Liam, when the world seemed to . . . stop. The disorientation of it all. You start thinking of everything *before* that moment as a different place somehow. The world after . . . it's as if it's shifted on its axis.'

Caleb is silent for a minute before meeting her gaze. 'Bea wanted to be there for you, you know, after Liam. She knew she'd let you down.' His voice is thick. 'I think she planned to speak to you about it at some point, but never got the chance.'

Hana blinks. 'I was surprised. She just seemed to drop off the radar.' She shrugs. 'But it wasn't just her. Most people did. I've never felt more alone.' She suddenly finds it hard to swallow, as if her throat has constricted. 'It made me question everything, everybody. If they couldn't be there for me after something like that, then when would they ever be?'

Caleb inclines his head. 'I get it, and I'm not trying to make excuses for her, but sometimes I think Bea struggled seeing you like that, with that level of emotion.'

'Did she ever say why?'

'Not explicitly, but I know she was traumatized by the fire, what happened to Sofia. When Liam died, it triggered something, I think. I'm pretty sure that's why she couldn't let herself get close to you at the time.'

Behind him a messy circle of insects are flitting around mid-air, an unruly gang with nowhere to go. Caleb flaps them away with the back of his hand.

Hana nods. 'I think we were all traumatized, but when you're a kid, you don't really process it. People think you've got over it, and then something happens as an adult and it all comes back as big and heavy as it was before. People thought Maya coped well, but I can tell she's struggling, even now. Jo, too, all the frenetic activity . . .'

He looks at her sideways. 'How's she holding up after Seth?'

She shrugs. 'Not good, but I suppose that's to be expected.'

Caleb nods, opening his mouth and then closing it again. *He's summoning up the courage to say something.* Finally, he meets her gaze. 'So do we know any more about what happened?'

'Not really, the detective didn't give much detail.'

Another awkward pause. 'It's just that last night, Jo and Seth – they were arguing. My room's next to theirs. It sounded pretty heated.'

'Could you hear what it was about?'

He pulls at the peak of his cap, clearly reluctant to reveal more.

'You can say, you know,' she interjects. 'I'm under no illusions that I've got the perfect family.'

'When they were talking, I heard Seth say something about Jo leaving the villa.'

'The night Bea arrived?'

'Yes.' He swallows jerkily. 'It sounded like "You've got to tell them it was you who left the villa. If they find out another way . . ."'

Hana looks at him, dumbstruck.

It was Jo who left the villa the night Bea died.

All this time, a question mark over it, and it was her.

'You're sure?'

'Certain.' As Caleb meets her eye, a shared awareness passes between them: they've interpreted what he overheard in the same way.

54

Neither of them speak for a moment.

Elin's breathing is shallow, her heart pounding.

On autopilot, she moves the beam of the torch lower, but she already knows what she's going to find.

Two more stones, positioned beneath Bea's and Seth's photographs.

'What the hell do you think this is?' Steed can barely get his words out.

'Well, either someone's keeping score for fun, some kind of macabre tally of people killed on this island, or the two cases . . . they're connected. This set-up . . . it implies a continuation of what was started when those teenagers were killed . . .' Her voice drops away as her eyes lock, once again, on the stones below the images.

'You think that Bea Leger's and Delaney's deaths might be connected to the Creacher case?'

Elin nods, moving the torch between the two sets of photographs. A generation apart, but together on the wall. 'Yes, and if they are, I've called this all wrong.' She fumbles over her words. 'I'm pretty sure whatever the motive is, it has nothing to do with drugs.'

It's about something more profound, she thinks, related to the rock looming large over the island. Had the killer hooked on to the curse, the island's history – the very topography – and used it to construct some kind of deranged motivation?

Steed shines his torch on the images of Bea and Seth. 'They look recent.'

She examines them more closely and it becomes clear that they've been taken at the retreat. The main lodge is visible in the background, the blurred shapes of the surrounding trees. Like the pictures of the Creacher victims, Bea and Seth hadn't known that they were being photographed. A zoom lens.

'But I don't understand how,' Steed continues. 'Creacher's in prison, isn't he?'

Elin nods. 'Put away for life, but . . .' Her mind churns it over, memories of the case, rumours that she never thought of as important until now.

'What is it?' Steed prompts.

'I don't know many details, but I remember the headlines. All the "have they got the right man?" stuff. Since then I've heard more. Talk at work. Creacher's always maintained his innocence, but people definitely had their doubts about his conviction.' Doubts she's taking a whole lot more seriously now.

'If they got it wrong with Creacher,' Steed says, 'and if Bea's and Seth's deaths *are* related to the murders of those teenagers, then why now, all these years on?'

'I know. Pretty big gap.' Elin looks around the cave again with a growing sense of apprehension as she realizes how much they'd miscalculated.

Steed moves in closer to Seth's photograph, scrutinizing it. 'And why choose Bea and Seth specifically? You think there's a chance they knew the teenagers or are there other parallels between them?'

'Maybe, but there's no echo in the MOs. Those teenagers were slashed, had stab wounds.'

'What about a copycat?' Steed says. 'Someone fixated with the Creacher case? Or like you said before, someone fetishizing what's happened on the island.'

'Could be.' Yet her gut is telling her that this isn't the work of a copycat. 'But this space, it's clearly been a while in the making. These photographs of the Creacher kids have been here for years, and the stones – it's telling *how* they've been placed.'

Steed frowns. 'Beneath the photographs, you mean?'

'Yes, and the fact there's one for every photograph. They resemble the rock, but it's as though' – she tries to find the right words – 'as though they're being used as some kind of tally, or a trophy, celebrating each killing. Would you really go to those lengths if you weren't involved?'

'And this powder everywhere.' Steed gestures around him. 'The fact that there's so much of it. I wonder if this room is being used as a workspace.'

'To shape the stones?' She swallows hard, her gaze once again locking on the stones.

'Yes. That's deliberate. Someone with a task in mind.'

Elin turns, about to take another look, when she feels her foot snag on something, material of some kind. She directs the torch at the ground, the handle damp with sweat, slippery between her fingers.

The dull glow of the beam illuminates heavy folds of fabric, all coated in a fine layer of dust. The tiny particles she's disturbed are aglow, swirling under the light. As she steadies the beam, more of the fabric is revealed; a hood, clearly visible on the left.

Some kind of cloak.

Her stomach lurches, her mind catching up with her eyes. Elin realizes what she's seeing: this cloak, what it's suggesting, it's tied to what's around her.

The Grim Reaper.

The Grim Reaper is usually depicted wearing a black hooded robe. A metaphor for death and the darkness it brings.

Could this be part of the killer's delusion?

It's not unusual in serial murders – the killer assuming the role of a powerful godlike figure, convinced that they have the right to decide between life and death.

Bile rises up in the back of her throat as the horror of the space strikes her: the realization that someone using this cloak, responsible for all of these deaths, was in here recently, not only painstakingly taping photographs to the wall, but creating macabre shapes from stone to place below them. She thinks about the powder they'd glimpsed near Seth's mouth, that Mieke found on Bea's body. *The killer hadn't actually put the stones in . . .*

Her hand, which had been holding her torch steady until this point, starts trembling, making the beam dance across the fabric. The more she looks, the more it seems like the cloak is moving. Her flesh crawls.

For a moment, she believes every word of what people whisper about this place.

The rumours. Curses.

She can feel it, taste it in the air, the evil at the very heart of this island. What Michael Zimmerman said was right. *There's something rotten here.*

Whatever it is doesn't want them here, and will stop at nothing until they're gone.

Overwhelmed by a heavy, visceral dread, she can feel her heart thudding in her chest, her throat.

Out. Out. She needs to get out.

55

Torch held aloft, Elin runs back the way they came, following the wall of the cave through to the space they first entered.

She turns this way and that, stumbling as she tries to find her way out, torch beam cutting erratic lines through the darkness. All she can see in her mind's eye are a frenzy of images: the cloak, the stones, the photographs. She takes in nothing but the exit in front, thin slices of sunlight from the opening streaking the walls a brilliant silver.

Elin bursts through the gap, jumping back down into the quarry. The sun is ferocious after the dim light of the cave, but she doesn't stop, feverishly running across the quarry floor towards the path.

Footsteps sound out behind her, Steed's voice calling her name, but it barely registers. She scrambles upwards, half on the path and half on the crumbling scree, clumps of rock coming loose beneath her fingers.

There's already a burning deep in her lungs from the exertion, but she keeps moving.

Eventually, she reaches the lip of the quarry. The rough imprint of the path pulls clear from the overgrowth – the foliage they'd trampled on their way here. Drawing on her last reserves of strength, she starts running again, but within minutes, every part of her body is screaming, sweat pooling beneath her top.

She stops, crouching low, and puts her hands to her head, her father's words ringing in her ears.

You're a coward, Elin. A coward.

'Hey . . .' Steed's caught up with her, still clutching his torch in his hand. 'What's wrong? You need your inhaler?'

Elin shakes her head, once again hearing her own rasping breath. 'I couldn't stay in there, I . . .' She tails off, realizing that her hands and forearms are stinging. Fine scratches zigzag across her skin, tiny speckles of blood, from climbing up the scree.

'You don't have to explain. It was terrifying.' Steed's voice wavers. 'Give me half a chance, and I'd have run too.' He shakes his head, and as she looks at him, she can see it in his face: fear.

He'd felt it too. That sense of something malevolent within the cave.

'But I think,' he says carefully, composing himself, 'that when you're faced with something like that, you can't help but read into it . . .'

Elin nods, playing along, because it's easier to, easier for the both of them to stick to that narrative. It's drilled into them. Rationality. Logic. Mind over matter.

Steed pulls out a can of Coke from his bag, passes it to her. 'Don't know about you but I'm running on empty.' He glances at his watch. 'Past two now.'

'Thanks,' she says softly, and as she meets his gaze, she smiles. 'You were right with the whole Boy Scout thing . . .'

'Got all my badges.' Steed busies himself pulling another can out, but not before she catches his smile too.

As Elin tears back the ring pull, she's warmed by the sheer normality of the act, can start to feel some of the terror slowly ebbing away. She hasn't even opened the can fully before Coke spurts out, gushing in a foaming streak down the metal. Tipping the can to the side, she slurps, catching the worst of it.

Steed laughs. 'Should have warned you. Had to run pretty fast to catch up.'

Mouth still bitter with bile, she gulps it back. The sugar hits her instantly, steadies her.

A few more glugs. She feels her breathing return to normal. 'Better?'

She nods. 'Before we call the Control Room, I want to get your take on what we found. It was a bit of a blur in there.'

'Walk and talk?'

Elin nods, but she soon finds that it's hard work doing both. Despite the rough path they'd trampled on their way in, it feels like they're having to fight their way through the undergrowth all over again. The sugar's triggered something: she can feel the first stirring of hunger pangs as she clambers over a fallen log.

'What was the evidence against Creacher?' Steed takes a long slug from his can.

'Can't remember, not off the top of my head, but a guy I know, who worked the case, said it was a tough one at the start. They didn't get much.'

'Who was the detective?'

'Johnson. Retired now. Before your time.' A career DS with a copper-coloured helmet of hair, Johnson had an earnestness about him that pissed people off, but he was diligent, hardworking, a details man who still put his hand up for jobs that others, including her, avoided at all costs. Elin remembers his palpable frustration as she'd talked over the Creacher case with him one day after work in the pub. The case had clearly got to him. 'He said there was a lot of pressure for a conviction.'

'That kind of case, there always is.'

'Yeah.' They lapse into silence, neither needing to voice what that means. *Teenagers killed while they were on a school trip.* The pressure to find someone would have been off the scale. That's when mistakes are made. Shortcuts taken. Elin swallows hard, struggling with the idea that someone's shortcut might have left the real offender free to kill again.

Steed takes another audible slug of his drink. 'I think that's my worst nightmare, you know, putting the wrong person away. It'd haunt me . . .'

'Me too. I'll give Johnson a call when we get back to the main lodge, see what insight he can give us.' It isn't strictly how she should go about getting information, but not only had Johnson been vocal in his concerns about the Creacher case, they already have a relationship of sorts, meaning she is less likely to be fobbed off. If there *was* any real doubt over Creacher's conviction, he'll have the inside track.

Trudging forwards, there's a rustling in the trees. Only a bird, flitting between the branches, but Elin stumbles, ankle turning. Steed reaches out. 'Hey . . . watch out . . .'

Elin nods. 'Tired.' She can feel the adrenaline slipping away, the quick sugar pick-me-up replaced by a horrible flatness, the light hunger pangs settling into something more pressing, insistent.

'The timing's still bothering me,' Steed says as they continue. 'If whoever killed Bea and Seth *is* the same person who killed those teenagers, then there's got to have been a trigger to act again after all these years. Not exactly the norm for a serial offender to decide to take a couple of decades off.'

'Maybe someone who was put away and only just got out. I think we need to do background checks on everyone here. See if there's anyone who was on the island around the same time as the Creacher murders. Any names that correlate with anyone from that case. Kids, teachers, camp leaders. Any connections at all.'

He nods. 'I'll get on it. And no one strikes you?'

Elin's thoughts immediately shift to Michael Zimmerman, but what does she have to go on? The fact that he'd looked at her strangely a few times? 'No, but given what we found in the shack, we can't discount someone not actually staying at the retreat, but accessing the resort illegally.' She hesitates. 'The one thing that *is* clear is that whoever we're looking for has a fascination with the rock, the curse. I'm no profiling expert, but I'd say it's likely that they're delusional, perhaps suffering from psychosis. In one of those kinds of episodes, someone can get hallucinations, hear voices instructing them to do something.'

'The Reaper?' Steed muses.

'Not out of the realm of possibility, particularly after finding that cloak. The visionary theory is plausible motivation, someone killing because they think they're being told to do it.'

Steed pushes his empty can into the side pocket of his rucksack. 'I get it, but surely anyone delusional wouldn't be capable of planning to the degree we saw in Bea's and Seth's deaths?'

'You're right.' She considers. 'They would usually be more chaotic. That fits with the MO of the teenagers' killer, which was pretty frenzied from all accounts, but not Bea and Seth.'

'What if it *is* a copycat, someone inspired by Creacher? Might explain the anomalies.' He shrugs. 'Or more than one person.'

Elin mulls it over, still unsure. Everything in that cave points to continuity. Someone carrying on with what they started during the Creacher murders. 'Maybe, but I'm wondering if perhaps it's not *how* they've been killed that's important, but the fact they've done it, recorded it, and celebrated it.'

'Either way,' Steed adds, 'the one thing we do know is that whoever's doing this carefully planned Bea's and Seth's deaths to lead us in a different direction.'

She nods. 'To give them time to act again.'

Neither of them speaks for a moment, the awareness of what this means weighing heavy.

The killer isn't done.

56

Hana can barely hold herself together as she paces up and down the corridor past the bedrooms, fuelled with an energy she doesn't know what to do with.

Caleb's words about Seth and Jo's argument are swirling in her head: *You've got to tell them that it was you who left the villa.*

Jo had lied to the detective and lied to them.

The thought spirals – lurid leaps of her imagination that make no sense. She knows Bea fell – the detective confirmed it – but she can't stop the questions mounting one on top of another.

Had Jo left the villa to see Bea that night? Had they argued? What if—?

Hana knows it won't stop until she confronts Jo. Gets answers.

Burnt out, she comes to a halt outside Jo's door.

She has to do it now. Before she persuades herself out of it.

Raising her hand, she raps loudly on the wood. The first knock results in the door pushing open, revealing a thin sliver of room: wooden floor, an upside-down Birkenstock. It was already ajar.

'Jo?'

No reply.

Hana raises her voice. 'Jo? You there?' Peering around the

door, she finds the room empty, piles of clothes – jumpsuits, shorts – laid across the bed as if Jo had already begun packing.

She's about to withdraw when she stops, noticing Jo's phone plugged in beside the bed, white charger snaking across the wooden frame.

A thought slips into her head: *she could look, couldn't she?*

It's something she'd never even consider doing usually, but these past few days, she feels different somehow. It's as if this trip has stripped a layer from her, revealed someone new.

Slipping inside, Hana walks in and stops beside the bed.

Seth.

He's everywhere: clothes still hanging in the wardrobe, Veja trainers under the bed, wallet on the bedside table. Despite the bravado, her heart is thudding in her ears.

Self-reprimands: *This is their space. It's wrong, especially after what's happened.*

But Hana steels herself. *No more guilt.* It's what's been holding her back all these years – a fear of being anything but good and nice, caring what people think of her.

Glancing quickly towards the door, she picks up the phone, unplugging it. No way of doing face recognition, but she doesn't need to – Hana's seen Jo tap in the code before: the first four digits of their old home landline number with her birth month at the end.

Once it's unlocked, Hana scrolls the screen until she finds WhatsApp – Jo's messaging platform of choice. If there's something to be found, it will be here.

Jo's messages to Seth are at the top, but as she scrolls through the chain, there's nothing but the banal type of messages you'd expect from the day-to-day.

Seth: Where are you?

Jo: Going for a run.

Seth: We're heading to breakfast.

Jo: Don't be long . . .

No reference to the night Bea arrived.

Hana goes back to the main list of messages. Her eyes leap down the names but fix on only one: *Bea.* She skips over the exchange. She sees right away that it's not the same kind of messages as the ones between Seth and Jo.

Punchy, aggressive language, the online continuation of an argument:

Bea: You have to tell Hana.

Jo: It's none of your business.

Bea: If you won't tell her, I will. It will devastate her, but it will be worse if she finds out from someone else.

Wildly scrolling and scrolling, Hana finds more of the same. It's obvious now that Jo had lied to her earlier. Whatever she and Bea were discussing here is at the heart of the letter she'd found on the jetty. It's clear that the scribbled-out note is nothing to do with Jo not supporting Hana after Liam's death.

Jo's hiding something else.

A terrible emptiness blooms inside her. This is what lies do, she thinks numbly – hollow you out. The bond between people – that mass of something certain and solid – is destroyed, and all you have left is the shell.

Hana puts the phone back on the side table with a clatter, watches it skitter off the surface and crash to the floor.

She lunges forwards to pick it up, and as she does so, her eyes hook on something protruding from the gap between Jo's mattress and the frame.

Dumbfounded, she presses her hand to her mouth.

57

'Can't get through to Johnson,' Elin says. 'It's going straight to voice mail.'

'He'll call back,' Steed murmurs. 'In the meantime, I got a list of everyone still here. The woman on reception has your kind of ruthless efficiency.' He smiles, but it quickly lapses when she fails to return it. 'That face, I don't like it. What's happened?'

Elin stops a little way from the reception desk. 'Before I called Johnson, I spoke to the force incident manager. Looks like we're on our own. MCIT are fully committed with a recent murder in Barnstaple and we've got several major incidents in Exeter.'

He raises an eyebrow. 'Several?'

'Yeah . . . a multiple fatal RTC and a fire in a shopping and residential development. People trapped. Sounds like all uniformed and community support officers are committed. Regional officers too. They're going to be delayed.'

Steed runs a hand through his hair. He looks flustered, unusual for him. 'So what are we meant to do now?'

'Lock down the retreat. Get everyone together. I need to find Farrah. I've called her, but she's going to voice mail too.' She glances down at her phone. 'I'll try again.' But her momentum falters as she absorbs the message on the screen.

It takes a moment for her to understand what it is.

A message from Will.

There's been another tweet. Have sent screenshot.

With a shaky hand, Elin steels herself, clicks on the image below. Her stomach drops.

It hits her all at once. Disbelief. Fear. Disgust.

Raw emotion washing over her like breakers.

It's her again, but unlike the last photograph, this hasn't been scraped off a public site. It shows her at the beach in her wet-suit with her friend Astrid.

They're both laughing at the camera, but the happy day has been spoilt. In the worst kind of way.

No. No.

They've gone for her eyes again; individual lines violently criss-crossing one another in a digital scrawl.

'What is it?' Steed asks, looking concerned.

'A tweet.'

He frowns. 'About what's happening?'

Shaking her head, she explains about the one Will had shown her before. 'This one, it's worse, somehow. The photo they've used . . . it was taken by my friend. Someone's gone trawling through her social media to find it.' This feels almost as bad as what they'd done to the image itself. It's as if some-one's taken her memory of that day and viciously trampled on it. *A violation.*

'Bloody trolls.' Steed shakes his head. 'I know it's no consola-tion, but another female officer I knew had a similar thing happen a few years ago. Not the photos, but someone kept posting this weird stuff to her house. She reported it, seemed to shut them up.' He hesitates. 'Probably not personal.'

Elin minimizes the image, her skin crawling. 'You're right. If it happens again, I will, but for now it'll have to wait. We need to find Farrah, set the wheels in motion for locking this place down.' She's desperately trying to project a confidence she doesn't feel, but as she walks to reception, her mind keeps stumbling on the photograph – her happiness erased in one violent scrawl.

The member of staff on duty at reception looks up and greets them with a practised smile. While Steed returns it, Elin doesn't, her eyes locked on the textile artwork on the wall behind her.

This time, as she looks, the small motifs of Reaper's Rock woven through the fabric no longer recede as they did on first sight – now they're all she can see. Tiny mirror images not only of the rock but the stones in the cave.

'Is everything okay?' The receptionist looks at her, forehead creased in concern.

'Yes.' It's an effort to tear her gaze away. 'I was wondering if you knew where Farrah is?'

The woman gestures to the corner of the room. 'She's over there.'

Elin follows her gaze to see Farrah sitting on one of the sofas with a man. Heads bowed, they're talking intently. 'Thank you,' she murmurs.

As they make their way across the room, the sandwich Elin hastily ate a few moments ago feels like lead in her stomach, acid crawling up the back of her throat.

Swallowing it away, she stops beside Farrah, lightly touches her arm. 'Sorry to interrupt, we—'

But before she's able to finish, Farrah cuts her off with a brittle smile, eyes widening slightly, in warning. 'Let me introduce you both to Ronan Delaney.'

58

Elin tries hard not to baulk and she knows that when it comes, her smile is forced.

Seth's father.

He gives a quick nod of greeting, and this close, Elin understands why she didn't recognize him at first; there's a marked contrast to the photograph she saw online.

It's not the clothes – the white shirt and linen trousers look as expensive as they did in the picture – but there's a rumpled, tired air about him. His silver hair is ruffled, his face creased with lines. *Grief does this to people.* Sucks the life from them, both mentally and physically.

Ronan extends a hand, the wristband of an expensive watch glinting under the spotlight overhead.

She reciprocates. 'DS Elin Warner. Good to meet you.'

Steed then introduces himself, but Ronan's eyes skim over him, come back to rest on Elin. 'You're the one who found Seth, I believe?'

'Yes, that's right,' Elin says gently.

'I was just asking Farrah if he'd' – he swallows hard – 'if you'd taken him away yet. I was in Devon anyway, for work. I wanted to see him.' Struggling to maintain his composure, he looks to the floor.

Elin exchanges a glance with Steed. This is always the worry in a situation like this; a bereaved relative taking matters into their own hands, not realizing what the reality of the situation might be. 'It's better you wait,' she says carefully. 'Until we're at the mortuary.'

He shakes his head. 'But I want to see him, with my own eyes.'

'Really, it's better if you wait.' Steed's tone is more forceful than hers.

Ronan meets his gaze and Elin senses him weighing Steed up, seeing if he can push him further. Finally he nods. 'I just can't understand it.' He looks bewildered. 'Why someone would want to hurt Seth. Everyone liked him.'

'That's what we've gathered,' Steed says delicately, 'but his girlfriend, Jo, did mention that recently he'd received threatening emails. Nasty stuff, from what she said.'

Ronan doesn't miss a beat. 'Par for the course when you're the son of someone like me. You piss people off just by existing. I get approached all the time, demands for money, conspiracy theorists sure they've got something on you. It's not unusual.'

Steed looks up from his notebook. 'We're also aware that he had a criminal record. You don't have any reason to suspect that he might still be involved in any—'

Ronan cuts him off. 'All that's stopped. Seth had cleaned up his act, did a lot of philanthropic work. Prison . . . changed his mindset, made him realize how short life is. He was determined not to waste it messing around, especially with drugs.' He turns the conversation back to them. 'So when are we going to get some answers about what happened to my son?'

'It's only day one, so it's very much early days for the investigation,' Elin says carefully. 'There's an incident on the mainland that is delaying our usual process.' Hearing the shakiness in her voice, she suppresses it. The last thing she needs is him working out that something bigger is afoot before she's briefed Farrah. 'We'll come back to you when we have more information.'

Nodding, Ronan shifts his attention to Farrah. 'I'm going to work from here for the time being. Can I use one of the meeting rooms?'

'Of course. The reception team will let you know which ones are available.'

'Thank you.' Saying goodbye, he gets to his feet.

Once he's out of earshot, Farrah shakes her head. 'Sorry, no idea he was coming.'

'Is he sticking around?'

'Yes.' Her expression is worried. 'He says he came here for Seth, but I get the sense he's also keeping an eye on things. Stuff's been leaked on social media, as you can imagine.'

'That might make what I'm about to say a bit more complicated.' Elin decides not to sugarcoat it. 'I think Bea's and Seth's deaths might be linked to another case. While I don't want to alarm you, I think there's every possibility that whoever is doing this is planning something else.'

Farrah inhales sharply.

Elin's body tightens in response to the sound: a reflection of Farrah's fear magnifying hers, which up until now she'd kept in check. 'Please, we need to keep this under wraps. If staff or any remaining guests pick up on what's going on . . .'

Her words hit home. 'I'm sorry, I just wasn't expecting . . .' Farrah composes herself. 'What do you need me to do?'

'Get the remaining guests together as quickly as you can, ready for evacuation once it's safe to do so. How many do you think are left?'

'Not a lot. More staff than guests.' Farrah pauses. 'At last count, fifteen, I believe. I can rope in staff to help, start to knock on doors if we can't get hold of people.'

'Good. Is there a large enough space to put everyone together?'

'Maybe the event room behind the restaurant. It's big enough.' She glances around her. 'But what am I meant to tell them? We're going to get questions.'

Elin hesitates. In her peripheral vision, she watches Ronan walking to the back of the room. 'All you need to say is that there's been an incident, and for their safety, it's imperative they follow our instructions. Once everyone's together, I'll speak to them, try to ward off any trouble. In the meantime, talk to key members of staff and brief them about the plan.'

'That makes sense.' Farrah tries to inject some energy into her tone, but it's belied by the vice-like grip she now has on her radio; her knuckles are laced with white.

Elin places a hand on her arm. 'Look, it'll be okay. Really.'

'I just . . .' Her lip trembles, the panicky tone edging back into her voice. 'It's not just this. I wanted to speak to you about something.' Farrah glances at Steed. 'In private . . .'

'Of course—' Elin breaks off, her phone loudly trilling. *DS Johnson.* 'Sorry, I need to get this. Can we chat in a minute?'

Farrah nods, tries to smile, but Elin catches the slight tremor of her lip.

59

*B*ea's phone.

Hana cradles it in her hands as carefully as if it were a baby.

The screen has been shattered, ragged lightning strikes across the glass. All that remains of the backplate is a fragmented corner of the case.

Utter incomprehension: *How could Jo have Bea's phone?*

But as her eyes trace the broken glass, her confusion soon gives way to a lurch of realization as she remembers why she'd snuck into Jo's room in the first place – what Caleb told her about Jo leaving the lodge.

Hana churns it over, but no matter how much she dissects the various elements, plays them this way and that, the picture they paint isn't pretty.

'I think you need to speak to her about it, Han, as soon as you can.' Maya shoves a vest top into her bag, looking at her helplessly. 'I don't know what else to say. She needs to give you some answers.'

Hana nods. She knew all along that would be Maya's response; coming into her room was simply a delay tactic. Putting off the moment, scared of what Jo will actually say.

'You're right.' She nods at Maya's bag, the messy heap of

clothes hastily thrown inside. 'I'll leave you to it. You're doing better than me. Haven't even started.'

'I just want to be ready for when they say we can go. Don't want to be here a minute longer than we have to.' Maya picks up a framed photo from her bedside table. She's about to push it into her bag, when Hana peers over her shoulder.

'It's lovely.' It's a beach shot: Maya's parents leaning over Sofia and Maya in swimming costumes. Clearly taken before the fire, it shows Sofia as she was before the stroke – smiling, gap-toothed, at the camera.

'Stupid.' Maya's voice wavers. 'I take it everywhere.'

'Not stupid, I love it,' Hana says softly. 'How are your mum and dad?'

'Okay, but they haven't been to see Sofia, not in weeks. They've changed, Han. We all knew how unlikely it was that something miraculous would happen, but I think Mum's always clung to the idea that she'd make a recovery. The miracle of hope – even when your brain is telling you one thing, your heart's able to stretch beyond that, cling on to things – someone else's story, a theory online, an obscure research paper . . .'

'But it does happen, doesn't it? People getting better years later.'

'Not with this level of brain damage. Doctors have said as much for years; we just haven't wanted to accept it.' Maya hesitates. 'But the past month or so, I think something's finally clicked. Mum's lost the last little bit of hope that she had. It's like a part of her has . . . gone with it. She's a completely different person.'

Hana finds herself blinking back tears. 'I'm sorry. I didn't know.'

'It is what it is.' Maya scoops up the last pile of books from the table. Mid turn, she loses her grip. They tumble to the floor and she gives a brittle laugh. 'Seems about right.' Hana steps forwards to help her pick them up. 'It's okay,' Maya says quickly, and Hana realizes that it isn't novels that have fallen.

It's the sketchbook she'd seen Maya with yesterday, fallen face-up. Hana picks it up, examining with curiosity the sketch on the right-hand side of the page: a profile of two people facing each other.

What strikes her first is the intimacy: not only in how close the faces are but in their expressions – lips turned up into a half smile, eye locked on eye.

The moment before a kiss.

'You're so talented,' Hana says, examining it more closely. 'I wish . . .' She stops, noticing something from the corner of her eye.

A photograph on the floor, fallen from the sketchbook.

With a panicked look on her face, Maya reaches down to get it, but she's not quick enough.

Hana's already picked it up.

Gazing at the image, she inhales sharply; it feels as if a fist has been slammed into her solar plexus.

She looks, looks again, wonders if she's hallucinating, some warped stretch of her imagination.

But she isn't.

The sketch is an almost perfect copy of this photograph.

Her sister, with Liam.

60

An unfamiliar dullness has consumed the afternoon as Elin steps on to the terrace, phone in hand. The clouds she'd glimpsed earlier are multiplying fast – a steely line hovering across the horizon, overwriting the blue.

Johnson's speaking, but his words are barely audible.

'You're going to have to speak up,' she says, raising her voice. 'I can't really hear you.' There's the high-pitched whine of a motorbike in the background. 'Sorry, I'm in a car park at the beach. I was just asking if everything was okay.' Hesitation in his voice. A random catch-up call isn't exactly the norm.

'All good.' They exchange a few pleasantries before she takes a breath. 'Look, this is a strange one, hence the call out of the blue. I wanted to pick your brains about the Creacher case. I'm out on the island now, another case, and I think I've got a possible link to the Creacher murders.' Elin shuffles closer to the barrier, making sure she's out of earshot of the staff clearing one of the tables near by.

A pause. 'Give me a second to peel this wetsuit down, get in the car.' Huffing and puffing. She hears a door slam. 'Right, I'm transferring you to speaker. Can you hear me?'

'Yes.' Elin cuts straight to the chase. 'Creacher, I know it was a long time ago, but I remember us talking, you mentioning there had been doubts, initially, about whether he was good for it.'

He pauses. 'I'll be honest, I did. Still do, for that matter. To me, at the beginning in particular, the evidence was flimsy at best.'

'Flimsy how?'

'There was DNA evidence on one of the victim's T-shirts, a match with Creacher. But in my opinion, it was circumstantial, could have been transferred another way. It didn't definitively put him at the scene. One of the experts for the defence also raised an interesting point about the *lack* of DNA on the victims, said that even if they hadn't put up any defence, he'd have expected more than a single spot on a shirt.'

'What else did you have?'

'Eyewitness account: the boatman said he'd seen Creacher hanging around, watching the kids. There were photographs too.'

'Photographs?' She thinks about the photographs they found in the cave.

'Yes. There were teenagers in the images we found, but there was landscape too, wildlife. He said he was simply a keen photographer.' Johnson gives a heavy sigh. 'Creacher was odd, that's for sure, someone you'd run a mile from if you bumped into him in a dark alley, but I felt there were assumptions made just *because* he was a bit of a loner.'

'An easy mark?'

'Something like that. Yes, Creacher struggled with eye contact, normal social stuff, and was a bit slow, but that didn't make him a killer. You get a feeling sometimes, whether someone's right for it, and I didn't get it with him. A loner, yes, but a murderer? I didn't see it. I kept suggesting we widen the net, particularly given the connection to the girl.'

'Girl?'

'Yes. I made an interesting connection almost as soon as we

picked up the case. Another girl, who went missing a few months before the Creacher murders.'

Another girl. Elin thinks about the fifth photograph on the wall. *Could that be her?*

'Her name was Lois Wade. All very strange. Her class went to the island for one of the Outward Bound courses, but she was one of the few who didn't. The week the kids were away, Lois was reported missing. The same night, a boy on the Outward Bound course reported he'd seen her on the island.'

'But you said she didn't go.'

'That's exactly the point. A group of them had snuck up to the rock on the island after the teachers had gone to sleep. They were drinking heavily, passed out. When the boy woke up, he was the only one still up there. Apparently he looked down, saw a body on the grass beneath the rock. Convinced it was Lois Wade, but by the time he climbed down, she'd gone. No sign. Not even a mark on the grass.'

'Weird.'

'Yes and no. The boy who saw her was the only one who did. Most people assumed it was the booze talking, possibly hallucinogens. Yet he was adamant, also admitted that they'd invited her to sneak on to the island that night, but he was alone in saying that; all the other kids gave the same story. Lois wasn't there, was never meant to be.'

Elin absorbs his words, glancing out at the water. A breeze has picked up, the turquoise of the sea striped with vivid, unfamiliar colour, bruising blue-blacks, tinny greys. 'But surely it must have been easy to check whether she *did* go out to the island. She'd had to have taken a boat.'

'No CCTV back then, so there was no real way of knowing if she had. Friends and acquaintances denied arranging anything on her behalf. We spoke to a few of the companies operating out of the harbour to see if they'd brought her across, but no. A few days later, the parents admitted Lois had form for running away. Then we had a sighting of her getting into a car on the mainland, and all resources went to that line of enquiry.'

'And the boy's statement about seeing her on the island?'

'Nothing came of it. Police scoured the woodland, spoke to staff, the other kids, the boatman, but we drew a blank.'

'But once the Creacher killings happened, you joined the dots.' Above Elin, the long branches of the pine shift, their shadows dancing sideways across the path.

'Yes. Understandably, I wondered if the cases were linked, if the girl might have potentially been Creacher's first victim, but that hypothesis tripped itself up before it even got out of the starting gate. A few days into questioning Creacher, we found out he wasn't on the island when Lois went missing.' Johnson hesitates, as if he's about to say something else, and then stops himself. 'And by that stage, the sighting of Lois on the mainland was substantiated by several people.'

'Did they ever find her?'

'No.'

'But surely that would imply what the boy was saying might have been the truth.'

Johnson sighs. 'I'm not sure. All I know is that the running away theory . . . it's what they rolled with at the time and they weren't keen on revisiting Lois Wade's case. If the wind's blowing one way, you know what it's like.'

Elin can read between the lines: Lois Wade's disappearance and the sighting of her on the island was very obviously a spoke in the wheel of Creacher's conviction. The police had made up their minds he was good for it, and Johnson's theory would have been an awkward inconvenience. If the cases *were* proven to be linked, and Creacher wasn't on the island when Lois Wade went missing, that would imply someone else was responsible. Having Lois Wade simply 'missing' made Creacher's conviction a whole lot easier to swallow.

Elin understands why: as she'd said to Steed, there would have been immense pressure on a case like this, from press and public, to get answers and fast. But in doing so, they'd possibly let the real killer go free. If that *was* the case, it has seismic implications for what's happening here; her theory that whoever killed those teenagers also killed Bea Leger and Seth Delaney is now looking increasingly likely.

'So what happened after that?'

'I persisted, foolishly, as it turned out. Couldn't let it go, but when I tried to broach it – and particularly the boy's testimony – it went nowhere. Shortly after, I got pulled off the case.' A pause. 'Someone more experienced came in.'

More experienced. They both know why he was pulled: his 'alternative' theory would have slowed the path to a conviction.

'I went to the SIO, asked him to take another look, given the fact that Lois Wade still hadn't turned up, but by that stage, the ball was rolling. With a case like this, it comes down to who is telling the best story, defence or prosecution, and in this instance the prosecution's story about Creacher . . . it was compelling. He fit the bill, and then when the girl came forward to give her testimony, it was pretty much game over.'

'Girl?'

Johnson clears his throat. 'Yes. One of the other kids from the Outward Bound course. Eyewitness. She came forward a little while after, said she saw Creacher the night of the murders.'

'Saw him where?'

'By the tents. Said she woke up, heard a disturbance. When

234

she put her head outside the tent, she saw him running away from the camp.'

'She could ID him in the dark?'

'Apparently so. Told us she flicked her torch on.'

'That quickly?'

'So she said.' There's a heavy silence.

'You had your doubts?'

Another sigh. 'Yes. I hate to say it. She was a kid, and clearly traumatized, but there was something odd about her statement. *Too perfect*, a colleague said at the time, and I knew what she meant. The way she spoke, the poise . . . it bothered me. And of course the fact that it took her a few days to come forward—'

'A few days?'

'Yes. Said she was scared to say anything before, thought he'd get to her too.'

'Do you remember the girl's name?'

'I do, all of that case is crystal clear to me. I probably shouldn't have, and this is to stay between you and me, but I've kept my old notebooks. Her name was Farrah.' Johnson hesitates. 'Farrah Riley.'

61

'Look.' Maya drags her gaze up to meet Hana's. 'I wanted Jo to tell you herself. As far as I knew, she was planning to.' Placing the sketchbooks on the bed, she rubs at the patch of hard, shiny skin on her palm.

Hana can't stop looking at the image of the two of them. *Jo and Liam, Jo and Liam.*

She's never put their names together before. It seems alien.

'Tell me what, exactly?' Hope creeps in. She might have misinterpreted this. A project for Maya maybe – she'd asked them to sit for her. A joke. Some kind of horseplay.

Maya's now pressing so hard on the callused skin on her palm that the flesh has turned white. Hana already knows that whatever she's about to say next is going to be bad, will reaffirm her initial assumption. She can tell from how Maya's face is crumpling, how she's already reaching out a hand to steady Hana. 'Jo and Liam – they had something, Han.' Her mouth seems to be moving in slow motion.

A vacuum opens up inside her.

She'd guessed right. *Had something. Had something.* Only one way to interpret that. 'An affair?' The word sits in her mouth, already souring.

'Yes. But I didn't know, not until a few weeks ago.' Hana feels her stomach turn at the robotic way Maya is talking.

'How did you find out?' She's not sure how she forces out the words, but she needs to have the truth. To hear it all.

'Bea saw a photo on Jo's phone, Han, of the two of them together, when they were out one night. She airdropped it to her phone, was going to speak to you about it, but then Liam had his fall and the last thing she wanted to do was upset you even more. A couple of weeks ago, Bea told me about it, said she couldn't keep it to herself any longer. She sent me the photo, wanted my opinion. I think she was hoping she'd misjudged it, wanted me to interpret it differently, but I couldn't. It was obvious . . . Jo had taken a selfie of the two of them, you could see her arm.' She falters. 'I told Bea to confront Jo. A few days later, she did. Said Jo had promised she'd tell you.'

'But she never did,' Hana finishes. Those words are still there in her head. *Jo and Liam. Jo and Liam.* She turns, focusing not on Maya but the sudden rain splatter on the window, fine snail trails of wet on the move.

'Do you know how long it went on for?'

Maya's eyes are wet with tears. 'A while, I think. From what Bea said, it started a few months before he died.'

Hana's mind leaps, trying to piece it together. It can't be true: *Liam didn't lie to her, never had. When would they have got together? Seen each other?*

But as she's thinking, Hana sees, with a strange, sickening clarity, how it might fit together: little parts start slotting into place. Things she'd never thought important before – the growing distance between her and Jo, the phone calls, already irregular, that tailed off entirely after she and Liam got together. Liam's dislike of Jo, never explicitly voiced, but obvious in how he cut conversations with her short at family gatherings, made jibes about her in their post-meet-up debriefings in bed.

Then how all-consuming work had been for her last year.

How emotionally absorbed she'd been, not only in mentoring a newly qualified teacher, but also in two of the children in her class who had taken hours of her time. Had she, without meaning to, pushed Liam away?

Was it then that it started?

Hana can see the lens through which Jo would have appeared – outdoorsy, fun, effortlessly easy-breezy – while Hana was chewing over meetings with parents, how best to advise the nervous new teacher on her lesson plans.

Perhaps Liam would have been flattered, unused to someone like Jo paying him attention. He'd have admired the way she could *ignite*, make even banal things more exciting.

'So when Jo didn't tell me, Bea confronted her?' Hana joins the dots. That was what the argument Caleb had overheard was about. The affair.

'Yes. Bea said Jo was planning to speak to you but bottled out at the last minute. Bea said to write to you, I think, if she couldn't say it to your face.'

So that was what the letter was really about.

The coward's way of confessing. Hana can picture it: Jo starting the letter and then not even having the courage to put pen to page and form the rest of the sentences.

'And when she couldn't even do that, she arranged the holiday instead.'

'I'm not sure. Perhaps she thought that if you spent some time together it would be—'

'What? Easier to break it to me? That I'd be happily sipping sundowners and suddenly be okay with it?' In part, she knows this is what Jo *would* think – that sensible, reliable Hana would take the hit and that Maya and Bea would be there to act as shock absorbers so she could distance herself from the inevitable fallout.

'I don't know what the plan was.' Maya's cheeks are red now.

'I need to talk to her. Now.' Hana stands up, the shock of a few moments ago evolving into a rolling energy. 'Have it out with her.'

'Han, wait. Not while you're upset.' Maya reaches out a hand.

'I have to, Maya. She needs to tell me the truth.'

62

Elin stares into an ever-darkening expanse of water in front of her, trying to wrap her mind around Johnson's words. *Farrah was on the island at the time of the Creacher killings. Farrah testified against Creacher.*

How is it even possible? Her mind flickers to Farrah's dismissal of the discussion about the island's past last night at dinner.

This was why.

She racks her brain, trying to remember if Will had ever mentioned Farrah coming to the island, but she's certain she'd have remembered if he had.

None of it makes sense, especially the fact that Farrah's chosen to work here. Given what had happened, why put yourself through that?

'Elin? Everything okay?' Johnson's voice startles her from her thoughts.

'Yes, sorry.' She glances across at the nearly empty restaurant, the staff still working to get it cleared.

'I'm thinking about what you said about the girl. Farrah.' She stumbles over her name. 'That you had doubts about her testimony.'

A long pause. 'I did, but Elin, to be clear, all this, it's my thoughts, nothing more, and I mean that. I was out on a limb. At the time, everyone else was all for Creacher.'

'No one else stood out for you? Aside from Creacher?'

'No, but I did keep going back to the idea that if it wasn't Creacher, and Lois *was* on the island that night the boy said, murdered by the same person who killed those teenagers, then the suspect had to have been on the island on both occasions. It narrowed the field a little more, but I drew a blank. The staff who'd supervised both of the Outward Bound courses all had solid alibis.'

Alibis she needs to scrutinize, because Johnson's right: the pool of potential people on the island at that time isn't huge. Camp leaders, teachers, other pupils . . . or someone else entirely? The island was certainly large enough for someone to hide.

'You didn't find evidence of anyone camping on the island? We found a shack on the beach that looked like it had been used—'

'No. We searched thoroughly. Didn't discount someone simply getting a boat, of course. But we struggled to provide a plausible alternative to Creacher. No one had motive as far as we could see. Those particular kids, they were well liked, popular. I was diligent in digging into background. Went for all angles. Family members, boyfriends, girlfriends, grudges. Potential gang involvement, drugs, mental health issues, anything that might have provoked an attack like that, but there was nothing.'

Elin mulls it over. 'Look, I know it's a big ask, but can you send over what you have on the case? You mentioned notebooks, but what about witness statements, anything else you thought significant at the time? I'm going to go via official channels, too, but having your take on things will be helpful.'

'All of the above. I'll need to dig them out, but please, in confidence, okay? It's not really the done thing to give yourself homework, as you know.'

'I understand.' She pauses. 'One last thing, the rock on the island. Reaper's Rock. Did any of the kids reference it when you were questioning them? Or the curse?'

A long silence. When he finally speaks, he gives a heavy sigh. 'Not explicitly, but we got the sense . . . those kids, they'd been spooked somehow . . . it bothered me. Initially, when we started questioning them, I suggested we talk in the old school building, but they wouldn't go near it. Someone had put the fear of God into them.' He hesitates. 'To be honest, after spending a few days there, I couldn't blame them. That place, half burnt like it was, and right underneath that rock . . . it wasn't somewhere you wanted to linger.'

The hairs on the back of her neck lift. 'I've not exactly heard good things about it. Did the teenagers you spoke to after the Creacher murders ever tell you who'd scared them?'

'No, but I always had the sense that we never got the full story. That was the trouble with the speed of Creacher's conviction, the case never got the chance to breathe. I'd have liked to go back to them again, once things had settled, but it was all sewn up by then.'

Elin thinks it through, discomforted by the idea that someone would try to scare the kids, about the school too. What was the fascination with the place? Things keep circling back to it . . .

As the conversation winds down and they say goodbye, Elin's thoughts shift back to Farrah. Nerves prickle her stomach. There's no escaping it; she's the only person who was on the island at the time of the Creacher murders and is here now. She needs to speak to her.

Making her way back to the main lodge, she's only a few metres from the entrance when Michael Zimmerman passes her. He's holding some kind of tarpaulin, an edge trailing across the floor.

He makes fleeting eye contact with Elin before she turns away.

63

'Farrah . . . shit . . .' Steed runs a hand through his hair. 'Take it she never mentioned it?'

'No. Neither did Will.' It's this that still stings: how he'd kept something of this magnitude from her. Her open book, as she'd always thought of him, had been anything but.

'So what do you make of it?'

'Not sure. Johnson clearly had doubts over whether Farrah was giving the full story. Given her testimony was key in the prosecution's case against Creacher, it starts to make the case against him look pretty shaky.'

'Particularly now you know he wasn't on the island when the other girl went missing.'

She nods, glances around reception. *No sign of Farrah.* 'Any progress on the cross-checking front?'

'Yeah. I've sent the list of guests and staff currently on the island to the intelligence unit. Might be a while before we get answers, though. The incident on the mainland is escalating from the sounds of it. They're pulling in people left, right, and centre.'

'Okay, let's find Farrah and then come up with a plan—' Elin is stopped by the shrill sound of raised voices near by.

'I think you need to tell us what the hell's going on.' A petite woman in a robe is standing close to the reception desk with a friend. The ends of their hair are wet, small droplets dotting the floor. Their swim's been disturbed by the news. 'No explanation. Just some garbled instructions that we need to pack our bags and come here.' She turns to her friend. 'We should have gone with everyone else. Not given them the benefit of the doubt.' A violent clatter as her key fob drops, skitters across the polished concrete floor.

Elin shrinks back, letting the member of staff deal with the situation.

'Only the start,' Steed murmurs.

She nods, aware that once everyone is together, she'll have to brief them properly. Deal with the inevitable onslaught of questions.

Circumnavigating the pair, she walks around to the other member of staff behind the reception desk. 'Sorry to disturb, but have you seen Farrah?'

'Yes, she was here a few minutes ago, speaking to Jared, one of the supervisors.'

The other receptionist leans over. Elin glances at the now-retreating couple; pacified for the moment. 'Actually, I think she went to her office, or at least in that direction. Said something urgent had come up.'

'Would you mind showing us where it is?'

'Of course.' The woman leads them towards the corridor at the back of the room. Fifty metres or so down, she stops, gestures in front of her. 'There. Hers is the corner office.'

'Thank you.' Elin clocks Farrah's name at the top of the door. Nerves clutch at her throat. Moving closer, she can see that the door is slightly ajar, but there's no movement inside.

Steed peers through the gap. 'Doesn't look like she's in there.'

Taking a deep breath, she knocks. 'Farrah?'

No response, so she tries again. *Nothing.*

Elin walks inside, Steed a few steps behind. She immediately catches the light scent of Farrah's perfume, but the room is empty.

The desk in the centre is almost bare, apart from several photo frames, a laptop, a neat pile of papers.

Elin's about to withdraw, then hesitates, a breeze lifting the hairs on her bare arm. She glances up, sees that the glass doors at the back of the room are partially open. 'She might be outside.'

But they haven't gone more than a metre towards the doors when Elin's eyes lock on Farrah's radio.

It's smashed; splintered pieces of black plastic littering the floor behind Farrah's desk.

Elin meets Steed's gaze, panic flaring in her chest.

Not Farrah. No.

64

The drooping branch of a pine is scratching at the window. Hana startles. Everything's been still for so long that any kind of movement like this feels alien somehow. Out of place.

But the weather only provides a brief distraction. *Where could Jo have gone?* Her room was empty, she wasn't outside . . . had she overheard the conversation between Hana and Maya? Taken herself out somewhere to escape the fallout?

All she can think about are the lies Jo told. Lies Bea tried to uncover for Hana. Hana feels a pang of guilt about Bea: she shouldn't have been so quick to judge. Even though Bea wasn't there for her after Liam died, she'd been looking out for her in another way.

Lying back on the bed, she scrolls through her phone to find the last photo she has of Bea and runs her finger across her sister's face. Memories of Bea consume her, memories she hadn't let in until now: Bea's towering book stacks around the house, how she'd clear her throat before saying anything confrontational. Bea's hippy phase, the only time she rebelled, the tattoo she got on her ankle during a camping trip in Bude, the defiance somewhat diminished by the fact that while the tattooist did their thing, Bea was doing revision.

Tears prick Hana's eyes. Twisting on the bed, she reaches for her tissues, but before she can pull one out there's a loud rap on the front door. She waits to see if someone else will get it, but a few moments later, the knock sounds out again. Louder this time.

Clambering off the bed, Hana heads into the corridor. When she pulls the door open, she finds a member of staff outside, iPad in hand. A crackling radio hangs from his belt loop.

The man greets her with a half smile, but his narrow face is set in a serious expression that tallies with the sombre scene surrounding him. Without the glare of the sun, there's an unfamiliar flatness to the surrounding foliage. It looks dulled.

'Ms . . .' The man glances down at the iPad, obviously trying to remind himself of her name. 'Ms Leger.'

'That's right.'

'I'm afraid I'm going to have to ask your group to pack up and leave your accommodation as soon as possible. There's been an . . .' He swallows, Adam's apple visibly bobbing. 'An incident. We need everyone to assemble at the main lodge.'

Hana looks at him, unnerved. 'What's happened?'

'I'm afraid that I can't share any more details, even if I had them.'

She starts to protest, but as the man nervously shifts from foot to foot, wiping his brow, she realizes that he's as shaken as she is. He's following instructions; no point grilling him. She nods. 'We'll get our things together and come up.'

'Thank you,' he replies, clearly relieved that she hasn't pushed back.

As she closes the door, she hears footsteps. Caleb appears, Jo behind him, a glazed expression on her face. Just the sight of her puts Hana on edge.

'I only caught the end of that. Didn't sound good.' Caleb

fiddles with his cap. It's turned backwards, a tuft of hair poking through the fastening at the front.

She nods, explains what the member of staff had told her.

'From bad to worse,' he says tightly. 'I just want to go. I haven't even told my mum yet, about Bea. I can't do this.' His voice splinters. 'Stay one more day on this bloody island. It's like some kind of torture.'

Jo's eyes flicker from him back to Hana. 'I'll keep going with the packing.' She's already turning. 'I've left my yoga things by the pool.'

Hana lightly grasps her arm. 'Hold on, I'll come with you. We need to talk.'

Jo eyes her warily, brow furrowed. 'What about?'

'Us, Jo,' Hana says heavily. 'You and me.'

65

Slowly, she turns in a circle. Steed does the same. 'No sign of any other disturbance,' he mutters.

Elin crouches down, scrutinizes the radio. The back cover is completely shattered, shards of plastic spilled in a wide circle around the radio itself.

'It would take significant force to do that,' she says uneasily. 'These radios are built to last, withstand heavy contact. This kind of damage wouldn't come from her simply dropping it. I don't like this. Given what Johnson said about her testimony. If our killer is aware Farrah knew Creacher wasn't responsible . . .'

Steed nods. 'Timing seems pretty bang on.'

Elin shakes her head. 'I shouldn't have taken Johnson's call, earlier, when she wanted to talk to me.'

'You weren't to know.'

'But what if it was about this case? . . . I'll call her.' Elin pulls out her phone, dials Farrah's number. It goes straight to voice mail. 'No answer. Let's check outside.'

Straightening up, she follows Steed through the open door. The outdoor area is a big space, as Farrah has the corner office, encompassing not just the back terrace but a portion of the side as well. Not a woodland view, but the sea, the islet with its dense thicket of trees. The growing bank of cloud is casting the islet into a dappled shade. The effect is curious, somehow isolating it from the rest of the vista, making it seem even more remote.

Steed steps down off the terrace on to the grass, where the land drops sharply away towards the cliff. 'Looks like there's access down to the rocks this way.'

She nods, noticing a handrail at the edge of the cliff – perhaps the start of steps. 'Any CCTV?'

Walking in a circle, Steed peers up at the building. 'Doesn't seem to be.'

Again, she feels a niggling sense of unease. 'Reckon someone could have gone unnoticed?'

'I'd say so. Pretty deserted around here. If you timed it right.'

She nods. 'Let's head in. Ask around.'

Back inside, they're only halfway across the room when her eyes alight on the bin beside Farrah's desk. From this angle, she picks up on something that wasn't visible as they entered. Among the crumpled paper and wrappers, there's a strip of card pressed against the wire mesh.

She tips her head. A photograph.

'Found something?' Steed asks.

Stopping beside the bin, Elin squats down to get a better look. 'I thought it was a photo, but it's too pixelated.'

He looks over her shoulder. 'A photocopy, from the looks of it. Maybe from a newspaper.'

'Could be.' Pulling a pair of gloves from her bag, Elin slips them on, gently tugging the strip out. No more than a few centimetres wide, it's been roughly torn, the edges ragged. While the image looks like a newspaper, the paper's far too thick. 'Definitely a photocopy.' Bringing it closer, she can make out not just one face now but several, one behind another, as if lined up for a group shot.

Elin flips it over but the back is blank. Curiosity piqued, she puts the first strip on Farrah's desk, then methodically starts fishing in the bin for the larger pieces of paper.

More strips, caught among the other rubbish. She lays them beside the first and carefully places them in order. Her hand wavers over the fourth strip as the image knits together: the faces, matching T-shirts, the old building looming behind.

'Looks like a photograph from one of the Outward Bound courses on the island.' Steed points. 'That's the school, isn't it, in the background?'

'Yeah.' One by one, she picks out the faces of what were assumed to be Creacher's victims, the same faces they'd discovered tacked to the wall of the cave. She swallows hard: it's unnerving – the cheery, carefree smiles of kids who had no idea what was coming.

Scouring the pixelated faces, she finds Farrah in the middle row, cap sitting slightly askew, looking directly at the camera.

Hard proof that she was there on the island during the Creacher killings.

'Why would she have this here?' Steed murmurs. 'And torn up like this . . .'

'Has to be connected to what's going on. Torn up because she probably doesn't want to shout about the fact she was on the island at the time. But if that's the case, why have a copy of it in the first place?' There's a glimmer in his eyes. 'Maybe the fact that it's a photo of the—'

'I get where you're going . . .'

'Perhaps she's also made a connection between what's going on and the Creacher murders. Refamiliarizing herself with the kids on the Outward Bound course.'

Steed narrows his eyes. 'She's recognized someone?'

'It's possible.' Looking back at the image, Elin's eyes move from face to face. Something stirs, a vague familiarity. The feeling nags at her until she's left with an overwhelming sense that her subconscious mind is trying to flag something.

But as she gathers the strips and puts them into a bag, she still can't place what it is.

'I'll take another look in the bin. She might have discarded something else.' Steed's already walking over.

He kneels down, thigh muscles visible through the thin fabric of his trousers. Elin watches as he carefully empties the contents on to the floor. A jumble of recyclables, empty snack wrappers, water bottles, typewritten documents.

'Doesn't look like anything else . . .' Steed tails off. 'Hold on.' He holds up a small scrap of paper. The page is lined, ragged edged, clearly torn from a notebook. 'There's writing on this. Pretty messy . . . It says . . . Rock House.' He tips the paper, screwing up his forehead. 'Yes, Rock House and then an *S*.'

'Rock House School,' Elin finishes uneasily, walking over.

'The writing hers?'

'Yes, I recognize it.'

'More digging?'

'Could be.' She frowns. 'This school . . . it's coming up everywhere. I'm wondering whether there's some kind of connection to the case.'

Steed raises an eyebrow. 'You reckon it might go further back than the Creacher murders?'

'Maybe.' She mulls it over. 'Might be just a coincidence, but the fact that it's in the bin with the photograph . . .'

He nods. 'Seeing this, I'm thinking about what the woman on reception mentioned. I wonder if the urgent thing was a ruse to draw her to her office?'

'Could be, but what would have pulled her back here?' Elin examines Farrah's desk. No sign of anything that might classify as urgent. It's all work related – training documents, health and safety protocols, stock overviews. She flips up the screen of Farrah's laptop, not expecting any luck: it's bound to be password protected.

But she doesn't need to go any further than the home screen. Elin's breath comes in one hard pull as a screen saver appears. Two sentences in a bold white font against a black background.

I KNOW WHAT YOU DID. I KNOW THAT YOU LIED.

66

A threat. It's the only interpretation.

A heavy pressure settles on Elin's chest.

'Looks like someone else thinks she lied in her testimony,' Steed murmurs.

'Yes.' She's unable to take her eyes off the blocky letters. 'The timing of this . . . it can't be a coincidence. If someone's threatening her now and it *does* refer to her testimony, it's more proof that this case links to the Creacher murders.'

Steed gives her a sideways glance. 'They always say, don't they, that a lie comes out in the end.'

She nods, knowing there's only one reason for Farrah to tell a lie of that magnitude. She had something so important to hide that she was willing to take Creacher down in the process.

A false conviction will have huge ramifications for this investigation.

Only one person might know what Farrah lied about.

'You're sure she's not somewhere else in the retreat?' Will's voice is muted, and while he might have been able to conceal how he was feeling had it been an ordinary call, the rapid blinks, the tight set to his jaw, visible on FaceTime, give him away.

'I'm certain. We've spoken to all the staff, they've radioed out. No one's seen her. Her phone keeps going to voice mail. I've got people looking inside and Steed's taken a group out to search the immediate vicinity.'

'Maybe she's taking a break, overwhelmed by what's going on.'

Elin hesitates, wanting to offer reassurances but unable to. After seeing the inside of that cave, she's frightened for Farrah. For Will. 'I'm sorry, but I don't think so.' She takes a breath. 'Will, the reason I'm concerned is because things have escalated. The deaths this weekend, we're pretty sure they're not accidental. Possibly linked to the Creacher murders.'

A pause, his face conflicted as he processes it. 'And you think' – he falters – 'you think Farrah going missing is related?'

'I'm not sure.' Elin clears her throat – a delay tactic. It's hard to find the words for what she's about to do: break open a decades-old lie, expose it to the light. 'Will, when Steed and I went to her office, we found a torn-up photograph in the bin of when Farrah was on the island as a kid. One of the Outward Bound courses.'

His face freezes. For a moment Elin thinks the signal has dropped, but no. A sudden intake of breath. 'So you know.'

She nods. 'It wasn't just the photo. I spoke to a detective who worked the Creacher case. He told me that Farrah's testimony was a key part of the prosecution's case.'

Will's gaze shifts away from the screen to the floor. A long silence, before he finally looks back. 'I'll be honest, all this is something I hoped would never come up. Farrah was traumatized by the whole thing. Still is. One of the few topics we don't really speak about.' The idea jars as his family always make a thing of their openness: *We don't hide things. We talk.* He looks back to her. 'If you knew what she went through . . .'

'I'm sorry,' she says quietly.

'Not your fault. They should never have bloody let kids on that island with that creep. People had reported him, you know? Years before the attack. The sicko had been photographing the kids while they were at the camp.'

Elin hates hearing the pain in his voice. It's still raw for him. 'I get it, but you can't blame yourself. Every family will have felt the same. Easy to say in hindsight.'

He meets her gaze. 'I know what you're about to ask. Why I pressed the button on LUMEN, why Farrah would want to work there.'

She shakes her head. 'You don't have to explain. People cope with trauma in all sorts of ways.'

'No, I want to tell you, explain why we were so touchy the other night. LUMEN, it was meant to be a fresh start for us both. When our team got the job, at first I couldn't even contemplate working on it, but in the end, I decided to put my hand up, turn the negative into a positive. I never imagined Farrah would want to work there herself, but when she suggested it, I thought, *That's my sister*. Doesn't run from a fight, but towards it. Ballsy.'

He's right, but Elin knows all too well that there's a fine line between ballsy and stupid. If it becomes a trigger . . . She hesitates. 'Look, I know this is hard, but we found something else, an odd screen saver on her laptop. Pretty threatening. Something along the lines of *I know what you did. I know that you lied.*' His face darkens. 'I'm wondering whether this note and Farrah's disappearance link to her testimony. The fact that I found a photo from her time on the island as well—'

'I don't get it,' Will says flatly.

'Maybe what it's implying about her lying connects in some

way to her testimony.' She stumbles over her words, hearing how it must sound.

'Ahh, now I understand.' He makes a small noise in his throat. 'Just come out and say it. You're asking if Farrah lied in her statement.'

'No,' Elin says quickly, floundering. *She's doing this wrong.* 'I'm just wondering if there's something about that night that she might have had doubts over.'

'Elin, stop. I can read between the lines. You've found this note and you've done what you always do with people. Immediately seen the worst.'

She doesn't reply right away, not because he isn't right; she *is* judgemental, but that's not the case here. 'This isn't about judging Farrah, it's about trying to find her. If she *did* lie, then it's important, because her testimony was central to Creacher's conviction. If that conviction was based on a lie, then it might mean he wasn't responsible. If that's the case, it means that whoever was might still be out there. On the island now.'

Will briefly closes his eyes. When he opens them, his expression is resigned. 'You're right. Farrah did lie about Creacher in her testimony, but it's not for whatever messed up reason you think. It's because of me.'

'You?' Her hand tightens around the phone, fingertips briefly eclipsing Will's face.

'Yes. Farrah did lie, but it was nothing to do with her. She did it to protect me.'

67

'So what exactly do you want to talk about?'

'Like I said, you and me.' Hana raises her voice above the strengthening sound of the wind. It's pulling at the tops of the pines overhanging the pool, making them shift and sway above them. 'And Liam?'

'Liam?' Jo echoes, walking around the pool. Bending at the waist, she rolls up her yoga mat, tucks it under one arm.

'Yes, Liam. I know what happened.' Hana's proud of herself then. Proud of how calm she is. In control. She knows now she'll remain steely throughout this conversation, won't be easily swayed by Jo's charm and easy patter. 'I know it all, how you lied. All this time.'

'You know it *all*.' Jo's voice stutters, misfires. 'How?'

'You don't need to know *how*. You just have to know that I know what you did.' Hana doesn't recognize her own voice, the deadened quality of each word.

The breeze gusts, jerking the half-open window behind them shut with a thud. There's a wild fear in Jo's eyes, her mouth twisting into an odd shape.

Then the words start coming out: 'Han, please, you have to know that I didn't mean to leave him. I panicked. I knew he was dead, I did. I wouldn't have left him if I wasn't certain. I'd have called an ambulance, stayed. But he was gone, I knew he

258

was. I keep going over it – wish I hadn't cycled away to do the other jump or persuaded him to come with me, but he was stubborn, said he wanted to try it again. I was out of sight, but I heard it. This thud ...' Jo briefly closes her eyes. 'I went straight back, and I swear, I checked to see if he was breathing, but he was gone, and I was going to tell you, but I couldn't. How could I?' She's wrapped her arms around herself, is doing a strange rocking motion, backwards and forwards on her heels.

Hana stares at her sister and feels a funny fizzing in her head. The awful heat that was there before, morphing into something colder, darker. 'You were *what*?' She has no idea where it's come from – this self-control that she's managed to muster. 'You were there when Liam died? At the bike park?'

'But that's what you're saying, isn't it?' Jo's face pales. Beads of sweat are dotting her forehead. 'That you knew it all. That I was with him when the accident happened.'

A horrible, weighty silence.

'No,' Hana says eventually. 'I found out about the affair, the *fling*, whatever it was. That was it.' The words are like acid in her mouth. 'Not *this*. That you were with him when he died and then you *left* him.'

She can't absorb it. She's played out Liam's final moments so many times in her head, forensically picked over the reports, it's as if she were there as it happened. This new narrative doesn't work, the pictures she's clung to now grinding to a juddering halt in her head.

'I panicked, Han, that's all it was, and I promise I've tried to tell you so many times, but there's no way I could have done it right after he died, and every moment since, it wouldn't happen. I'd open my mouth or start writing a letter and the words wouldn't come.' Jo drags her gaze up to meet hers. 'I never wanted to tell you like this, you have to know that. It's the last thing I wanted. I planned to do it properly, but Bea's accident, and then Seth . . .' Tears are forming in her eyes. 'There was never the right moment.'

'Bea knew, didn't she?' Hana watches a tiny insect crawl up the underside of the yoga mat towards Jo's hand.

Jo nods, a jerky, puppetlike movement. 'Yes. She saw a photo on my phone of the two of us together. A few weeks ago she confronted me and it all came out. She said I had to tell you. I promised I would, said I'd do it here, on the holiday. That night, when Bea got to the island, she called me, asked if I'd done it.'

'And that's when you went to meet her, wasn't it? It was you who left the villa that night.'

'You knew it was me?' Jo's grip on the yoga mat tightens.

'Caleb overheard you talking to Seth.'

As the insect on the mat reaches her thumb, Jo looks down, flicks it away. 'She asked me to meet her there. I've no idea why she wanted to talk there and then. She was in an odd mood, kept going on about needing to make things right, telling the truth.' She frowns. 'But we cleared it up, I promise. I told Bea I'd tell you the next day and she seemed happy with that.'

'And you definitely left her on the beach?'

'Yes. She said she was going to get her stuff and then come to the villa. She still wanted it to be a surprise for the rest of you.'

'But what about this?' Hana pulls Bea's broken phone from her pocket. 'I found it in your room.' Her voice cracks. 'You took her phone, Jo. Something we might have been able to give to the police. You destroyed it, took the memory card. Why would you do that?'

Jo looks at her, stricken. 'I didn't destroy it. It was like that when I found it, the morning Bea was discovered. I saw it under one of the planters near the yoga pavilion. The memory card was gone when I picked it up.'

Hana mulls over her words, a thought edging out from the corner of her mind. 'So that's what you were looking for when I saw you by the pavilion after I spoke to the detective. You knew what people would think if they realized you'd met Bea that night, the messages between you. How it would seem, out of context.'

Jo flinches at the words. 'Yes, and I feel shitty about it, Han, but I didn't know what else to do. I never found the memory card, honestly. Either it's still there somewhere or it was taken by whoever smashed the phone in the first place.' She meets Hana's gaze. 'I acted stupidly, impulsively, like I always do, but I'd never hurt Bea, Han. You know that.'

'But you'd *leave* Liam . . .' Hana's never had a noise inside her brain like this before, this loud buzzing. It's as if her skull is filled with a teeming mass of tiny, angry flies.

Jo doesn't reply, just steps towards her, but Hana edges away, on to the grass.

'You left him, Jo,' Hana spits out. The buzzing inside her head is morphing into a strange kind of electric energy. 'You left him there, to die.'

She thinks of all of the moments prior to Liam's accident and after it when Jo could have told her. All the moments on the way to the hospital, the way home, at the funeral. The weeks that came after.

Moment after moment seared upon her brain and Jo has taken them all and she will never remember them without hate again.

But the worst thing that Jo's stolen from her is the only thing she really has left, the most precious thing of all.

Her memory of Liam.

'You think you can get away with this? Stealing everything from me? Because that's what you do. Take everything.'

'I don't know what you mean . . .' Jo can't look at her and Hana knows why. Jo, more than anyone, knows that it's a pattern – Jo steals from people, always has. Jo stole her hobbies, her friends, and made them hers. And for a short while, Jo would feel better about herself simply because she'd beaten someone.

'I'll tell you.' Hana lists them all, coldly, brutally: petty things that only a sister would remember or find important. Hana tells Jo about the barbed comments she always makes, how she took up ice-skating just because Hana did, and how she practised and practised until she was better than Hana. How she'd talk over Bea when she did well at something and how she'd try to drop in a sly negative when someone else had something good to say.

The words keep coming. Hana's hot when she finishes speaking, her skull pounding.

Jo is watching her, silent, but her body language – shoulders sagging, head hanging low – says it all. *It's hit home.* Finally something has penetrated the barrier.

'I'm sorry,' she says finally, her voice muffled by tears. 'I'm so, so sorry.'

It's actually the worst thing she can say: Hana wants something meaty in return, something she can toy with and rebut. She doesn't want Jo's apologies, because there's pity in that and that's the last thing she wants. Pity makes her feel silly and small, and she wants to wipe it off Jo's face.

Hana doesn't plan what happens next, and she surprises even herself because she has never been physical – has always been the one to run away from conflict and not towards it. Bea and Jo were more likely to scrap it out, wrestle on the sofa, but never her.

Striding forwards, Hana roughly grabs Jo's wrist. 'But I don't think you are sorry.'

Jo recoils. 'Stop, you're hurting me.' She tries to twist away, mascara now smudged in watery black streaks beneath her eyes.

'No,' Hana replies. The buzzing in her head, the black flies, are taking over. 'I want you to say it properly.'

'Please, Han,' Jo pleads, trying to dislodge her hand. 'You're scaring me.'

But it's as if Hana can't hear her. Looking at Jo's face, the fear in her eyes, all Hana can concentrate on is the feeling this is giving her, a heady sense of power.

'Han . . .'

But Hana's silent.

She squeezes harder on Jo's wrist, so hard that she can feel the rigid line of bone beneath her sister's skin.

68

'You.'

It's all that Elin can manage. There's a strange, slippery feeling beneath her breastbone, an internalized sensation of the rug being pulled from beneath her feet.

'Yes, but she was protecting me, Elin. Being the big sister.' His voice breaks.

Elin tries to collect herself. *Don't judge. You're in no position to judge.* 'So what happened?' she says softly. 'When she was out there?'

'When *we* were out there. I was on the island that week too. Farrah's year group and mine were small, so we went together.'

She frowns. 'But the photo I found . . . you weren't in it.'

'That was of Farrah's year, not mine.' Will pauses. 'The night of the murders, I was with Thea, one of the girls, when she was attacked. We'd wandered into the woods, Thea took herself off to pee. I didn't even have a chance to turn my back when, out of nowhere, someone hit her.' He falters. 'Hit her again and again, and I . . .' A fleeting grimace. 'I ran. Left her there.'

Elin gropes for reassurances, but it's hard because she's thrown by what he's saying. 'You were scared,' she says finally. 'Wanted to help, but thought he'd attack you too.'

'No.' Will's voice is flat. 'I didn't even think about helping her. Can't even say it entered my head. I ran. What you were saying the other day about being a coward, you weren't, that day with Sam. You froze, but you didn't run. I saved myself over helping Thea. I still think about all the what-ifs. If I'd tried to defend her ...' He shakes his head, the pain evident in his eyes.

'I understand. I did the same,' she says quietly. 'Kept going over it, making it play out a different way.'

He nods. 'After it happened, I hid for a while. When I came out, there was no one there, only this stone on the sand. It was odd, it had been shaped to look like the rock.' Elin's pulse quickens. *Shaped*, like the stones in the cave. 'I picked it up – that's when someone attacked me from behind. I couldn't see properly, but I got glimpses of a dark cloak, the hood pulled over their face.'

A cloak: like the one they found in the cave.

What he's told her proves, beyond doubt, the connection between the two cases.

'Somehow, I got past them, ran back through the woods. That's when I found her, still there, in the clearing.' Will clasps a hand over his mouth. 'There was so much blood, and she was so still, Elin. Unnatural. I stayed there for a while, part of me hoping she'd wake up, say it was all a joke, but in the end, I knew.' A sob emerges from behind his hand. 'Eventually, I made my way back to camp to tell the teachers, but then I saw Josh and David's tent slashed, and you could see, even from outside, that they were dead. The stone I found ...' His voice pitches higher. 'It was lying beside them, covered in blood. I thought, I thought—'

'That it was the same one you found on the beach.' Elin fills in the gap. She knows where this is going.

He nods. Another hiccupy sob. 'I assumed I'd dropped it on the beach, so when I saw it there, I thought the worst. Knew my fingerprints would be on it. I panicked and grabbed it.'

'And that's when you told Farrah?'

'Yes. She said that I couldn't say anything, that my DNA would be all over the stone, and when they found Thea, they'd think it was me. Farrah hid it in the woods.'

Elin nods, one thing still bothering her about this story – the idea that the killer had brought the stone to the tent, to the scene of the crime. There's no evidence, as far as she can tell, that the killer did this with Bea Leger and Seth Delaney.

Is it important, a deviation, or does it imply something else?

'So when did Farrah decide to make the statement about Creacher?'

'After he was arrested. Farrah said we couldn't be sure that the police wouldn't find any other evidence linking back to me, so she came up with the idea of saying she'd seen Creacher lurking about by the tents.'

'It was Farrah's idea?'

'Yes, but she only said what she did because we thought Creacher *was* responsible. The lie was meant to cement what the police already suspected. We weren't thinking about the consequences.' Will drags his gaze up to meet hers, shaking his head. 'I should have said something when you started investigating, but I didn't even want to consider that there might be a connection.'

'Don't blame yourself. I can see it would have been hard to go there, and with Creacher in prison . . .' But saying the words, a seed of doubt creeps in. *This was about protecting him and Farrah.*

'I have to, if Farrah's lie for me has to do with her going missing.' He shakes his head. 'I should have faced it, told the police. You were right when you said you couldn't paper over the past, but I've been doing it my whole life. The retreat, my name—'

'Your *name*?'

He nods. 'I changed it after it happened. Parents did the full

266

deed poll thing. I kept having these nightmares, Thea calling out my name. It was Oliver, but she always called me Ollie.' Tears are welling in his eyes, and he brings a hand up to wipe them away.

Ollie. Elin has the strange, jarring sensation of her life being balanced on what are now unstable foundations.

'So if Creacher wasn't the killer, then you think whoever was' – he visibly swallows – 'whoever was, they might have . . . Farrah . . .'

She nods. 'I'm sorry, but yes, it's possible.'

'But if Creacher didn't kill Thea, my other friends, then why would the killer come after Farrah now? What Farrah did helped them, surely? Planted suspicion even more firmly on Creacher.'

'I don't know what their motive is yet. Given the photograph in her bin, I'm thinking that maybe she's done some digging, recognized someone. If that's the case, then they probably recognized her too. This might be their way of warning her off.'

'Do you think you're going to be able to find her?' There's desperation in his voice. 'I've got to tell Mum and Dad and I want to give them something positive.'

'I'll do everything I can, you know that, but with two of us, and the location . . . it isn't easy . . .' She pauses. 'Will, do you remember anything about the person who attacked Thea?'

'I wish I did.' His voice is subdued. 'All I know is that they were strong, and that they'd have killed me if they could. I could feel the violence, somehow, emanating from them. That's what stayed with me, even after all these years. That . . . brutality.'

'I'm so sorry,' she says quietly. 'And I hate to have to make you relive it again, but one last question: did anyone mention anything about the school? The detective said the kids during the Creacher case were scared of going into the old school building, and we've found reference to it in Farrah's things.'

A long pause, then Will nods. 'People were talking about it from the moment we set foot on the island. Rumours. Someone said that they knew someone who'd been to the school, that the teachers were obsessed with the rock. Used to take the kids into this room . . .'

Elin's skin prickles. 'What kind of room?'

'They didn't give any more detail. You know what it's like at that age. Probably all hearsay.'

She's silent. *Hearsay.*

Will might be right, but after everything she's learnt about the place, she's not so sure.

69

'What's wrong? I heard shouting,' Caleb says as Hana makes her way into her room. He stops beside her in the doorway, rucksack already fastened over his shoulders. It's too tight: the straps are pulling up his T-shirt, revealing several inches of pale stomach.

'Jo,' Hana says flatly, bumping her case around the door.

His face softens. 'Upset about Seth?'

'Actually, no.' Hana glances down, finding it hard to articulate her thoughts. 'A bit of a bombshell. I found out she was having an affair with Liam, and' – her voice catches – 'she told me that she was with him . . . when he died.' She falters, unable to stop her mind from going there again; picturing the two of them together.

Caleb baulks. '*With* him?'

'Yes, they were cycling together. Jo saw the accident and she left him to it. Never told anyone.' She has to bite down on her lip to stop herself from crying. 'Keeping the affair secret was obviously more important.'

'Oh, God.' He shakes his head, lip curling. Hana knows what he's thinking: none of this is a surprise. It's pretty clear that Caleb has low expectations of their family, particularly Jo. 'I'm so sorry,' he says quietly. 'I never met Liam, but I knew what you two had. I can't even begin to imagine how you're feeling.'

Hana nods, and although she wasn't planning on saying it, some horrible part of her wants him to understand, just a tiny bit, the emotions swirling inside her. *Share the burden.* 'It wasn't the only thing she fessed up to. I found Bea's phone in her room. She admitted to taking it.'

'*Bea's* phone?' His voice is shaking.

'What's left of it. It's smashed up. Jo said she found it like that, got a glimpse of it near the yoga pavilion when the forensic guy was searching.'

'And her first instinct wasn't to give it to the detective?'

'Apparently not. She said there was stuff on there she didn't want getting out. About Liam.'

'But by doing that—'

'I know.'

Silence stretches out between them. 'You buy it?' Caleb says eventually. 'That she just found it there?'

Hana shrugs, silent, but she doesn't need to say anything. As she meets his gaze, yet again, words pass between them, unspoken.

'Where's Jo now?' Caleb breaks the silence.

'Packing the last of her stuff.'

'And Maya?'

'In her room. I said I'd meet her there to walk up.' Hana frowns. 'She's thrown, I think, by the whole thing.'

'Aren't we all? You know, when I googled this place, after Jo first sent through the details, I laughed at all the conspiracy theories, but now . . .'

Hana nods numbly. 'I know.' It would have happened eventually, she thinks: the fallout from all these lies, whether they'd come to the island or not. But still, she can't help feeling robbed, like the island keeps taking from them and will continue to take until they have nothing left to give.

'Storm's set in pretty bad.' Caleb glances out the window. 'Not going to be a nice walk up.'

He's right, she thinks, following his gaze. Everything suddenly feels dark and melancholy, the clouds growing not just in number but in size – obliterating the blue. The strengthening breeze has already transformed the once-tranquil setting into chaos – tiny branches now littering the terrace, flattened imprints of blossoms marking the smooth expanse of stone.

Hana's about to turn away when the wind gusts. A sudden sharp crack, a blistering movement.

Caleb flinches.

They watch, frozen, as a large branch from the pine above plummets to the ground.

An amputation; the raw, white innards of the branch exposed where it's been brutally wrenched from the tree.

Neither of them speak.

They simply stare at the branch as it writhes from side to side in the wind before a ferocious gust sends it tumbling past the window, lifting it up in the air before dropping it again.

An ugly, tortuous dance.

70

Elin recounts to Steed what Will told her, her eyes darting between the staff and remaining guests swelling the lobby.

The work that Farrah started is in full swing: staff shepherding guests towards the corridor at the back of reception. The lobby is ringing with sound. Voices. Suitcase wheels. The erratic slap-slap of sandals on the floor.

'And Will didn't get anything identifiable on who attacked him?' Steed asks, his eyes tracking the frenzied movements of a group of guests near by. They're arguing about something, a man pointing down at his case.

'No.'

Steed frowns a little. 'Well, bad news on that front. I pulled a favour, got someone to run those names through the database . . . but no joy. It's pulled up nothing apart from Farrah, and obviously we're aware of that.'

'Should have known it wouldn't be that easy.'

He nods. 'I think it's worth going back to basics. Speaking to everyone who's left, see if anything comes up about the last few days. Someone might have witnessed something without knowing it was significant.'

'Good idea. Same for Farrah. Someone might have—'

But she doesn't get to finish her sentence.

'Still no sign of Farrah?'

It's Jared, the supervisor. His angular face is puckered with worry.

'Afraid not. We've searched the immediate vicinity . . . nothing.'

'Should we widen the search? There's staff we can spare. Most of the remaining guests are already here, and the others are on their way.' Jared casts an anxious look outside at the growing mass of clouds, the fine spits of rain now pocking the window. 'The storm's really coming in now. If she's out there on her own . . .'

Elin glances outside. She's stuck: do as he says and they risk staff safety. Do nothing and the odds of finding Farrah narrow further. If they *were* to extend the search, the quarry and cave are an obvious place to start, but she can't let anyone go that far.

'No, I don't think—' Her words are lost amid the loud crackle from Jared's radio, a sudden flurry of speech.

'Hello?' He brings the radio up close to his ear. 'Can you repeat yourself?'

The person does, but it's still inaudible.

Whoever's calling must be outside, voice blurred by the howling of the wind.

'Let me go somewhere quieter.' Jared slips behind the reception desk into the small room behind.

Hovering outside, Elin shifts from foot to foot, nerves playing in her stomach.

A few moments later, he emerges from behind the desk. 'One of the staff has found a bag on the rocks. Says it looks like Farrah's.'

'I'll go.' Elin turns to Steed. 'You start speaking to the staff.'

When Elin steps outside, it's like walking into another world.

The dull scene of just a few moments ago has become something wilder, more desolate, clouds scudding across the sky, the sea crested with white foaming peaks.

273

'He still down there?' she calls.

'Yes.' Jared runs ahead towards the steps down to the beach.

Elin follows. When they reach the beach, a gust of wind grabs a layer of sand and flings it into her face. She rubs at her eyes as Jared leads her left, past the beach shack. It's been locked up, but in a hurry – one of the freestanding kayak racks has been left out. The wind is rattling it, kayaks shifting from side to side on their rests.

'There he is.' Jared raises a hand, points.

Looking up, Elin sees a member of staff beside the rocks, raising a hand in the air in greeting. It's Michael Zimmerman. He's wearing a thin raincoat, unzipped, the rounded dome of his belly pulling at his polo shirt. Once again, that sense of recognition flares.

Why can't she place him?

It takes a few minutes to reach him and when they finally stop beside him, both Elin and Jared are breathing heavily.

'I haven't touched anything.' Michael gestures to the bag. 'As soon as I saw it, I radioed.' He shakes his head. 'Don't understand it. We searched this right at the beginning. Nothing was here.'

Elin follows his gaze to the tote bag lying half on the rocks and half on the beach. It's open, spilling its guts on to the sand – a brush, a sunglasses case, a battered tube of sun cream – but it's not the contents that catch her attention, it's the bag itself. The tan colour, the wide strap . . . it's Farrah's, she's certain.

But why would it be here, of all places? It's possible that the attacker dumped it, but why *this* location? From here, all she can see is water. A wide expanse of grey-blue, getting angrier by the minute.

Her thoughts swirl. There's nowhere to go from here other than off the island. Could the placement of the bag be deliberate? Some kind of set-up or diversion?

Or had Farrah run, scared by the threat? It's not implausible that she'd found a way to leave.

There's also another possibility – and her heart drops as she considers it. Had Farrah gone off of her own accord, for a more sinister reason? She can't prove that Farrah didn't put that screen saver in place to confuse them.

At this stage, she can't discount the idea that Farrah might be involved in some capacity. Farrah lied to the police and they have only Will's word as to why. Perhaps something happened that he isn't aware of, something Farrah was desperate to keep hidden, and so lied in her testimony? Could her questions about the school relate to that?

Her mind teases apart the different scenarios as she wriggles her phone from her pocket. Crouching down, she takes a photograph of the bag as they found it, before pulling on a new pair of gloves, sifting through the contents. Items she recognizes: sunglasses case, hairbrush, planner. She's about to zip the bag back up when she notices a piece of paper protruding askew from the address book.

Her pulse picks up.

A torn edge. The same as the paper from the notebook in Farrah's office.

As she carefully unfolds it, her eyes lock on the handwriting at the very top. Again, the same.

Farrah's: the last part of the word on the piece of paper they'd found in the bin.

The word is now complete: *School.*

She was right: Farrah had written down the name of Rock House School.

But that's not the only thing on the page.

Her eyes move down. Another name below it.

Michael Zimmerman.

71

Elin keeps her back turned, the piece of paper flapping against her fingers in the breeze.

Rock House School. Michael Zimmerman.

Part of her had known somehow that the school was connected to this case, to the Creacher murders too. Clearly Farrah had come to the same conclusion. But how does it link to Michael? Fear prickles the back of her neck as she remembers him watching her.

Slowly, she turns to him, holding the paper out in front of her. 'I've found this, in Farrah's bag. She's made a note referring to the old school . . . your name is under it. Do you know what it means?'

Michael glances down at the paper and then nods. 'She was doing some research, as far as I could gather.' *Farrah was doing some digging of her own.* Looking at Jared, Michael lowers his voice to a murmur. 'But look, what she told me, I don't think it was meant for public consumption.'

Elin steps away, so they're out of earshot of Jared. 'If it's about the fact she was on the island at the time of the Creacher murders, I'm already aware.'

Michael's shoulders relax. He nods. 'She was asking what I knew about the school. Said someone had put the fear of God into her and her friends about the place when they came to the island for the Outward Bound course, but she'd never really understood what it was all about. The curse, she got, but not the connection to the school. Said it had always bothered her.'

'Did she say who it was who spoke to her?'

He shakes his head.

Elin looks back down at the piece of paper, her thoughts whirling. If Farrah *was* trying to get information about the school, then surely it indicates that it plays a role in this case. 'And why did she come to you?'

'Farrah overheard me talking to that guest, the one I mentioned to you, the artist, who'd been to the school. She thought I might know something.'

'And I take it you do?' Her question is punctuated by a shrill shriek from a gull swooping overhead.

There's no reply at first, before he nods. 'When we spoke before, I didn't quite give you the whole story. The artist, he was actually pretty emotional, seeing his piece in situ.' He tugs at his cap, a slight grimace on his face. 'We got talking and he opened up a little about what went on at the school. Pretty odd punishments, from what I gathered.'

'In what way?'

'Said there was a room, hidden away, that they used to take the kids to. I didn't probe, but he looked haunted, you know?' Michael shakes his head. 'I knew it had to be pretty bad if it was still tearing him up, all these years later.'

Elin absorbs his words, heart starting to thud in her chest. *A room. Like Will mentioned. Could this be somewhere they've taken Farrah?* 'Did he say anything else?'

A beat of hesitation. 'Not explicitly, no, but the person I told you about, that I saw walking near the rock at night? It was the artist. When I clocked it was him, I wondered if he was all right, after what he told me, so I went out there, after him. I was about to approach him, but then he walked away, went *past* the rock.'

'*Past* it?' Her heart starts to beat a little faster. 'There's only woodland there, isn't there?'

'Yeah, that's what got me wondering. I followed.' Michael pauses. 'He went a little way into the woods, to some kind of old bunker structure. I wondered if it was the room he'd mentioned, figured he might be trying to get some kind of closure.'

'Did you tell Farrah this?'

'I did, but when I showed her, she found, like I did, that nothing's there. Definitely a bunker from what I could make out. When the retreat was built, the construction team blocked it in. Chucked half a ton of concrete down the steps leading there from the looks of it.'

Elin's heart sinks. 'There's no way someone could access it now? No other entrance points?'

'Not unless they've excavated it. It's fully blocked. I can show you if you like.'

Worth checking, she thinks, *but it sounds like a dead end in more ways than one.* 'Thank you for being so honest.'

He nods. 'Of course.'

Elin turns her attention back to the bag, frustrated. What Michael's told her indicates they're on the right track, assuming Farrah's been doing some digging of her own, but it still doesn't explain either where Farrah is now or why her bag would be here.

Bending down, she picks up the bag. 'We need to get back. This storm's picking up.' As if on cue, the wind gusts, sand blown in gritty bursts towards them. She shivers. 'Let's go.'

The relief on Jared's and Michael's faces is clear. They don't want to be here any more than she does.

Halfway across the beach, their walk is punctuated by another, more violent surge of wind. *It's picked up a notch*, she thinks warily. There's an ominous creaking. Tipping up her head, she sees the trees on the cliff above bowing in the wind, trunks bending at an impossible angle.

'Let's pick up the pace,' she says, rounding the corner. 'I think—' Elin stops abruptly.

A splash of bright white in the sand beneath the overhang of the cliff.

She breaks into a jog, her eyes picking out a definitive shape: a profile. Head, torso, legs.

A flash of pale blonde hair.

72

Elin sprints across the beach, fine spits of rain hitting her full in the face. Blinking them away, she stops just before the overhang, gasping for breath. Here, the cliff face has been carved away, striated with deep grooves, to form a natural lip. Just in front, blood marks the sand, little wells of red, then a messy arc of spray and spatter.

Her eyes catch the furrows of sand behind, blurred echoes of footprints.

The blood is pounding out in her ears as she assesses; *Farrah was attacked here, then dragged under the overhang.*

Stepping forward, Elin ducks her head – a semi-crouch until she's under the rocky lip.

The first thing to hit her is the smell – not just the saline dampness, the mustiness of undisturbed sand; but the metallic tang of blood.

Strong enough to overpower all the other odours.

The small space is throbbing with a blisteringly violent energy, a siren call telling her: *something terrible has happened here.*

A rolling wave of nausea hits, but Elin forces herself to look at Farrah: fair hair, bloodstained creases of her white shirt.

Desperate, she looks for any movement, any signs of life.

Despite the blood and the body's position, Elin is still holding on to a thread of hope that Farrah might still be alive.

She circles the body until she can see her face.

It's not Farrah.

73

I t's Jo Leger.

Her eyes are closed, but she looks anything but peaceful. A huge bloody contusion has burst open the skin above her right eye. The skull above is caved in, the surrounding hair messy and tangled with a gritty liquid mix of blood and sand.

The white top that Elin had mistaken for Farrah's shirt is speckled with sand, smeared drops of blood alternating with spatter.

It's obvious now that she knows it's Jo – the harder musculature of her limbs, darker skin tone. Only superficial similarities.

Stepping forwards for a closer look, Elin can't stop swallowing, her throat impossibly dry.

She tugs on a pair of gloves, reaching out a hand to Jo's neck to feel for a pulse. As her fingers rest there, her breath is high in her chest in anticipation, but the skin gives her nothing, only a residual warmth.

Her heart drops. *Jo's dead, but hasn't been for long.*

Michael must have been close by when he discovered the bag, and she and Jared, too, had been in striking distance when they'd run to meet him. The stakes are inevitably raised; a killer who has shed their fear of being discovered – or the consequences – is capable of anything.

Elin carefully examines the wound. Cause of death seems to be blunt force trauma to the skull. But where's the weapon?

Her eyes dart around the enclosed space, the area outside. No sign of any kind of implement.

But still, a glimmer of hope: their choice of Jo as a victim has revealed something fundamental.

Three deaths from the same group of people. Bea. Seth. Jo. What might have been rationalized before as a coincidence now seems to be a pattern.

Why this specific group of victims?

After seeing the set-up in the cave, they'd been leaning towards the idea that the victim selection might be random, circumstantial, tallying with the group of teenagers the killer had chosen before, but now she wonders if it is in fact more deliberate.

While the killer's motive might still stem from a delusional belief about the curse or Reaper's Rock, they might also have reason to target this particular group.

'Farrah?'

Elin jumps, but it's only Jared, stood outside the overhang, Michael behind him.

'No,' she says quickly. 'It's a guest.'

He steps back, visibly shaken. 'Is she . . .?'

'Yes. Not long.' After taking some photographs, Elin edges her way back from under the overhang. Jared asks her another question, but his words are drowned out by the noise of the ever-growing storm.

It's as though the island, silent and still for so long, has finally found its voice – a voice sounding out through the sea and rain and the whistling of the wind, an angry caterwauling of gulls.

The energy that was only simmering before – the faint crackle – has become a roar.

'Shall we go?' Jared's voice jerks her from her reverie.

Elin nods, an insistent pulse of fear thudding in her chest. She needs to get an update on backup and then speak to the group – what's left of them.

Hana, Maya, Caleb.

It's time to push harder.

74

'Sorry, Elin, no more levers I can pull, I've tried. Fire and rescue are still in the process of evacuating, but they're nearly there. A few hours, I'm hoping.'

'But Farrah's still missing.' Elin hears the desperation in her voice. Things have changed. Surely Anna understands that. 'We need more resources, to search.' Her gaze moves to the window. The glass walls opposite are streaming with rainwater, the movement blurring with the shapes of the staff around her, distributing a makeshift dinner of sandwiches and fruit.

'I get it, but there's nothing I can say except sit tight. We'll be with you as soon as we can.'

'Okay. I'll keep in touch.' It takes all her willpower to drive some positivity into her tone. Moments like this – and there are always moments like this in an investigation – when things don't go your way: this is when you show your mettle. She needs to draw on the strength she felt earlier.

'Guess it's a no-can-do?' Steed says heavily as she says goodbye.

'For now, yes. They're still snowed under. Looks like we're in for a long night.'

'At least we've got a plan.' But the confidence in his tone is belied by the concern marring his face.

He's scared too. Doesn't want to show it.

She nods. 'First, we need to speak to what's left of the Leger group. Get some answers.'

'Two from the same group, you might still be looking at coincidence, but three . . .'

'Yep. I think there's a reason why the killer's targeting them. Has to be.'

Steed looks past her at the member of staff who's clearly scoping out the sandwich offering. 'But doesn't that mess with the whole Reaper motivation?'

'Might do. It's tricky. If there is some overall plan to take out this group, it suggests something very personal. But then those teenagers' deaths back in the day – and Jo's murder on the beach – imply someone more delusional, acting on impulse.' Her mind flip-flops.

Steed runs a hand over his forehead. 'The differences could be the result of erratic taking of meds. More lucid at some points than others.'

'Or even two different people working together.' Elin chews on her lip. 'I just can't square it away. Everything we found in the cave and the issues with Creacher's conviction imply it's the same killer, but the anomalies bother me. The different levels of planning, why those stones were near the teenagers' bodies, yet no sign of them here . . .'

He shrugs. 'Perhaps the selection of those kids *was* more intentional than we know.'

'True, but then what's the connection between them and the Legers?'

'It might just be coincidence they're from the same group,' Steed says slowly. 'There aren't many people left on the island. The killer could be opportunistic.'

'Perhaps. I just feel like we're missing something, particularly about the school.'

'But how does that fit with the Legers?' Steed frowns. 'Unless they're extremely genetically blessed, they weren't alive when that school was around.'

'I know. I think it's worth double-checking to see if any of them have ties to the school.'

'Well, we can ask them now.' Steed nods to the door. 'They've just arrived.'

75

'I'll do it,' Elin says, but as she speaks her voice splinters, the weight of the news she's about to impart suddenly overwhelming. It's as if the sight of Hana, Caleb, and Maya has breached the barrier she's had in place since the beach. The memory hits her afresh – Jo Leger's bloodied body on the sand.

'You can take a moment,' Steed says, watching her.

'I think it's only just . . . sunk in. A double shock, in a way; I was so convinced that it was Farrah, and then to find someone else . . .' She blinks, reliving the moment.

'Understandable. You want me to do the honours?'

Elin smiles, grateful. 'Please.'

Hana stops a few metres away. Elin and Steed make their way over. Hana's hair is wet, legs stained with mud splatter. Caleb and Maya are standing awkwardly behind, equally bedraggled. Maya's dark curls, freed from their usual headscarf, are clinging in damp clumps to her shoulders. Caleb tugs out an AirPod as they greet him, but he looks discombobulated as he fiddles with the hem of his blue T-shirt. Numb.

'Sorry to jump on you right away, but we need to speak with you privately.' Steed steers them into a corner. He lowers his voice. 'What I'm about to say is going to be a shock, but I need you to try not to react or draw attention to what I'm saying. Does that make sense?'

It's only Hana who seems to pick up on something in his expression, or perhaps his tone of voice. 'Something's happened, hasn't it?' she says quickly.

Steed cuts straight to the chase. 'I'm afraid I have to tell you that Jo is dead. We found her a little while ago.'

A sharp intake of breath. A sudden change in the air; it's charged with emotion. The group's eyes lock as a collective first on Steed's face and then Elin's, as if waiting for the punchline of a joke, but there's none to give.

'It's not possible,' Maya stutters. 'She was with us not long ago. At the villa.' She turns to Hana. 'You said she was packing, didn't you?'

Hana's face is ashen, tight. 'Yes. I thought she was.' A note of hysteria creeps into her voice. 'We knocked for her before we left, but there was no answer. We assumed she was making her way up here.' She lets out a low moan. 'Who would do something like this? Why us?'

Caleb puts his arm around her shoulders. 'What did I say?' he mutters. 'This place, it's not—'

'How?' Maya says desperately, cutting across him. 'What happened?'

'We found her on the beach. It looks like someone attacked her there.'

Hana starts to cry, shoulders heaving. The emotions pull at Elin. Despite the fact that Caleb and Maya are next to her, she looks alone. Vulnerable.

Clearing his throat, Steed looks between them. 'I'm sorry to have to ask this right now,' he says, voice soft, 'but have you all been together these past few hours?'

'Yes, we've been in the villa, getting our stuff ready to come here.' Tears are welling in Maya's eyes too. 'I mean, not together every minute ... We were in our rooms, but no one left, did they?'

'Wouldn't go anywhere here on my own.' Caleb gives a small, bitter laugh, but it doesn't detract from the wobble of his lip. A sob breaks loose and he turns away, embarrassed as another guest, on their right, looks their way.

'Nor me.' Hana shakes her head, tears now streaming down her face. 'I can't believe it. Jo as well ...'

Maya bites down on her lip, but she can't stop it from coming; she too starts audibly crying.

Steed leaves it a beat before speaking again. 'Look, I'm sorry to keep bombarding you with questions, but it would be helpful if you can tell us exactly when you last saw Jo so we can get a clear picture of her movements.'

'That's probably easiest for me to answer.' Caleb turns the AirPod case over in his hands. 'I haven't really seen her today, not since breakfast. I haven't left the villa either, apart from getting some food, a few hours ago.'

Maya tries to compose herself, wiping at her eyes. 'The last time I saw her was after breakfast.'

'And you?' Steed addresses Hana.

Drawing up her chest, Hana blows out through her cheeks. 'I think I probably saw her last outside, by the pool. We ... we argued. I grabbed her ...' She stops, another sob breaking free. 'I grabbed her and I ...'

76

Beside her, Maya freezes, eyes wide with fear. For a moment it's as if they're all teetering on a knife-edge, none of them able to move or speak.

The silence thickens.

'I kept squeezing her wrist . . .' Hana says finally. Her words come out choky, strangulated. 'Jo was crying, but it was like I couldn't stop. I just kept doing it, squeezing and squeezing. I had this rage I'd never felt before, like something had snapped inside me. All I could think was that I wanted to hurt her, more than she hurt me.' Elin's heart lurches as she recalls the simmering tension they'd picked up on in the group. 'For a moment . . .' Hana pauses, tears streaming messily down her cheeks. 'God, for a moment . . .' She uses the back of her hand to wipe her cheeks. 'But I couldn't . . . I wanted to, but I let go.'

Elin exhales. 'And what happened to Jo after that?'

'She went back inside.' Hana meets her gaze. 'I assumed she'd just gone to her room.'

An uneasy silence settles, Maya and Caleb staring at Hana, as if they're still struggling to process her words.

'Can I ask what the argument was about?' Steed says.

Hana blinks. 'My boyfriend. He died last year. I only just found out that' – she takes a deep breath, her eyes shiny with both tears and emotion – 'that he and Jo were having an affair, and that she was with him when he died. She'd kept it from me.' Her shoulders start trembling. 'All this time.' She's struggling to get the words out, fighting back tears. 'She also admitted that she had Bea's phone.'

Elin exchanges a glance with Steed. *The missing phone.* 'Did she explain why she had the phone?'

'She said she spotted it the morning Bea was found, near the yoga pavilion. It was smashed up, the memory card missing. Jo was worried that if you found Bea's phone, knew they'd met up that night . . .'

'We'd suspect her.'

'And I did,' Hana says, trembling so much that her voice comes out as an unintelligible rattle. 'I practically accused her.'

'Do you know what she did with the memory card?' Steed says gently.

'She said she never found it. It's still missing.'

Elin's stomach clenches. *Or the killer has it.*

Hana briefly closes her eyes. 'I thought Jo was lying, you know, that she might have actually had something to do with this . . .' A sob racks her body.

'I'm sorry,' Elin says quietly. 'I know this is hard, but we have a few more questions: are there any reasons you can think of why someone would be targeting Jo, the rest of your group? You haven't been aware of anyone acting suspiciously?'

One by one, they shake their heads.

'And have any of you a connection to the island outside of this holiday? Do you know anything about the school that used to be here?'

Hana and Caleb give another round of negatives, but Maya nods. 'My father's friend worked at the old school, but it wasn't for long. Said it was an awful place.' She hesitates. 'I don't know any more than that, I'm sorry. He didn't give any details.'

Elin glances at Steed, disappointed. She wasn't expecting a sudden breakthrough, but still . . .

'Thank you. Again, we're so sorry for your loss. If you do think of anything else, we—' She breaks off, feeling her phone vibrate. Detective Johnson. *Have emailed through files as requested.* 'Sorry, I'm going to have to leave this here.'

As they move away, Steed looks at her. 'So what do you make of that?'

'Hard to say at this point. Most interesting is the memory card. Can you chase up the phone data application?'

'Of course.'

'While you do that, I'm going to take a minute. Johnson's emailed through his files from the Creacher case.' She tugs loose two chairs from the stack in front of her. Steed helps her drag them over near the window, so they're out of sight of the group. The dense expanse of woodland beyond is just visible. In the dim light it looks even more impenetrable.

Pulling out her notebook, Elin opens the first attachment. But she's only just started reading when a muffled cry sounds out.

Caleb. He's sat on the floor, head in his hands.

'I'll go,' Elin murmurs, standing back up.

By the time she reaches them, Maya has her arm around Caleb's shoulders.

'Anything I can do?' Elin says softly.

Hana shakes her head, eyes still wet with tears. 'I think he's at breaking point. His dad died fairly recently. From what he's said, it was pretty bad circumstances. I don't think he's really processed it yet. To have one loss on top of another like this, now Jo . . . it's a lot.'

Elin nods, glancing around at the remaining guests and staff in the room. Most have finished eating and the activity has left a lull in which a palpable tension hovers; frantic fingers tapping on phones. Fevered conversation.

A pressure cooker. That's what this feels like. A pressure cooker, ready to pop.

77

Johnson's laboriously photographed the documents. High res, they're too big for one email so one long chain fills her inbox.

Steed glances over. 'Phone data application is a go. Want a hand?'

'Please. I'll forward some.' Elin opens the first few attachments: statements from the night Lois Wade went missing. The narrative is uniform: *Lois Wade wasn't on the island. Was never meant to be. No one saw her.*

She skims the ones taken during the Creacher case. Camp leaders, teachers. The same story: how they woke to screams, what they found when they emerged from their tents. Creacher's briefly mentioned; how they found him odd, noticed him watching the kids.

'Anything useful?'

Elin shakes her head. 'Bit of a pattern . . . similar story. How about you?'

'Same.' Steed shakes his head. 'Can't get my head around the fact that no one was awake when the killer went for them. A school trip, you'd expect them all to be up.'

'Maybe the killer waited until they were sure the kids were all down,' she says, opening the teenagers' statements. The narrative is the same as the adults', but there's raw emotion too;

none of the contained formality of the adult accounts, some-how subconsciously absorbed from books or TV dramas. *How a Statement Should Be Given 101.*

'Any arguments mentioned?' Steed looks up. 'Nothing in mine.'

'Not yet. This is Farrah's,' she murmurs, grimacing at what she knows are lies.

'Hard reading?'

She nods, putting Farrah's and Will's documents aside to review the last statement, the boatman's. It begins with his recollection of bringing the group from the mainland, his observations about Creacher. He, too, had found Creacher's behaviour odd, had noticed him watching not just this group of teenagers, but others too. *Hadn't wanted to say anything before, you know?*

Elin's about to close the file when her eye is drawn to the boatman's name; it hadn't registered the first time she looked.

Porter Jackson.

Something pulls up and out from her subconscious. Rolling it about in her head for a few moments, it comes to her: a Porter Jackson was briefly mentioned in the article she'd read about the development of the island, the protester opposing Ronan Delaney's plans.

Elin taps his name into Google together with the words *Reaper's Rock.*

Several pages of results appear. The first few are versions of the initial story she'd read, local news, then national, the story amplified by the mass-market dailies. LOCALS PROTEST OVER DEVELOPMENT OF INFAMOUS ISLAND. No surprise: nationals loved reporting on local infighting, a newcomer upsetting the apple cart.

Elin clicks into the first, adrenaline pulsing through her.

She's right: Porter Jackson *was* the vocal complainant. It can't be a coincidence, but does it actually mean anything? If you'd worked on the island, albeit as a boatman, when it was in its natural state, it wouldn't be a stretch to imagine you'd complain when a development of this scale was proposed.

But as she scans lower in the search results, she pauses, finger hovering over the screen. The only article that isn't connected to the development of the island.

A Reddit thread. She spots Porter Jackson's name mentioned in the subhead directly below a headline that immediately intrigues her: *Does anyone remember being on the island at the school between 1963–1967?*

Surely the thread is referring to Rock House School? Quickly scrolling, she scans the comments below.

Hi, my name is Alain Dunne, I was at Rock House from 1963–1967. Look-ing back, it's clear it was a dumping ground, for local authorities all over the UK to send 'maladjusted' children (as we were referred to as) with behav-iour problems.

Someone else comments:

I like the term 'naughty boys' boarding school, I think that the PC phrase would be 'educationally challenged' boys boarding school. I know I was.

Several comments down, a photograph appears in the thread of the old school. Elin reads on.

A friend of my father was a Master at Rock House in the sixties and seven-ties. I was a child at the time, but he scared the life out of me, so goodness knows what those boys went through.

Below that, another comment:

Anyone remember Porter Jackson? He was in my class. The only one I haven't kept in touch with.

Elin stares, her heartbeat now sounding in her ears.

There in black and white: Porter Jackson, boatman at the time of the Creacher murders and vocal complainant about the development, had attended the school.

His connection to the island went even further back than the Creacher murders.

'You found something?' Steed glances up from his phone.

'Yes. The boatman, Porter Jackson.' Briefing Steed on the connection to the article she read, she then skims the rest of the thread, reminiscences about teachers and questionable food. Finger over screen, she pauses on a post about halfway down.

Does anyone remember that strange room they used to take us to? It had these odd things on the floor – stones that looked like that rock.

Elin blinks, rereading it with a strange, sickening lurch: the room, surely the same room Michael Zimmerman mentioned.

A room with stones on the floor. Like the cave in the quarry.

It can't be coincidence. She tilts the phone screen towards Steed. 'Read this.'

He whistles under his breath. 'Bloody hell.'

Elin's skin prickles as she thinks it through. The rumours she's heard about the school make sense now; the numbed faces of the boys in the photographs, Zimmerman's words about the artist's preoccupation with his time at the school.

Confounded, she continues reading.

Do you remember where it was?

No. They blindfolded us, didn't they? But it wasn't far from the house. I remember going down some steps.

It worked though. Putting us down there on our own all night . . . a horrible punishment, but I know I never played up again.

I still have nightmares about it now. I've started putting it into my art . . . it's the only way I can go about processing it.

Let's take this private. I don't think a public forum is the place to discuss.

Elin keeps reading, but that's the last mention of the room.

'I don't know what drives some people.' Steed grimaces. 'Vulnerable kids . . .'

'Yeah. The very people who were there to protect them too . . .' As Elin scrolls back to a particular part of the conversation, her eyes hook on one phrase: *I've started putting it into my art.* 'This bit, about the art, it's got me thinking about the piece in reception with the motifs of the rock woven through it. What if, rather than motifs, they're representations of the stones described in this room?'

'Maybe a way of trying to process it, like this guy says here.'

'And perhaps our killer never has. I think we've got pretty substantial motive here; what if our killer is echoing their experience of this room through the murders? Going through this . . . a massive trauma. If you're delusional as well . . .'

Steed slowly nods. 'But if that *is* the case, then surely it implies that the killer has to be someone who was at the school, went through it? Or at least has knowledge of it.'

'You're right.' Elin's mind darts to the one person whose

name drew her attention to this thread in the first place. 'The only person who fits is Porter Jackson, but the question is whether he was also on the island when Lois Wade went missing. I'll message Johnson.'

He replies almost instantly. Elin turns back. 'Jackson *was* the boatman when Lois went missing. Johnson never thought it significant: Jackson apparently dropped the kids and left, and people verified that.'

She catches a fleeting light in Steed's eyes. 'But just because he left doesn't mean he didn't come back.'

'Exactly.' It's a theory, but one she can't help stumbling on – while Jackson was on or around the island at the time of the Creacher murders, there's no evidence he is now.

'Let's see if we can get anything on current whereabouts.' Elin quickly searches his name on her phone, but it brings up pages of results. 'Bad idea. This will take hours to trawl through. Let's call the intel unit, get their help. In the meantime, I want to speak to Michael, get a look at this building he mentioned. He reckons it's been blocked up, but after seeing this, I'm wondering if there's another access point.'

'You're thinking somewhere the killer might be holding Farrah?'

'It's a possibility. You keep an eye on things here and I'll find Michael.' Reaching for her bag, she feels a sharp prickle of excitement, adrenaline rising in her so fast, she stumbles as she makes her way across the room.

They're getting there. Piece by piece things are pulling together.

78

'That's it. The entrance, at least.' Reaching up, Michael tugs at the mass of tree branches smothering what remains of the doorway.

A faint smell of old vegetation wafts towards her as Elin holds up her torch, the beam highlighting an intricate spider's web, tiny water droplets clinging to the filigree. A guttural rumble of thunder sounds out, followed by a gust of wind that makes the branches above thrash wildly from side to side. As the wind subsides, Elin surveys what's beneath with disappointment: a packed-out infill of rubble and cement.

No mistaking it: the entrance to the room is completely blocked.

'Hard to see now, but there's the outline of the doorway.' Michael gestures to the left of the infill, the hood of his mac slipping down as he moves. Above him, lightning flares: an explosion of harsh white light. Trees, leaf litter, Michael, bounce out of monochrome into fleeting, brittle colour.

As the light fades, Elin scopes out the structure. It looks like a bunker of some description, presumably leading downstairs to the room he'd described. The hairs on the back of her neck stand to attention. Despite the infill, a horrible atmosphere pervades the area. The more she sees, the more she can't stop herself envisioning what might have happened down there.

Elin walks further, past the entrance. 'And you're sure there's no other way to access it?'

Michael shakes his head, blinking rainwater out of his eyes. 'Unless someone's tunnelled in, I think it's highly unlikely, and besides, once they got down there, the room would be filled.'

Elin nods. He's right. It's clear: the place is blocked up.

'Sorry it's not more helpful,' Michael says, the last part of his sentence drowned out by the rain. It's picked up in intensity, drumming hard against the sodden ground. 'From what the guy said, the idea was that this place was buried forever, and they pretty much achieved that goal.' He glances around him. 'Can't blame them. Not a nice feeling here, is it?'

'No,' Elin replies, but her discomfort is quickly supplanted by a creeping realization as she picks up on what he just said – new information, subtly different to what he told her on the beach. 'What you said, about it being buried forever . . . Was someone explicit about that, then? It wasn't just a safety instruction to fill in an old building?'

'Yeah.' Michael pulls his mac tighter. The heavy rain is flattening his hair to his skull, revealing a bald patch beneath. 'Apparently the owner was insistent. That's what made me think the room the artist mentioned *was* underneath all this. He wanted all of it filled, not just the entrance. From what I gathered, he went to the school too.'

Elin looks at him, chilled.

Ronan Delaney.

79

'Jackson?' Ronan Delaney flips down the screen of his laptop, a flare of recognition in his eyes.

Elin nods. 'Am I right in thinking that you went to school together, here on the island?'

Ronan's eyes move warily between her face and Steed's. 'Yes. We were classmates. Both football fans too, though rival teams.'

Steed gives a half smile. 'And he was also a vocal opponent to the development of the retreat?'

'He was.' Ronan's mouth puckers. 'Set against it, caused no end of problems. Started campaigns, protests, but if I'm honest, that comes with the job. You piss people off. Locals especially. No one likes change. I don't think it helped we were at school together.' He pauses. 'And I always thought it was a little . . . personal, because of what happened before.'

Elin falters, something about him that she can't quite get a handle on. While he's obviously grieving, his body language is that of a professional interviewee, sitting uneasily with what they're discussing: big, bold gestures, mouth lapsing into a smile at the end of each sentence. Someone used to extending a hand to colleagues, charming investors. She knows it's probably automatic, a reflex, but it's disconcerting nonetheless.

'And what was that?' Steed asks.

'I advised Jackson, along with several other school friends, to make an investment. All went belly-up in the end, but that's part of the risk. Some you win, some you lose. Jackson took it to heart, but if you're that way inclined, you shouldn't put your chips on the board.'

Elin nods. Clearly bad blood between them, but how does it fit with the bigger picture?

'Going back to the school, we've learnt about a room, outside the school, being used as a punishment. Were you ever aware of that?'

Several beats pass. 'Yes,' he says finally, clearing his throat. 'But it's not something I've ever talked about.'

'Are you able to tell us what happened?' Steed says quietly.

Ronan nods, and when he meets her gaze, Elin glimpses a raw fear in his eyes.

'From the minute I arrived at the school, something was . . . off. Kids that age, you'd expect them to be bouncing off the walls, but they were broken, physically shaking when an adult came into the room. A few days in, I found out why.' A small silence. 'I was woken up in the early hours by a figure in this odd' – he grimaces – 'this cloak. That's the only way I can describe it.'

Elin tenses. *A cloak.* It's starting to paint a pretty compelling picture.

'We were blindfolded, led out of the school and into a room outside.' Ronan shakes his head, as if trying to dislodge the memory. 'All I remember is the blindfold coming off. It was dark, but after a while, your eyes would adjust. There were these . . . stones on the floor, shaped to look like the rock.' His voice falters.

Her pulse picks up. *Stones . . . shaped to look like the rock.*

'Did something happen in there?' she asks gently.

Ronan nods, and for the first time, the veneer slips away completely. His body seems to collapse from the core, his face crumpling.

80

'They kept us in there for hours.' Ronan stares at his hands. It's the first time she's noticed his bitten-down nails, the inflamed skin around them. 'We knew about the curse, so the stones . . . they were terrifying. After a while, your mind started playing tricks on you. I always had this horrible sense that they were watching us.' He shakes his head. 'It's something the teachers always said. *The Reaper's watching.* If we did anything wrong, he'd find us.'

'Must have been so frightening,' Elin murmurs, struggling to imagine how or why someone would want to inflict such fear on kids.

'It was. A warped, psychological terror meted out on us for no other reason than to have control over someone who couldn't fight back. As an adult, I can see it for what it was: an abuse of power. But as a kid . . .'

'I'm sorry.' She swallows hard, the weight of what he's told them sitting heavily on the room. All the things she'd imagined about this case, but not *this*. 'Was there any pattern to it happening?'

'Not really.' Again, the professional smile appears, quickly falls away.

'Did you ever find out who was acting as the Reaper character?' Steed asks. 'Which teacher?'

'No.' Ronan's left hand comes up to his mouth, teeth finding the raw skin around the nails.

Steed is writing in his notebook. 'No one ever spoke up about it?'

'We were too scared. One boy said he was planning to tell his parents, but the next day, he fell during a trip to the quarry. No one dared mention it after that. At the time, we really believed' – he makes quote marks with his fingers – '"the Reaper" was responsible. We weren't little kids, but the fear we had . . .'

Someone wanted to shut them up, Elin thinks, and in the cleverest way – a way that would only cement the terrible narrative that the reaper would hurt them if they stepped out of line. 'Manipulation,' she murmurs.

'Yes,' Ronan says heavily. 'Of the worst kind.'

'And Porter Jackson, I'm assuming he'd have experienced the same thing?'

'I expect so. I'm pretty sure none of us were excluded from it.'

Steed looks up from his notebook. 'And were you aware that Porter Jackson was working as a boatman on the island at the time of the Creacher murders?'

A pause before he nods. 'Now you've mentioned it, yes. I think I read about it.'

'Did it surprise you? After his time at the school?'

'Strangely enough, no. I felt the same thing, the urge to come back here, to try to put some kind of a lid over what went on.' Ronan shrugs.

Like Will and Farrah, Elin thinks, and the artist who'd created the textile work. 'And after the planning issues, you haven't been in contact with Jackson?'

'No, but that's not surprising.' Ronan looks up. 'A school friend told me a few months ago that Jackson had died. He mentioned a funeral in Jackson's hometown, Ashburton. The November before last, maybe.'

Elin meets Steed's gaze, sees her own dismay reflected in his eyes. Grabbing her phone, she searches both his name and hometown. The more specific search terms yield an immediate result: a memorial page from over two years ago. There's a photograph at the top. She tips the screen to show Ronan. 'This him?'

He nods. Elin scans the text below the image, which details the specifics of Jackson's funeral. There's also a brief biography mentioning his time at the school, and his working life, including on the island.

It's him. There's no doubting it. Porter Jackson's dead.

Bea's, Seth's and Jo's deaths – there's no way he can be responsible.

'Guess that's not what you both wanted to hear?' Ronan asks, watching them.

'Not exactly.' She's still processing it. 'Do you know if he has any family?'

'I'm not sure. I'm sorry.'

'And no one else who attended the school has been in touch recently?' Elin hears the desperation in her voice. *She'd been so convinced. Jackson not only had genuine motive . . . but he was at the school and on the island during the Creacher murders.*

'No.' Ronan hesitates, shaking his head. 'But honestly, I'm struggling to understand why someone who'd been through what we endured would want to do the same thing to someone else.'

'Sometimes it can be part of a pattern. A cycle. Someone abused in that way becomes an abuser themselves. Mostly, of course, that's not the case, but it can happen. I—' She stops. Her phone's ringing. Will. 'Sorry, I need to take this.'

'Of course. If you need anything else, I'll be with the group.' Ronan gathers his stuff together. 'I've been given pretty strong instructions to get on my way.'

'I've missed it . . .' Elin murmurs as they leave the room.

'Who was it?' Steed asks.

'Will. I'd better call him back.'

Steed lightly grasps her arm. 'Wait, before you do, I was thinking of heading down to the old shack on the beach, if you're okay here . . .'

Elin frowns. 'The shack? We agreed no one would leave the lodge and Seth . . .'

He nods, his expression serious. 'I'll put on my gear, be as quick as I can. Something's bothering me about what we saw in there. When Delaney mentioned football then, it came to me. The mug I spotted, on that shelf, it was celebrating a tourna-ment that was only *last* year.'

Elin's pulse picks up. 'Someone's been in there using it recently.'

Steed meets her gaze. 'Yes, after the retreat was built.'

81

No greeting from Will, just: 'Any news?'

Elin swallows hard, reluctant to quash the hope in his voice. 'No sign, I'm sorry. The only thing we've found is her bag on the beach.'

'That means she was there, right?' he says quickly. 'You need to search the area.'

'We have, but it's not safe to send anyone out again, not without backup.'

A pause. 'What about the threats, there's got to be some clue there, surely?'

'Yes, but she didn't give specifics.' Elin feels the telltale prickle of heat on her neck. As soon as the words are out, she realizes her mistake, not only in what she's let slip – that Farrah confided in her about the earlier threats – but in what she'd done. The reason Farrah didn't give specifics is because Elin put her off, hadn't connected it to what was happening. Farrah had tried to confide and Elin batted her away.

'*She didn't give specifics.*' Will's voice is ominously calm. 'What you said then, it sounds like Farrah had already told you about the threats. I don't see how that's possible, she was missing when you found them on her computer.'

The burning heat is now creeping up her neck. 'I didn't

know, Will – still don't – if what she told me before is related. She told me it was her ex. Trying to scare her.'

A heavy silence. 'Let me get this straight,' Will says finally. 'Farrah told you *before* she went missing that she was being threatened. Did you take the time to check it out?'

'No, but—' Elin's talking on autopilot because the enormity of what she's done is only just hitting home. She'd failed Farrah – hadn't taken seriously what she said.

'You were too busy playing the hero, weren't you?'

'What do you mean?' she says, taken aback by the aggression in his tone.

'What you're saying is that you didn't have time for her, but this . . . this *situation*, you're all over it, and you shouldn't have been. You said it yourself, you weren't ready for this kind of case, but you did it anyway. You had doubts – doubts that were justified, because you've missed vital stuff – and now Farrah's missing. If you'd looked into Farrah's concerns properly, we could have protected her . . . but no.'

'Look, we don't even know if Farrah *is* missing.'

'What do you mean?'

'Well, I was thinking that there's a possibility she might have run, or—'

'Or what,' he says flatly.

'Well, I was wondering,' – she's blundering now, in the dark. *Why had she brought it up? Wrong time. Wrong tone.* 'If you did know everything about what happened on the island that night, if Farrah was entirely honest with you. Maybe something else happened.'

He cuts across her. 'Despite what I told you about why Farrah lied, to protect *me*, you're still doubting her? What do you think really happened, Elin? That she lied to protect herself? And now, what? She's involved in this somehow? Hasn't gone missing at all?'

310

Elin knows she should come back right away with a denial, because she doesn't think that, not really, she just said it because it was there, in her head, and she wanted to stop him talking, saying all those words about her.

'No, that's not what I think,' she says quickly, but even to her own ears, her reply sounds insubstantial. 'I have to look into everything, you know that.'

There's a long silence. 'I get that, Elin,' he says finally. 'That you have to explore it, but you don't have to *believe* it too.'

'I don't.'

'Rubbish, I can hear it in your voice. You're doubting her, and by default, that means you're doubting me too. What does that say about us?' His voice wobbles. 'Actually, I forgot, us – our relationship – comes second best, doesn't it? Second best to the job.'

'That's not true.' Turning, she looks through the window in front of her. Her reflection comes back speckled with debris from the storm.

'It is, and what's so screwed up is that you don't even realize it. You took a shortcut with Farrah, and rather than taking responsibility, you're trying, in some warped way, to point the finger at her. And what you don't understand is that when it comes to family, you don't take shortcuts, or maybe *you* do because your family is so messed up that you don't know what it's like to care about someone.'

'Will, I—'

'No, Elin, you don't get it. What Farrah did for me after Thea died, lying to the police, it was wrong, absolutely, but that's love. What you've done here is the antithesis of that. Tossed away family for your ego.'

'I made a mistake, that's all.'

'Yes, but a mistake that could have been prevented. You

know, all this time, you were worried about being a coward because of *not* doing something, but sometimes that's the bravest thing of all. Acknowledging your limits.' His voice has an unfamiliar chill – the one he reserves for the few times someone's really upset him. 'Farrah's my sister, Elin. My sister.' A long, shuddering breath. 'If you had any doubts, any doubts what-so-fucking-ever, you should have told me.'

Elin presses the phone harder to her ear. A horrible, ugly shame washes over her. 'I'm sorry. I didn't know that what she was going to tell me was about something important like this, the case . . .'

A pause. 'That sums it up. You didn't think it was about anything important *like the case*. Our relationship will never be as important as your job. It's where you're alive, Elin. I glimpsed it in Switzerland, thought it was because the case was personal, but it's not.'

His words hit like a cold splash of water on her face.

Elin can hear the wretchedness in his voice, which she knows is mainly down to what's happened with Farrah, but it still cuts her to the core. She wants to protest, push back, but she can't.

Part of her knew from the minute she stepped on to the island that she was making a mistake, but she did it because she wanted to, *had* to, felt compelled to. Maybe it *was* because her brother died so young. She'd never consciously acknowledged it, but since it happened, she was acutely aware that she didn't want to live a bland life. She wanted to live a life on the edge, full of electric, vibrant emotion, because Sam never would.

'I'm sorry. I'm sorry I haven't been able to find her.' It's all she has. Although it feels like her heart is breaking, the words on the tip of her tongue to express that, words that would make this better – the proper sorrys and I-love-yous – they won't come out. That part of her . . . it's malfunctioning. Stuck.

'I know you are, but there'll always be something. Another case, another bit between your teeth. Nothing I do or say will be able to compete with that.'

Elin's numb. It's as if Will's ripped away the protective veneer she's wrapped around herself. Left her exposed. The person she trusts the most has been the one to pull back the veil. 'I'm not giving up on finding her.'

'I know that, but what's happened, it's made me think about things. When you come home, I think it's best if we talk, Elin. Decide how we best move forwards.'

82

Elin's legs are shaky as she makes her way to the event room. She feels empty, hollowed out after hearing Will's words.

He wants to talk – how ominous that sounds. She can't help feeling that Will's seen her properly for the first time, and he doesn't like what he's glimpsed. What if they can't get back from this? How will she cope if he doesn't trust her like he did before?

But as she reaches the door to the event room, she forces the thoughts away.

Steel yourself. You've still got to do the job.

The member of staff outside pulls open the door to reveal a chaotic scene; bags and clothes scattered across the once-pristine floor. Snippets of frustrated conversation drift over: *Why won't they give us more information? I want to leave now. Get home.* Staff are in the process of dragging in mattresses, but most people are already settled – in makeshift beds of their own clothes, or awkwardly perched on chairs.

With night almost set in, the long strip lights above them are the only illumination. The artificial light thrown out is unforgiving, picking out the dark shadows settling beneath people's eyes, livid streaks of sunburn.

'How did it go?' Steed says, as she stops beside him.

'Not great. How about you?'

'Okay. Seth . . . nothing disturbed there.' He pauses. 'But I was right, we weren't the first to get in there since the Outward Bound days. I found newspapers dated from last year, and this, tucked at the back. Pre-LUMEN. Copies of a plan.' Removing a folded piece of paper from his bag, Steed passes it to her. 'Looks like an alternative development for the island.' His finger hovers over a pencilled box on the top right. Elin leans in. Written in pencil is a proposal to have the site protected, a formal conservation designation as a Site of Special Scientific Interest.

'This SSSI thing came up when I read that article about Porter Jackson complaining about the development . . .'

Steed's still looking at the plan. 'There's also a name, Christopher someone . . . can't make out the rest.'

She examines the neat lettering, something stirring in her head, but she can't quite grasp what it is. 'Anything else?'

'A case study about the impact of this kind of development on the ecosystem, wildlife . . . data on energy usage, habitat disruption . . .'

'Maybe they were planning some kind of exposé on the retreat.'

'Looks likely.' He shrugs. 'Sorry it's not more helpful. I was hoping it would kick up something else.'

'It's fine.' Elin takes a breath. 'Right, I'm going to make an attempt to reassure everyone. Take it you haven't heard about backup?'

He shakes his head. 'No, but I've spoken to them. Good and bad news. I'll start with the good, but not actually sure if it deserves that classification . . . phone data is back from Bea Leger. Verifies what the water sports guy told you. She made several calls the night she arrived on the island. One to what we know is her sister's phone and one to an unknown number. I've tried it, but it's dead. I've asked for any data we have on the number.'

'A burner?'

'Probably, and the sister was right. The SIM card *was* taken from her phone. It's been used several times since Bea Leger's body was found.'

'Chances are it's the killer. Info deletion exercise.'

'Seems that way.' Steed shrugs. 'But finding out whose phone it was put into might be a needle in the proverbial haystack.'

'And the bad news?'

'I spoke to Anna on my way back from the beach. You must have been on the phone . . . she tried to get hold of you.' He hesitates, clearly uncomfortable with what he's about to say. 'There's been another tweet, Elin.'

It takes a moment for her mind to catch up with what he's saying. 'Another one?'

'Yes.' He looks troubled. 'Anna called because this time, there's a photo of you . . .'

'But there was a photo in the other one.' His tone of voice unnerves her: not the casual, genuine reassurances of the past few days, but something more forced. He's frightened for her.

'No, this is different.' He fumbles for his phone. 'Anna's taken a screenshot. Look.'

Steed passes her his phone. Elin stares at the tweet.

For a split second, it feels like her heart has stopped beating.

She immediately understands why he was so hesitant to tell her.

It's not just that they've done the same thing as before – they've etched-out hollows for her eyes – but it's what the backdrop of the image tells her.

The photograph was taken the day she arrived at the retreat, standing by the yoga pavilion.

Whoever is sending these tweets is here, on the island, with her.

83

Moments from the last few days flash through her mind. Her alone at the back of the lodge, the person searching, the cliff fall . . .

Had she been in real danger?

Steed takes the phone back. 'I reckon someone's trying to warn you off, that's all.'

'But if that's the case, why aren't they targeting you too?'

He hesitates. 'I don't know,' he says eventually.

Elin's mind starts spiralling: *What if it's not the killer who's sending them? Could it be the same troll who'd sent similar things during the Hayler case? Hayler himself? It's not implausible. He's never been found. Zimmerman? She thought she recognized him . . .*

'It might not mean anything,' Steed says quickly. 'Could be just a prank, someone realizing you were police, wants to scare you. As horrible as it is, I think as a woman you're more susceptible to this kind of stuff. We both know the stick female officers put up with. Most of these people are cowards, hiding behind their keyboards. Doesn't mean they'll act on it.'

Elin nods. He's right, the majority don't, but that isn't reassuring. She's worked with victims of stalkers and she knows that the real fear lies in the *threat* of violence, the knowing that someone's watching. Waiting. The unpredictability of what they'll do next.

'Look, it's just something we need to be aware of.' Steed's voice is steadier now, as if he's gaining confidence in the idea as he says it aloud. 'Someone, whether it's the killer or not, is trying to get inside your head, mess up the investigation. You can't let it. Not now you've come this far.' He inclines his head towards the people behind them. 'Everyone here, they're relying on you. They need to know what's going on.'

'You're right.' Her words belie the turmoil inside her; she's starting to get a bad feeling about this.

Taking a moment to collect herself, Elin makes her way to the front of the room.

'Excuse me, I'd like to say a few words.'

Zero response. No one even looks her way.

Loudly clapping her hands together, Elin raises her voice. 'Excuse me, if you can please give me your attention, I want to say a few words—'

'About time,' someone calls, but Elin ploughs on. 'I understand that the situation is worrying, and you probably have more questions than I have answers. Right now, all I can tell you is that we're dealing with an incident here on the island, and for your safety it's in your best interests to stay together.' More murmurs of discontent, but she continues. 'Rest assured that the police on the mainland know of our situation. As soon as they can get someone out to us, they will.'

Another voice: 'So what exactly *is* going on?'

'I'm afraid I can't say, not until we have more information.' Sweat pricks the back of her neck.

More muttering, shaking of heads. A pulsing tension ripples through the room, a raw hostility in the faces assembled before her.

Elin knows why: people are usually relieved when someone's there to take control of a situation, but not when there are no answers. Without it, the imagination takes over.

Continuing to talk, she mentally works through the loose script she'd prepared in her head – instructions on what to do if they need to use the toilet, or what to do in an emergency. She's only halfway through when a man steps forwards, features already tight with displeasure. He jams his hands in his pockets, thumbs pointing at her, a hostile gesture.

'Can't you tell us any more?' The raw streak of sunburn on his left cheek makes it look like he's been slapped. 'A vague mention of an incident isn't really going to cut it. My wife's terrified, and all we're getting is hearsay. Someone heard a member of staff saying that a body's been found on the beach.'

Meeting his gaze, Elin feels exposed. 'I'm afraid I don't have any further information at this stage. All we're doing now is trying to keep everyone safe.'

The man keeps his eyes locked on her as if in challenge, the moment broken only by the loud whine of the wind outside. It sounds frenzied, out of control, as if it's pulling at the very foundations of the building.

The room falls into an uneasy silence.

But Elin's aware that they've only been given a respite because it's late – nearly midnight; people are tired, unable to think straight. *They're on borrowed time.* When everyone wakes up tomorrow, they'll be fired up. She needs to be ready.

Stepping back, she says to Steed: 'I'm going to look through my notes again, the statements Johnson sent through.'

'I'll do the same.'

Taking a seat on the far side of the room, Elin starts reading, looking for something, anything. She has plausible motive now, but if Jackson's dead, who can be responsible?

It has to be someone linked to all three time frames – the school, the Creacher killings, the present day. The possibilities seem scarce and at the same time overwhelming, and as she scrolls through the files, the conversation with Will replays in her head.

Sometimes not doing something is the bravest thing of all. Acknowledging your limits.

Tears prick her eyes. What if he's right? What if this *is* beyond her? Past doubts consume her and her thoughts start to spiral. *What if something happens to Farrah overnight? On her watch? What about the tweet?*

The thoughts still churning over in her mind, the stress of the day hits her like a battering ram.

She leans back against the chair, closing her eyes for a moment's respite.

84

Day 4

Elin's not sure how long she's been asleep for when a voice sounds out, stirring at the back of her consciousness.

Opening her eyes, she startles. Ronan's standing over her, phone in hand, turning it between his fingers.

'Sorry to wake you.'

'It's fine.' She hauls herself into a more upright position. 'I shouldn't have fallen asleep.'

Around her, the room is dimly lit, people asleep on chairs and the floor. A few are still awake – the telltale glow of mobile phones lending their faces an eerie glow. Glancing across at Steed, she sees that he, too, has succumbed, fast asleep in his chair, head lolling to the side. Elin puts out a foot to nudge him awake, but all it does is prompt a soft snore.

Ronan nods. 'Understandable, and I should have done the same, but my mind's been on a loop ever since we spoke. I've been thinking about Jackson, what you asked about whether he had any family.' He shakes his head. 'It's just come to me. The day of the protests, Jackson *was* with someone. He half introduced me to him, his son, I think, said they were working together. There were so many people there, it was a bit of a blur.'

'Can you recall anything about him?'

'Not much. He was wearing a cap, and he had a beard, and similar eyes to Jackson ... close set.' A pause. He furrows his brow. 'Actually, there *is* something. He had a slight stutter, like Jackson. That's probably how I came to the conclusion that they were related. I know it can run in families. My uncle had a stammer and my cousin had one too.'

A stutter. As Elin absorbs his words, something stirs in her brain. Something she'd picked up in the very first conversation they had; the very deliberate way he spoke. An almost imperceptible pause at the beginning of each sentence, as if he were having to line up the words in his head. Another association: the blue T-shirt she'd glimpsed on the figure she'd seen heading into the woodland. The same colour as the T-shirt he's wearing now.

The ages worked.

'Give me a moment.' Elin reaches into her bag, pulls out the plastic bag containing the torn-up image. With fumbling fingers, she lines the strips of paper up roughly on her lap and scrutinizes the photograph.

Faces appear from the jumble. Girls. Boys. Teachers. Camp leaders.

Her eyes scour them again, until they come to rest on one in particular.

Caleb.

There, in the back row; one of the camp leaders.

For a moment she doesn't see Caleb at all; it appears to be an entirely different person, the soft jawline of today eclipsed by the presence of a beard, long straggly hair that elongates his face. The cap pulled down over his face camouflages him even more as she looks closer.

Now she knows what she's looking for, the similarities are clear. The eyes, the set of his mouth. It's this her subconscious had flagged to her when she'd first found the photograph in Farrah's bin, put the torn-up pieces in order.

Her pulse is pounding as her mind draws the once disparate strands together: the stutter, Steed's observations about Caleb being disparaging about Seth, the retreat, Hana's words about Caleb losing his father.

That father was Porter Jackson.

'It's him,' Elin murmurs. The wind again keens against the side of the building, muffling her words.

Caleb was on the island at the time of the Creacher murders.

85

Struggling to keep her voice steady, Elin addresses Ronan, gesturing at the image on her lap. 'Was this the person you saw Jackson with?'

Leaning over, he examines it. 'I'm sorry, it's hard to say, it was so long ago. Similar, if that helps.' He hesitates. 'Do you recognize him?' She nods. Despite the dim light, he casts his gaze around the room. 'You really think if he *is* Jackson's son, that he's involved?'

'I'm not sure.' Until now, she was certain that the killer must have a direct connection to the school, what happened there, but Caleb wouldn't even have been born at the time. His father had plausible motive as an ex-pupil, but not Caleb. *What are they missing in terms of motive?* 'I'm going to wake my colleague. We'll let you know once we have more information. If you think of anything else—'

'Of course.' Ronan nods, trudging back to his seat.

Once he's left, Elin tries to rouse Steed. He's out cold; it takes a minute to stir him.

'What time is it?' He rubs his eyes. 'I didn't mean to go off . . .'

'Just after five.' She takes him through what Ronan told her. Yawns, poorly suppressed, punctuate every other word and she's not sure how much he's absorbed until he abruptly straightens, glances in the direction of the Leger party. 'What do you reckon? Get a jump on him before he clocks what's going on?'

'Good shout.' Picking up their bags, they carefully weave their way between the sleeping bodies to the group.

Elin directs the beam of her torch over them. The light picks up Hana first, curled foetal-style. Maya's asleep beside her, phone still clasped loosely in her hand.

'No Caleb,' Elin murmurs as she gently shakes Hana's arm. There's a look of surprise when she sees Elin, her eyes widening. 'Sorry to disturb,' she whispers. 'But do you know where Caleb is?'

Bleary-eyed, Hana shakes her head. 'He was here earlier . . .' She tails off, picking up on their urgency. 'Is something wrong?'

'Yes. I need to speak to him.'

'I'll wake Maya.' Sitting up, Hana squeezes Maya's hand, talking quietly in her ear.

Still lying down, Maya looks between them, hair mussed over her face. 'He was here when I fell asleep,' she says groggily. 'He passed out before I did, I could hear from his breathing.'

'He didn't wake up in the night, say he was leaving the room?' Elin turns slowly, confused. If Caleb *has* left, how has he done it? The member of staff on the door had been instructed not to let anyone in or out unless in supervised pairs for toilet breaks and to raise the alarm if no one returned. How could he have got past that?

'No . . .' But Maya stops, face stricken. 'Actually, I *did* hear footsteps, a few hours ago. I didn't properly wake though, so I don't know if it was him.'

Elin nods. *She doesn't like this.* 'Have you noticed anything odd about his behaviour over the past few days? Anything out of character?'

Hana shakes her head. 'Not really, but I've been in my own

325

bubble. He's been upset, like you saw last night, but apart from that . . .'

'The same,' Maya affirms.

'He hasn't mentioned something about any of you? Any disagreements?' Steed asks.

Hana pauses. 'Well, not disagreements, exactly, but Caleb's been pretty vocal about his dislike for Seth. Jo too. I assumed that was just a personal thing, they'd rubbed him up the wrong way.'

Steed bends down. 'Is this Caleb's?' He gestures to the large backpack by Hana's feet.

Hana nods. 'He has a case too,' she says, pointing.

With brutal efficiency, Steed rummages through the backpack first, before unzipping the suitcase. Maya and Hana watch in silence as he riffles through the contents.

'Nothing here,' Steed says a few moments later, zipping it back up. 'He doesn't have any other luggage?'

'No,' Maya murmurs, but her brow furrows. 'Actually . . .' She turns to Hana. 'Before we left the villa to come here, you guys met me in my room, didn't you? Han, you went to do a final check, see if we'd left anything outside.' She pauses. 'While you were gone, Caleb and I were talking. I went to the loo, and when I came back, he was fiddling with the zip on your suitcase. He said it had come undone. I didn't think anything of it at the time, but . . .'

Elin looks at Steed, raises an eyebrow. *Would he really be so brazen?* 'Do you have an overnight bag with you?'

'Yes, that one,' Hana says, pointing.

Elin thinks it through: Caleb may have assumed that there would be no reason for them to open their cases again until they got to the mainland, particularly if they had overnight

326

bags for the travel back. As good a place as any to stash something.

Steed pulls the case towards him. 'You okay if I open it?'

Hana nods.

Reaching for the zips, Steed tugs them apart, flipping up the lid. For a moment, it looks like Maya's theory is wrong: all Elin can see is crumpled balls of clothing shoved against one another, no semblance of order.

'There,' Maya says slowly, pointing. 'That's not yours, Han, is it?'

Pushed down the far side, against her swimwear, is a washbag. Hana shakes her head as Steed reaches for it. 'Looks fairly innocuous,' he observes.

'Maybe he just ran out of room in his case,' Maya offers, as if she, too, is struggling to see anything sinister in the mundanity of it.

'So why not just ask me if he could put it there?' Hana frowns. 'Why hide it?'

Opening it, Steed rakes through the contents: toothbrush, paste, hair gel.

'Just toiletries,' Maya says, tailing off as Steed fishes something out.

As he holds it aloft, she opens her mouth to speak again, but no words come out.

86

'A passport.' Elin holds up her torch, the dull light illuminating the words. *Christopher Jackson.* 'A different name and a different face . . .' She scrutinizes the photograph. A bushy beard, darker than his hair, lengthens his face, lending the skin around it a sallow colour. The image bears a striking resemblance to the photograph she'd fished from Farrah's bin.

Her gaze slips back to the name, pulse quickening: *Christopher.* 'Wasn't the name Christopher on the plans for the SSSI you found in the shack?'

Steed nods.

'So if Caleb is actually Christopher, chances are those were Caleb and Porter Jackson's plans for the island.' Her mind flickers to the article she'd read about the development, the thwarted plans for ensuring SSSI status. A Chris was mentioned there too, she's certain.

Little cogs in her head start cranking into gear. 'Didn't you say Caleb was pretty disparaging about the retreat?'

'He was,' Steed replies. 'It struck me as a bit over the top, given what had happened.'

Hana glances at her. 'He's said similar to me . . .'

'You think Ronan Delaney knew about these plans when he proposed the development?' Steed says slowly.

'I don't know. But if this *was* Caleb and Porter Jackson's

project, and it never got off the ground, it certainly gives credence to the idea that Jackson had a vested interest in opposing Delaney's plans for the island.'

'Yes, I—' Steed stops. 'Hold on, there's something else.' He's still fumbling in the washbag.

Elin looks over his shoulder, past a faded packet of painkillers to the rounded edge of a phone.

As he withdraws it, they exchange a loaded glance. *The missing memory card.*

Steed presses down on the side button. No password protection: the screen goes straight to home. An ordered stack of icons.

'That's Bea's home screen,' Hana says quickly, her face draining of colour.

Steed clicks on the envelope icon at the bottom. 'Must be her work account,' he mutters.

Elin looks at the massive thread of unread emails, more loading on top.

Steed searches using Caleb's name, then methodically works his way around the icons – WhatsApp, iPhone messages. 'Looks like he's done a pretty thorough job. Can't see anything on here between him and Bea.'

Frowning, Hana points to an icon in a folder on the top of Bea's screen. 'Check this – her Yahoo account. We set those accounts up together, as kids. I didn't know she still had it.'

Steed opens the app. New messages flood the inbox.

Elin waits, expectant.

When the most recent emails download, it's not Caleb's name that appears at the very top of the email chain; it's Bea's.

87

'These look like emails she's sent to herself, copies of messages she's sent to Caleb,' Steed says. 'From what I can see, Bea sent Caleb the messages the morning the group arrived on the island.' He taps the screen. 'Looks like she's found the passport too. She's taken a photo of it, asked him: *What's this?*' He pauses, still scrolling. 'She's also questioning him about emails she's found, written from a different account. Threatening, from the sounds of it. Seems he never replied.'

'Any dates on them?'

He moves his finger down the screen. 'The first we've got here was sent about eighteen months ago.'

Eighteen months ago. The timing can't be a coincidence. 'Around the same time the hotel was being built. Not long after Porter Jackson's memorial.'

Maya turns to Hana. 'Caleb told you his father died, didn't he?'

Hana nods. 'Pretty tragic circumstances, apparently. He said the other day that someone had taken his father's money in a scam not long before he died. Reckoned he'd just started to get his life on track when it happened.'

Elin absorbs her words, casting her mind back to what Ronan Delaney had told her about Jackson's investment gone wrong, an investment he'd encouraged him to make.

Little pieces start to pull together in her mind and, for the first time, form a coherent narrative – one that would give Caleb a clear motive for dispatching Seth Delaney. And from what they've found, it looks like Bea stumbling on his true identity would give him motive for killing her as well.

Disbelief plays out in Elin's mind as she realizes that this case isn't about the curse at all. Caleb's motivation is something else entirely.

'I think we've got the perfect storm here,' she says slowly, moving to the side, out of earshot of Hana and Maya. 'What if the SSSI Caleb and his father had planned for the island never came to fruition because Delaney scammed Porter Jackson of his money, money that might have helped his application? Delaney then goes on to build the retreat.'

'Bit of a slap in the face.'

'Exactly. The Jacksons try to protest the development, but fail, and then shortly afterwards, Porter Jackson dies.' She looks at Steed. 'It would give Caleb a pretty compelling motive.'

'Revenge.'

She nods. 'A far more compelling motive than the curse surrounding Reaper's Rock.'

'But what about what we found in the cave, the Creacher kids?' Steed says slowly. 'How does that fit?'

'I think it fits perfectly. The cave, I'm sure, was Porter Jackson's work, and for him, the motive of the curse, the Reaper, still stands. The anomalies we picked up on between the cases is a result of the fact they were committed by two different people. I think Porter Jackson was obsessed with the rock and killed those teenagers in 2003, and Caleb was simply using that connection to throw us off the scent.'

'That makes sense, but the one thing I don't get is why the SSSI matters so much to the Jacksons in the first place.'

'Think about what Caleb told Hana about how his father was getting his life back on track just before he died, the threatening emails Seth Delaney was receiving. The message was similar in both; Ronan Delaney had prevented people from getting on with their lives. If it *was* Caleb Jackson who sent the emails, maybe it refers to this. Perhaps the SSSI was a way of ensuring his father wasn't compelled to kill again. If it became a nature reserve, it would never be inhabited, so no temptation.'

'Breaking the spell.'

'Exactly. I—' Elin stops as they hear footsteps approach. They turn to find Tom, the water sports instructor, picking his way around the sleeping forms. 'There's something you should know,' he says quickly. 'I've just seen a man outside, running across the bridge to the islet.'

Elin takes a breath. 'When?'

'Ten minutes or so ago . . . I woke up just before, heard a thudding. Thought it was the storm at first, then I remembered that I'd forgotten to put the last rack of boards away. Didn't want them damaging the shack, so I went out to sort it.'

'I'm guessing you didn't go out the main doors?'

Sheepishly, Tom shakes his head, points to a room divider halfway across the side wall, sitting parallel to the wall itself. 'There's a door, behind there.' He pauses. 'I was only out there a few minutes when I saw him.'

'Not staff?'

'Not sure,' Tom replies. 'It's only dimly lit . . . no lights on the bridge itself.'

Elin's stomach tightens.

The islet.

Turning to Steed, she drops her voice a notch. 'You searched there, didn't you?'

'Pretty thoroughly.'

'Any chance you missed something?'

'It's possible. Tree cover's fairly thick in places.'

'I want to take another look.' Elin looks at him. 'I'll go.'

He frowns. 'Alone?'

'I'll have to, we can't risk leaving the lodge unattended.'

'Are you heading out now?'

She nods, adrenaline pulsing through her as she glances outside. 'If that's our killer, possibly Caleb, I'm thinking there's a good explanation as to why he's gone out there.'

'Farrah.'

88

Once the detectives have gone, Maya lies down, dark curls splaying out over the pale fabric of her coat. 'Han, try to go back to sleep. There's nothing you can do. Not now. You need to sleep.'

Hana looks at her, incredulous. *How can Maya even think about resting?*

A wave of nausea pushes through her as she thinks about the group arriving on the jetty only a few days ago, reduced to *this*. The two of them. She can't bear it. 'I just don't understand.' Tears are welling up, hot behind her eyes. 'Caleb . . . he loved Bea. How he talked about her – you can't fake that.' Hana scrolls through their conversations in her mind, a ball of anger and frustration burning in her chest. She recalls his palpable grief. *How had she missed something so vital?*

'People lie, Han, you know that.' Maya's voice is dull.

'I know, but how would he have had the opportunity? We've been together most of the time.'

'Not all. I was just thinking about it, we've been in our own little bubbles after everything that's happened, taken for granted that he's been in his room, but he could have snuck out. There've been loads of times that he went up alone to the restaurant, said he was getting drinks or something to eat, but

God knows what he was doing. I couldn't tell you the exact movements of any of us, not really.'

Hana nods, churning it over. 'But how could he do something like this? Something so *wrong*? Even if you hated someone's guts it doesn't give you the right to—' She breaks off, tears escaping, spilling down her cheeks.

'I don't know. How do you ever get inside someone else's head?' Maya pauses. 'And Han, it's not up to you to find answers. We've been through enough. Jo . . . she's dead.' She tries to catch Hana's eye. 'We haven't even talked about what's happened yet, have we? Jo, I mean.'

Hana nods, and all at once she feels it catching up with her. All the anger she's felt about Jo mixed with a strange kind of guilt. Regret. Love. A complex blend that she's unable to understand, let alone grapple with. She can actually feel it, thick in her throat, all the emotion somehow stuck, clotted there.

'I can't forgive her for what she did with Liam, but I loved her, Maya,' she says falteringly. 'Bea too.' She swallows. 'I loved them so much, and now they're gone.'

'I know.' Maya takes her hand in hers, and it's there, on the floor of the room with strangers asleep all around them, that the tears and the real feelings come rushing out. The tears are not just for her, but for Bea, Liam, all of it. All the emotions knotted together in one big ball, and it's only now unravelling.

'I'm alone, Maya,' Hana says, for the first time not just saying it aloud but acknowledging it in her own head. 'I'm all alone. My sisters are dead.' Her chest is heaving as it hits her. A sledgehammer of grief.

Maya looks at her. For a moment, Hana thinks she's about to cry too, but then she reaches for Hana, pulls her down beside her, wraps her body tightly around hers.

Hana remembers them doing this as kids, the last time, the night of the fire. Maya always had bad nightmares, so Hana would curl up behind her until she went back to sleep.

'You're not alone,' Maya says softly. 'I promise you. You've got me. And this time, Han, I won't leave you. I'm here for you as long as you need.'

89

Outside, Elin finds herself in the eye of the storm. Though it's past dawn, the sky has barely lightened. Rain is torrential – coming at her sideways, lashing her face and neck. She can even taste it, the ground giving up what remained of the dry and dust, a heady, earthy scent.

The storm has wreaked devastation: chairs tossed around the terrace, broken branches scattering the path. Trees are ominously creaking around her, their trunks bending in the gusts.

On reaching the beach, there's more damage: a pine uprooted and snarled across the sand, a Medusa. The rack Tom described has tipped over, the boards being lifted by the wind on one side before slamming hard back down to the beach on the other.

Looking around, Elin has the feeling that the retreat won't survive this – that the storm and the island, the rock itself, won't be sated until it's swept the place clean, all traces of the man-made removed.

Slowly, she makes her way up on to the rocks leading to the wooden bridge. On the first, she hesitates, finding them slick with water. Each step is carefully taken, arms outstretched for balance. It takes several minutes before she reaches the start of the bridge. The thin slats are slippery too, and Elin watches with trepidation as it sways violently from side to side.

Clamping her hands tightly around the ropes of the handrail, she tentatively begins moving forwards. Fine spats of rain whip her face, into her eyes, blurring her view of the islet, but she keeps her gaze fixed ahead, determined to avoid looking down through the gaps. The water between them is no longer flat, the beautiful minty green of before, but dark and angry, frothing thin spumes of white into the air.

Fear pulses relentlessly in her chest, and it's a relief when she finally steps on to solid ground on the other side. She rushes up the path and through the trees, the dense canopy a respite from the rain but not the wind, the branches above shaking furiously.

Through the gloom, the villa appears. It looks like it's barely holding on; the structure seems too fragile for the storm raging around it. Stopping by the front door, she peers through the rain-splattered glass. The space appears to be empty, a scene undisturbed from when she'd come to the islet with Farrah, searched the room.

Fumbling for her security pass, she holds it up to the door. It opens with a click. Breath high in her throat, Elin walks slowly into the room – instant relief from the storm – but there's no one there.

'Farrah?' she calls.

No response.

She checks the bathroom. *Empty.*

Elin's heart is pounding, the isolation she felt the last time she was here even more acute. Moving back to the centre of the room, she keeps looking, but listens this time too, straining her ears over the sound of the storm.

It's then that she feels a tingling at the base of her neck.

Though the room is deserted, she has the distinct feeling that she's being watched. Her thoughts dart to the photograph in the tweet.

Could someone be watching her at this very moment?

Uneasy, she heads for the door, walking around the side of the building to the terrace. Waves are thrashing against the decking, water pooling in the wooden slats, washing through the legs of the chairs and table. No one would be out here, she thinks, not unless they had a death wish. One surge and you'd be in the water.

She plunges into the copse on the right of the terrace, but the higgledy-piggledy line of trees reveals nothing except muddy puddles and damp, slippery shadows of leaf litter.

Elin keeps moving. The tree cover gets denser; she's having to force her way between the trunks. The darkness beneath the canopy plays tricks with her mind. As she fights her way through, she glimpses a shadow dissolve into the thicket, but she puts it down to the storm, the sense of relentless motion it's created.

A few steps on and the land starts sloping downwards, fast-moving streams of rainwater flowing towards the sea. It meets resistance in broken branches and stones, forming winding tributaries.

Within minutes, she's sweating heavily, breathing hard. It's taking all her concentration to remain upright on the slippery ground.

She's nearly at the waterline.

Inching forwards, all she can see through the trees is the sea – choppy, slapping peaks surging on to the rocks then sucking back with such force it's as though it's trying to take a piece of the island with it.

Glancing around her, she's about to turn back, when she notices something in the very periphery of her vision.

A leg, protruding from behind a tree, a pale slice of calf.

Elin's heart is in her mouth as she pushes forwards.

No.

As she rounds the tree, she can see all of her: Farrah, lying on her back on the dirty, sodden ground, a blindfold tied around her head.

No movement. Nothing at all.

An ugly, dogged panic fills her chest.

Elin's stomach twists, her heart beating furiously as she sees a dark smear of blood matting Farrah's hair. She steps closer. A large head wound is now visible, more blood, on the left-hand side of her temple.

Caleb had hit her, just like he hit Jo Leger.

But any disgust she has for him is superseded by disgust with herself.

A sob escapes her throat. *She'd let Farrah down. Failed her.*

Moments flicker in Elin's head: when Farrah had tried to confide. She'd pushed her away, made the wrong call. Elin pictures herself a few hours ago, her naivety as she'd torn around the island.

Had she really thought this would end any differently?

With a shaking hand, she lightly touches Farrah's neck.

A small flicker of hope shimmers, then rapidly fades to nothing. No rise and fall, nothing at all except the hot, relentless pulse of her own blood inside her.

Another sob breaks loose. Grief is already there, taking shape inside her, a grief not just for Farrah but for Will, because she knows what this will do to him. How the sadness will take root inside him and grow and keep growing until it changes him irrevocably.

'I'm sorry,' she murmurs. 'I'm so sorry.'

Elin is about to pull her hand away when something stirs, so faint that at first she thinks it's her own heartbeat.

Shifting closer, she presses her finger slightly harder against Farrah's skin.

A pulse?

90

Elin presses again.

There. A pulse. Thank God. Relief surges through her.

'Farrah,' she says quickly. 'Can you hear me?'

She's unconscious. Breathing but unresponsive.

Elin kneels down on the ground beside her, carefully moving her into the recovery position. Easing the blindfold off, she gently tilts Farrah's head back, lifts her chin, checking that nothing is blocking her airway.

Whether it's the movement that's stirred her or she's simply coming to, Elin hears a faint moan. Farrah's eyes briefly flicker open before closing again.

Agonizingly slow seconds pass before Farrah's eyelids flutter again and she opens her eyes properly, trying to focus.

'It's me, Elin. You're safe.'

Farrah tries to sit up as Elin watches, panicked. With possible neck and spinal injuries, the last thing she should be doing is moving before she's been assessed. 'Don't try to move,' she urges. 'You've got a nasty head injury.'

But Farrah's already trying to sit up. 'I'm cold.' She's violently shivering. She wraps her arms around herself. 'So cold. I can't stay here.'

Elin hesitates. Farrah's right. She's soaked through, and the storm isn't showing any sign of dying down. If they stay put, she's at risk of hypothermia. 'Okay, but before we get you stand-ing, let me do some basic checks. Can you move your fingers and toes?'

But a few minutes later, she's forced to admit defeat on her once-over as Farrah starts getting to her feet. Elin helps, instructing Farrah to lean on her. Inching them towards the villa, she's unable to take her eyes off Farrah's face, the pain etched across her features as they navigate the slippery ground. Every tree root, puddle, an obstacle.

It's a relief when they reach the villa. 'Let's get you inside. Warmed up.' But when Elin opens the door, the air conditioning's blasting, the chill biting through her wet clothing.

She quickly finds the AC control and turns it off. As she leads Farrah across the room to the bed, under the glare of the lights, nothing about her face is familiar – purplish bruises and broken skin. A milky pallor.

Once Farrah's lying down, Elin reaches for the duvet, tugs it up to her shoulders. She's still shivering, her teeth chattering as she lies back, flinching as her head touches the pillow.

Retrieving a glass from the bedside table, Elin fills it with water, hands it to her. Farrah pulls herself up a little and slowly sips.

'So what happened?' Elin says softly and then checks herself. 'Don't worry, I understand if you don't feel like talking.'

'No, it's okay.' Putting the glass down, Farrah leans back again, wincing with the movement. 'It was Caleb . . . he' – she's still struggling to get the words out – 'he hit me with some-thing . . . left me for dead.' She briefly closes her eyes.

Feeling a lump in her throat, Elin has to swallow hard. 'When did he attack you?'

'A few hours ago maybe.' As Farrah looks at Elin, she notices new details: dirt and tiny scratches on Farrah's cheeks and forehead. A gash below her eye is thick with blood. 'I've been hiding over here since yesterday.'

'Caleb came to your office, didn't he?'

Farrah nods. A flicker in her eyes as if she's reliving the memory. 'I got a message from reception saying a detective wanted to meet in my office. I assumed it was you, but when I got there . . .' She swallows.

'It's okay, take your time.'

Farrah composes herself, starts again: 'When I got there, it was him, waiting for me. I tried to defuse the situation at first, grabbed my bag, said I had to go, but the look on his face . . .' She makes a small, strangled sound. 'I knew there was no chance he was going to let me go. I ran out of the back doors, managed to get some distance between us, got down the steps leading to the rocks near the islet. I knew there's a maintenance room below ground, just behind this villa. It was the only place I could think of. I thought he might not know about it.' She hesitates. 'I was right, he didn't. I lost him in the trees.' Her eyes drift, as if she's starting to lose focus.

'You didn't have your phone on you to call anyone?'

'It was in my bag, I dropped it when I was running.' Farrah's eyes slip away again as she toys with the duvet, pinching it between her fingers before releasing it.

'We found your bag when we were looking for you. No phone.' Elin stops. A loud thud.

Startling, Farrah's head jerks up, her gaze darting towards the door.

Elin's pulse quickens. There's every possibility that Caleb's still lurking out there. Could be watching them right now . . .

She springs to her feet, but before she can make a move, the sound comes again, together with a sudden, lurching movement she glimpses from the corner of her eye.

91

Elin whirls around, but then her eyes catch on a large branch, hanging down about a metre from the top of the window. It's moving in the wind, limp, at an awkward angle, as if it's been pulled down.

'Just a branch.' Elin settles back on the bed, but she's still on high alert, eyes roaming around the room.

'You were saying,' she prompts, 'about the bag.'

Farrah nods. 'I think Caleb probably took it, discarded the rest.' She winces again as she shifts position. 'This morning, I was going to try to get back to the main island, to warn you, but he must have seen me . . . or maybe he knew I was there all along and was waiting for the right moment. I tried running again, but he caught up with me this time. I think he thought he'd done it. That I was . . .' Tailing off, she blinks back tears.

'And do you know why he came after you?' Elin says gently.

'Yes.' Farrah drags her gaze up to meet hers. 'I take it . . .' a pause, 'that you know I was on the island when the Creacher murders happened.'

Elin nods. 'I've already spoken to Will. He explained it all.'

Relief softens Farrah's features before her face darkens. 'Caleb, or Chris, as we knew him then, was a camp leader at the time. A few months ago, he came to the retreat, with a friend. I recognized him immediately, but I thought I was imagining it, that it was someone who just looked similar. My head's not exactly been straight, with my ex. I didn't think about it until he appeared again, several weeks ago. When I heard his voice, it got me wondering, but still, I thought it's probably the guilt talking, that I was being paranoid.' Farrah shakes her head. 'But then I noticed him looking at me. He came up to the bar a few times, under the guise of getting a beer, but I could tell he was watching me. Not just idly, you know?'

'He recognized you too.'

'Yeah, I think so. That's when I dug out the old newspaper clipping from the school trip. I couldn't be certain, but I was pretty sure.' Farrah rubs her fingertips against her temple. 'It wouldn't have been such a big deal, but then when Bea fell, and Seth was found dead, and I knew Caleb was with that group . . . I remembered that when he was camp leader, he kept banging on about the old school, Reaper's Rock, trying to scare us. He always came off as a bit strange, you know?'

'That's when you thought Caleb might have something to do with it?'

She nods. 'I think he must have guessed I was suspicious, maybe realized that if he'd recognized me, that I'd done the same. I started wondering if those messages I'd been getting were from him, if he was trying to scare me off the island before he came this time.'

'And he had no way to know that you'd thought it was your ex sending them.'

'Yeah, and I suppose when I didn't leave like he'd hoped, he knew he had to do something else.' She bites down on her lip. 'I should have been on my guard.'

Watching her, Elin's riddled with guilt, heat creeping into her cheeks. 'Don't blame yourself. I didn't listen when you said you wanted to talk. I fobbed you off.' She shakes her head. 'I'm sorry. I should have taken it more seriously.'

'No,' Farrah replies, her expression fierce. 'No apologies. Finding me like you did, it more than makes up for it. If I'd been out there much longer . . .' She reaches for Elin's hand, squeezes hard. Her eyes search Elin's face and as their eyes meet, something passes between them, just as it had outside the villa that first day.

A connection on a level she'd never thought possible.

Elin drops her gaze, a lump in her throat. She knows that in finding Farrah, she's been given a reprieve, not just from Will, but herself. Seeing Farrah motionless back then, on the sodden ground, she'd felt like she was teetering on the brink of something that would not just change Will forever, but her too. A shame and regret that would always haunt her.

Farrah's watching her. 'Will you let Will know I'm okay?'

'Of course. He's been out of his mind.' Elin tugs her phone from her pocket, realizing that she also needs to warn Steed about Caleb – that their suspicions were correct. 'But before that, you need to be checked over. I'm going to try to get you some medical help.'

Yet as she looks at the choppy water through the window, Elin feels a looming sense of foreboding. Even if the team are ready to come, will they really give the okay to sending a boat in these conditions? Further out, the waves are huge, towering walls of water, metres high. Given the wind, a helicopter is looking even less likely.

About to dial, Elin stops, noticing the no-signal icon on her screen. 'Signal's down.' She tries to keep her voice steady.

'It isn't great here, not compared to the main island.' Farrah gestures towards the bedside table. 'Try the landline.'

Elin stands, reaches for the phone. But all she gets is silence. 'It's dead. Either the storm's taken it out or Caleb's cut the line.' She bites down on her lip. 'I don't want to leave you like this,

346

but I'm going to have to go to the main island to call. I'll get one of the first-aiders over to you at the same time.'

Farrah picks up on the hesitancy in her tone. 'It's fine, really. You go.'

Still reluctant to leave her, Elin mulls it over. With no idea of Caleb's whereabouts, it's a risk. But *not* going back to the main island is also risky.

'Go.' Farrah squeezes her hand. 'Honestly, I'm fine.'

'Okay, but you need to lock the door behind me, from the inside.'

Farrah nods. After giving her one last once-over, Elin lets herself out of the villa, the door slamming shut behind her.

Water, everywhere.

Pools formed in the dirty hollows, bigger streams carved out between the leaf litter.

Jumping between them, Elin finds the path, slips between the trees. She breaks into a jog, the saturated ground kicking up a mix of spray and dirt.

As she powers through the final thicket of trees, a gust catches her hair, sending it lashing around her face. It momentarily blinds her, and she skids to a stop.

Reaching up, Elin roughly tugs it away, but too late: a sudden movement at the edge of her vision.

A searing, sharp pain.

Everything goes hazy, a liquid blackness that seems to push up from the base of her skull, pouring over and through her like a wave. For a moment, it sounds like the rain is inside her skull, a soft pitter-patter.

Her vision seems to tunnel, an inky black surging from the outside in.

Then total darkness.

92

When Elin comes to, she's soaked through, bitterly cold. For a moment she thinks she's in the water, floating, waves breaking around her, but as her ankle judders – a jerky up and down – she realizes that while she *is* moving, she's not on water, but land.

She blinks once, twice, but can see nothing; she's been blindfolded.

Panic flares as she tries to move her arms, tug it away, but she's on her back, her hands tied behind her.

Fingers dig hard against her ribs.

Caleb. Holding her under her arms, dragging her backwards.

All she can hear is the wild thrashing of the sea. With every step, the sound gets louder, more intimidating.

Bile rises up the back of her throat. *He's pulling her towards the water.*

While there's a chance he might just throw her in, there's an equal chance that he'll make sure she really is unconscious before doing so. In these conditions, if that happens, it's all over.

Fear closes over her throat, makes it hard to swallow.

Questions dart through her mind: *How long has she been unconscious? Has he already got to Farrah? Done the same to her?*

Think, Elin, think.

For a moment, she can't process it, but then her brain stutters into gear.

A decision: if she stands any chance of getting out of this, she has to play for time. Pretend that she's still unconscious, wait until he stops, and then make her move.

A spray of water hits her face. They're only a metre from the sea; she has to act now.

In one smooth motion, she propels herself forwards; a clumsy jerk of head and torso.

But it works: unbalanced, Caleb rocks from side to side, the hands clamped under her arms briefly slackening.

Falling forwards with a thud, Elin scrambles awkwardly to her knees, inches herself onwards.

Her ribs are heaving, sore from his grip. A few metres on, she puts her right foot out, tries to stand, but Caleb's already rallied.

His hand grabs her leg, jerks her back, towards him.

Elin attempts to wrench herself forwards again, out of reach, but he's quicker. Stronger.

The grip on her ankle tightens; his fingers are just beneath her ankle bone, pushing, pressing.

No time to think: she simply has to move. Elin rolls, cheek pressed stickily to the ground. The movement dislodges not only the grip on her leg, but loosens the tie around her wrists; the pressure from the ligature gives, ever so slightly. Sliding her wrists backwards and forwards across the ground, she tries to loosen it further.

One, two, three, hard strokes across the ground.

It works: Elin wriggles her fingers free with a sudden euphoria, bringing her hands back around in front of her, but she didn't think about what might come after – the vulnerability of being on her back.

She tries scrabbling backwards, crablike, but part of her already knows it's useless. Lurching towards her, Caleb pins her down, his legs on hers.

Elin claws at him, but her hands find nothing but air. She reaches up to try to rip off her blindfold, get a sight of where he is, but before she can even grasp the fabric, he finds her.

A punch to her chest, her face.

Hit after hit that come in time with his grunts. She can smell his breath; it's rancid, stale and sour.

Another blow – one that seems to take over her face, a pain that springs from below her eye, radiating outwards.

Elin can't think.

She's all sensation, can feel every bruised part of herself, tastes iron-bitter blood at the back of her throat.

Punches, one after another. Punches that stun and dazzle, tiny shimmers amongst the black. Her brain seems to dip in and out of consciousness.

Caleb grips her under her arms again, hauling and heaving, as if she's simply a package he has to get rid of, and she wonders if he did this to Seth with the same grim functionality. Hit him and then coldly wedged him into that gap.

Closer again. The sea sounds like it's right behind them.

Her jacket and top have ridden up at the back and she can feel the scratch of the wet ground on her skin. Just grunts from him now, this is workmanlike.

Her reserves of strength are ebbing away; the opposite of the sea, full of power.

Part of her wants to give in, make it easy now.

Elin closes her eyes, bracing herself for the choppy swell of the water.

93

I t doesn't come.

As Caleb grabs her arms, she hears her father's voice in her head again.

You're a coward, Elin. A coward.

The words turn the spark into a fire inside her. Elin throws herself back, the crown of her head hitting something hard with a crack.

His jaw? A cheek? She can't see, but whatever she struck jolts him backwards, off guard. She uses the momentary vulnerability to kick out behind her. He's already unstable and it's enough to make him stumble.

Elin manages to turn, finally gets her hands up to her face to rip off her blindfold.

But the sudden influx of light is too much; she's blinded, her vision blurred. All she can see is a vague outline of him as he staggers sideways.

Caleb seems to hesitate, step towards her, then back. Elin's already anticipating him lunging towards her again, but instead, he's moving away.

Footsteps, thudding hard into the distance.

Elin lies back, closing her eyes and then opening them, waiting for her vision to steady, the giddy spinning beneath her eyelids to cease.

A sob escapes her throat.

It's hard to believe she's safe; she can still feel the violence in the air around her. Caleb was close to killing her, wanted desperately to do it; she could feel the anger in every part of him, every limb, every sinew.

As she eases herself up to a sitting position, questions tear through her head: *why had he left her when he did?* The attack felt so . . . intimate. Something you wouldn't leave unfinished. *Had she hurt him more than she realized? Did he fear he couldn't finish the job?*

But the thoughts are immediately supplanted by the realization that if he's left her, the chances are that he's going after someone else. Farrah, if he hasn't already, Ronan Delaney, Steed, who's on his own back there.

With a huge effort, Elin pulls herself upright, but it's a struggle to get to her feet; the blows have made her dizzy. Still punch-drunk, swaying slightly on her feet, resolve settles on her as she thinks about what lies ahead.

She's reached a pivot point – either she gives up now, or she goes after him.

It only takes a moment to decide as her fear recedes and something else replaces it. Outrage.

Overwhelming, raw anger. Caleb made her feel weak just then. A coward.

She doesn't want to feel like that any more.

Making her way back to the front of the villa, Elin peers through the glass, relief unfolding inside her as she sees Farrah, lying, eyes closed, on the bed. *He didn't come back for her.*

She gently raps on the glass. Farrah's eyes flicker open, widening in alarm before she realizes that it's Elin.

Clambering out of bed, she makes her way to the door. 'Is

everything okay?' she murmurs, pulling the door open. 'Your face...'

Elin raises a hand, lightly grazes her cheek. She winces. 'Caleb.'

Farrah's eyes dart past Elin in panic, but there's no sign of any movement bar the storm: the frenzy it's created, water pounding the glass, still collecting in dirty puddles on the path.

'He's not here.' Elin follows her inside. 'I think he's gone over to the main island. You haven't seen him?'

'No, but I've been drifting in and out of sleep.'

Elin nods and she realizes that Caleb hadn't come back for Farrah because whether she lived or died was irrelevant to him. Coming to the islet was an exercise in distracting Elin, one of the only obstacles in his path, drawing her away from the main island. Winning him enough time to get to his real target.

Ronan.

Farrah climbs back into bed, relaxing against the pillow. 'I'm tired.'

'I know. Let me quickly check you over again and then I'll get help. Try to rest.'

'Okay.' Farrah opens her mouth as if she's about to say something, but her eyes droop closed again.

Back outside a few minutes later, Elin starts picking her way through the trees towards the bridge. Slower this time: every step she takes hurts from Caleb's blows – a dull throbbing in every limb. She's never felt so drained, the heavy, numbing fatigue settling over her, making it hard even to put one foot in front of another.

It seems like an age before she makes it through the trees. She's only a metre or so from the water when her stomach lurches.

The bridge is gone.

94

The swaying slats of the bridge have become a void: all Elin can see is the sea swirling below.

The bridge itself is hanging from its fastening.

Caleb's cut it from the other side.

Up close, she can see that the full length of the structure is now submerged in the water, wooden slats being tossed around in the waves.

She can't get back to the main island.

Elin's gaze lurches to the foaming water. Even with the bridge down, it marks the narrowest point between the islet and the main island. Swimming across is the only way.

Ordinarily, she wouldn't baulk at it, it's only fifty metres at most, yet Elin looks at it with a feeling of trepidation. She's over her fear of water now, has conquered the ugly memories of the Hayler case, but still.

Since the storm, the water has become something *other*, entirely unrecognizable. It's boiling and rolling, worse than when she'd walked over just a little while ago. Waves crashing against the boulders closest to the surface are merging noisily with the backlash from the rocks on the main island, surging upwards in wild peaks.

But Elin doesn't think, she just moves.

Tearing off her shoes and jacket, she slips her phone into a zipped pocket. Inch by inch, she climbs down with her back to the water, using the boulders at the very edge of the islet as a makeshift ladder.

A sharp inhalation as the water surges at her ankles and calves, her body already stiffening, but she rapidly submerges herself. No hesitation.

Flipping over, Elin starts swimming left, away from the bridge that is still being tossed around in the water. Seawater flicks up as it pounds the rocks in front of her, the salt stinging her eyes.

Immediately she feels the churning current created by the backwash, pummelling her back towards the islet. She forces herself on, ploughing through in a clumsy attempt at a front crawl, but it's impossible to get any kind of rhythm with the water tugging at her clothes, the fabric heavy. She should have taken off another layer.

Her breathing is growing staccato. Not from the pain or exertion, but fear. She tries to clear her mind, remember the basics – use her legs more. The strongest part of her.

Swimming forwards, she kicks out. It works – inch by inch, the motion giving her added propulsion.

Eventually, she finds herself a few metres from the rocks. Steadying herself with her hands, she starts clambering up, but the exertion of the swim has made her clumsy. She's misjudging handholds, footholds, crying out as her knee scrapes the sharp protrusions of rock.

Nevertheless, she finally reaches the top, slowly makes her way across the rocks to the beach, water streaming down her face, body. When she jumps on to the sand, it's tacky against her bare feet, no longer simply being peeled off in layers, but whipped into a vortex.

The water sports area has been further decimated – paddleboards scattered far and wide across the beach. One has hit something as it's travelled, a lightning bolt of a crack ripping through the fibreglass.

Elin slowly makes her way across the beach and up the steps to the lodge. Halfway there, she has to stop, her breathing shallow, the pain in her ribs making it hard to take a deeper inhalation.

As the adrenaline drains from her, she can feel bruises blossoming across her body.

Everything's hazy, the vision in her left eye slowly becoming compromised. She can only hope that it's swelling from the punches rather than damage to the eye itself.

She pulls her phone from her pocket. It's wet, the screen blurred with water droplets, but still functioning. Swiping at the screen, she looks for the signal bar.

Nothing.

It wasn't just the islet. The storm has taken everything out.

For a moment, the wind dies, allows Elin to gather her breath and her thoughts, but the quiet is soon broken.

A gunshot, ripping through the silence.

95

Elin's heart thumps in her chest: Caleb's armed . . . this changes everything.

Still unsteady on her feet, she careers up the path towards the main lodge. The gravel is slippery, collected in uneven pockets. Every step, each jolt and jar, brings new pain.

The tarpaulin draped over the restaurant bar on her left has half come loose and is flapping in the wind; sharp cracks that cut right through her. Bottles jostle against each other, several rolling drunkenly backwards and forwards across the countertop.

As she reaches the automatic doors, a bottle loudly smashes to the floor. Elin ploughs on, slipping through the doors.

Inside, she slows, glancing around warily, no idea what she's about to find. Yet the room is eerily empty; sofas bare, reception unmanned. There's a strange sense of desolation. Total abandonment. A sharp contrast to how she'd seen it last.

Moving further in, she notices a trail of wet footprints leading towards the corridor at the back. The prints are spread out, surrounded by a messy splatter of water and sand.

It tells a story: someone running from outside. Someone on a mission.

To find Ronan Delaney.

Elin pushes on, sprinting towards the event room. Halfway across, she tries to take a breath, but her chest is sore, searing jabs of pain around her ribs. By the time she reaches the door, she's gasping.

No time to recover. Tugging her pass from her pocket, she puts it up to the sensor, then pushes.

An immediate resistance.

Shoulder to door, Elin shoves harder, but it only gives a little. Pain radiates across her diaphragm, but she attempts it again; steps back, then forwards, slamming against it with the full force of her body, shoulder first.

The sudden movement makes her cry out, the throbbing around her ribs unbearable, but it's enough: the door gives a little more – enough for her to see a thin sliver of what's behind.

Table legs. Chairs.

They've barricaded themselves in with furniture.

Grabbing the edge of the door, she holds it slightly ajar, peering inside. The room is dimly lit, the space beyond indecipherable. Fumbling for her torch, she switches it on, directing it inwards.

'It's DS Elin Warner,' she calls. The beam of the torch bounces off the metal legs of the chairs, making it hard to see anything past the jumble of furniture. Just a blur of featureless faces in the dim light.

Despite the lack of movement, the fear inside the space is almost tangible. It's as if everyone in the room is taking a collective breath.

Her mind runs riot. *What if Steed hasn't made it?* It would make sense for Caleb to take him out first so he would then have free rein to do whatever else he had planned to Delaney.

But only a few moments later, she hears footsteps. The light of the torch picks out Steed's face peering past the furniture, through the barricade.

'Are you okay?' she says quickly.

'We're all fine, but Delaney's gone.' His voice wavers as he starts tugging at the furniture to let her inside. 'Nothing I could do. Jackson's armed, let off a few warning shots. No way of taking him down.' He lowers his voice. 'Delaney went willingly. Pretty clear what Jackson would do if he didn't.'

Elin scrambles over an upturned table into the room. The group of people left are huddled in the far corner, their eyes locked on her, wide, frightened.

Taking her to one side, Steed's gaze slides over her face, body, his eyes clouded with concern. 'What happened? You're soaked.'

'I was . . .' Swallowing hard, she re-forms the sentence. 'Caleb – he attacked me, on the islet. I got away, but he cut the bridge down, I had to swim across.'

'Jesus.' He takes a breath. 'And Farrah?'

'I found her over there. He's hit her . . . she's got a head injury, but she'll make it.'

'She still over there?'

'Yes.' Elin shudders, feeling the unpleasant sensation of cold water dripping down the base of her neck from her hair. 'I didn't want to leave her, but I had no signal to contact anyone and I knew he was coming here. I've left her in the villa.'

'We could try to get a member of staff across.'

'I thought that before I saw the bridge was down. The water's too wild to swim. Too risky to send anyone.'

A beat. Steed looks troubled. 'And you're sure that *you're* okay?'

'I'm fine.' But as she speaks, the pain from her ribs flares again, takes the breath from her.

'Elin . . .'

She bats away his concern with a question. 'Did you see which way he went?'

Still watching her, Steed gestures towards the doors behind. 'He took Delaney through those.'

'How long ago?'

'Five minutes, maybe ten.'

Elin follows his gaze, calculating. Those doors are on the same side of the building as Farrah's office. Not many places for Caleb to go from there. 'I need to change and then I'll head out.'

Steed's gaze locks on hers. 'Elin, no, Caleb's armed. We need to wait for the team.'

Elin hesitates and, in that brief moment, fear slides into the silence between them as she remembers the violence of Caleb's attack on the islet. In her mind's eye, she feels it all over again, blow after angry blow, the oily lurch in her gut as he'd dragged her to the water.

But as the memory subsides, the echoes of his violence only steel her resolve. 'With the phone lines down, we've got no idea when the team's coming or if they can even get here, given the storm. That might be too late for Ronan. I think now we know why Caleb's doing this, I can talk him down.'

Steed's silent as Elin tugs off her wet jacket. Every jerky movement sends little ripples of pain through her ribcage. Grabbing her bag, she steps behind the barrier to change, but despite her words to Steed, she feels panic rising in her throat.

She fights it back, stooping to pull on a pair of shorts. A new pain: a dull throbbing not just around her ribs but *from* them, as if the very bone itself is protesting.

Doubt strikes again: is she really capable of stopping him in this state?

As she steps out from behind the barrier, Steed catches her eye. 'Elin, I've been thinking about it. You can't go alone. At least let me—'

But she's already heading for the doors.

96

Stepping through the doors, Elin's under siege, the world moving frenetically around her.

Trees. Furniture. Parasols. A merry-go-round of sand and dirt.

Adrenaline squeezes at her chest. Every sound, every movement is like a warning: telling her to go back to the main lodge. Protect them. Protect herself.

But she can't. Ronan and Caleb are out here somewhere.

Looking around, she assesses where they could have gone. Her gaze lurches left, then right, locking on the sloping patch of grass leading down to the cliff. No access to the beach below apart from the steps she glimpsed when she and Steed were looking for Farrah. Too steep, surely, for Delaney, if he's restrained?

Elin shuffles forwards, listening for any sounds, but it's impossible: the storm is the only voice to be heard. There's no chance of hearing anything beyond the howling wind and ugly spatter of the rain.

She moves towards the front of the lodge: *no sign of Caleb or Ronan.*

When she reaches the restaurant terrace and bar a few moments later, she's stopped in her tracks.

It's been decimated. The neat piles of chairs she'd glimpsed on her way in have been toppled, flung around, several jammed up against the balustrade.

Lifting her leg over the broken remains of a table to get closer to the bar, she notices that the tarpaulin is no longer flapping; it's completely gone.

Without any shelter, the wind's wreaked havoc: bottles rolling across the floor. Glass smashed beneath her feet, crunching as she moves. Amber liquid from a broken bottle is pooling between the pieces of glass. The acrid smell of alcohol hits her nose.

A movement makes Elin glance up: one of the strings of festoon lights has been ripped from its fastening on one side, careering wildly backwards and forwards. Another has come fully down, now snaking along the floor between the broken glass and puddles of alcohol.

She's about to turn, head for the balustrade to look at the level below, when something shifts in her vision.

A dark mass swinging towards her.

In a split second she realizes: the tarpaulin. *It hasn't gone.* It's still attached at the top, a gust hauling it out of sight for a moment before pulling it back down.

Elin steps away but too late: the tarp slaps her in the face, chest. The sudden movement nearly knocks her off her feet. Quickly steadying herself, a wave of dizziness washes over her, blood rushing to her head.

One deep breath. Another.

It's a few moments before she's ready to move again. Winding through the debris, she picks her way across the restaurant terrace and peers over the balustrade to the pool. For a moment, she thinks she sees a person before she realizes that it's only a daybed, half submerged in the pool, one end bobbing up and through the water.

She shifts right to get a vantage point to the beach.

Chaos.

More sand is being whirled up into mini-vortexes. Trees, uprooted from the cliff, have now taken rocks down with them, vast lumps of stone studding the sand. She looks left, towards the islet. From this angle, she can just about make out the rope swing, individual ropes being wildly tossed about by the wind.

No one's there.

Turning, she moves quickly towards the yoga pavilion – long, loping strides. Obstacles wherever she goes: puddles, clods of churned-up earth, debris. From the corner of her eye, she's convinced she sees movements, but it's only her own erratic, jerky gestures reflected in the glass walls of the main lodge.

Once she reaches the yoga pavilion, she takes another look around her. Still no sign.

The only place left outside, at this level, is the back of the main lodge. If they're not there, she'll have to search the building itself. There's a small chance they might have doubled back, gone inside.

As Elin starts to half walk, half run, a dogged panic settles in her chest. Out here, exposed like this, she can't help but feel that she's being watched: that Caleb Jackson's aware that she escaped the islet and is lying in wait for her somewhere.

Skin crawling, she has to force the thought away, keep moving. At the corner of the lodge, she forks right. Back to the wall, she skirts around the side, finding cover as best she can. This close to the woodland, the path is littered with twigs, whole branches, wrenched from the trees. It's as if the island isn't just turning on the retreat, but on itself, won't stop until it's stripped itself bare.

Stopping at the back of the lodge, she scans the terrace, the grass in front dipping away into woodland.

Her eyes lock on the dark mass of the forest beyond, the only colour the bright triangles of trail markers tacked to the trees. If she thought it was wild the last time she'd glimpsed it, it's become something other; as though the whole forest is moving as one entity, trees not just thrashing wildly, individually, but beating together.

A force.

As Elin stares into the depths, finding Caleb and Ronan suddenly seems an impossible task. Too much ground to cover on her own.

Should she abandon hope? Do as Steed suggested and wait for backup?

But it's then that she hears something.

Stilling every muscle, Elin strains her ears.

A voice: Caleb's.

Low muttered tones. Getting louder. Another voice, a cry of pain.

She holds her breath.

Ronan and Caleb are heading her way.

97

Caleb must have been lying low, somewhere close to where she'd exited the building, waiting until he thought it was clear.

Elin looks wildly around her. If he finds her here, out in the open, she loses any element of surprise. With Caleb armed, she stands no chance.

Her gaze lurches towards the lodge, the doors. Too late: she goes that way and she'll be heading straight towards them, plus she needs her pass to get in. It'll take too long.

The woods.

The throbbing in her ribs, chest, is now insistent, but she tries to force a jog across the grass, towards the first thicket of trees. Wood chippings and pine needles spray out as her feet clumsily pound the ground.

She's only a few metres from the forest when her foot slides out from under her. No purchase on the slippery ground.

Tumbling forwards, her hands jerk out to break her fall. A brutal jarring as her palms slam against the ground, the impact surging up her arms to her chest. The pain around her ribs grips tighter and she gasps, drawing herself up on to her hands and knees.

Elin glances in the direction of the lodge.

They're closer. Another metre and they'll be almost parallel to her.

Aghast, she lies flat, tries not to make a sound, draw attention to herself. The soil is damp, tiny stones within it digging into her cheeks.

Holding her breath, she can feel her heart pounding.

The wind drops so she can hear voices again. Caleb's, growing louder.

Did they see her fall? Are they heading her way now?

If they hadn't seen her then, once they get parallel to her, they're certain to.

Move. She has to move.

Hauling herself forwards, staying low, she plunges into the dense undergrowth. Brambles and twigs poke and prod at her face, snagging on her clothing.

A voice sounds out again – some kind of shouted directive.

Still crouching, Elin pushes deeper, thorns catching in her neck, hair. She winces as one snags the soft skin of her scalp.

Between the gusts of wind, Caleb's voice is audible again.

Panic flares.

She lifts her head a fraction, but all she can see is the undergrowth in front of her: spikes of pine needles, churned-up soil. Leaf litter, sodden and creased. Her nostrils are filled with the scent of fresh soil, undertones of decay.

'You see that?' Caleb's voice sounds out: a shout that drifts in the wind. 'Down there?'

Whether he's talking to himself or Ronan, she has no idea.

A flurry of movement.

Heart racing, Elin lies frozen on the spot, eyes wide open, staring into the undergrowth. The effort of holding the position is too much; her muscles twitch. She's going to have to move.

There's a guttural rumble of thunder.

As it fades, Caleb speaks again. 'Let's go. Nothing here.'

The relief is instantaneous, but still, she lets a few minutes pass until she moves.

Slowly breathing out, she gradually hauls herself up, using the woodland as cover while she surveys the grass in front, the space around her. Her legs are numb and stiff; it takes a moment until they feel like hers again.

Still looking about, on her guard, she stumbles up the grass towards the main lodge. No sign of them, but she guesses they've continued in the same direction – away from where they'd exited the building, towards the rock.

Back to the wall, she moves slowly around the side of the building, once again struck by paranoia: that Caleb's watching somewhere. Waiting. Fleeting glimpses of the interior of the lodge only heighten her unease: in the shifting shadows beyond the glass there's movement everywhere.

Elin passes the base of the rock, about to start down the steps to the villas, when there's a brief lull in the wind. The thrashing of the trees is stilled, the swirling sand and dirt settling to the ground. She catches the strains of speech, then a harsh, scraping noise. More speech. Short, angry sounds. Lost as the wind gusts again.

Heart pounding, she waits, poised, willing another moment of quiet.

Elin only has to wait a minute or so for it to arrive. A moaning noise: Ronan?

Straining her ears, she tries to isolate the source of the sound.

It's only when the noise gets louder that Elin realizes that it's coming from above her.

The rock.

98

Elin looks up, can't see anything. But as she moves a few feet around the rock, she sees it: a ladder, propped against the stone.

More sounds: something scraping. Voices.

He's taking Ronan up there.

Despite the acute pain in her ribs, she walks as quickly as she can to the base of the rock to find Caleb scrambling up the ladder, Ronan in front of him.

Elin ducks behind a small overhang, waits, silent, but Caleb gives no sign that he's seen her. She's about to reach for the ladder, when it moves. *He's knocking it away from the rock.*

The ladder sways precariously backwards then forwards before Elin manages to grab it, haul it back into position. She looks up, but Caleb either hasn't spotted her or is already gone.

Gingerly, she steps on to the first rung, starts to climb. The wind has picked up again, violent gusts tugging at her wet clothes, her hair. She immediately feels its strength as she hauls herself upwards, biting her lip at the pain sparked by every movement.

Inching herself up the last rung and on to a plateau, Elin exhales, scoping out the space. The rock juts inwards here, the plateau formed by a natural shelf, about a metre wide, wrapping itself around the main body of the rock on her right, which continues upwards, soaring above her.

Caleb and Ronan are nowhere to be seen. They must be on the other side of the rock.

Breathing fast, she starts moving around the plateau, but the stone beneath her feet is rough, slippery. A few paces on, the wind gusts. Swaying, Elin forces herself to look straight ahead. Focus on the tips of the trees in the distance.

Don't look down.

The wind surges again. Fists clenched tight, Elin steps closer to the rock for shelter, arms outstretched for balance.

Rounding the corner a few moments later, she stops in her tracks.

Caleb, holding a gun, is pointing it at Ronan. Slumped at the base of the rock, a large gash splitting a ragged line through Ronan's temple, trickles of blood snaking down towards his shirt. Below, a massive swelling around his eye has closed it to a slit. His lips are pressed together as if he's trying to stop himself from crying.

Caleb doesn't even look in her direction. He's doing something curious: talking at Ronan, a stream of words with no pause or punctuation. A focused, verbal violence. He's enjoying the sound of himself.

This is what he wanted, Elin thinks, why he didn't kill Ronan on sight; he wanted to explain exactly what Ronan had done to his family. He wants Ronan to *see* him, see them.

She imagines all the moments that will have built to this point: one lie, every misstep, on top of another.

Elin steps closer. Caleb's head whips around, his eyes deadened as they meet hers. She wonders how she didn't see it before, the chilling vacancy in his face. Someone who had lost his connection to the world.

'I know you'd like to help him, but I'm afraid no can do.' Caleb shakes his head, almost sorrowfully. 'You've disturbed us when I was just getting into my flow.' Behind him, heavy clouds hang low, making dark pockets in the sky.

'Caleb, this isn't how you want this to play out, I know,' Elin says, raising her voice above the sounds of the storm. 'There's still time to stop this going any further.'

'But I *want* this to go further. This is what it's all about. This moment.' Even this close, the end of his sentence is muffled by the wind.

Elin takes another step. 'You might think that, but it's not the answer to anything.'

'Stop.' Caleb jerks his arm upwards. 'Don't come any closer.' He lowers the gun until it's pointing directly at Ronan's face, giving a light flick of the wrist as if in warning. Ronan flinches, starts to tremble, a barely audible noise coming from the back of his throat. 'He needs to be punished, here, on the rock, where it all began.'

Keep him talking. 'But what you're doing here, it isn't about Reaper's Rock, is it?'

His eyes flash. 'It is. It's what's happening here, right now, the Reaper taking the souls of people who deserve to die.' Caleb glances down at Ronan. 'People like him.'

Steadying her voice, Elin looks him in the eye. 'You really believe that?'

He seems surprised by the question. Something flickers in his expression before he composes himself. 'Of course I do. Look what happened at the school, the Creacher kids.'

'But it was your father who killed those teenagers on the course. There is no Reaper. You know as well as I do that your father was delusional, killed those teenagers because of what happened to him at that school. But what you've done, it's about something else.'

Caleb tips his head, watching her, as if he's trying to calculate what she might know. A smirk, but it falters. 'Go on, then, seeing as you've got it all worked out. Tell me what that is.'

'Revenge. Revenge for the fact that your father lost money to Ronan. Money he was going to use to buy the island, ensure its status as an SSSI, and revenge for the fact that Ronan went on to develop it himself, something that sent your father to an early grave.'

Caleb starts to speak, as if he's about to push back, before he seems to crumple, shoulders rounding. His fingers come up to pinch the skin at the bridge of his nose as if to stop himself from crying. 'That SSSI . . . it was supposed to be a fresh start for my father. Do you know what that school did to him?' He shakes his head. 'It consumed him, turned him into a monster. He spent hours in that cave, shaping those stones, convincing himself he was some bloody reaper.' His voice wobbles. 'But after he killed those kids, he tried to change, you know? He took the right meds, determined it wasn't going to happen again.' He jerks his arm towards Ronan. 'But *he* trampled all over that by taking my father's money.'

Ronan's eyes flicker open. 'A tip, that's all it was.' His voice is low, muffled by pain. Despite his protestation, it's clear that he's lying. Like a cloud weighing heavy above him, she can see it: shame. Etched into every part of his face. 'I didn't mean anything by it.'

Caleb's mouth drops open, incredulous. 'Even now, you're lying. The company that ran the scheme, you were behind it. I found out. All you've ever done, Delaney, is take. You destroyed my father. Financially. Mentally. Until he couldn't take it any more, until he . . .'

The words stop him in his tracks, the hand clamped around the gun starting to tremble, making the barrel move up and down. His eyes are smarting when he looks at her, and Elin can see it marked in them: grief. Grief and pain, and utter bewilderment – as if he's looking at the world and not understanding it any more.

'I'm sorry,' Ronan says, his face ashen. He sucks in a gaspy breath, clutching his side. 'I never wanted anything like that to happen.'

Elin's struck by a sharp needle of fear at the wheedling, pleading tone to Ronan's voice. *No*, she wants to tell him, *don't try to garner sympathy, because that will make him hate you even more, because you haven't shown sympathy for him, not the slightest bit. You took from him, everything he had, and now you're trying to take more.*

Tears stream down Caleb's face. 'You dismissed me when I contacted you, tried explaining what the SSSI meant to my father. Like what you'd done – taking my father's savings, trampling on his fucking dream – meant *nothing*.' He draws breath. 'One bit I never understood was how it doesn't get to you. How you can't feel it.' Caleb reaches up a hand to his chest. 'Feel it in here. Seth was the same. I thought he might have a shred more moral conscience, but no. People like you, you think that because you've got money and power, the rules don't apply. But I'm making you care now, aren't I? You deserve every bit of what's coming to you.'

'But the others didn't,' Elin says softly. A glimmer of hope; how Caleb's sharing like this, opening up – it might be enough. The lever she needs. If she can just keep him talking, she might be able to break the spell and help him see the rationale in letting Ronan go free. 'Bea and Seth and Jo.'

'Jo?' Caleb's eyes narrow. 'But I didn't kill her.' He cocks his head, breathing hard. 'Is this some part of your strategy, try to confuse me by accusing me of things I *haven't* done?'

Another upwards jerk of the gun. Ronan shrinks backwards.

Elin edges closer. 'Caleb, I know what Ronan did was terrible, but by hurting him, you're also doing something wrong. I know you can see that—'

'Keep away. I mean it.' The gun shifts from Ronan to her and then back again, the barrel shaking because Caleb's trembling, the muscles in his forearm visibly twitching. 'I know I'm doing something wrong. I'm well aware, but you know, it's right that it ends here, on this rock.' A brittle laugh. 'I still can't believe my poor father believed all that shit, but people believe it for a reason, don't they?' His words are emerging faster and faster. 'It's a projection; they're putting the darkest parts of themselves into something else. Strange to call it a safe space, but it is. When you put all the bits of yourself that you hate and fear into a rock like this, it's no longer a part of you. It's what my father did.' He shakes his head. 'But I know where the darkness really lies. In us. In you. *We* do bad things. Not some piece of stone.'

Caleb lifts his face to meet hers. For a moment she thinks he's wavering, his hand loosening around the gun, but then he looks back to Ronan. His gaze hardens, eyes flinty, his expression fixed in a way that's making her nervous.

He raises his hand a notch, fingers twitching around the gun before he steadies them.

Panic clawing at her chest, Elin reaches out a hand, steps forwards, starts to say something, but Caleb's already compressing the trigger.

A deafening bang.

99

Ronan's body spasms, an erratic flailing of limbs. Horrified, Elin forces herself to look, expecting Caleb to have aimed for his head or chest, but instead sees blood gushing from a wound in his thigh.

As Caleb steps towards her, she realizes why: he has unfinished business with Ronan. The shot wasn't fired to kill him, but to immobilize him, so Caleb can come for her.

Panicked, she thinks: *Engage him. Make him see you as a person. Not a threat.*

But as she opens her mouth to speak, Caleb's already talking. 'I didn't want to do this.' He swings the gun around to point it at her. 'I meant what I said before. I didn't want to hurt anyone else. This was supposed to be all about Ronan and Seth, but, you know, I haven't quite finished explaining *exactly* what he did to my family, and while you're here, I'm not going to be able to get my words out properly.' He sounds almost apologetic, rueful. 'I'm sorry it has to be this way.'

His finger twitches around the trigger. Another loud bang.

Elin lurches sideways. She doesn't know where the speed comes from, the strength to move, but it's not enough.

There's an almost instantaneous pressure followed by a hot, searing pain, unlike anything she's ever felt before. A sudden and strange heat overwhelms the left-hand side of her body, as if something fiery is inside her, trying to burn its way through from the inside out.

She glances down at herself, startles. *Blood.* So much blood.

Gasping, she stumbles backwards. All at once, her legs give out from under her and she crumples to the stone. Head spinning, she clutches at her side, reeling as her fingers come away red.

Caleb steps towards her. He's frowning, head tipped to one side, examining, a world-weary expression on his face. Elin realizes that he's telling the truth. He doesn't want to do this, but it's become necessary. A job to be done.

He raises the gun again.

Elin's throat slackens in resignation. For the first time, she isn't scared. She's too tired to be scared. All she feels is a weird kind of longing. For quiet. Peace.

Caleb takes another step closer, arm outstretched.

But just as she braces herself, his arm drops a notch. She watches as he slips, almost in slow motion, his foot, perhaps slick with blood and rainwater, going out from underneath him.

There's a loud cry of exclamation as he falls heavily on to the stone.

He seems unable to move at first and Elin watches him, confused. His shoulders are heaving. *He's crying*, she realizes. As he glances up, tears are streaming down his cheeks.

A glimmer of hope: she has a brief window of time in which to do something.

Elin tries to focus. While the pain is excruciating, it has a clarity about it now; no longer everywhere but tunnelling into an urgent throbbing, not in her torso as she'd thought, but her arm.

The knowledge galvanizes her: it might not be as bad as she believed.

A sudden head rush as she gets to her feet; every part of her pulling together into this one moment. Every last bit she has. Strength. Willpower. Fear. It's all the momentum she'll ever have.

The voice in her head calling her a coward is there again, but Elin pushes it away. It doesn't scare her, nor does it motivate her. She doesn't need to prove herself. She's done that already, time and time again.

Lurching forwards, she knows that what she's about to do is *her* decision, no one else's. The right decision in the circumstances.

Elin staggers, hearing her own ragged breath in her ears. Caleb's head snaps back to look at her, he starts to speak, but his words lift up into the wind, quickly fading away.

Caleb tries to scramble to his feet, but he can't get purchase.

Elin's already there; she rams her body against him, against the pain, against every doubt she's had, the speed of the move taking even her by surprise. The jolt as she hits him pushes the breath from her lungs, sending an agonizing jab of pain through her ribs.

Caleb's gun skitters out of his grasp, coming to rest on the stone a metre away. He lunges towards it and tries to grab it, but she slams herself on top of him again, the full weight of her body on his, grinding his torso into the stone.

He squirms beneath her, but Elin holds fast, using all her strength to haul his arms behind his back, forcing herself to ignore the pain screaming from her wound.

As she pins him down, everything is muted. She can barely hear the wind and the rain, even her own heaving breath.

It's just the two of them. Him versus her.

Caleb's twisting beneath her, trying to move, but Elin pushes down harder, so hard she can feel the muscles in her arms pulsing with the effort.

She knows she has no choice but to keep hold of him. Her strength is all she has – if she makes a move for her handcuffs, he'll try to use the opportunity to get the better of her.

'He was my father,' Caleb says between sobs. 'The only family I ever had. Without family, you've got nothing, have you? Nothing.'

Elin's gaze see-saws between him and Ronan. Ronan's eyes are still closed. He's making a high-pitched keening sound. It's clear that he's cut himself off, closed his eyes and mind to what's happening around him.

Caleb moves again, trying to dislodge her. Elin starts to panic, unsure how much longer she can hold him. Her hands are slippery with sweat and blood, the pain in her arm excruciating.

She pulls in a deep breath, trying to summon up the last of her strength, when she registers another hand, in front of hers.

'It's okay, Elin, I've got him.'

Steed's voice. For a moment she thinks she's imagining it, until she tips up her head and sees Steed there, kneeling beside her. 'Elin, I've got hold of him. You can let go now.'

Blinking, Elin meets Steed's gaze, nods. She can't quite read his expression, but there's something in his eyes that she understands on a level that defies words.

Slowly, carefully, she shifts out of Steed's way.

Relief washes over her. *He's right: she can let go now.*

Watching Steed restrain him, she realizes that what Caleb said was true. Family *is* all you have, but it isn't found only in a blood connection. Family shows itself in the unlikeliest of moments: the split-second glances, a gesture, the hand next to yours when you need it the most.

Epilogue

'Guessing it's still raining, then?' Elin hauls herself upright in her hospital bed. Her eyes run over Anna's damp hair, fine droplets of water caught in the hairs escaping her ponytail.

'Hasn't stopped.' Anna smiles, too hearty and healthy-looking for the clinical surroundings in her blue hoodie and running tights.

Steed, sitting on the right of her bed, shuffles his chair closer. Reaching into his bag, he pulls out a pack of grapes, passes them to her. 'Thought I'd do the whole cliché grape thing. Might keep you going until lunch.'

Elin laughs, but as she takes the pack, there's a pull in her ribs. She winces.

Steed looks at her, concerned. 'Still got pain?'

'Yeah, but it's getting better. To be honest, I'm tired more than anything. The infection took it out of me. Thought I was ready to go home, then I got hit by that.'

'And the ribs? Fracture healing?'

Slipping a grape into her mouth, she nods. 'Just about. I hate the whole not-moving thing, but Will says it's doing me good. Enforced relaxation.' Smiling, she looks out the window. Cars are winding past the hospital car park, making their way to the bottom of the hill.

'How are things between you and Will?' Anna asks, then casts a panicked look at Steed, clearly wondering if she's got too personal in front of him. 'Sorry,' she mouths.

'It's fine. He knows all the nitty-gritty.' Elin flashes him a smile. 'To be honest, we haven't really had a chance to speak properly yet, not on that level anyway. Probably wait until I get home.'

Anna nods. 'And Farrah? She's recovered okay?'

'Physically at least, yes, she was lucky, only superficial damage, but mentally . . . I think she's still in shock.'

'Understandable. It'll take time to work through.' Leaning across, Anna plucks a grape from her packet. 'So what's next? Still planning on the holiday?'

'Yeah. Going with Isaac. We're heading out to the sticks for a bit. His friend has recommended a place.' Elin's stomach dips. She's nervous, she realizes, about seeing him. No Will this time. Just the two of them. Alone. Nowhere to hide. 'The time away will do me good. Sat in here, I've had time to think . . . I've decided I need to try to understand me a bit more.'

'Headspace?'

Elin nods. 'I keep going over it, and I've realized that I've always convinced myself that what's been driving me is some noble thing about getting answers – living life to the max because Sam couldn't – but it's not that.' She gives a brittle laugh. 'During this case, it's my father's voice I've heard in my head, calling me a coward. That's what's been driving me. Trying to prove to him, other people, that I'm not.'

'And to yourself?' Anna says quietly.

'Yes, I think so, but up there on the rock, the move I made on Caleb, I reckon it's the first time I ever made a decision just for me.' She hesitates, thinking about the best way to phrase it. 'I'm not a coward, like Will said, for doing something I shouldn't, or for doing nothing, like my dad made me believe. The only really cowardly thing I've done is not be true to myself.'

'Doing what *you* want,' Steed murmurs.

'Exactly. I need to get to know myself, all the good bits, but the bad bits too.' She shrugs. 'I want to be sure that when I come back, I'll do what I did up on that rock every time. Make decisions that are mine, no one else's.'

Anna's quiet for a moment, before nodding. 'As long as you *are* coming back.' She looks between them, smiles. 'You two – you're the dream team.'

Steed tips his head to one side, as if considering. 'Tough decision, but I think I'm okay to work with her again.'

Elin grins at him. 'Seriously though, thanks, for everything. I didn't get a chance to say it properly before.'

'S'all right. For a moment there . . .' Steed tails off.

She meets his gaze. Neither of them can begin to say it. And they don't need to.

Making a fuss of moving the grapes to her side table, she grabs the packet of Yumnuts Will left her. 'Saved one for you.' She passes him the box.

Giving her a grateful smile, he digs his hand in, pulls it out. It's gone in two bites.

'So what's happened now, with the case?' Elin asks.

'Post-mortems confirmed what we suspected,' Anna replies. 'Jackson confessed to it all, gave details. Bea Leger was collateral damage, as we thought. From the sound of it, the cliff fall was another option he had planned for dispatching Delaney, but then Bea threw a spanner in the works, forced him to improvise.'

'And the cave, the Reaper stuff?'

'You were right. All a ruse once he realized that the accident narrative wouldn't stick. Wanted to distract us into thinking the case was linked to the Creacher murders, so he could crack on with getting rid of Ronan Delaney.' Steed wipes his mouth with the back of his hand. 'He told us his father was responsible for the murders Creacher was meant to have committed. Lois Wade, too.'

'What about Jo Leger?' Elin clears her throat.

Anna frowns, pausing. 'That's the one thing that's still bothering me,' she says finally. 'Jackson's still saying he didn't do it. Steed reckons he's toying with us.'

Steed eyes the empty Yumnut box, nods. 'I know it happens. A power thing. Not giving every piece of the puzzle away.'

'And the tweets? He ever fess up to those?'

Anna falters. 'No, but we're pretty sure he's responsible. The fact there's been no messages since . . .'

Elin nods, discomforted. Until Anna and Steed arrived, she wasn't even sure whether she was going to bring it up. 'It's just—'

'What?'

'I'm probably being paranoid, but I've still got this feeling that someone's' – she clears her throat – 'someone's been watching me.'

'You've seen them?' Steed's brow furrows in concern.

'No, it's more a *feeling*.' Elin flushes, unsure of how to word it. 'The other day someone came past the ward and I thought—' She shrugs, forcing a laugh. 'Forget it, probably all the meds making me loopy.'

Anna and Steed exchange a glance.

Elin changes the subject. 'How's it going with Creacher?'

Steed places a newspaper on the table. 'Funny you say that. It's all in here. Not exactly light bedtime reading, so don't feel you have to look if you don't want to.' He hesitates. 'There's mention of Farrah and Will too.'

She scans the headlines, the subhead.

Larson Creacher has been released from HMP Exeter ... The police are satisfied that there is sufficient evidence to prove that Porter Jackson was responsible for the murders of five teenagers in 2003. The police have confirmed that they are not looking for anyone else in relation to these deaths.

Her eyes skip over the text: no further police action will be taken against Farrah and Will Riley.

A rush of relief. Closure. She leans back against the pillow, suddenly tired.

'You look knackered,' Anna says, watching her. 'We'll leave you to it.' Standing up, she leans over the bed, hugs Elin.

Steed bends down, lightly pecks her on the cheek. 'If I don't see you before you go on holiday, I want photos, okay? Lots of them.'

'Guaranteed. You won't be able to escape my ugly mug. I'm going to be one of those annoying holiday braggers, posting photos every day.'

Steed grins, grabbing a last grape from her pack as they leave the room.

Watching through the glass as they make their way down the corridor, Elin picks up the newspaper Steed left. She starts flicking, trying to find the article on Creacher, when her phone buzzes.

A message, from a number she doesn't recognize: a screenshot of a tweet.

Her heart seems to stop in her chest mid-beat: she doesn't want to look, but at the same time, can't stop herself.

They've tagged Torhun police station again, but this time there's text next to it.

Two lines.

Want to know a story about this detective?
A clue: this one doesn't always tell the truth . . .

Elin sucks in a breath, but any fear she has of the wording is supplanted by a raw terror at the image below.

A photograph of her in her hospital bed, Steed's newspaper in hand, taken a few moments ago.

Two Weeks Later

It's a couple of weeks since she got home, but only now Maya feels ready to unpack. She hauls her bag into the kitchen, empties it beside the washing machine. The crumpled clothes smell of beach and sea. Sand is embedded in the folds of the fabric; little off-white grains, fragments of shell – tiny half-moons, purplish slivers of mussel.

Maya loves this bit after every trip, the sense of possibility that comes with a freshly emptied bag, waiting for the next adventure.

Her trainers are at the very bottom, the ones she'd worn on the beach that day. Shaking them vigorously into the sink, sand skitters out over the stainless steel, and with it comes a flash of Jo's face as Maya had stepped towards her.

She'd found Jo staring out to sea, snivelling, self-indulgent. Maya could tell that when Jo turned, she thought it was Hana, ready to continue their argument about Liam. Jo's mouth was already half open, ready to apologize, worm her way back into her sister's affections.

When she saw it was Maya instead, she smiled in relief. Jo didn't notice the rock in Maya's hand – it wouldn't even enter her mind that her cousin would hurt her. Maya's always been in the background, meant to be grateful. Grateful that Jo had got her a job, a job that she'd then taken away. Grateful that Jo and Bea and Hana had absorbed her into their family unit after what had happened to Sofia.

But what Jo didn't know is that Maya *saw* her. Really saw her. Saw who she was inside: someone grasping, selfish, the kind of selfish that doesn't even recognize itself because it's cloaked in laughter and teasing and couldn't care less. Maya saw that Jo was jealous of her – even as a child – just like she was jealous of everyone who had what she didn't have. Jealous of Maya's pretty room, her matching curtains, her kind mother and father.

Maya saw that Jo was the type of person who'd take a match and light up her cousin's striking embroidered curtains when she thought Maya was asleep, not stopping to think of the consequences.

For years, Maya thought she'd dreamt it – waking up to see Jo by the curtain, watching the flames lick the fabric, eyes wide open, reflecting the glow of the fire, match still held aloft in her hand.

Maya knew Jo wouldn't do anything like that. She loved Maya. She was *family*. There was no way that her cousin would start a fire, a fire that went on to change Sofia's life forever.

But then, as they grew up, she saw a pattern repeated – not just with Maya, but with Hana too; and most recently, with Liam.

Jo saw something new and shiny of Hana's which she had to take, and if she couldn't take, she destroyed.

Maya, watching from inside, had admired Hana's self-control after Jo confessed everything, how she'd released her grip on Jo's wrist and walked away.

But Maya didn't have the same self-control, she had something better – a plan. And because of that plan, Jo wouldn't be able to take anything from anyone again.

She lifts up her bag. There's still sand everywhere. She'll have to shake it outside against the patio furniture. If that doesn't work, she'll raise the stakes: wedge the handheld hoover inside.

It takes time and effort to remove something so persistent, but she'll get there.

Get rid of every little trace.

ACKNOWLEDGEMENTS

It was never going to be easy to write a book during a global pandemic and I'd like to express my thanks to the people who helped bring this book to life during this challenging time.

Firstly, a huge thanks to my amazing literary agent, Charlotte Seymour. Your ongoing support and kindness is something I value so much and has meant the world over the past eighteen months. What a journey so far and hopefully a lot further to travel!

A massive thank you to my talented editors at Transworld – Frankie Gray and Finn Cotton. I can't thank you enough for your hard work under such tricky circumstances and investing so much time into honing the story. I'm privileged to benefit from your expertise. Another enormous thank you to Tom Hill, my tireless publicist. Your attention to detail and organization is a joy to behold and something I know ensures the book finds more readers.

More sparkly thank yous need to go to the indefatigable Em Burton for her creative marketing and to Holly Minter, Queen of Digital. Your campaigns really think outside of the box and never fail to wow me. I also want to thank Rich Shailer in the UK for his brilliant cover design. I love how you bring the book to life so well.

Another big thank you has to go to Reese Witherspoon and

the wonderful team at Reese's Book Club – selecting my debut as the Feb '21 pick changed my world in the best possible way and proved to be such a motivation whilst I was writing this book. I'll always be grateful.

I also need to thank the wider team at Andrew Nurnberg Associates and Johnson & Alcock for their support and for helping the book find new readers both here and abroad. Thank you also to my foreign publishers for believing in the story and wanting to bring it to your readers.

I would also like to thank the wonderful Stuart Gibbon for his detailed and always brilliant help with police procedure and terminology and for putting up with my endless questions. Any factual inaccuracies in police procedure are either my error or to fit the story.

Secondly, an enormous thank you to my wonderful friends for their support for my writing and for cheering me on every step of the way. I haven't seen as many of you as I'd have liked thanks to lockdown but your ongoing kindness means the world. Equally to all those who follow and connect with me on social media, readers and booksellers alike, who don't just support me, but show what a positive place social media can be. Your comments and messages have more impact than you know.

Thank you also to my local booksellers for your support with a special mention to Emily and Tanya in Waterstones Torquay – your displays of my books are really something else and your ongoing kindness and enthusiasm throughout my writing journey has been everything an author could dream of!

I am blessed by the best family you could wish for and want to say a huge thank you to them (thankfully nothing like the family in the book!). We were tight-knit before the pandemic (some people say scarily so!), but this challenging year for our family has only brought us even closer. I don't know what I'd have done without our daily (sometimes twice-daily) chats and your support.

Finally, thank you to my daughters and my husband. This novel was written in lockdown while we were juggling home-school, family illness, and just about everything in between but you kept me sane and provided me with endless cups of decaf. Thank you also to my two cats, Elsa and Anna, for always being at the end of the bed when I'm tackling a tricky plot point – I love how you seem to fall asleep best to the sound of me tapping on my keyboard. I don't know what I would do without you all. Once again . . . FTB.

ABOUT THE AUTHOR

Sarah Pearse lives by the sea in South Devon with her husband and two daughters. She studied English and Creative Writing at the University of Warwick and worked in brand PR for a variety of household brands before following her passion for writing.

Her experiences living in the Swiss Alps in her early twenties inspired her acclaimed debut novel, *The Sanatorium*, which was an instant *Sunday Times* No.1 and *New York Times* Top Ten bestseller, and a Reese Witherspoon Book Club pick. *The Retreat* is her second novel.

You can find Sarah on Twitter @SarahVPearse and Instagram @sarahpearseauthor

If you loved *The Retreat*, read on for an extract from Sarah Pearse's debut novel.

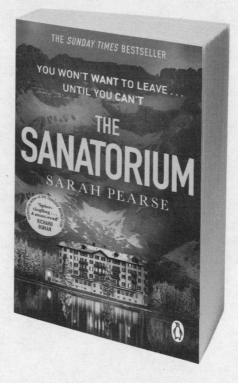

Available now!

Prologue

January 2015

Discarded medical equipment litters the floor: surgical tools blistered with rust, broken bottles, jars, the scratched spine of an old invalid chair. A torn mattress sits slumped against the wall, bile-yellow stains pocking the surface.

Hand clamped tight around his briefcase, Daniel Lemaitre feels a sharp wave of revulsion: it's as if time has taken over the building's soul, left something rotten and diseased in its place.

He moves quickly down the corridor, footsteps echoing on the tiled floor.

Keep your eyes on the door. Don't look back.

But the decaying objects pull at his gaze, each one telling stories. It doesn't take much to imagine the people who'd stayed here, coughing up their lungs.

Sometimes he thinks he can even smell it, what this place used to be – the sharp, acrid scent of chemicals still lingering in the air from the old operating wards.

Daniel's halfway down the corridor when he stops.

A movement in the room opposite – a dark, distorted blur. His stomach drops. He stares, motionless, his gaze picking over the shadowy contents of the room – a slew of papers scattered across the floor, the contorted tubes of a breathing apparatus, a broken bedframe, frayed restraints hanging loose.

His skin is prickling with tension, but nothing happens. The building is quiet, still.

He exhales heavily, starts walking again.

Don't be stupid, he tells himself. *You're tired. Too many late nights, early mornings.*

Reaching the front door, Daniel pulls it open. The wind howls angrily, jerking it back on its hinges. As he steps forward, he's blinded by an icy gust of snowflakes, but it's a relief to be outside.

The sanatorium unnerves him. Though he knows what it will become – has sketched every door, window and light switch of the new hotel – at the moment he can't help but react to its past, what it used to be.

The exterior isn't much better, he thinks, glancing up. The stark, rectangular structure is mottled with snow. It's decaying, neglected – the balconies and balustrades, the long verandah, crumbled and rotting. A few windows are still intact, but most are boarded up, ugly squares of chipboard studding the facade.

Daniel thinks about the contrast with his own home in Vevey, overlooking the lake. The contemporary blockish design is constructed mostly of glass to take in panoramic views of the water. It has a rooftop terrace, a small mooring.

He designed it all.

With the image comes Jo, his wife. She'll have just got back from work, her mind still churning over advertising budgets, briefs, already corralling the kids into doing their homework.

He imagines her in the kitchen, preparing dinner, auburn hair falling across her face as she efficiently chops and slices. It'll be something easy – pasta, fish, stir-fry. Neither of them is good at the domestics.

The thought buoys him, but only momentarily. As he crosses

the car park Daniel feels the first flickers of trepidation about the drive home.

The sanatorium wasn't easy to get to in the best of weather, its position isolated, high among the mountains. This was a deliberate choice, engineered to keep the tuberculosis patients away from the smog of the towns and cities and keep the rest of the population away from them.

But the remote location meant the road leading to it was nightmarish, a series of hairpin bends cutting through a dense forest of firs. On the drive up this morning the road itself was barely visible – snowflakes hurling themselves at the windscreen like icy white darts, making it impossible to see more than a few metres ahead.

Daniel's nearly at the car when his foot catches on something – the tattered remains of a placard, half covered by snow. The letters are crude, daubed in red.

NON AUX TRAVAUX!! NO TO BUILDING WORKS!!

Anger spiking, Daniel tramples it underfoot. The protestors had been here last week. Over fifty of them, shouting abuse, waving their gaudy placards in his face. It had been filmed on mobile phones, shared on social media.

That was just one of the endless battles they'd had to fight to bring this project to fruition. People claimed they wanted progress, the tourist francs that followed, but when it came down to actually building, they baulked.

Daniel knew why. People don't like a winner.

It's what his father had said to him once, and it was true. The locals had been proud at the start. They'd approved of his small successes – the shopping mall in Sion, the apartment block in Sierre overlooking the Rhone – but then he'd become *too much,* hadn't he? Too much of a success, a personality.

Daniel got the feeling that, in their eyes, he'd had his share of the pie and was now being greedy by taking more. Only thirty-three, and his architectural practice is thriving – offices in Sion, Lausanne, Geneva. One planned for Zurich.

It was the same with Lucas, the property developer and one of his oldest friends. Mid-thirties, and he already owned three landmark hotels.

People resented them for their success.

And this project had been the nail in the coffin. They'd had it all: online trolls, emails, letters to the office. Planning objections.

They came for him first. Rumours began circulating on local blogs and social media that the business was struggling. Then they'd started on Lucas. Similar stories, stories he could easily dismiss, but one in particular stuck.

It bothered Daniel, more than he cared to admit.

Talk of bribes. Corruption.

Daniel had tried to speak to Lucas about it, but his friend had shut the conversation down. The thought nags at him, an itch, like so many things on this project, but he forces the thought away. He has to ignore it. Focus on the end result. This hotel will cement his reputation. Lucas's drive and his compulsion for detail have propelled Daniel to a spectacularly ambitious design, an end-point he hadn't thought possible.

Daniel reaches the car. The windscreen is thick with fresh snow; too much for the wipers. He'll have to scrape it off.

But as he reaches into his pocket for his key he notices something.

A bracelet, lying beside the front tyre.

He bends down, picks it up. It's thin and made of copper. Daniel twists it between his fingers. He can make out a row of numbers engraved on the interior . . . a date?

Daniel frowns. It has to belong to someone who'd been up there today, surely? Otherwise it would already be covered in snow.

But what were they doing so close to his car?

Images of the protestors flicker through his mind, their angry, jeering faces.

Could it be them?

Daniel makes himself take a long, deep breath, but as he pushes the bracelet into his pocket he catches a glimpse of something: a movement behind the ridge of snow that's built up against the wall of the car park.

A hazy profile.

His palms are sweaty around his key fob. Pushing down hard on the fob to open the boot, he freezes as he looks up.

A figure, standing in front of him, positioned between him and his car.

Daniel stares, briefly paralysed, his brain frantically trying to process what he's seeing – how could someone have moved so quickly towards him without him noticing?

The figure is dressed in black. Something is covering their face.

It resembles a gas mask; the same basic form, but it's missing the filter at the front. Instead, there's a thick rubber hose running from mouth to nose. A connector. The hose is ribbed, black; it quivers as the figure shifts from foot to foot.

The effect is horrifying. Monstrous. Something scraped from the darkest depths of the unconscious mind.

Think, he tells himself, *think*. His brain starts churning through possibilities, ways to make this something innocuous, benign. It's a prank, that's all: one of the protestors, trying to scare him.

Then the figure steps towards him. A precise, controlled movement.

All Daniel can see is the lurid magnified close-up of the black rubber stretched across the face. The ribbed lines of the hose. Then he hears the breathing; a strange, wet sucking sound coming from the mask. Liquid exhalations.

His heart is pounding against his ribcage.

'What is this?' Daniel says, hearing the fear in his voice. A tremble he tries to stamp out. 'Who are you? What are you trying to do?' A drip trickles down his face. Snow melting against the heat of his skin, or sweat? He can't tell.

Come on, he tells himself. *Get control of yourself.* It's some stupid prick messing around.

Just walk past and get into your car.

It's then, from this angle, that he notices another car. A car that wasn't there when he arrived. A black pick-up. A Nissan.

Come on, Daniel. Move.

But his body is frozen, refusing to obey. All he can do is listen to the strange breathing sound coming from the mask. It's louder now, faster, more laboured.

A soft sucking noise and then a high-pitched whistle.

Over and over.

The figure lurches closer, something in their hand. A knife? Daniel can't make it out. The thick gloves they're wearing are concealing most of it.

Move, move.

He manages to propel himself forwards, one step, then two, but fear makes his muscles seize. He stumbles in the snow, right foot sliding out from under him.

By the time he straightens it's too late: the gloved hand clamps over his mouth. Daniel can smell the stale mustiness of the glove but also the mask – the curious burnt-plastic odour of rubber, laced with something else.

Something familiar.

But before his brain can make the connection something pierces his thigh. A single, sharp pain. His thoughts scatter, then his mind goes quiet.

A quiet that, within seconds, tips over into nothingness.

Press Release – under embargo until midnight, 5 March 2018

Le Sommet
Hauts de Plumachit
Crans-Montana 3963
Valais
Switzerland

5-STAR HOTEL SET TO OPEN IN THE SWISS RESORT OF CRANS-MONTANA

Located on a sunny mountain plateau above Crans-Montana, high in the Swiss Alps, Le Sommet is the brainchild of Swiss property developer Lucas Caron.

After eight years of extensive planning and construction, one of the town's oldest sanatoriums is set to reopen as a luxury hotel.

The main building was designed in the late nineteenth century by Caron's great-grandfather Pierre. It became renowned worldwide as a centre for treating tuberculosis before the advent of antibiotics forced its diversification.

More recently, it gained international recognition for its innovative architecture, earning the elder Caron a posthumous Swiss Arts award in 1942. Combining clean lines with large panoramic windows, flat roofs and unadorned geometrical shapes, one judge described the building as 'groundbreaking – purpose-designed to fulfil its function as a hospital while also creating a seamless transition between the interior and exterior landscapes'.

Lucas Caron said: 'It was time we breathed new life into this building. We were confident that, with the right vision, we could create a sensitively restored hotel that would pay homage to its rich past.'

Under the guidance of Swiss architectural firm Lemaitre SA, a team has been assembled to renovate the building and also add a state-of-the-art spa and events centre.

Subtly refurbished, Le Sommet will make innovative use of natural, local materials such as wood, slate and stone. The hotel's elegant modern interiors will not only echo the powerful topography outside but will draw on the building's past to create a new narrative.

Philippe Volkem, CEO of Valais Tourism, said, 'This will doubtless be the jewel in the crown of what is already one of the finest winter resorts in the world.'

For press enquiries, please contact Leman PR, Lausanne.

For general enquiries/bookings, please visit www.lesommet cransmontana.ch.

A beautiful, eerie hotel in the Swiss Alps, recently converted from an abandoned sanatorium, is the last place Detective Elin Warner wants to be. But her estranged brother has invited her there for his engagement party, and she feels she has no choice but to accept.

Arriving in the midst of a threatening storm, Elin immediately feels on edge. And things only get worse when they wake the next morning to find her brother's fiancée is missing. With access to the hotel cut off, the guests begin to panic.

But this is only the first disappearance. Everyone's in danger – and anyone could be next . . .

'Spine-tingling . . . A must-read' **Richard Osman**

'I absolutely loved *The Sanatorium* – it gave me all the wintry thrills and chills' **Lucy Foley**

'An addictive, creepy and twisting read' *Stylist*

'A chillingly vivid thriller' **T. M. Logan**

'A menacing, creepy debut [. . .] echoes of Hitchcock and du Maurier' *Daily Mail*

dead good

Looking for more gripping must-reads?

Head over to Dead Good —
the home of killer crime books,
TV and film.

Whether you're on the hunt for an intriguing
mystery, an action-packed thriller
or a creepy psychological drama,
we're here to keep you in the loop.

Get recommendations and reviews from
crime fans, grab discounted books at bargain
prices and enter exclusive giveaways
for the chance to read brand-new releases
before they hit the shelves.

Sign up for the free newsletter:
www.deadgoodbooks.co.uk/newsletter